VARNEY
THE VAMPYRE;
or,
The Feast of Blood
A Romance.

$3.00

D1554967

Book One
The Feast of Blood

Other works by James Malcolm Rymer

The Black Monk; or, The Secret of the Grey Turret
Ada the Betrayed; or, The Murder at the Old Smithy
The First False Step; or, The Path to Crime

VARNEY
THE VAMPYRE

James Malcolm Rymer

Book One

The Feast of Blood

WILDSIDE PRESS
Berkeley Heights, New Jersey

Originally published as a serial by E. Lloyd, of Fleet Street, London,
in 1845-1847; reprinted as a book E. Lloyd in 1847.
This Wildside edition contains significant editorial alterations and
is copyright © 2000 by The Wildside Press.
All rights reserved.

Varney the Vampyre;
or,
The Feast of Blood
Book One: The Feast of Blood
A publication of
Wildside Press

www.wildsidepress.com

TWENTY-FIRST CENTURY EDITION

— *"How graves give up their dead,*
And how the night air hideous grows
With shrieks!"

Preface.

*T*he unprecedented success of the romance of "Varney the Vampyre," leaves the Author but little to say further, than that he accepts that success and its results as gratefully as it is possible for any one to do popular favors.

A belief in the existence of vampyres first took its rise in Norway and Sweden, from whence it rapidly spread to more southern regions, taking a firm hold of the imaginations of the more credulous portion of mankind.

The following romance is collected from seemingly the most authentic sources, and the Author must leave the question of credibility entirely to his readers, not even thinking that he his peculiarly called upon to express his own opinion upon the subject.

Nothing has been omitted in the life of the unhappy Varney which could tend to throw a light upon his most extraordinary career, and the fact of his death just as it is here related made a great noise at the time through Europe, and is to be found in the public prints for the year 1713.

With these few observations, the Author and Publisher are well content to leave the work in the hands of the public, which has stamped it with an approbation far exceeding their most sanguine expectations, and which is calculated to act as the strongest possible incentive to the production of other works, which in a like, or perchance a still further degree, may be deserving of public patronage and support.

To the whole of the Metropolitan Press for their laudatory notices, the Author is peculiarly obliged.

— London, Sept. 1847

Chapter I.

MIDNIGHT. – THE HAILSTORM. – THE DREADFUL VISITOR.
– THE VAMPYRE.

*T*he solemn tones of an old cathedral clock have announced midnight – the air is thick and heavy – a strange, deathlike stillness pervades all nature. Like the ominous calm which precedes some more than usually terrific outbreak of the elements, they seem to have paused even in their ordinary fluctuations, to gather a terrific strength for the great effort. A faint peal of thunder now comes from far off. Like a signal gun for the battle of the winds to begin, it appeared to awaken them from their lethargy, and one awful, warring hurricane swept over a whole city, producing more devastation in the four or five minutes it lasted than would a half century of ordinary phenomena.

It was as if some giant had blown upon some toy town, and scattered many of the buildings before the hot blast of his terrific breath; for as suddenly as that blast of wind had come did it cease, and all was as still and calm as before.

Sleepers awakened, and thought that what they had heard must be the confused chimera of a dream. They trembled and turned to sleep again.

All is still – still as the very grave. Not a sound breaks the magic of repose. What is that – a strange pattering noise, as of a million fairy feet? It is hail – yes, a hailstorm has burst over the city. Leaves are dashed from the trees, mingled with small boughs; windows that lie most opposed to the direct fury of the pelting particles of ice are broken, and the rapt repose that before was so remarkable in its intensity, is exchanged for a noise which, in its accumulation, drowns every cry of surprise or consternation which here and there arose from persons who found their houses invaded by the storm.

Now and then, too, there would come a sudden gust of wind that in its strength, as it blew laterally, would, for a moment, hold millions of the hailstones suspended in midair, but it was only to dash them with redoubled force in some new direction, where more mischief was to be done.

Oh, how the storm raged! Hail — rain — wind. It was, in very truth, an awful night.

*T*here was an antique chamber in an ancient house. Curious and quaint carvings adorn the walls, and the large chimneypiece is a curiosity of itself. The ceiling is low, and a large bay window, from roof to floor, looks to the west. The window is latticed, and filled with curiously painted glass and rich stained pieces, which send in a strange, yet beautiful light, when sun or moon shines into the apartment. There is but one portrait in that room, although the walls seem paneled for the express purpose of containing a series of pictures. That portrait is of a young man, with a pale face, a stately brow, and a strange expression about the eyes, which no one cared to look on twice.

There is a stately bed in that chamber, of carved walnut-wood is it made, rich in design and elaborate in execution; one of those works which owe their existence to the Elizabethan era. It is hung with heavy silken and damask furnishing; nodding feathers are at its corners — covered with dust are they, and they lend a funereal aspect to the room. The floor is of polished oak.

God! how the hail dashes on the old bay window! Like an occasional discharge of mimic musketry, it comes clashing, beating, and cracking upon the small panes; but they resist it — their small size saves them; the wind, the hail, the rain, expend their fury in vain.

The bed in that old chamber is occupied. A creature formed in all fashions of loveliness lies in a half sleep upon that ancient couch — a girl young and beautiful as a spring morning. Her long hair has escaped from its confinement and streams over the blackened coverings of the bedstead; she has been restless in her sleep, for the clothing of the bed is in much confusion. One arm is over her head, the other hangs nearly off the side of the bed near to which she lies. A neck and bosom that would have formed a study for the rarest sculptor that ever Providence gave genius to, were half disclosed. She moaned slightly in her sleep, and once or twice the lips moved as if in prayer — at least one might judge so, for the name of Him who suffered for all came once faintly from them.

She had endured much fatigue, and the storm does not awaken her; but it can disturb the slumbers it does not possess the power to destroy entirely. The turmoil of the elements wakes the senses, although it cannot entirely break the repose they have lapsed into.

Oh, what a world of witchery was in that mouth, slightly parted, and exhibiting within the pearly teeth that glistened even in the faint light that came from that bay window. How sweetly the long silken eyelashes lay upon the cheek. Now she moves, and one shoulder is entirely visible — whiter, fairer than the spotless clothing of the bed on which she lies, is the smooth skin of that fair creature, just budding into womanhood, and in that transition state which presents to us all the charms of the girl — almost of the child, with the more matured beauty and gentleness of advancing years.

Was that lightning? Yes — an awful, vivid, terrifying flash — then a roaring peal of thunder, as if a thousand mountains were rolling one over the other in the blue vault of Heaven! Who sleeps now in that ancient city? Not one living soul. The dread trumpet of eternity could not more effectually have awakened any one.

The hail continues. The wind continues. The uproar of the elements seems at its height. Now she awakens — that beautiful girl on the antique bed; she opens those eyes of celestial blue, and a faint cry of alarm bursts from her lips. At least it is a cry which, amid the noise and turmoil without, sounds but faint and weak. She sits upon the bed and presses her hands upon her eyes. Heavens! what a wild torrent of wind, and rain, and hail! The thunder likewise seems intent upon awakening sufficient echoes to last until the next flash of forked lightning should again produce the wild concussion of the air. She murmurs a prayer — a prayer for those she loves best; the names of those dear to her gentle heart come from her lips; she weeps and prays; she thinks then of what devastation the storm must surely produce, and to the great God of Heaven she prays for all living things. Another flash — a wild, blue, bewildering flash of lightning streams across that bay window, for an instant bringing out every color in it with terrible distinctness. A shriek bursts from the lips of the young girl, and then, with eyes fixed upon that window, which, in another moment, is all darkness, and with such an expression of terror upon her face as it had never before known, she trembled, and the perspiration of intense fear stood upon her brow.

"What — what was it?" she gasped; "real or delusion? Oh, God, what was it? A figure tall and gaunt, endeavoring from the outside to unclasp the window. I saw it. That flash of lightning revealed it to me. It stood the whole length of the window."

There was a lull of the wind. The hail was not falling so thickly — moreover, it now fell, what there was of it, straight, and yet a strange clattering sound came upon the glass of that long window. It could not be a delusion — she is awake, and she hears it. What can produce it? Another flash of lightning — another shriek — there could be now no delusion.

A tall figure is standing on the ledge immediately outside the long window. It is its fingernails upon the glass that produces the sound so like the hail, now that the hail has ceased. Intense fear paralyzed the limbs of the beautiful girl. That one shriek is all she can utter — with hand clasped, a face of marble, a heart beating so wildly in her bosom, that each moment it seems as if it would break its confines, eyes distended and fixed upon the window, she waits, froze with horror. The pattering and clattering of the nails continue. No word is spoken, and now she fancies she can trace the darker form of that figure against the window, and she can see the long arms moving to and fro, feeling for some mode of entrance. What strange light is that which now gradually creeps up into the air? red and terrible — brighter and brighter it grows. The lightning has set fire to a mill, and the reflection of the rapidly consuming building falls upon that long window. There can be no mistake. The figure is there, still feeling for an entrance, and clattering against the glass with its long nails, that appear as if the growth of many years had been untouched. She tries to scream again but a choking sensation comes over her, and she cannot. It is too dreadful — she tries to move — each limb seems weighted down by tons of lead — she can but in a hoarse faint whisper cry, —

"Help — help — help — help!"

And that one word she repeats like a person in a dream. The red glare of the fire continues. It throws up the tall gaunt figure in hideous relief against the long window. It shows, too, upon the one portrait that is in the chamber, and the portrait appears to fix its eyes upon the attempting intruder, while the flickering light from the fire makes it look fearfully lifelike. A small pane of glass is broken, and the form from without introduces a long gaunt hand, which seems utterly destitute of flesh. The fastening is removed, and one-half of the window, which opens like folding doors, is swung wide open upon its hinges.

And yet now she could not scream — she could not move. "Help! — help! — help!" was all she could say. But, oh, that look of terror that sat upon her face, it was dreadful — a look to haunt the memory for a lifetime — a look to obtrude itself upon the happiest moments, and turn them to bitterness.

The figure turns half round, and the light falls upon its face. It is perfectly white — perfectly bloodless. The eyes look like polished tin; the lips are drawn back, and the principal feature next to those dreadful eyes is the teeth — the fearful looking teeth — projecting like those of some wild animal, hideously, glaringly white, and fang-like. It approaches the bed with a strange, gliding movement. It clashes together the long nails that literally appear to hang from the finger ends. No sound comes from its lips. Is she going mad — that young and beautiful girl exposed to so much terror? she has drawn up all her limbs; she cannot even now say help. The power of articulation is gone, but the power of movement has returned to her; she can draw herself slowly along to the other side of the bed from that towards which the hideous appearance is coming.

But her eyes are fascinated. The glance of a serpent could not have produced a greater effect upon her than did the fixed gaze of those awful, metallic-looking eyes that were bent down on her face. Crouching down so that the gigantic height was lost, and the horrible, protruding white face was the most prominent object, came on the figure. What was it? — what did it want there? — what made it look so hideous — so unlike an inhabitant of the earth, and yet be on it?

Now she has got to the verge of the bed, and the figure pauses. It seemed as if when it paused she lost the power to proceed. The clothing of the bed was now clutched in her hands with unconscious power. She drew her breath short and thick. Her bosom heaves, and her limbs tremble, yet she cannot withdraw her eyes from that marble-looking face. He holds her with his glittering eye.

The storm has ceased — all is still. The winds are hushed; the church clock proclaims the hour of one: a hissing sound comes from the throat of the hideous being, and he raises his long, gaunt arms — the lips move. He advances. The girl places one small foot on to the floor. She is unconsciously dragging the clothing with her. The door of the room is in that direction — can she reach it? Has she power to walk? — can she withdraw her eyes from the face of the intruder, and so break the hideous charm? God of Heaven! is it real, or some dream so like reality as to nearly overturn judgment forever?

The figure has paused again, and half on the bed and half out of it that young girl lies trembling. Her long hair streams across the entire width of the bed. As she has slowly moved along she has left it streaming across the pillows. The pause lasted about a minute — oh, what an age of agony. That minute was, indeed, enough for madness to do its full work in.

With a sudden rush that could not be foreseen — with a strange howling cry that was enough to awaken terror in every breast, the figure seized the long tresses of her hair, and twining them round his bony hands he held her to the bed. Then she screamed — Heaven granted her then power to scream. Shriek followed shriek in rapid succession. The bedclothes fell in a heap by the side of the bed — she was dragged by her long silken hair completely on to it again. Her beautifully rounded limbs quivered with the agony of her soul. The glassy, horrible eyes of the figure ran over that angelic form with a hideous satisfaction — horrible profanation. He drags her head to the bed's edge. He forces it back by the long hair still entwined in his grasp. With a plunge he seizes her neck in his fang-like teeth — a gush of blood, and a hideous sucking noise follows. *The girl has swooned, and the vampyre is at his hideous repast!*

Chapter II.

THE ALARM. – THE PISTOL SHOT. – THE PURSUIT AND ITS CONSEQUENCES.

*L*ights flashed about the building, and various room doors opened; voices called one to the other. There was an universal stir and commotion among the inhabitants.

"Did you hear a scream, Harry?" asked a young man, half-dressed, as he walked into the chamber of another about his own age.

"I did — where was it?"

"God knows. I dressed myself directly."

"All is still now."

"Yes; but unless I was dreaming there was a scream."

"We could not both dream there was. Where do you think it came from?"

"It burst so suddenly upon my ears that I cannot say."

There was a tap now at the door of the room where these young men were, and a female voice said, —

"For God's sake, get up!"

"We are up," said both the young men, appearing.

"Did you hear anything?"

"Yes, a scream."

"Oh, search the house — search the house; where did it come from, can you tell?"

"Indeed we cannot, mother."

Another person now joined the party. He was a man of middle age, and, as he came up to them, he said, —

"Good God! what is the matter?"

Scarcely had the words passed his lips, than such a rapid succession of shrieks came upon their ears, that they felt absolutely stunned by them. The elderly lady, whom one of the young men had called mother, fainted, and would have fallen to the floor of the corridor in which they all stood, had she not been promptly supported by the last comer, who himself staggered, as those piercing cries came upon the night air. He, however, was the first to recover, for the young men seemed paralyzed.

"Henry," he cried, "for God's sake support your mother. Can you doubt that these cries come from Flora's room?"

The young man mechanically supported his mother, and then the man who had just spoken darted back to his own bed-room, from whence he returned in a moment with a pair of pistols, and shouting, —

"Follow me who can!" he bounded across the corridor in the direction of the antique apartment, from whence the cries proceeded, but which were now hushed.

That house was built for strength, and the doors were all of oak, and of considerable thickness. Unhappily, they had fastenings within, so that when the man reached the chamber of her who so much required help, he was helpless, for the door was fast.

"Flora! Flora!" he cried; "Flora, speak!"

All was still.

"Good God!" he added; "we must force the door."

"I hear a strange noise within," said the young man, who trembled violently.

"And so do I. What does it sound like?"

"I scarcely know; but it closest resembles some animal eating, or sucking some liquid."

"What on earth can it be? Have you no weapon that will force the door? I shall go mad if I am kept here."

"I have," said the young man. "Wait here a moment."

He ran down the staircase, and presently returned with a small, but powerful, iron crowbar.

"This will do," he said.

"It will, it will. — Give it to me."

"Has she not spoken?"

"Not a word. My mind misgives me that something very dreadful must have happened to her."

"And that odd noise!"

"Still goes on. Somehow, it curdles the very blood in my veins to hear it."

The man took the crow-bar, and with some difficulty succeeded in introducing it between the door and the side of the wall — still it required great strength to move it, but it did move, with a harsh, crackling sound.

"Push it!" cried he who was using the bar, "push the door at the same time."

The younger man did so. For a few moments the massive door resisted. Then, suddenly, something gave way with a loud snap — it was part of the lock, — and the door at once swung wide open.

How true it is that we measure time by the events which happen within a given space of it, rather than by its actual duration.

To those who were engaged in forcing open the door of the antique chamber, where slept the young girl whom they named Flora, each moment was swelled into an hour of agony; but, in reality, from the first moment of the alarm to that when the loud cracking noise heralded the destruction of the fastenings of the door, there had elapsed but very few minutes indeed.

"It opens — it opens," cried the young man.

"Another moment," said the stranger, as he still plied the crowbar — "another moment, and we shall have free ingress to the chamber. Be patient."

This stranger's name was Marchdale; and even as he spoke, he succeeded in throwing the massive door wide open, and clearing the passage to the chamber.

To rush in with a light in his hand was the work of a moment to the young man named Henry; but the very rapid progress he made into the apartment prevented him from observing accurately what it contained, for the wind that came in from the open window caught the flame of the candle, and although it did not actually extinguish it, it blew it so much on one side, that it was comparatively useless as a light.

"Flora — Flora!" he cried.

Then with a sudden bound something dashed from off the bed. The concussion against him was so sudden and so utterly unexpected, as well as so tremendously violent, that he was thrown down, and, in his fall, the light was fairly extinguished.

All was darkness, save a dull, reddish kind of light that now and then, from the nearly consumed mill in the immediate vicinity, came into the room. But by that light, dim, uncertain, and flickering as it was, some one was seen to make for the window.

Henry, although nearly stunned by his fall, saw a figure, gigantic in height, which nearly reached from the floor to the ceiling. The other young man, George, saw it, and Mr. Marchdale likewise saw it, as did the lady who had spoken to the two young men in the corridor when first the screams of the young girl awakened alarm in the breasts of all the inhabitants of that house.

The figure was about to pass out at the window which led to a kind of balcony, from whence there was an easy descent to a garden.

Before it passed out they each and all caught a glance of the side-face, and they saw that the lower part of it and the lips were dabbled in blood.

They saw, too, one of those fearful-looking, shining, metallic eyes which presented so terrible an appearance of unearthly ferocity.

No wonder that for a moment a panic seized them all, which paralyzed any exertions they might otherwise have made to detain that hideous form.

But Mr. Marchdale was a man of mature years; he had seen much in life, both in this and in foreign lands; and he, although astonished to the extent of being frightened, was much more likely to recover sooner than his younger companions, which, indeed, he did, and acted promptly enough.

"Don't rise, Henry," he cried. "Lie still."

Almost at the moment he uttered these words, he fired at the figure, which then occupied the window, as if it were a gigantic figure set in a frame.

The report was tremendous in that chamber, for the pistol was no toy weapon, but one made for actual service, and of sufficient length and bore of barrel to carry destruction along with the bullets that came from it.

"If that has missed its aim," said Mr. Marchdale, "I'll never pull trigger again."

As he spoke he dashed forward, and made a clutch at the figure he felt convinced he had shot.

The tall form turned upon him, and when he got a full view of the face, which he did at that moment, from the opportune circumstance of the lady returning at the instant with a light she had been to her own chamber to procure, even he, Marchdale, with all his courage, and that was great, and all his nervous energy, recoiled a step or two, and uttered the exclamation of, "Great God!"

That face was one never to be forgotten. It was hideously flushed with color — the color of fresh blood; the eyes had a savage and remarkable luster whereas, before, they had looked like polished tin — they now wore a ten times brighter aspect, and flashes of light seemed to dart from them. The mouth was open, as if, from the natural formation of the countenance, the lips receded much from the large canine looking teeth.

A strange howling noise came from the throat of this monstrous figure, and it seemed upon the point of rushing upon Mr. Marchdale. Suddenly, then, as if some impulse had seized upon it, it uttered a wild and terrible shrieking kind of laugh; and then turning, dashed through the window, and in one instant disappeared from before the eyes of those who felt nearly annihilated by its fearful presence.

"God help us!" ejaculated Henry.

Mr. Marchdale drew a long breath, and then, giving a stamp on the floor, as if to recover himself from the state of agitation into which even he was thrown, he cried, —

"Be it what or who it may, I'll follow it."

"No — no — do not," cried the lady.

"I must, I will. Let who will come with me — I follow that dreadful form."

As he spoke, he took the road it took, and dashed through the window into the balcony.

"And we, too, George," exclaimed Henry; "we will follow Mr. Marchdale. This dreadful affair concerns us more nearly than it does him."

The lady who was the mother of these young men, and of the beautiful girl who had been so awfully visited, screamed aloud, and implored them to stay. But the voice of Mr. Marchdale was heard exclaiming aloud, —

"I see it — I see it; it makes for the wall."

They hesitated no longer, but at once rushed into the balcony, and from thence dropped into the garden.

The mother approached the bedside of the insensible, perhaps murdered girl; she saw her, to all appearance, weltering in blood, and, overcome by her emotions, she fainted on the floor of the room.

When the two young men reached the garden, they found it much lighter than might have been fairly expected; for not only was the morning rapidly approaching, but the mill was still burning, and those mingled lights made almost every object plainly visible, except when deep shadows were thrown from some gigantic trees that had stood for centuries in that sweetly wooded spot. They heard the voice of Mr. Marchdale, as he cried, —

"There — there — towards the wall. There — there — God! how it bounds along."

The young men hastily dashed through a thicket in the direction from whence his voice sounded, and then they found him looking wild and terrified, and with something in his hand which looked like a portion of clothing.

"Which way, which way?" they both cried in a breath.

He leant heavily on the arm of George, as he pointed along a vista of trees, and said in a low voice, —

"God help us all. It is not human. Look there — look there — do you not see it?"

They looked in the direction he indicated. At the end of this vista was the wall of the garden. At that point it was full twelve feet in height, and as they looked, they saw the hideous, monstrous form they had traced from the chamber of their sister, making frantic efforts to clear the obstacle.

They saw it bound from the ground to the top of the wall, which it very nearly reached, and then each time it fell back again into the garden with such a dull, heavy sound, that the earth seemed to shake again with the concussion. They trembled — well indeed they might, and for some minutes they watched the figure making its fruitless efforts to leave the place.

"What — what is it?" whispered Henry, in hoarse accents. "God, what can it possibly be?"

"I know not," replied Mr. Marchdale. "I did seize it. It was cold and clammy like a corpse. It cannot be human."

"Not human?"

"Look at it now. It will surely escape now."

"No, no — we will not be terrified thus — there is Heaven above us. Come on, and, for dear Flora's sake, let us make an effort yet to seize this bold intruder."

"Take this pistol," said Marchdale. "It is the fellow of the one I fired. Try its efficacy."

"He will be gone," exclaimed Henry, as at this moment, after many repeated attempts and fearful falls, the figure reached the top of the wall, and then hung by its long arms a moment or two, previous to dragging itself completely up.

The idea of the appearance, be it what it might, entirely escaping, seemed to nerve again Mr. Marchdale, and he, as well as the two young men, ran forward towards the wall. They got so close to the figure before it sprang down on the outer side of the wall, that to miss killing it with the bullet from the pistol was a matter of utter impossibility, unless willfully.

Henry had the weapon, and he pointed it full at the tall form with steady aim. He pulled the trigger — the explosion followed, and that the bullet did its office there could be no manner of doubt, for the figure gave a howling shriek, and fell headlong from the wall on the outside.

"I have shot him," cried Henry, "I have shot him."

Chapter III.

THE DISAPPEARANCE OF THE BODY. – FLORA'S RECOVERY
AND MADNESS. – THE OFFER OF ASSISTANCE FROM SIR
FRANCIS VARNEY.

"*H*e is human!" cried Henry; "I have surely killed him."

"It would seem so," said M. Marchdale. "Let us now hurry round to the outside of the wall, and see where he lies."

This was at once agreed to, and the whole three of them made what expedition they could towards a gate which let into a paddock, across which they hurried, and soon found themselves clear of the garden wall, so that they could make way towards where they fully expected to find the body of him who had worn so unearthly an aspect, but who it would be an excessive relief to find was human.

So hurried was the progress they made, that it was scarcely possible to exchange many words as they went; a kind of breathless anxiety was upon them, and in the speed they disregarded every obstacle, which would, at any other time, have probably prevented them from taking the direct road they sought.

It was difficult on the outside of the wall to say exactly which was the precise spot which it might be supposed the body had fallen on; but, by following the wall its entire length, surely they would come upon it.

They did so; but, to their surprise, they got from its commencement to its further extremity without finding any dead body, or even any symptoms of one having lain there.

At some parts close to the wall there grew a kind of heath, and, consequently, the traces of blood would be lost among it, if it so happened that at the precise spot at which the strange being had seemed to topple over, such vegetation had existed. This was to be ascertained; but now, after traversing the whole length of the wall twice, they came to a halt, and looked wonderingly in each other's faces.

"There is nothing here," said Harry.

"Nothing," added his brother.

"It could not have been a delusion," at length said Mr. Marchdale, with a shudder.

"A delusion?" exclaimed the brothers. "That is not possible; we all saw it."

"Then what terrible explanation can we give?"

"By heavens! I know not," exclaimed Henry. "This adventure surpasses all belief, and but for the great interest we have in it, I should regard it with a world of curiosity."

"It is too dreadful," said George; "for God's sake, Henry, let us return to ascertain if poor Flora is killed."

"My senses," said Henry, "were all so much absorbed in gazing at that horrible form, that I never once looked towards her further than to see that she was, to appearance, dead. God help her! poor — poor, beautiful Flora. This is, indeed, a sad, sad fate for you to come to. Flora — Flora —"

"Do not weep, Henry," said George. "Rather let us now hasten home, where we may find that tears are premature. She may yet be living and restored to us."

"And," said Mr. Marchdale, "she may be able to give us some account of this dreadful visitation."

"True — true," exclaimed Henry; "we will hasten home."

They now turned their steps homewards, and as they went they much blamed themselves for all leaving home together, and with terror pictured what might occur in their absence to those who were now totally unprotected.

"It was a rash impulse of us all to come in pursuit of this dreadful figure," remarked Mr. Marchdale; "but do not torment yourself, Henry. There may be no reason for your fears."

At the pace they went, they very soon reached the ancient house; and when they came in sight of it, they saw lights flashing from the windows, and the shadows of faces moving to and fro, indicating that the whole household was up, and in a state of alarm.

Henry, after some trouble, got the hall door opened by a terrified servant, who was trembling so much that she could scarcely hold the light she had with her.

"Speak at once, Martha," said Henry. "Is Flora living?"

"Yes; but —"

"Enough — enough! Thank God she lives; where is she now?"

"In her own room, Master Henry. Oh, dear — oh, dear, what will become of us all?"

Henry rushed up the staircase, followed by George and Mr. Marchdale, nor paused he once until he reached the room of his sister.

"Mother," he said, before he crossed the threshold, "are you here?"

"I am, my dear — I am. Come in, pray come in, and speak to Flora."

"Come in, Mr. Marchdale," said Henry — "come in; we will make no stranger of you."

They all entered the room.

Several lights had been now brought into that antique chamber, and, in addition to the mother of the beautiful girl who had been so fearfully visited, there were two female domestics, who appeared to be in the greatest possible fright, for they could render no assistance whatever to anybody.

The tears were streaming down the mother's face, and the moment she saw Mr. Marchdale, she clung to his arm, evidently unconscious of what she was about, and exclaimed, —

"Oh, what is this that has happened — what is this? Tell me, Marchdale! Robert Marchdale, you whom I have known even from my childhood, you will not deceive me. Tell me the meaning of all this?"

"I cannot," he said, in a tone of much emotion. "As God is my judge, I am as much puzzled and amazed at the scene that has taken place here tonight as you can be."

The mother wrung her hands and wept.

"It was the storm that first awakened me," added Marchdale; "and then I heard a scream."

The brothers tremblingly approached the bed. Flora was placed in a sitting, half-reclining posture, propped up by pillows. She was quite insensible, and her face was fearfully pale; while that she breathed at all could be but very faintly seen. On some of her clothing, about the neck, were spots of blood, and she looked more like one who had suffered some long and grievous illness, than a young girl in the prime of life and in the most robust health, as she had been on the day previous to the strange scene we have recorded.

"Does she sleep?" said Henry, as a tear fell from his eyes upon her pallid cheek.

"No," replied Mr. Marchdale. "This is a swoon, from which we must recover her."

Active measures were now adopted to restore the languid circulation, and, after persevering in them for some time, they had the satisfaction of seeing her open her eyes.

Her first act upon consciousness returning, however, was to utter a loud shriek, and it was not until Henry implored her to look around her, and see that she was surrounded by none but friendly faces, that she would venture again to open her eyes, and look timidly from one to the other. Then she shuddered, and burst into tears as she said, —

"Oh, Heaven, have mercy upon me — Heaven, have mercy upon me and save me from that dreadful form."

"There is no one here, Flora," said Mr. Marchdale, "but those who love you, and who, in defense of you, if needs were would lay down their lives."

"Oh, God! Oh, God!"

"You have been terrified. But tell us distinctly what has happened? You are quite safe now."

She trembled so violently that Mr. Marchdale recommended that some stimulant should be give to her, and she was persuaded, although not without considerable difficulty, to swallow a small portion of some wine from a cup. There could be no doubt but that the stimulating effect of the wine was beneficial, for a slight accession of color visited her cheeks, and she spoke in a firmer tone as she said, —

"Do not leave me. Oh, do not leave me, any of you. I shall die if left alone now. Oh, save me — save me. That horrible form! That fearful face!"

"Tell us how it happened, dear Flora?" said Henry.

"No — no — no," she said, "I do not think I shall ever sleep again."

"Say not so; you will be more composed in a few hours, and then you can tell us what has occurred."

"I will tell you now. I will tell you now."

She placed her hands over her face for a moment, as if to collect her scattered thoughts, and then she added, —

"I was awakened by the storm, and I saw that terrible apparition at the window. I think I screamed, but I could not fly. Oh, God! I could not fly. It came — it seized me by the hair. I know no more. I know no more."

She passed her hand across her neck several times, and Mr. Marchdale said, in an anxious voice, —

"You seem, Flora, to have hurt your neck — there is a wound."

"A wound!" said the mother, and she brought a light close to the bed, where all saw on the side of Flora's neck a small punctured wound; or, rather two, for there was one a little distance from the other.

It was from these wounds the blood had come which was observable upon her night clothing.

"How came these wounds?" said Henry.

"I do not know," she replied. "I feel very faint and weak, as if I had almost bled to death."

"You cannot have done so, dear Flora, for there are not above half-a-dozen spots of blood to be seen at all."

Mr. Marchdale leaned against the carved head of the bed for support, and he uttered a deep groan. All eyes were turned upon him, and Henry said, in a voice of the most anxious inquiry, —

"Have you something to say, Mr. Marchdale, which will throw some light upon this affair."

"No, no, no, nothing!" cried Mr. Marchdale, rousing himself at once from the appearance of depression that had come over him. "I have nothing to say, but that I think Flora had better get some sleep if she can."

"No sleep — no sleep for me," again screamed Flora. "Dare I be alone to sleep?"

"But you shall not be alone, dear Flora," said Henry. "I will sit by your bedside and watch you."

She took his hand in both hers, and while the tears chased each other down her cheeks, she said, —

"Promise me, Henry, by all your hopes of Heaven, you will not leave me."

"I promise."

She gently laid herself down, with a deep sigh, and closed her eyes.

"She is weak, and will sleep long," said Mr. Marchdale.

"You sigh," said Henry. "Some fearful thoughts, I feel certain, oppress your heart."

"Hush — hush!" said Mr. Marchdale, as he pointed to Flora. "Hush! not here — not here."

"I understand," said Henry.

"Let her sleep."

There was a silence of some few minutes' duration. Flora had dropped into a deep slumber. That silence was first broken by George, who said, —

"Mr. Marchdale, look at that portrait."

He pointed to the portrait in the frame to which we have alluded, and the moment Marchdale looked at it he sunk into a chair as he exclaimed, —

"Gracious Heaven, how like!"

"It is — it is," said Henry. "Those eyes —"

"And see the contour of the countenance, and the strange shape of the mouth."

"Exact — exact."

"That picture shall be moved from here. The sight of it is at once sufficient to awaken all her former terrors in poor Flora's brain if she should chance to awaken and cast her eyes suddenly upon it."

"And is it so like him who came here?" said the mother.

"It is the very man himself," said Mr. Marchdale. "I have not been in this house long enough to ask any of you whose portrait that may be?"

"It is," said Henry, "the portrait of Sir Runnagate Bannerworth, an ancestor of ours, who first, by his vices, gave the great blow to the family prosperity."

"Indeed. How long ago?"

"About ninety years."

"Ninety years. 'Tis a long while — ninety years."

"You muse upon it."

"No, no. I do wish, and yet I dread —"

"What?"

"To say something to you all. But not here — not here. We will hold a consultation on this matter tomorrow. Not now — not now."

"The daylight is coming quickly on," said Henry; "I shall keep my sacred promise of not moving from this room until Flora awakens; but there can be no occasion for the detention of any of you. One is sufficient here. Go all of you, and endeavor to procure what rest you can."

"I will fetch you my powder-flask and bullets," said Mr. Marchdale; "and you can, if you please, reload the pistols. In about two hours more it will be broad daylight."

This arrangement was adopted. Henry did reload the pistols, and placed them on a table by the side of the bed, ready for immediate action, and then, as Flora was sleeping soundly, all left the room but himself.

Mrs. Bannerworth was the last to do so. She would have remained, but for the earnest solicitation of Henry, that she would endeavor to get some sleep to make up for her broken night's repose, and she was indeed so broken down by her alarm on Flora's account, that she had not power to resist, but with tears flowing from her eyes, she sought her own chamber.

And now the calmness of the night resumed its sway in that evil-fated mansion; and although no one really slept but Flora, all were still. Busy thought kept every one else wakeful. It was a mockery to lie down at all, and Henry, full of strange and painful feelings as he was, preferred his present position to the anxiety and apprehension on Flora's account which he knew he should feel if she were not within the sphere of his own observation, and she slept as soundly as some gentle infant tired of its playmates and its sports.

Chapter IV.

THE MORNING. – THE CONSULTATION. – THE FEARFUL SUGGESTION.

W hat wonderfully different impressions and feelings, with regard to the same circumstances, come across the mind in the broad, clear, and beautiful light of day to what haunt the imagination, and often render the judgment almost incapable of action, when the heavy shadow of night is upon all things.

There must be a downright physical reason for this effect – it is so remarkable and so universal. It seems that the sun's rays so completely alter and modify the constitution of the atmosphere, that it produces, as we inhale it, a wonderfully different effect upon the nerves of the human subject.

We can account for this phenomenon in no other way. Perhaps never in his life had he, Henry Bannerworth, felt so strongly this transition of feeling as he now felt it, when the beautiful daylight gradually dawned upon him, as he kept his lonely watch by the bedside of his slumbering sister.

The watch had been a perfectly undisturbed one. Not the least sight or sound or any intrusion had reached his senses. All had been as still as the very grave.

And yet while the night lasted, and he was more indebted to the rays of the candle, which he had placed upon a shelf, for the power to distinguish objects than to light of the morning, a thousand uneasy and strange sensations had found a home in his agitated bosom.

He looked so many times at the portrait which was in the panel that at length he felt an undefined sensation of terror creep over him whenever he took his eyes off it.

He tried to keep himself from looking at it, but he found it vain, so he adopted what, perhaps, was certainly the wisest, best plan, namely, to look at it continually.

He shifted his chair so that he could gaze upon it without any effort, and he placed the candle so that a faint light was thrown upon it, and there he sat, a prey to many conflicting and uncomfortable feelings, until the daylight began to make the candle flame look dull and sickly.

Solution for the events of the night he could find none. He racked his imagination in vain to find some means, however vague, of endeavoring to account for what occurred, and still he was at fault. All was to him wrapped in the gloom of the most profound mystery.

And how strangely, too, the eyes of that portrait appeared to look upon him — as if instinct with life, and as if the head to which they belonged was busy in endeavoring to find out the secret communings of his soul. It was wonderfully well executed that portrait; so life-like, that the very features seemed to move as you gazed upon them.

"It shall be removed," said Henry. "I would remove it now, but that it seems absolutely painted on the panel, and I should awake Flora in any attempt to do so."

He arose and ascertained that such was the case, and that it would require a workman, with proper tools adapted to the job, to remove the portrait.

"True," he said, "I might now destroy it, but it is a pity to obscure a work of such rare art as this is; I should blame myself if I were. It shall be removed to some other room of the house, however."

Then, all of a sudden, it struck Henry how foolish it would be to remove the portrait from the wall of a room which, in all likelihood, after that night, would be uninhabited; for it was not probable that Flora would choose again to inhabit a chamber in which she had gone through so much terror.

"It can be left where it is," he said, "and we can fasten up, if we please, even the very door of this room, so that no one need trouble themselves any further about it."

The morning was now coming fast, and just as Henry thought he would partially draw a blind across the window, in order to shield from the direct rays of the sun the eyes of Flora, she awoke.

"Help — help!" she cried, and Henry was by her side in a moment.

"You are safe, Flora — you are safe," he said.

"Where is it now?" she said.

"What — what, dear Flora?"

"The dreadful apparition. Oh, what have I done to be made thus perpetually miserable?"

"Think no more of it, Flora."

"I must think. My brain is on fire! A million of strange eyes seem to be gazing on me."

"Great Heaven! she raves," said Henry.

"Hark — hark — hark! He comes on the wings of the storm. Oh, it is most horrible — horrible!"

Henry rang the bell, but not sufficiently loudly to create any alarm. The sound reached the waking ear of the mother, who in a few moments was in the room.

"She has awakened," said Henry, "and has spoken, but she seems to me to wander in her discourse. For God's sake, soothe her, and try to bring her mind round to its usual state."

"I will, Henry — I will."

"And I think mother, if you were to get her out of this room, and into some other chamber as far removed from this one as possible, it would tend to withdraw her mind from what has occurred."

"Yes; it shall be done. Oh, Henry, what was it — what do you think it was?"

"I am lost in a sea of wild conjecture. I can form no conclusion; where is Mr. Marchdale?"

"I believe in his chamber."

"Then I will go and consult with him."

Henry proceeded at once to the chamber, which was, as he knew, occupied by Mr. Marchdale; and as he crossed the corridor, he could not but pause a moment to glance from a window at the face of nature.

As is often the case, the terrific storm of the preceding evening had cleared the air, and rendered it deliciously invigorating and lifelike. The weather had been dull, and there had been for some days a certain heaviness in the atmosphere, which was now entirely removed.

The morning sun was shining with uncommon brilliancy, birds were singing in every tree and on every bush; so pleasant, so spirit-stirring, health-giving a morning, seldom had he seen. And the effect upon his spirits was great, although not altogether what it might have been, had all gone on as it usually was in the habit of doing at that house. The ordinary little casualties of evil fortune had certainly from time to time, in the shape of illness, and one thing or another, attacked the family of the Bannerworths in common with every other family, but here suddenly had arisen a something at once terrible and inexplicable.

He found Mr. Marchdale up and dressed, and apparently in deep and anxious thought. The moment he saw Henry, he said, —

"Flora is awake, I presume?"

"Yes, but her mind appears to be much disturbed."

"From bodily weakness, I dare say."

"But why should she be bodily weak? she was strong and well, ay, as well as she could ever be in all her life. The glow of youth and health was on her cheeks. It is possible that, in the course of one night, she should become bodily weak to such an extent?"

"Henry," said Mr. Marchdale, sadly, "sit down. I am not, as you know, a superstitious man."

"You certainly are not."

"And yet, I never in all my life was so absolutely staggered as I have been by the occurrences of tonight."

"Say on."

"There is a frightful, a hideous solution for them; one which every consideration will tend to add strength to, one which I tremble to name now, although, yesterday, at this hour, I should have laughed it to scorn."

"Indeed!"

"Yes, it is so. Tell no one that which I am about to say to you. Let the dreadful suggestion remain with ourselves alone, Henry Bannerworth."

"I — I am lost in wonder."

"You promise me?"

"What — what?"

"That you will not repeat my opinion to any one."

"I do."

"On your honor."

"On my honor, I promise."

Mr. Marchdale rose, and proceeding to the door, he looked out to see that there were no listeners near. Having ascertained then that they were quite alone, he returned, and drawing a chair close to that on which Henry sat, he said, —

"Henry, have you never heard of a strange and dreadful superstition which, in some countries, is extremely rife, by which is it supposed that there are beings who never die?"

"Never die!"

"Never. In a word, Henry, have you never heard of — of — I dread to pronounce the word."

"Speak it. God of Heaven! let me hear it."

"*A vampyre!*"

Henry sprung to his feet. His whole frame quivered with emotion; the drops of perspiration stood upon his brow, as, in a strange, hoarse voice, he repeated the words, —

"A vampyre!"

"Even so; one who has to renew a dreadful existence by human blood — one who eats not and drinks not as other men — a vampyre."

Henry dropped into his seat, and uttered a deep groan of the most exquisite anguish.

"I could echo that groan," said Marchdale, "but that I am so thoroughly bewildered I know not what to think."

"Good God — good God!"

"Do not too readily yield to belief in so dreadful a supposition, I pray you."

"Yield belief!" exclaimed Henry, as he rose, and lifted up one of his hands above his head. "No; by Heaven, and the great God of all, who there rules, I will not easily believe aught so awful and so monstrous."

"I applaud your sentiment, Henry; not willingly would I deliver up myself to so frightful a belief — it is too horrible. I merely have told you of that which you saw was on my mind. You have surely before heard of such things."

"I have — I have."

"I much marvel, then, that the supposition did not occur to you, Henry."

"It did not — it did not, Marchdale. It — it was too dreadful, I suppose, to find a home in my heart. Oh! Flora, Flora, if this horrible idea should once occur to you, reason cannot, I am quite sure, uphold you against it."

"Let no one presume to insinuate it to her, Henry. I would not have it mentioned to her for worlds."

"Nor I — nor I. Good God! I shudder at the very thought — the mere possibility; but there is no possibility, there can be none. I will not believe it."

"Nor I."

"No; by Heaven's justice, goodness, grace and mercy, I will not believe it."

"'Tis well sworn, Henry; and now, discarding the supposition that Flora has been visited by a vampyre, let us seriously set about endeavoring, if we can, to account for what has happened in this house."

"I — I cannot now."

"Nay, let us examine the matter; if we can find any natural explanation, let us cling to it, Henry, as the sheet-anchor of our very souls."

"Do you think. You are fertile in expedients. Do you think, Marchdale; and, for Heaven's sake, and for the sake of our worn peace, find out some other way of accounting for what has happened, than the hideous one you have suggested."

"And yet my pistol bullets hurt him not; and he has left the tokens of his presence on the neck of Flora."

"Peace, oh! peace. Do not, I pray you, accumulate reasons why I should receive such a dismal, awful superstition. Oh, do not, Marchdale, as you love me!"

"You know my attachment to you," said Marchdale, "is sincere; and yet, Heaven help us!"

His voice was broken by grief as he spoke, and he turned aside his head to hide the bursting tears that would, despite all his efforts, show themselves in his eyes.

"Marchdale," added Henry, after a pause of some moments' duration, "I will sit up tonight with my sister."

"Do — do!"

"Think you there is a chance it may come again?"

"I cannot — I dare not speculate upon the coming of so dreadful a visitor, Henry; but I will hold watch with you most willingly."

"You will, Marchdale?"

"My hand upon it. Come what dangers may, I will share them with you, Henry."

"A thousand thanks. Say nothing, then, to George of what we have been talking about. He is of a highly susceptible nature and the very idea of such a thing would kill him."

"I will; be mute. Remove your sister to some other chamber, let me beg of you, Henry; the one she now inhabits will always be suggestive of horrible thoughts."

"I will; and that dreadful-looking portrait, with its perfect likeness to him who came last night."

"Perfect indeed. Do you intend to remove it?"

"I do not. I thought of doing so; but it is actually on the panel in the wall, and I would not willingly destroy it, and it may as well remain where it is in that chamber, which I can readily now believe will become henceforward a deserted one in this house."

"It may well become such."

"Who comes here? I hear a step."

There was a tap at the door at this moment, and George made his appearance in answer to the summons to come in. He looked pale and ill; his face betrayed how much he had mentally suffered during the night, and almost directly he got into the bed-chamber he said, —

"I shall, I am sure, be censured by you both for what I am going to say; but I cannot help saying it, nevertheless, for to keep it to myself would destroy me."

"Good God, George! what is it?" said Mr. Marchdale.

"Speak it out!" said Henry.

"I have been thinking of what has occurred here, and the result of that thought has been one of the wildest suppositions that ever I thought I should have to entertain. Have you never heard of a vampyre?"

Henry sighed deeply, and Marchdale was silent.

"I say a vampyre," added George, with much excitement in his manner. "It is a fearful, a horrible supposition; but our poor, dear Flora has been visited by a vampyre, and I shall go completely mad!"

He sat down, and covering his face with his hands, he wept bitterly and abundantly.

"George," said Henry, when he saw that the frantic grief had in some measure abated — "be calm, George, and endeavor to listen to me."

"I hear, Henry."

"Well, then, do not suppose that you are the only one in this house to whom so dreadful a superstition has occurred."

"Not the only one?"

"No; it has occurred to Mr. Marchdale also."

"Gracious Heaven!"

"He mentioned it to me; but we have both agreed to repudiate it with horror."

"To — repudiate — it?"

"Yes, George."

"And yet — and yet —"

"Hush, hush! I know what you would say. You would tell us that our repudiation of it cannot affect the fact. Of that we are aware; but yet will we disbelieve that which a belief in would be enough to drive us mad."

"What do you intend to do?"

"To keep this supposition to ourselves, in the first place; to guard it most zealously from the ears of Flora."

"Do you think she has never heard of vampyres?"

"I never heard her mention that in all her reading she had gathered even a hint of such a fearful superstition. If she has, we must be guided by circumstances, and do the best we can."

"Pray Heaven she may not!"

"Amen to that prayer, George," said Henry. "Mr. Marchdale and I intend to keep watch over Flora tonight."

"May not I join you?"

"Your health, dear George, will not permit you to engage in such matters. Do you seek your natural repose, and leave it to us to do the best we can in this most fearful and terrible emergency."

"As you please, brother, and as you please, Mr. Marchdale. I know I am a frail reed, and my belief is that this affair will kill me quite. The truth is, I am horrified — utterly and frightfully horrified. Like my poor, dear sister, I do not believe I shall ever sleep again."

"Do not fancy that, George," said Marchdale. "You very much add to the uneasiness which must be you poor mother's portion, by allowing this circumstance to so much affect you. You will know her affection for you all, and let me therefore, as a very old friend of hers, entreat you to wear as cheerful an aspect as you can in her presence."

"For once in my life," said George, sadly, "I will, to my dear mother, endeavor to play the hypocrite."

"Do so," said Henry. "The motive will sanction any such deceit as that, George, be assured."

The day wore on, and Poor Flora remained in a very precarious situation. It was not until mid-day that Henry made up his mind he would call in a medical gentleman to her, and then rode to the neighboring market town, where he knew an extremely intelligent practitioner resided. This gentleman Henry resolved upon, under a promise of secrecy, making a confidant of; but, long before he reached him, he found he might well dispense with the promise of secrecy.

He had never thought, so engaged had he been with other matters, that the servants were cognizant of the whole affair, and that from them he had no expectation of being able to keep the whole story in all its details. Of course such an opportunity for tale-bearing and gossiping was not likely to be lost; and while Henry was thinking over how he had better act in the matter, the news that Flora Bannerworth had been visited in the night by a vampyre — for the servants named the visitation such at once — was spreading all over the county.

As he rode along, Henry met a gentleman on horseback who belonged to the county, and who, reining in his steed, said to him,

"Good morning, Mr. Bannerworth."

"Good morning," responded Henry, and he would have ridden on, but the gentleman added, —

"Excuse me for interrupting you, sir; but what is the strange story that is in everybody's mouth about a vampyre?"

Henry nearly fell off his horse, he was so much astonished, and, wheeling the animal around, he said, —

"In everybody's mouth!"

"Yes; I have heard it from at least a dozen persons."

"You surprise me."

"Is it untrue? Of course I am not so absurd as really to believe about the vampyre; but is there no foundation at all to it? We generally find that at the bottom of these common reports there is a something around which, as a nucleus, the whole has formed."

"My sister is unwell."

"Ah, and that's all. It really is too bad, now."

"We had a visitor last night."

"A thief, I suppose?"

"Yes, yes — I believe a thief. I do believe it was a thief, and she was terrified."

"Of course, and upon such a thing is grafted a story of a vampyre, and the marks of his teeth being upon her neck, and all the circumstantial particulars."

"Yes, yes."

"Good morning, Mr. Bannerworth."

Henry bade the gentleman good morning, and much vexed at the publicity which the affair had already obtained, he set spurs to his horse, determined that he would speak to no one else upon so uncomfortable a theme. Several attempts were made to stop him, but he only waved his hand and trotted on, nor did he pause in his speed till he reached the door of Mr. Chillingworth, the medical man whom he intended to consult.

Henry knew that at such a time he would be at home, which was the case, and he was soon closeted with the man of drugs. Henry begged his patient hearing, which being accorded, he related to him at full length what had happened, not omitting, to the best of his remembrance, any one particular. When he had concluded his narration the doctor shifted his position several times, and then said, —

"That's all?"

"Yes — and enough too."

"More than enough, I should say, my young friend. You astonish me."

"Can you form any supposition, sir, on the subject?"

"Not just now. What is your own idea?"

"I cannot be said to have one about it. It is too absurd to tell you that my brother George is impressed with a belief a vampyre has visited the house."

"I never in all my life heard a more circumstantial narrative in favor of so hideous a superstition."

"Well, but you cannot believe —"

"Believe what?"

"That the dead can come to life again, and by such a process keep up vitality."

"Do you take me for a fool?"

"Certainly not."

"Then why do you ask me such questions?"

"But the glaring facts of the case?"

"I don't care if they were ten times more glaring, I won't believe it. I would rather believe you were all mad, the whole family of you — that at the full of the moon you all were a little cracked."

"And so would I."

"You go home now, and I will call and see your sister in the course of two hours. Something may turn up yet, to throw some new light on this strange subject."

With this understanding Henry went home, and he took care to ride as fast as before, in order to avoid questions, so that he got back to his old ancestral home without going through the disagreeable ordeal of having to explain to any one what had disturbed the peace of it.

When Henry reached his home, he found that the evening was rapidly coming on, and before he could permit himself to think upon any other subject, he inquired how his terrified sister had passed the hours during his absence.

He found that but little improvement had taken place in her, and that she had occasionally slept, but to awaken and speak incoherently, as if the shock she had received had had some serious effect upon her nerves. He repaired at once to her room, and finding that she was awake, he leaned over her, and spoke tenderly to her.

"Flora," he said, "dear Flora, you are better now?"

"Harry, is that you?"

"Yes, dear."

"Oh, tell me what has happened?"

"Have you not a recollection, Flora?"

"Yes, yes, Henry; but what was it? They none of them will tell me what it was, Henry."

"Be calm, dear. No doubt some attempt to rob the house."

"Think you so?"

"Yes; the bay window was particularly adapted for such a purpose; but now that you are removed here to this room, you will be able to rest in peace."

"I shall die of terror, Henry. Even now those eyes are glaring on me so hideously. Oh, it is fearful — it is very fearful, Henry. Do you not pity me, and no one will promise to remain with me at night."

"Indeed, Flora, you are mistaken, for I intend to sit by your bedside armed, and so preserve you from all harm."

She clutched his hand eagerly, as she said, —

"You will, Henry. You will, and not think it too much trouble, dear Henry."

"It can be no trouble, Flora."

"Then I shall rest in peace, for I know that the dreadful vampyre cannot come to me when you are by."

"The what, Flora?"

"The vampyre, Henry. It was a vampyre."

"Good God, who told you so?"

"No one. I have read of them in the book of travels in Norway, which Mr. Marchdale lent us all."

"Alas, alas!" groaned Henry. "Discard, I pray you, such a thought from your mind."

"Can we discard thoughts. What power have we but from the mind, which is ourselves?"

"True, true."

"Hark, what noise is that? I thought I heard a noise. Henry, when you go, ring for some one first. Was there not a noise?"

"The accidental shutting of some door, dear."

"Was it that?"

"It was."

"Then I am relieved. Henry, I sometimes fancy I am in the tomb, and that some one is feasting on my flesh. They do say, too, that those who in life have been bled by a vampyre, become themselves vampyres, and have the same horrible taste for blood as those before them. Is it not horrible?"

"You only vex yourself with such thoughts, Flora. Mr. Chillingworth is coming to see you."

"Can he minister to a mind diseased?"

"But yours is not, Flora. Your mind is healthful, and so, although his power extends not so far, we will thank Heaven, dear Flora, that you need it not."

She sighed deeply, and she said, —

"Heaven help me! I know not, Henry. The dreadful being held on to my hair. I must have it all taken off. I tried to get away, but it dragged me back — a brutal thing it was. Oh, then at that moment, Henry I felt as if something strange took place in my brain, and that I was going mad! I saw those glazed eyes close to mine — I felt a hot, pestiferous breath upon my face — help — help!"

"Hush! my Flora, hush! Look at me."

"I am calm again. It fixed its teeth in my throat. Did I faint away?"

"You did, dear; but let me pray you to refer all this to imagination; or at least the greater part of it."

"But you saw it."

"Yes —"

"All saw it."

"We all saw some man — a housebreaker — it must have been some housebreaker. What more easy, you know, dear Flora, than to assume some such disguise?"

"Was anything stolen?"

"Not that I know of; but there was an alarm, you know."

Flora shook her head, as she said, in a low voice, —

"That which came here was more than mortal. Oh, Henry, if it had but killed me, now I had been happy; but I cannot live — I hear it breathing now."

"Talk of something else, dear Flora," said the much-distressed Henry; "you will make yourself much worse, if you indulge yourself in these strange fancies."

"Oh, that they were but fancies!"

"They are, believe me."

"There is a strange confusion in my brain, and sleep comes over me suddenly, when I least expect it. Henry, Henry, what I was, I shall never, never be again."

"Say not so. All this will pass away like a dream, and leave so faint a trace upon your memory, that the time will come when you will wonder it ever made so deep an impression on your mind."

"You utter these words, Henry," she said, "but they do not come from your heart. Ah, no, no, no! Who comes?"

The door was opened by Mrs. Bannerworth, who said, —

"It is only me, my dear. Henry, here is Dr. Chillingworth in the dining-room."

Henry turned to Flora, saying, —

"You will see him, dear Flora? You know Mr. Chillingworth well."

"Yes, Henry, yes, I will see him, or who-ever you please."

"Shew Mr. Chillingworth up," said Henry to the servant.

In a few moments the medical man was in the room, and he at once approached the bedside to speak to Flora, upon whose pale countenance he looked with evident interest, while at the same time it seemed mingled with a painful feeling — at least so his own face indicated.

"Well, Miss Bannerworth," he said, "what is all this I hear about an ugly dream you have had?"

"A dream?" said Flora, as she fixed her beautiful eyes on his face.

"Yes, as I understand."

She shuddered and was silent.

"Was it not a dream, then?" added Mr. Chillingworth.

She wrung her hands, and in a voice of extreme anguish and pathos, said, —

"Would it were a dream — would it were a dream! Oh, if any one could but convince me it was a dream!"

"Well, will you tell me what it was?"

"Yes, sir, it was a vampyre."

Mr. Chillingworth glanced at Henry, as he said, in reply to Flora's words, —

"I suppose that is, after all, another name, Flora, for the nightmare?"

"No — no — no!"

"Do you really, then, persist in believing anything so absurd, Miss Bannerworth?"

"What can I say to the evidence of my own senses?" she replied. "I saw it, Henry saw it, George saw, Mr. Marchdale, my mother — all saw it. We could not all be at the same time the victims of the same delusion."

"How faintly you speak."

"I am very faint and ill."

"Indeed. What wound is that on your neck?"

A wild expression came over the face of Flora; a spasmodic action of the muscles, accompanied with a shuddering, as if a sudden chill had come over the whole mass of blood took place, and she said, —

"It is the mark left by the teeth of the vampyre."

The smile was a forced one upon the face of Mr. Chillingworth.

"Draw up the blind of the window, Mr. Henry," he said, "and let me examine this puncture to which your sister attaches so extraordinary a meaning."

The blind was drawn up, and a strong light was thrown into the room. For full two minutes Mr. Chillingworth attentively examined the two small wounds in the neck of Flora. He took a powerful magnifying glass from his pocket, and looked at them through it, and after his examination was concluded, he said, —

"They are very trifling wounds, indeed."

"But how inflicted?" said Henry.

"By some insect, I should say, which probably — it being the season for many insects — has flown in at the window."

"I know the motive," said Flora, "which prompts all these suggestions: it is a kind one, and I ought to be the last to quarrel with it; but what I have seen, nothing can make me believe I saw not, unless I am, as once or twice I have thought myself, really mad."

"How do you now feel in general health?"

"Far from well; and a strange drowsiness at times creeps over me. Even now I feel it."

She sunk back on the pillows as she spoke, and closed her eyes with a deep sigh.

Mr. Chillingworth beckoned Henry to come with him from the room, but the latter had promised that he would remain with Flora; and as Mrs. Bannerworth had left the chamber because she was unable to control her feelings, he rang the bell, and requested that his mother would come.

She did so, and then Henry went down stairs along with the medical man, whose opinion he was certainly eager to be now made acquainted with.

As soon as they were alone in the old-fashioned room which was called the oak closet, Henry turned to Mr. Chillingworth, and said, —

"What, now, is your candid opinion, sir? You have seen my sister, and those strange indubitable evidences of something wrong."

"I have; and to tell you candidly the truth, Mr. Henry, I am sorely perplexed."

"I thought you would be."

"It is not often that a medical man likes to say so much, nor is it, indeed, often prudent that he should do so, but in this case I own I am much puzzled. It is contrary to all my notions upon all such subjects."

"Those wounds, what do you think of them?"

"I know not what to think. I am completely puzzled as regards them."

"But, but do they not really bear the appearance of being bites?"

"They really do."

"And so far, then, they are actually in favor of the dreadful supposition which poor Flora entertains."

"So far they certainly are. I have no doubt in the world of their being bites; but we must not jump to a conclusion that the teeth which inflicted them were human. It is a strange case, and one which I feel assured must give you all much uneasiness, as, indeed, it gave me; but, as I said before, I will not let my judgment give in to the fearful and degrading superstition which all the circumstances connected with this strange story would seem to justify."

"It is a degrading superstition."

"To my mind your sister seems to be laboring under the effect of some narcotic."

"Indeed?"

"Yes; unless she really has lost a quantity of blood, which loss has decreased the heart's action sufficiently to produce the languor under which she now evidently labors."

"Oh, that I could believe the former supposition, but I am confident she has taken no narcotic; she could not even do so by mistake, for there is no drug of the sort in the house. Besides, she is not heedless by any means. I am quite convinced that she has not done so."

"Then I am fairly puzzled, my young friend, and I can only say that I would freely have given half of what I am worth to see that figure you saw last night."

"What would you have done?"

"I would not have lost sight of it for the world's wealth."

"You would have felt your blood freeze with horror. The face was terrible."

"And yet let it lead me where it liked I would have followed."

"I wish you had been here."

"I wish to Heaven I had. If I thought there was the least chance of another visit I would come and wait with patience every night for a month."

"I cannot say," replied Henry. "I am going to sit up tonight with my sister, and, I believe, our friend Mr. Marchdale will share my watch with me."

Mr. Chillingworth appeared to be for a few moments lost in thought, and then, suddenly rousing himself, as if he found it either impossible to come to any rational conclusion upon the subject, or had arrived at one which he chose to keep to himself, he said, —

"Well, well, we must leave the matter at present as it stands. Time may accomplish something towards its development; but at present so palpable a mystery I never came across, or a matter in which human calculation was so completely foiled."

"Nor I — nor I."

"I will send you some medicines, such as I think will be of service to Flora, and depend upon seeing me by ten o'clock tomorrow morning."

"You have, of course, heard something," said Henry to the doctor, as he was pulling on his gloves, "about vampyres."

"I certainly have, and I understand that in some countries, particularly Norway and Sweden, the superstition is a very common one."

"And in the Levant."

"Yes. The ghouls of the Mahometans are of the same description of beings. All that I have heard of the European vampyre has made it a being which can be killed, but is restored to life again by the rays of a full moon falling on the body."

"Yes, yes, I have heard as much."

"And that the hideous repast of blood has to be taken very frequently, and that if the vampyre gets it not he wastes away, presenting the appearance of one in the last stage of a consumption, and visibly, so to speak, dying."

"That is what I have understood."

"Tonight, do you know, Mr. Bannerworth, is the full of the moon." Henry started.

"If now you had succeeded in killing — . Pshaw, what am I saying. I believe I am getting foolish, and that the horrible superstition is beginning to fasten itself upon me as well as upon all of you. How strangely the fancy will wage war with the judgment in such a way as this."

"The full of the moon," repeated Henry, as he glanced towards the window, "and the night is near at hand."

"Banish these thoughts from your mind," said the doctor, "or else, my young friend, you will make yourself decidedly ill. Good evening to you, for it is evening. I shall see you tomorrow morning."

Mr. Chillingworth appeared now to be anxious to go, and Henry no longer opposed his departure; but when he was gone a sense of great loneliness came over him.

"Tonight," he repeated, "is the full of the moon. How strange that this dreadful adventure should have taken place just the night before. 'Tis very strange. Let me see — let me see."

He took from the shelves of a bookcase the work which Flora had mentioned, entitled, "Travels in Norway," in which work he found some account of the popular belief in vampyres.

He opened the work at random, and then some of the leaves turned over of themselves to a particular place, as the leaves will frequently do when it has been kept open a length of time at that part, and the binding stretched there more than anywhere else. There was a note at the bottom of one of the pages at this part of the book, and Henry read as follows: —

"With regard to these vampyres, it is believed by those who are inclined to give credence to so dreadful a superstition, that they always endeavor to make their feast of blood, for the revival of their bodily powers, on some evening immediately preceding a full moon, because if any accident befall them, such as being shot, or otherwise killed or wounded, they can recover by lying down somewhere where the full moon's rays will fall on them."

Henry let the book drop from his hands with a groan and a shudder.

Chapter V.

THE NIGHT WATCH. – THE PROPOSAL. – THE MOONLIGHT. – THE FEARFUL ADVENTURE.

A kind of stupefaction came over Henry Bannerworth, and he sat for about a quarter of an hour scarcely conscious of where he was, and almost incapable of anything in the shape of rational thought. It was his brother, George, who roused him by saying, as he laid his hand upon his shoulder, –

"Henry, are you asleep?"

Henry had not been aware of his presence, and he started up as if he had been shot.

"Oh, George, is it you?" he said.

"Yes, Henry, are you unwell?"

"No, no; I was in a deep reverie."

"Alas, I need not ask upon what subject," said George, sadly. "I sought you to bring you this letter."

"A letter to me?"

"Yes, you see it is addressed to you, and the seal looks as if it came from some one of consequence."

"Indeed!"

"Yes, Henry. Read it, and see from whence it comes."

There was just sufficient light by going to the window to enable Henry to read the letter, which he did aloud.

It ran thus: –

"Sir Francis Varney presents his compliments to Mr. Beaumont, and is much concerned to hear that some domestic affliction has fallen upon him. Sir Francis hopes that the genuine and loving sympathy of a neighbor will not be regarded as an intrusion, and begs to proffer any assistance or counsel that may be within the compass of his means.

"Ratford Abbey."

"Sir Francis Varney!" said Henry, "who is he?"

"Do you not remember, Henry," said George, "we were told a few days ago, that a gentleman of that name had become the purchaser of the estate of Ratford Abbey."

"Oh, yes, yes. Have you seen him?"

"I have not."

"I do not wish to make any new acquaintance, George. We are very poor — much poorer indeed that the general appearance of this place, which, I fear, we shall soon have to part with, would warrant any one believing. I must, of course, return a civil answer to this gentleman, but it must be such a one as shall repress familiarity."

"That will be difficult to do while we remain here, when we come to consider the very close proximity of the two properties, Henry."

"Oh, no, not at all. He will easily perceive that we do not want to make acquaintance with him, and then, as a gentleman, which doubtless he is, he will give up the attempt."

"Let it be so, Henry. Heaven knows I have no desire to form any new acquaintance with any one, and more particularly under our present circumstances of depression. And now, Henry, you must permit me, as I have had some repose, to share with you your night watch in Flora's room."

"I would advise you not, George; your health, as you know, is far from good."

"Nay, allow me. If not, then the anxiety I shall suffer will do me more harm than the watchfulness I shall keep up in her chamber."

This was an argument which Henry felt himself the force of too strongly not to admit it in the case of George, and he therefore made no further opposition to his wish to make one in the night watch.

"There will be an advantage," said George, "you see, in three of us being engaged in this matter, because, should anything occur, two can act together, and yet Flora may not be left alone."

"True, true, that is a great advantage."

Now a soft gentle silvery light began to spread itself over the heavens. The moon was rising, and as the beneficial effects of the storm of the preceding evening were still felt in the clearness of the air, the rays appeared to be more lustrous and full of beauty than they commonly were.

Each moment the night grew lighter, and by the time the brothers were ready to take their places in the chamber of Flora, the moon had risen considerably.

Although neither Henry nor George had any objection to the company of Mr. Marchdale, yet they gave him the option, and rather in fact urged him not to destroy his night's repose by sitting up with them; but he said —

"Allow me to do so; I am older, and have calmer judgment than you can have. Should anything again appear, I am quite resolved that it shall not escape me."

"What would you do?"

"With the name of God upon my lips," said Mr. Marchdale, solemnly, "I would grapple with it."

"You laid hands upon it last night."

"I did, and have forgotten to show you what I tore from it. Look here, — what should you say this was?"

He produced a piece of cloth, on which was an old-fashioned piece of lace, and two buttons. Upon a close inspection, this appeared to be a portion of the lapel of a coat of ancient times, and suddenly, Henry, with a look of intense anxiety, said, —

"This reminds me of the fashion of garments very many years ago, Mr. Marchdale."

"It came away in my grasp as if rotten and incapable of standing any rough usage."

"What a strange unearthly smell it has!"

"Now that you mention it yourself," added Mr. Marchdale, "I must confess it smells to me as if it had really come from the very grave."

"It does — it does. Say nothing of this relic of last night's work to any one."

"Be assured I shall not. I am far from wishing to keep up in any one's mind proofs of that which I would fain, very fain refute."

Mr. Marchdale replaced the portion of the coat which the figure had worn in his pocket, and then the whole three proceeded to the chamber of Flora.

*I*t was within a very few minutes of midnight, the moon had climbed high in the heavens, and a night of such brightness and beauty had seldom shown itself for a long period of time.

Flora slept, and in her chamber sat the two brothers and Mr. Marchdale, silently, for she had shown symptoms of restlessness, and they much feared to break the light slumber into which she had fallen.

Occasionally they had conversed in whispers, which could not have the effect of rousing her, for the room, although smaller than the one she had before occupied, was still sufficiently spacious to enable them to get some distance from the bed.

Until the hour of midnight now actually struck, they were silent, and when the last echo of the sounds had died away, a feeling of uneasiness came over them, which prompted some conversation to get rid of it.

"How bright the moon is now," said Henry in a low tone.

"I never saw it brighter," replied Marchdale. "I feel as if I were assured that we shall not tonight be interrupted."

"It was later than this," said Henry.

"Do not then yet congratulate us upon no visit."

"How still the house is!" remarked George; "it seems to me as if I had never found it so intensely quiet before."

"It is very still."

"Hush! she moves."

Flora moaned in her sleep, and made a slight movement. The curtains were all drawn closely round the bed to shield her eyes from the bright moonlight which streamed into the room so brilliantly. They might have closed the shutters of the window, but this they did not like to do, as it would render their watch there of no avail at all, inasmuch as they would not be able to see if any attempt was made by any one to obtain admittance.

A quarter of an hour longer might have thus passed when Mr. Marchdale said in a whisper —

"A thought has just stuck me that the piece of coat I have, which I dragged from the figure last night, wonderfully resembles in color and appearance the style of dress of the portrait in the room which Flora lately slept in."

"I thought of that," said Henry, "when first I saw it; but, to tell the honest truth, I dreaded to suggest any new proof connected with last night's visitation."

"Then I ought not to have drawn your attention to it," said Mr. Marchdale, "and regret I have done so."

"Nay, do not blame yourself on such an account," said Henry. "You are quite right, and it is I who am too foolishly sensitive. Now, however, since you have mentioned it, I must own I have a great desire to test the accuracy of the observation by a comparison with the portrait."

"That may easily be done."

"I will remain here," said George, "in case Flora awakens, while you two go if you like. It is but across the corridor."

Henry immediately rose, saying —

"Come, Mr. Marchdale, come. Let us satisfy ourselves at all events upon this point at once. As George says it is only across the corridor, and we can return directly."

"I am willing," said Mr. Marchdale, with a tone of sadness.

There was no light needed, for the moon stood suspended in a cloudless sky, so that from the house being a detached one, and containing numerous windows, it was as light as day.

Although the distance from one chamber to the other was only across the corridor, it was a greater space than these words might occupy, for the corridor was wide, neither was it directly across, but considerably slanting. However, it was certainly sufficiently close at hand for any sound of alarm from one chamber to reach the other without any difficulty.

A few moments sufficed to place Henry and Mr. Marchdale in that antique room, where, from the effect of the moonlight which was streaming over it, the portrait on the panel looked exceedingly life like.

And this effect was probably the greater because the rest of the room was not illuminated by the moon's rays, which came through a window in the corridor, and then at the open door of that chamber upon the portrait.

Mr. Marchdale held the piece of cloth he had close to the dress of the portrait, and one glance was sufficient to show the wonderful likeness between the two.

"Good God!" said Henry, "it is the same!"

Mr. Marchdale dropped the piece of cloth and trembled.

"This fact shakes even your skepticism," said Henry.

"I know not what to make of it."

"I can tell you something which bears upon it. I do not know if you are sufficiently aware of my family history to know that this one of my ancestors, I wish I could say worthy ancestors, committed suicide, and was buried in his clothes."

"You — you are sure of that?"

"Quite sure."

"I am more and more bewildered as each moment some strange corroborative fact of that dreadful supposition we so much shrink from seems to come to light and to force itself upon our attention."

There was a silence of a few moments duration, and Henry had turned towards Mr. Marchdale to say something, when the cautious tread of a footstep was heard in the garden, immediately beneath that balcony.

A sickening sensation came over Henry, and he was compelled to lean against the wall for support, as in scarcely articulate accents he said —

"The vampyre — the vampyre! God of heaven, it has come once again!"

"Now, Heaven inspire us with more than mortal courage," cried Mr. Marchdale, and he dashed open the window at once, and sprang into the balcony.

Henry in a moment recovered himself sufficiently to follow him, and when he reached his side in the balcony, Marchdale said, as he pointed below, —

"There is some one concealed there."

"Where — where?"

"Among the laurels. I will fire a random shot, and we may do some execution."

"Hold!" said a voice from below; "don't do any such thing, I beg of you."

"Why, that is Mr. Chillingworth's voice," cried Henry.

"Yes, and it's Mr. Chillingworth's person, too," said the doctor, as he emerged from among some laurel bushes.

"How is this?" said Marchdale.

"Simply that I made up my mind to keep watch and ward tonight outside here, in the hope of catching the vampyre. I got into here by climbing the gate."

"But why did you not let me know?" said Henry.

"Because I did not know myself, my young friend, till an hour and a half ago."

"Have you seen anything?"

"Nothing. But I fancied I heard something in the park outside the wall."

"Indeed!"

"What say you, Henry," said Mr. Marchdale, "to descending and taking a hasty examination of the garden and grounds?"

"I am willing; but first allow me to speak to George, who otherwise might be surprised at our long absence."

Henry walked rapidly to the bed-chamber of Flora, and he said to George, —

"Have you any objection to being left alone here for about half an hour, George, while we make an examination of the garden?"

"Let me have some weapon and I care not. Remain here while I fetch a sword from my own room."

Henry did so, and when George returned with a sword, which he always kept in his bed-room, he said, —

"Now go, Henry. I prefer a weapon of this description to pistols much. Do not be gone longer than necessary."

"I will not, George, be assured."

George was then left alone, and Henry returned to the balcony, where Mr. Marchdale was waiting for him. It was a quicker mode of descending to the garden to do so by clambering over the balcony than any other, and the height was not considerable enough to make it very objectionable, so Henry and Mr. Marchdale chose that way of joining Mr. Chillingworth.

"You are, no doubt, much surprised at finding me here," said the doctor; "but the fact is, I half made up my mind to come while I was here; but I had not thoroughly done so, therefore I said nothing to you about it."

"We are much indebted to you," said Henry, "for making the attempt."

"I am prompted to it by a feeling of the strongest curiosity."

"Are you armed, sir?" said Marchdale.

"In this stick," said the doctor, "is a sword, the exquisite temper of which I know I can depend upon, and I fully intended to run through any one whom I saw that looked in the least of the vampyre order."

"You would have done quite right," replied Mr. Marchdale. "I have a brace of pistols here, loaded with ball; will you take one, Henry, if you please, and then we shall be all armed."

Thus, then, prepared for any exigency, they made the whole round of the house; but found all the fastenings secure, and everything as quiet as possible.

"Suppose, now, we take a survey of the park outside the garden wall," said Mr. Marchdale.

This was agreed to; but before they had proceeded far, Mr. Marchdale said, —

"There is a ladder lying on the wall; would it not be a good plan to place it against the very spot the supposed vampyre jumped over last night, and so, from a more elevated position, take a view of the open meadows. We could easily drop down on the outer side, if we saw anything suspicious."

"Not a bad plan," said the doctor. "Shall we do it?"

"Certainly," said Henry; and they accordingly carried the ladder, which had been used for pruning the trees, towards the spot at the end of the long walk, at which the vampyre had made good, after so many fruitless efforts, his escape from the premises.

Then made haste down the long vista of trees until they reached the exact spot, and then they placed the ladder as near as possible, exactly where Henry, in his bewilderment on the evening before, had seen the apparition from the grave spring to.

"We can ascend singly," said Marchdale; "but there is ample space for us all there to sit on the top of the wall and make our observations."

This was seen to be the case, and in about a couple of minutes they had taken up their position on the wall, and, although the height was but trifling, they found that they had a much more extensive view than they could have obtained by any other means.

"To contemplate the beauty of such a night as this," said Mr. Chillingworth, "is amply sufficient compensation for coming the distance I have."

"And who knows," remarked Marchdale, "we may yet see something which may throw a light upon our present perplexities? God knows that I would give all I can call mine in the world to relieve you and your sister, Henry Bannerworth, from the fearful effect which last night's proceedings cannot fail to have upon you."

"Of that I am well assured, Mr. Marchdale," said Henry. "If the happiness of myself and family depended upon you, we should be happy indeed."

"You are silent, Mr. Chillingworth," remarked Marchdale, after a slight pause.

"Hush!" said Mr. Chillingworth — "hush — hush!"

"Good God, what do you hear?" cried Henry.

The doctor laid his hand upon Henry's arm as he said, —

"There is a young lime tree yonder to the right."

"Yes — yes."

"Carry your eye from it in a horizontal line, as near as you can, towards the wood."

Henry did so, and then he uttered a sudden exclamation of surprise, and pointed to a rising spot of ground, which was yet, in consequence of the number of tall trees in its vicinity, partially enveloped in shadow.

"What is that?" he said.

"I see something," said Marchdale. "By Heaven! it is a human form lying stretched there."

"It is — as if in death."

"What can it be?" said Chillingworth.

"I dread to say," replied Marchdale; "but to my eyes, even at this distance, it seems like the form of him we chased last night."

"The vampyre?"

"Yes — yes. Look, the moonbeams touch him. Now the shadows of the trees gradually recede. God of Heaven! the figure moves."

Henry's eyes were riveted to that fearful object, and now a scene presented itself which filled them all with wonder and astonishment, mingled with sensations of the greatest awe and alarm.

As the moonbeams, in consequence of the luminary rising higher and higher in the heavens, came to touch this figure that lay extended on the rising ground, a perceptible movement took place in it. The limbs appeared to tremble, and although it did not rise up, the whole body gave signs of vitality.

"The vampyre — the vampyre!" said Mr. Marchdale. "I cannot doubt it now. We must have hit him last night with the pistol bullets, and the moonbeams are now restoring him to a new life."

Henry shuddered, and even Mr. Chillingworth turned pale. But he was the first to recover himself sufficiently to propose some course of action, and he said, —

"Let us descend and go up to this figure. It is a duty we owe to ourselves as much as to society."

"Hold a moment," said Mr. Marchdale, as he produced a pistol. "I am an unerring shot, as you well know, Henry. Before we move from this position we now occupy, allow me to try what virtue may be in a bullet to lay that figure low again."

"He is rising!" exclaimed Henry.

Mr. Marchdale leveled the pistol — he took sure and deliberate aim, and then, just as the figure seemed to be struggling to its feet, he fired, and, with a sudden bound, it fell again.

"You have hit it," said Henry.

"You have indeed," exclaimed the doctor. "I think we can go now."

"Hush!" said Marchdale — "Hush! Does it not seem to you that, hit it as often as you will, the moonbeams will recover it?"

"Yes — yes," said Henry, "they will — they will."

"I can endure this no longer," said Mr. Chillingworth, as he sprung from the wall. "Follow me or not, as you please, I will seek the spot where this being lies."

"Oh, be not rash," cried Marchdale. "See, it rises again, and its form looks gigantic."

"I trust in Heaven and a righteous cause," said the doctor, as he drew the sword he had spoken of from the stick, and threw away the scabbard. "Come with me if you like, or I go alone."

Henry at once jumped down from the wall, and then Marchdale followed him, saying, —

"Come on; I will not shrink."

They ran towards the piece of rising ground; but before they got to it, the form rose and made rapidly towards a little wood which was in the immediate neighborhood of the hillock.

"It is conscious of being pursued," cried the doctor. "See how it glances back, and then increases its speed."

"Fire upon it, Henry," said Marchdale.

He did so; but either his shot did not take effect, or it was quite unheeded, if it did, by the vampyre, which gained the wood before they could have a hope of getting sufficiently near it to effect, or endeavor to effect, a capture.

"I cannot follow it there," said Marchdale. "In open country I would have pursued it closely; but I cannot follow it into the intricacies of a wood."

"Pursuit is useless there," said Henry. "It is enveloped in the deepest gloom."

"I am not so unreasonable," remarked Mr. Chillingworth, "as to wish you to follow into such a place as that. I am confounded utterly by this affair."

"And I," said Marchdale. "What on earth is to be done?"

"Nothing — nothing!" exclaimed Henry, vehemently; "and yet I have, beneath the canopy of Heaven, declared that I will, so help me God! spare neither time nor trouble in the unraveling of this most fearful piece of business. Did either of you remark the clothing which this spectral appearance wore?"

"They were antique clothes," said Mr. Chillingworth, "such as might have been fashionable a hundred years ago, but not now."

"Such was my own impression," added Marchdale.

"And such my own," said Henry, excitedly. "Is it at all within the compass of the wildest belief that what we have seen is a vampyre, and no other than my ancestor who, a hundred years ago, committed suicide?"

There was so much intense excitement, and evidence of mental suffering, that Mr. Chillingworth took him by the arm, saying, —

"Come home — come home; no more of this at present; you will make yourself seriously unwell."

"No — no — no."

"Come home — come home; I pray you; you are by far too much excited about this matter to pursue it with the calmness which should be brought to bear upon it."

"Take advice, Henry," said Marchdale, "take advice, and come home at once."

"I will yield to you; I feel that I cannot control my own feelings — I will yield to you, who, as you say, are cooler on this subject than I can be. Oh, Flora, Flora, I have no comfort for you now."

Poor Henry Bannerworth appeared to be in a complete state of mental prostration, on account of the distressing circumstances that had occurred so rapidly and so suddenly in his family, which had had quite enough to contend with without having superadded to every other evil the horror of believing that some preternatural agency was at work to destroy every hope of future happiness in this world, under any circumstances.

He suffered himself to be led home by Mr. Chillingworth and Marchdale; he no longer attempted to dispute the dreadful fact concerning the supposed vampyre; he could not contend now against all the corroborating circumstances that seemed to collect together for the purpose of proving that which, even when proved, was contrary to all his notions of Heaven, and at variance with all that was recorded and established as part and parcel of the system of nature.

"I cannot deny," he said, when they had reached home, "that such things are possible; but the probability will not bear a moment's investigation."

"There are more things," said Marchdale, "in Heaven, and on earth, than are dreamed in our philosophy."

"There are indeed, it appears," said Mr. Chillingworth.

"Are you a convert?" said Henry, turning to him.

"A convert to what?"

"To a belief in — in — these vampyres?"

"I? No, indeed; if you were to shut me up in a room full of vampyres, I would tell them all to their teeth that I defied them."

"But after what we have seen tonight?"

"What have we seen?"

"You are yourself a witness."

"True; I saw a man lying down, and then I saw a man get up; he seemed then to be shot, but whether he was or not he only knows; and then I saw him walk off in a desperate hurry. Beyond that, I saw nothing."

"Yes; but, taking such circumstances into combination with others, have you not a terrible fear of the truth of the dreadful appearance?"

"No — no; on my soul, no. I will die in my disbelief of such an outrage upon Heaven as one of these creatures would most assuredly be."

"Oh! that I could think like you; but the circumstance strikes too nearly to my heart."

"Be of better cheer, Henry — be of better cheer," said Marchdale; "there is one circumstance which we ought to consider, it is that, from all we have seen, there seems to be some things which would favor an opinion, Henry, that your ancestor, whose portrait hangs in the chamber which was occupied by Flora, is a vampyre."

"The dress is the same," said Henry.

"I noted it was."

"And I."

"Do you not, then, think it possible that something might be done to set that part of the question at rest?"

"What — what?"

"Where is your ancestor buried?"

"Ah! I understand you now."

"And I," said Mr. Chillingworth; "you would propose a visit to his mansion?"

"I would," added Marchdale; "anything that may in any way tend to assist in making this affair clearer, and divesting it of its mysterious circumstances, will be most desirable."

Henry appeared to rouse for some moments, and then he said, —

"He, in common with many other members of the family, no doubt occupies a place in the vault under the old church in the village."

"Would it be possible," asked Marchdale, "to get into that vault without exciting general attention?"

"It would," said Henry; "the entrance to the vault is in the flooring of the pew which belongs to the family in the old church."

"Then it could be done?" asked Mr. Chillingworth.

"Most undoubtedly."

"Will you undertake such an adventure?" said Mr. Chillingworth. "It may ease your mind."

"He was buried in the vault, and in his clothes," said Henry, musingly; "I will think of it. About such a proposition I would not decide hastily. Give me leave to think of it until tomorrow."

"Most certainly."

They now made their way to the chamber of Flora, and they heard from George that nothing of an alarming character had occurred to disturb him on his lonely watch. The morning was now again dawning, and Henry earnestly entreated Mr. Marchdale to go to bed, which he did, leaving the two brothers to continue as sentinels by Flora's bedside, until the morning light should banish all uneasy thoughts.

Henry related to George what had taken place outside the house, and the two brothers held a long and interesting conversation for some hours upon that subject, as well as upon others of great importance to their welfare. It was not until the sun's early rays came glaring in at the casement that they both rose, and thought of awakening Flora, who had now slept soundly for so many hours.

Chapter VI.

A GLANCE AT THE BANNERWORTH FAMILY. – THE PROBABLE CONSEQUENCES OF THE MYSTERIOUS APPARITION'S APPEARANCE.

*H*aving thus far, we hope, interested our readers in the fortunes of a family which had become subject to so dreadful a visitation, we trust that a few words concerning them, and the peculiar circumstances in which they are now placed, will not prove altogether out of place, or unacceptable. The Bannerworth family then were well known in the part of the country where they resided. Perhaps, if we were to say they were better known by name than they were liked, on account of that name, we should be near the truth, for it had unfortunately happened that for a very considerable time past the head of the family had been the very worst specimen of it that could be procured. While the junior branches were frequently amiable and most intelligent, and such in mind and manner as were calculated to inspire goodwill in all who knew them, he who held the family property, and who resided in the house now occupied by Flora and her brothers, was a very so-so sort of character.

This state of things, by some strange fatality, had gone on for nearly a hundred years, and the consequence was what might have been fairly expected, namely — that, what with their vices and what with their extravagancies, the successive heads of the Bannerworth family had succeeded in so far diminishing the family property that, when it came into the hands of Henry Bannerworth, it was of little value, on account of the numerous encumbrances with which it was saddled.

The father of Henry had not been a very brilliant exception to the general rule, as regarded the head of the family. If he were not quite so bad as many of his ancestors, that gratifying circumstance was to be accounted for by the supposition that he was not quite so bold, and that the changes in habits, manners, and laws, which had taken place in a hundred years, made it not so easy for even a landed proprietor to play the petty tyrant.

He had, to get rid of those animal spirits which had prompted many of his predecessors to downright crimes, had recourse to the gaming table, and, after raising whatever sums he could upon the property which remained, he naturally, and as might have been fully expected, lost them all.

He was found lying dead in the garden of the house one day, and by his side was his pocket-book, on one leaf of which, it was the impression of the family, he had endeavored to write something previous to his decease, for he held a pencil firmly in his grasp.

The probability was that he had felt himself getting ill, and, being desirous of making some communication to his family which pressed heavily upon his mind, he had attempted to do so, but was stopped by the too rapid approach of the hand of death.

For some days previous to his decease, his conduct had been extremely mysterious. He had announced an intention of leaving England for ever — of selling the house and grounds for whatever they would fetch over and above the sums for which they were mortgaged, and so clearing himself of all encumbrances.

He had, but a few hours before he was found lying dead, made the following singular speech to Henry, —

"Do not regret, Henry, that the old house which has been in our family so long is about to be parted with. Be assured that, if it is but for the first time in my life, I have good and substantial reasons now for what I am about to do. We shall be able to go to some other country, and there live like princes of the land."

Where the means were to come from to live like a prince, unless Mr. Bannerworth had some of the German princes in his eye, no one knew but himself, and his sudden death buried with him that most important secret.

There were some words written on the leaf of his pocket book, but they were of by far too indistinct and ambiguous a nature to lead to anything. They were these: —

"The money is —"

And then there was a long scrawl of the pencil, which seemed to have been occasioned by his sudden decease.

Of course nothing could be made of these words, except in the way of a contradiction, as the family lawyer said, rather more facetiously than a man of law usually speaks, for if he had written "The money is not," he would have been somewhere remarkably near the truth.

However, with all his vices he was regretted by his children, who chose rather to remember him in his best aspect than to dwell upon his faults.

For the first time then, within the memory of man, the head of the family of the Bannerworths was a gentleman, in every sense of the word. Brave, generous, highly educated, and full of many excellent and noble qualities — for such was Henry, whom we have introduced to our readers under such distressing circumstances.

And now, people said, that the family property having been all dissipated and lost, there would take place a change, and that the Bannerworths would have to take some course of honorable industry for a livelihood, and that then they would be as much respected as they had before been detested and disliked.

Indeed, the position which Henry held was now a most precarious one — for one of the amazingly clever acts of his father had been to encumber the property with overwhelming claims, so that when Henry administered to the estate, it was doubted almost by his attorney if it were at all desirable to do so.

An attachment, however, to the old house of his family, had induced the young man to hold possession of it as long as he could, despite any adverse circumstance which might eventually be connected with it.

Some weeks, however, only after the decease of his father, and when he fairly held possession, a sudden and a most unexpected offer came to him from a solicitor in London, of whom he knew nothing, to purchase the house and grounds, for a client of his, who had instructed him so to do, but whom he did not mention.

The offer made was a liberal one, and beyond the value of the place.

The lawyer who had conducted Henry's affairs for him since his father's decease, advised him by all means to take it; but after a consultation with his mother and sister, and George, they all resolved to hold by their own house as long as they could, and, consequently, he refused the offer.

He was then asked to let the place, and to name his own price for the occupation of it; but that he would not do: so the negotiation went off altogether, leaving only, in the minds of the family, much surprise at the exceeding eagerness of some one, whom they knew not, to get possession of the place on any terms.

There was another circumstance perhaps which materially aided in producing a strong feeling on the minds of the Bannerworths, with regard to remaining where they were.

That circumstance occurred thus: a relation of the family, who was now dead, and with whom had died all his means, had been in the habit, for the last half dozen years of his life, of sending a hundred pounds to Henry, for the express purpose of enabling him and his brother George and his sister Flora to take a little continental or home tour, in the autumn of the year.

A more acceptable present, or for a more delightful purpose, to young people, could not be found; and, with the quiet, prudent habits of all three of them, they contrived to go far and to see much for the sum which was thus handsomely placed at their disposal.

In one of those excursions, when among the mountains of Italy, an adventure occurred which placed the life of Flora in imminent hazard.

They were riding along a narrow mountain path, and, her horse slipping, she fell over the ledge of a precipice.

In an instant, a young man, a stranger to the whole party, who was traveling in the vicinity, rushed to the spot, and by his knowledge and exertions, they felt convinced her preservation was effected.

He told her to lie quiet; he encouraged her to hope for immediate succor; and then, with much personal exertion, and at immense risk to himself, he reached the ledge of rock on which she lay, and then he supported her until the brothers had gone to a neighboring house, which, by-the-bye, was two good English miles off, and got assistance.

There came on, while they were gone, a terrific storm, and Flora felt that but for him who was with her she must have been hurled from the rock, and perished in an abyss below, which was almost too deep for observation.

Suffice it to say that she was rescued; and he who had, by his intrepidity, done so much towards saving her, was loaded with the most sincere and heartfelt acknowledgments by the brothers as well as by herself.

He frankly told them that his name was Holland; that he was traveling for amusement and instruction, and was by profession an artist.

He traveled with them for some time; and it was not at all to be wondered at, under the circumstances, that an attachment of the tenderest nature should spring up between him and the beautiful girl, who felt that she owed to him her life.

Mutual glances of affection were exchanged between them, and it was arranged that when he returned to England, he should come at once as an honored guest to the house of the family of the Bannerworths.

All this was settled satisfactorily with the full knowledge and acquiescence of the two brothers, who had taken a strange attachment to the young Charles Holland, who was indeed in every way likely to propitiate the good opinion of all who knew him.

Henry explained to him exactly how they were situated, and told him that when he came he would find a welcome from all, except possibly his father, whose wayward temper he could not answer for.

Young Holland stated that he was compelled to be away for a term of two years, from certain family arrangements he had entered into, and that then he would return and hope to meet Flora unchanged as he should be.

It happened that this was the last of the continental excursions of the Bannerworths, for, before another year rolled round, the generous relative who had supplied them with the means of making such delightful trips was no more; and, likewise, the death of the father had occurred in the manner we have related, so that there was no chance, as had been anticipated and hoped for by Flora, of meeting Charles Holland on the continent again, before his two years of absence from England should be expired.

Such, however, being the state of things, Flora felt reluctant to give up the house, where he would be sure to come to look for her, and her happiness was too dear to Henry to induce him to make any sacrifice of it to expediency.

Therefore was it that Bannerworth Hall, as it was sometimes called, was retained, and fully intended to be retained at all events until after Charles Holland had made his appearance, and his advice (for he was, by the young people, considered one of the family) taken, with regard to what was advisable to be done.

With one exception this was the state of affairs at the hall, and that exception relates to Mr. Marchdale.

He was a distant relation of Mrs. Bannerworth, and, early in life, had been sincerely and tenderly attached to her. She, however, with the want of steady reflection of a young girl, as she then was, had, as is generally the case among several admirers, chosen the very worst: that is, the man who had treated her with the most indifference and who paid her the least attention, was, of course, thought the most of, and she gave her hand to him.

That man was Mr. Bannerworth. But future experience had made her thoroughly awake to her former error; and, but for the love she bore her children, who were certainly all that a mother's heart could wish, she would often have deeply regretted the infatuation which had induced her to bestow her hand in the quarter she had done so.

About a month after the decease of Mr. Bannerworth, there came one to the hall, who desired to see the widow. That one was Mr. Marchdale.

It might have been some slight tenderness towards him which had never left her, or it might be the pleasure merely of seeing one whom she had known intimately in early life, but, be that as it may, she certainly gave him a kindly welcome; and he, after consenting to remain for some time as a visitor at the hall, won the esteem of the whole family by his frank demeanor and cultivated intellect.

He had traveled much and seen much, and he had turned to good account all he had seen, that not only was Mr. Marchdale a man of sterling sound sense, but he was a most entertaining companion.

His intimate knowledge of many things concerning which they knew little or nothing; his accurate modes of thought, and a quiet, gentlemanly demeanor, such as is rarely to be met with, combined to make him esteemed by the Bannerworths. He had a small independence of his own, and being completely alone in the world, for he had neither wife nor child, Marchdale owned that he felt a pleasure in residing with the Bannerworths.

Of course he could not, in decent terms, so far offend them as to offer to pay for his subsistence, but he took good care that they should really be no losers by having him as an inmate, a matter which he could easily arrange by little presents of one kind and another, all of which he managed should be such as were not only ornamental, but actually spared his kind entertainers some positive expense which otherwise they must have gone to.

Whether or not this amiable piece of maneuvering was seen through by the Bannerworths it is not our purpose to inquire. If it was seen through, it could not lower him in their esteem, for it was probably just what they themselves would have felt a pleasure in doing under similar circumstances, and if they did not observe it, Mr. Marchdale would, probably, be all the better pleased.

Such then may be considered by our readers as a brief outline of the state of affairs among the Bannerworths — a state which was pregnant with changes, and which changes were now likely to be rapid and conclusive.

How far the feelings of the family towards the ancient house of their race would be altered by the appearance at it of so fearful a visitor as a vampyre, we will not stop to inquire, inasmuch as such feelings will develop themselves as we proceed.

That the visitation had produced a serious effect upon all the household was sufficiently evident, as well among the educated as among the ignorant. On the second morning, Henry received notice to quit his service from the three servants he had with difficulty contrived to keep at the hall. The reason why he received such notice he knew well enough, and therefore he did not trouble himself to argue about a superstition to which he felt now himself almost compelled to give way; for how could he say there was no such thing as a vampyre, when he had, with his own eyes, had the most abundant evidence of the terrible fact?

He calmly paid the servants, and allowed them to leave him at once without at all entering into the matter, and, for the time being, some men were procured, who, however, came evidently with fear and trembling, and probably only took the place, on account of not being able to procure any other. The comfort of the household was likely to be completely put an end to, and reasons now for leaving the hall appeared to be most rapidly accumulating.

Chapter VII.

THE VISIT TO THE VAULT OF THE BANNERWORTHS, AND ITS UNPLEASANT RESULT. – THE MYSTERY.

*H*enry and his brother roused Flora, and after agreeing together that it would be highly imprudent to say anything to her of the proceedings of the night, they commenced a conversation with her in encouraging and kindly accents.

"Well, Flora," said Henry, "you see you have been quite undisturbed tonight."

"I have slept long, dear Henry."

"You have, and pleasantly too, I hope."

"I have not had any dreams, and I feel much refreshed, now, and quite well again."

"Thank Heaven!" said George.

"If you will tell dear mother that I am awake, I will get up with her assistance."

The brothers left the room, and they spoke to each other of it as a favorable sign, that Flora did not object to being left alone now, as she had done on the preceding morning.

"She is fast recovering, now, George," said Henry. "If we could now but persuade ourselves that all this alarm would pass away, and that we should hear no more of it, we might return to our old and comparatively happy condition."

"Let us believe, Henry, that we shall."

"And yet, George, I shall not be satisfied in my mind, until I have paid a visit."

"A visit? Where?"

"To the family vault."

"Indeed, Henry! I thought you had abandoned that idea."

"I had. I have several times abandoned it; but it comes across my mind again and again."

"I much regret it."

"Look you, George; as yet, everything that has happened has tended to confirm a belief in this most horrible of all superstitions concerning vampyres."

"It has."

"Now, my great object, George, is to endeavor to disturb such a state of thing, by getting something, however slight, or of a negative character, for the mind to rest upon on the other side of the question."

"I comprehend you, Henry."

"You know that at present we are not only led to believe, almost irresistibly, that we have been visited by a vampyre, but that that vampyre is our ancestor, whose portrait is on the panel of the wall of the chamber into which he contrived to make his way."

"True, most true."

"Then let us, by an examination of the family vault, George, put an end to one of the evidences. If we find, as most surely we shall, the coffin of the ancestor of ours, who seems, in dress and appearance, so horribly mixed up in this affair, we shall be at rest on that head."

"But consider how many years have elapsed."

"Yes, a great number."

"What then, do you suppose, could remain of any corpse placed in a vault so long ago?"

"Decomposition must of course have done its work, but still there must be a something to show that a corpse has so undergone the process common to all nature. Double the lapse of time surely could not obliterate all traces of that which had been."

"There is reason in that, Henry."

"Besides, the coffins are all of lead, and some of stone, so that they cannot have all gone."

"True, most true."

"If in the one which, from the inscription and date, we discover to be that of our ancestor whom we seek, we find the evident remains of a corpse, we shall be satisfied that he has rested in his tomb in peace."

"Brother, you seem bent on this adventure," said George; "if you go, I will accompany you."

"I will not engage rashly in it, George. Before I finally decide, I will again consult with Mr. Marchdale. His opinion will weigh much with me."

"And in good time, here he comes across the garden," said George, as he looked from the window of the room in which they sat.

It was Mr. Marchdale, and the brothers warmly welcomed him as he entered the apartment.

"You have been early afoot," said Henry.

"I have," he said. "The fact is, that although at your solicitation I went to bed, I could not sleep, and I went out once more to search about the spot where we had seen the — the I don't know what to call it, for I have a great dislike to naming it a vampyre."

"There is not much in a name," said George.

"In this instance there is," said Marchdale. "It is a name suggestive of horror."

"Made you any discovery?" said Henry.

"None whatever."

"You saw no trace of any one?"

"Not the least."

"Well, Mr. Marchdale, George and I were talking over this projected visit to the family vault."

"Yes."

"And we agreed to suspend our judgments until we saw you, and learned your opinion."

"Which I will tell you frankly," said Mr. Marchdale, "because I know you desire it freely."

"Do so."

"It is, you should make the visit."

"Indeed."

"Yes, and for this reason. You have now, as you cannot help having, a disagreeable feeling, that you may find that one coffin is untenanted. Now, if you do fine it so, you scarcely make matters worse, by an additional confirmation of what already amounts to a strong supposition, and one which is likely to grow stronger by time."

"True, most true."

"On the contrary, if you find indubitable proofs that your ancestor has slept soundly in the tomb, and gone the way of all flesh, you will find yourselves much calmer, and that an attack is made upon the train of events which at present all run one way."

"That is precisely the argument I was using to George," said Henry, "a few moments since."

"Then let us go," said George, "by all means."

"It is so decided then," said Henry.

"Let it be done with caution," replied Mr. Marchdale.

"If any one can manage it, of course we can."

"Why should it not be done secretly and at night? Of course we lose nothing by making a night visit to a vault into which daylight, I presume, cannot penetrate."

"Certainly not."

"Then let it be at night."

"But we shall surely require the concurrence of some of the church authorities."

"Nay, I do not see that," interposed Mr. Marchdale. "It is to the vault actually vested in and belonging to yourself you wish to visit, and, therefore, you have a right to visit it in any manner or at any time that may be most suitable to yourself."

"But detection in a clandestine visit might produce unpleasant consequences."

"The church is old," said George, "and we could easily find means of getting into it. There is only one objection that I see, just now, and that is, that we leave Flora unprotected."

"We do, indeed," said Henry. "I did not think of that."

"It must be put to herself, as a matter for her own consideration," said Mr. Marchdale, "if she will consider herself sufficiently safe with the company and protection of your mother only."

"It would be a pity were we not all three present at the examination of the coffin," remarked Henry.

"It would, indeed. There is ample evidence," said Mr. Marchdale, "but we must not give Flora a night of sleeplessness and uneasiness on that account, and the more particularly as we cannot well explain to her where we are going, or upon what errand."

"Certainly not."

"Let us talk to her, then, about it," said Henry. "I confess I am much bent upon the plan, and fain would not forego it; neither should I like other than that we three should go together."

"If you determine, then, upon it," said Marchdale, "we will go tonight; and, from your acquaintance with the place, doubtless you will be able to decide what tools are necessary."

"There is a trap-door at the bottom of the pew," said Henry; "it is not only secured down, but it is locked likewise, and I have the key in my possession."

"Indeed!"

"Yes; immediately beneath is a short flight of stone steps, which conduct at once into the vault."

"Is it large?"

"No; about the size of a moderate chamber, with no intricacies about it."

"There can be no difficulties, then."

"None whatever, unless we meet with actual personal interruption, which I am inclined to think is very far from likely. All we shall require will be a screwdriver, with which to remove the screws, and then something with which to wrench open the coffin."

"Those we can easily provide, along with lights," remarked Mr. Marchdale. "I hope to heaven that this visit to the tomb will have the effect of easing your minds, and enable you to make a successful stand against the streaming torrent of evidence that has poured in upon us regarding this most fearful of apparitions."

"I do, indeed, hope so," added Henry; "and now I will go at once to Flora, and endeavor to convince her she is safe without us tonight."

"By-the-bye, I think," said Marchdale, "that if we can induce Mr. Chillingworth to come with us, it will be a great point gained in the investigation."

"He would," said Henry, "be able to come to an accurate decision with respect to the remains — if any — in the coffin, which we could not."

"Then have him, by all means," said George. "He did not seem averse last night to go on such an adventure."

"I will ask him when he makes his visit this morning upon Flora; and should he not feel disposed to join us, I am quite sure he will keep the secret of our visit."

All this being arranged, Henry proceeded to Flora, and told her that he and George, and Mr. Marchdale wished to go out for about a couple of hours in the evening after dark, if she felt sufficiently well to feel a sense of security without them.

Flora changed color, and slightly trembled, and then, as if ashamed of her fears, she said, —

"Go, go; I will not detain you. Surely no harm can come to me in presence of my mother."

"We shall not be gone longer than the time I mentioned to you," said Henry.

"Oh, I shall be quite content. Besides, am I to be kept thus in fear all my life? Surely, surely not. I ought, too, to learn to defend myself."

Henry caught at the idea, as he said, —

"If fire-arms were left you, do you think you would have courage to use them?"

"I do, Henry."

"Then you shall have them; and let me beg of you to shoot any one without the least hesitation who shall come into your chamber."

"I will, Henry. If ever human being was justified in the use of deadly weapons, I am now. Heaven protect me from a repetition of the visit to which I have now been once subjected. Rather, oh, much rather would I die a hundred deaths than suffer what I have suffered."

"Do not allow it, dear Flora, to press too heavily upon your mind in dwelling upon it in conversation. I still entertain a sanguine expectation that something may arise to afford a far less dreadful explanation of what has occurred than what you have put upon it. Be of good cheer, Flora, we shall go one hour after sunset, and return in about two hours from the time at which we leave here, you may be assured."

Notwithstanding this ready and courageous acquiescence of Flora in the arrangement, Henry was not without his apprehension that when the night should come again, her fears would return with it; but he spoke to Mr. Chillingworth upon the subject, and got that gentleman's ready consent to accompany them.

He promised to meet them at the church porch exactly at nine o'clock, and matters were all arranged, and Henry waited with much eagerness and anxiety now for the coming night, which he hoped would dissipate one of the fearful deductions which his imagination had drawn from recent circumstances.

He gave to Flora a pair of pistols of his own, upon which he knew he could depend, and he took good care to load them well, so that there could be no likelihood whatever of their missing fire at a critical moment.

"Now, Flora," he said, "I have seen you use fire-arms when you were much younger than you are now, and therefore I need give you no instructions. If any intruder does come, and you do fire, be sure you take a good aim, and shoot low."

"I will, Henry, I will; and you will be back in two hours?"

"Most assuredly I will."

The day wore on, evening came, and then deepened into night. It turned out to be a cloudy night, and therefore the moon's brilliance was nothing near equal to what it had been on the preceding night. Still, however, it had sufficient power over the vapors that frequently covered it for many minutes together, to produce a considerable light effect upon the face of nature, and the night was consequently very far, indeed, from what might be called a dark one.

George, Henry, and Marchdale, met in one of the lower rooms of the house, previous to starting upon their expedition; and after satisfying themselves that they had with them all the tools that were necessary, inclusive of the same small, but well-tempered iron crow-bar with which Marchdale had, on the night of the visit of the vampyre, forced open the door of Flora's chamber, they left the hall, and proceeded at a rapid pace towards the church.

"And Flora does not seem much alarmed," said Marchdale, "at being left alone?"

"No," replied Henry, "she has made up her mind with a strong natural courage which I knew was in her disposition to resist as much as possible the depressing effect of the awful visitation she has endured."

"It would have driven some really mad."

"It would, indeed; and her own reason tottered on its throne, but, thank Heaven, she has recovered."

"And I fervently hope that, through her life," added Marchdale, "she may never have such another trial."

"We will not for a moment believe that such a thing can occur twice."

"She is one among a thousand. Most young girls would never at all have recovered the fearful shock to the nerves."

"Not only has she recovered," said Henry, "but a spirit, which I am rejoiced to see, because it is one which will uphold her, of resistance now possesses her."

"Yes, she actually — I forgot to tell you before — but she actually asked me for arms to resist any second visitation."

"You much surprise me."

"Yes, I was surprised, as well as pleased, myself."

"I would have left her one of my pistols had I been aware of her having made such a request. Do you know if she can use fire-arms?"

"Oh, yes; well."

"What a pity. I have both of them with me."

"Oh, she is provided."

"Provided?"

"Yes; I found some pistols which I used to take with me on the continent, and she has them both well loaded, so that if the vampyre makes his appearance, he is likely to meet with rather a warm reception."

"Good God! was it not dangerous?"

"Not at all, I think."

"Well, you know best, certainly, of course. I hope the vampyre may come, and that we may have the pleasure, when we return, of finding him dead. By the bye, I — I — . Bless me, I have forgot to get the materials for lights, which I pledged myself to do."

"How unfortunate."

"Walk on slowly, while I run back and get them."

"Oh, we are too far —"

"Hilloa!" cried a man at this moment, some distance in front of them.

"It is Mr. Chillingworth," said Henry.

"Hilloa," cried the worthy doctor again. "Is that you, my friend, Henry Bannerworth?"

"It is," cried Henry.

Mr. Chillingworth now came up to them, and said, —

"I was before my time, so rather than wait at the church porch, which would have exposed me to observation perhaps, I thought it better to walk on, and chance meeting with you."

"You guessed we should come this way?"

"Yes, and so it turns out, really. It is unquestionably your most direct route to the church."

"I think I will go back," said Mr. Marchdale.

"Back!" exclaimed the doctor; "what for?"

"I forgot the means of getting lights. We have candles, but no means of lighting them."

"Make yourselves easy on that score," said Mr. Chillingworth. "I am never without some chemical matches of my own manufacture, so that as you have the candles, that can be no bar to our going on at once."

"That is fortunate," said Henry.

"Very," added Marchdale; "for it seems a mile's hard walking for me, or at least half a mile from the hall. Let us now push on."

They did push on, all four walking at a brisk pace. The church, although it belonged to the village, was not in it. On the contrary, it was situated at the end of a long lane, which was a mile nearly from the village, in the direction of the hall; therefore, in going to it from the hall, that amount of distance was saved, although it was always called and considered the village church.

It stood alone, with the exception of a glebe house and two cottages, that were occupied by persons who held situations about the sacred edifice, and who were supposed, being on the spot, to keep watch and ward over it.

It was an ancient building of the early English style of architecture, or rather Norman, with one of those antique, square, short towers, built of flint stones firmly embedded in cement, which, from time, had acquired almost the consistency of stone itself. There were numerous arched windows, partaking something of the more florid gothic style, although scarcely ornamental enough to be called such. The edifice stood in the center of a graveyard, which extended over a space of about half an acre, and altogether it was one of the prettiest and most rural old churches within many miles of the spot.

Many a lover of the antique and of the picturesque, for it was both, went out of his way while traveling in the neighborhood to look at it, and it had an extensive and well-deserved reputation as a fine specimen of its class and style of building.

In Kent, to the present day, are some fine specimens of the old Roman style of church building; and, although they are as rapidly pulled down as the abuse of modern architects, and the cupidity of speculators, and the vanity of clergymen can possibly encourage, in order to erect flimsy, Italianised structures in their stead, yet sufficient of them remain dotted over England to interest the traveler. At Willesden there is a church of this description, which will well repay a visit. This, then, was the kind of building into which it was the intention of our four friends to penetrate, not on an unholy, or an unjustifiable errand, but on one which, proceeding from good and proper motives, it was highly desirable to conduct in as secret a manner as possible.

The moon was more densely covered by clouds than it had yet been that evening, when they reached the little wicket-gate which led into the churchyard, through which was a regularly used thoroughfare.

"We have a favorable night," remarked Henry, "for we are not so likely to be disturbed."

"And now, the question is, how are we to get in?" said Mr. Chillingworth, as he paused, and glanced up at the ancient building.

"The doors," said George, "would effectually resist us."

"How can it be done, then?"

"The only way I can think of," said Henry, "is to get out one of the small, diamond-shaped panes of glass from one of the low windows, and then we can one of us put in our hands, and undo the fastening, which is very simple, when the window opens like a door, and it is but a step into the church."

"A good way," said Marchdale. "We will lose no time."

They walked round the church till they came to a very low window indeed, near to an angle of the wall, where a huge abutment struck far out into the burial-ground.

"Will you do it, Henry?" said George.

"Yes. I have often noticed the fastenings. Just give me a slight hoist up, and all will be right."

George did so, and Henry with his knife easily bent back some of the leadwork which held in one of the panes of glass, and then got it out whole. He handed it down to George, saying, —

"Take this, George. We can easily replace it when we leave, so that there can be no signs left of any one having been here at all."

George took the piece of thick, dim-colored glass, and in another moment Henry had succeeded in opening the window, and the mode of ingress to the old church was fair and easy before them all, had there been ever so many.

"I wonder," said Marchdale, "that a place so inefficiently protected has never been robbed."

"No wonder at all," remarked Mr. Chillingworth. "There is nothing to take that I am aware of that would repay anybody the trouble of taking."

"Indeed!"

"Not an article. The pulpit, to be sure, is covered with faded velvet; but beyond that, and an old box, in which I believe nothing is left but some books, I think there is no temptation."

"And that, Heaven knows, is little enough, then."

"Come on," said Henry. "Be careful; there is nothing beneath the window, and the depth is about two feet."

Thus guided, they all got fairly into the sacred edifice, and then Henry closed the window, and fastened it on the inside, as he said, —

"We have nothing to do now but to set to work opening a way into the vault, and I trust that Heaven will pardon me for thus desecrating the tomb of my ancestors, from a consideration of the object I have in view by so doing."

"It does seem wrong thus to tamper with the secrets of the tomb," remarked Mr. Marchdale.

"The secrets of a fiddlestick!" said the doctor. "What secrets has the tomb, I wonder?"

"Well, but, my dear sir —"

"Nay, my dear sir, it is high time that death, which is, then, the inevitable fate of us all, should be regarded with more philosophic eyes than it is. There are no secrets in the tomb but such as may well be endeavored to be kept secret."

"What do you mean?"

"There is one which very probably we shall find unpleasantly revealed."

"Which is that?"

"The not over pleasant odor of decomposed animal remains — beyond that I know of nothing of a secret nature that the tomb can show us."

"Ah, your profession hardens you to such matters."

"And a very good thing that it does, or else, if all men were to look upon a dead body as something almost too dreadful to look upon, and by far too horrible to touch, surgery would lose its value, and crime, in many instances of the most obnoxious character, would go unpunished."

"If we have a light here," said Henry, "we shall run the greatest chance in the world of being seen, for the church has many windows."

"Do not have one, then, by any means," said Mr. Chillingworth. "A match held low down in the pew may enable us to open the vault."

"That will be the only plan."

Henry led them to the pew which belonged to his family, and in the floor of which was the trap door.

"When was it last opened?" inquired Marchdale.

"When my father died," said Henry; "some ten months ago now, I should think."

"The screws, then, have had ample time to fix themselves with fresh rust."

"Here is one of my chemical matches," said Mr. Chillingworth, as he suddenly irradiated the pew with a clear and beautiful flame, that lasted about a minute.

The heads of the screws were easily discernible, and the short time that the light lasted had enabled Henry to turn the key he had brought with him in the lock.

"I think that without a light now," he said, "I can turn the screws well."

"Can you?"

"Yes, there are but four."

"Try it, then."

Henry did so, and from the screws having very large heads, and being made purposely, for the convenience of removal when required, with deep indentations to receive the screw-driver, he found no difficulty in feeling for the proper places, and extracting the screws without any more light than was afforded to him from the general whitish aspect of the heavens.

"Now, Mr. Chillingworth," he said, "another of your matches, if you please. I have all the screws so loose that I can pick them up with my fingers."

"Here," said the doctor.

In another moment the pew was as light as day, and Henry succeeded in taking out the few screws, which he placed in his pocket for their greater security, since, of course, the intention was to replace everything exactly as it was found, in order that not the least surmise should arise in the mind of any person that the vault had been opened, and visited for any purpose whatever, secretly or otherwise.

"Let us descend," said Henry. "There is no further obstacle, my friends. Let us descend."

"If any one," remarked George, in a whisper, as they slowly descended the stairs which conducted into the vault — "if any one had told me that I should be descending into a vault for the purpose of ascertaining if a dead body, which had been nearly a century there, was removed or not, and had become a vampyre, I should have denounced the idea as one of the most absurd that ever entered the brain of a human being."

"We are the very slaves of circumstances," said Marchdale, "and we never know what we may do, or what we may not. What appears to us so improbable as to border even upon the impossible at one time, is at another the only course of action which appears feasibly open to us to attempt to pursue."

They had now reached the vault, the floor of which was composed of flat red tiles, laid in tolerable order the one beside the other. As Henry had stated, the vault was by no means of large extent. Indeed, several of the apartments for the living, at the hall, were much larger than was that one destined for the dead.

The atmosphere was damp and noisome, but not by any means so bad as might have been expected, considering the number of months which had elapsed since last the vault was opened to receive one of its ghastly and still visitants.

"Now for one of your lights, Mr. Chillingworth. You say you have the candle, I think, Marchdale, although you forgot the matches."

"I have. Here they are."

Marchdale took from his pocket a parcel which contained several wax candles, and when it was opened, a smaller packet fell to the ground.

"Why, these are instantaneous matches," said Mr. Chillingworth, as he lifted the small packet up.

"They are; and what a fruitless journey I should have had back to the hall," said Mr. Marchdale, "if you had not been so well provided as you are with the means of getting a light. These matches, which I thought I had not with me, have been, in the hurry of our departure, enclosed, you see, with the candles. Truly, I should have hunted for them at home in vain."

Mr. Chillingworth lit the wax candle which was now handed to him by Marchdale, and in another moment the vault from one end of it to the other was quite discernible.

Chapter VIII.

THE COFFIN. – THE ABSENCE OF THE DEAD. – THE MYSTERIOUS CIRCUMSTANCE, AND THE CONSTERNATION OF GEORGE.

*T*hey were all silent for a few moments as they looked around them with natural feelings of curiosity. Two of that party had of course never been in that vault at all, and the brothers, although they had descended into it upon the occasion, nearly a year before, of their father being placed in it, still looked upon it with almost as curious eyes as they who now had their first sight of it.

If a man be at all of a thoughtful or imaginative cast of mind, some curious sensations are sure to come over him, upon standing in such a place, where he knows around him lie, in the calmness of death, those in whose veins have flowed kindred blood to him — who bore the same name, and who preceded him in the brief drama of his existence, influencing his destiny and his position in life probably largely by their actions compounded of their virtues and their vices.

Henry Bannerworth and his brother George were just the kind of persons to feel strongly such sensations. Both were reflective, imaginative, educated young men, and, as the light from the wax candle flashed upon their faces, it was evident how deeply they felt the situation in which they were placed.

Mr. Chillingworth and Marchdale were silent. They both knew what was passing in the minds of the brothers, and they had too much delicacy to interrupt a train of thought which, although from having no affinity with the dead who lay around, they could not share in, yet they respected. Henry at length, with a sudden start, seemed to recover himself from his reverie.

"This is a time for action, George," he said, "and not for romantic thought. Let us proceed."

"Yes, yes," said George, and he advanced a step towards the center of the vault.

"Can you find out among all these coffins, for there seem to be nearly twenty," said Mr. Chillingworth, "which is the one we seek?"

"I think we may," replied Henry. "Some of the earlier coffins of our race, I know, were made of marble, and others of metal, both of which materials, I expect, would withstand the encroaches of time for a hundred years, at least."

"Let us examine," said George.

There were shelves or niches built into the walls all round, on which the coffins were placed, so that there could not be much difficulty in a minute examination of them all, the one after the other.

When, however, they came to look, they found that "decay's offensive fingers" had been more busy than they could have imagined, and that whatever they touched of the earlier coffins crumbled into dust before their very fingers.

In some cases the inscriptions were quite illegible, and, in others, the plates that had borne them had fallen on to the floor of the vault, so that it was impossible to say to which coffin they belonged.

Of course, the more recent and fresh-looking coffins they did not examine, because they could not have anything to do with the object of that melancholy visit.

"We shall arrive at no conclusion," said George. "All seems to have rotted away among those coffins where we might expect to find the one belonging to Marmaduke Bannerworth, our ancestor."

"Here is a coffin plate," said Marchdale, taking one from the floor.

He handed it to Mr. Chillingworth, who, upon an inspection of it, close to the light, exclaimed, —

"It must have belonged to the coffin you seek."

"What says it?"

> "YE MORTALE REMAINS OF
> MARMADUKE BANNERWORTH, YEOMAN.
> GOD RESTE HIS SOULE.
> A.D. 1640."

"It is the plate belonging to his coffin," said Henry, "and now our search is fruitless."

"It is so, indeed," exclaimed George, "for how can we tell to which of the coffins that have lost the plates this one really belongs?"

"I should not be so hopeless," said Marchdale. "I have, from time to time, in the pursuit of antiquarian lore, which I was once fond of, entered many vaults, and I have always observed that an inner coffin of metal was sound and good, while the outer one of wood had rotted away, and yielded at once to the touch of the first hand that was laid upon it."

"But, admitting that to be the case," said Henry, "how does that assist us in the identification of the coffin?"

"I have always, in my experience, found the name and rank of the deceased engraved upon the lid of the inner coffin, as well as being set forth in a much more perishable manner on the plate which was once secured to the outer one."

"He is right," said Mr. Chillingworth. "I wonder we never thought of that. If your ancestor was buried in a leaden coffin, there will be no difficulty in finding which it is."

Henry seized the light, and proceeding to one of the coffins, which seemed to be a mass of decay, he pulled away some of the rotted wood work, and then suddenly exclaimed, —

"You are quite right. Here is a firm strong leaden coffin within, which, although quite black, does not appear otherwise to have suffered."

"What is the inscription on that?" said George.

With difficulty the name on the lid was deciphered, but it was found not to be the coffin of him whom they sought.

"We can make short work of this," said Marchdale, "by only examining those leaden coffins which have lost the plates from off their outer cases. There do not appear to be many in such a state."

He then, with another light, which he lighted from the one that Henry now carried, commenced actively assisting in the search, which was carried on silently for more than ten minutes.

Suddenly Mr. Marchdale cried, in a tone of excitement, —

"I have found it. It is here."

They all immediately surrounded the spot where he was, and then he pointed to the lid of a coffin, which he had been rubbing with his handkerchief, in order to make the inscription more legible, and said, —

"See. It is here."

By the combined light of the candles they saw the words, —

"MARMADUKE BANNERWORTH, YEOMAN. 1640."

"Yes, there can be no mistake here," said Henry. "This is the coffin, and it shall be opened."

"I have the iron crowbar here," said Marchdale. "It is an old friend of mine, and I am accustomed to the use of it. Shall I open the coffin?"

"Do so — do so," said Henry.

They stood around in silence, while Mr. Marchdale, with much care, proceeded to open the coffin, which seemed of great thickness, and was of solid lead.

It was probably the partial rotting of the metal, in consequence of the damps of that place, what made it easier to open the coffin than it otherwise would have been, but certain it was that the top came away remarkably easily. Indeed, so easily did it come off, that another supposition might have been hazarded, namely, that it had never been effectively fastened.

The few moments that elapsed were ones of very great suspense to every one there present; and it would, indeed, be quite safe to assert, that all the world was for the time forgotten in the absorbing interest which appertained to the affair which was in progress.

The candles were now both held by Mr. Chillingworth, and they were so held as to cast a full and clear light upon the coffin. Now the lid slid off, and Henry eagerly gazed into the interior.

There lay something certainly there, and an audible "Thank God!" escaped his lips.

"The body is there!" exclaimed George.

"All right," said Marchdale, "here it is. There is something, and what else can it be?"

"Hold the lights," said Mr. Chillingworth; "hold the lights, some of you; let us be quite certain."

George took the lights, and Mr. Chillingworth, without any hesitation, dipped his hands at once into the coffin, and took up some fragments of rags which were there. They were so rotten, that they fell to pieces in his grasp, like so many pieces of tinder.

There was a death-like pause for some few moments, and then Mr. Chillingworth said, in a low voice, —

"There is not the least vestige of a dead body here."

Henry gave a deep groan, as he said, —

"Mr. Chillingworth, can you take upon yourself to say that no corpse has undergone the process of decomposition in this coffin?"

"To answer your question exactly, as probably in your hurry you have worded it," said Mr. Chillingworth, "I cannot take upon myself to say any such thing; but this I can say, namely, that in this coffin there are no animal remains, and that it is quite impossible that any corpse enclosed here could, in any lapse of time, have so utterly and entirely disappeared."

"I am answered," said Henry.

"Good God!" exclaimed George, "and has this but added another damning proof, to those we have already on our minds, of one of the most dreadful superstitions that ever the mind of man conceived?"

"It would seem so," said Marchdale sadly.

"Oh, that I were dead! This is terrible. God of heaven, why are these things? Oh, if I were but dead, and so spared the torture of supposing such things possible."

"Think again, Mr. Chillingworth; I pray you think again," cried Marchdale.

"If I were to think for the remainder of my existence," he replied, "I could come to no other conclusion. It is not a matter of opinion; it is a matter of fact."

"You are positive, then," said Henry, "that the dead body of Marmaduke Bannerworth has not rested here?"

"I am positive. Look for yourselves. The lead is but slightly discolored; it looks tolerably clean and fresh; there is not a vestige of putrefaction — no bones, no dust even."

They did all look for themselves, and the most casual glance was sufficient to satisfy the most skeptical.

"All is over," said Henry; "let us now leave this place; and all I can now ask of you, my friends, is to lock this dreadful secret deep in your own hearts."

"It shall never pass my lips," said Marchdale.

"Nor mine, you may depend," said the doctor. "I was much in hopes that this night's work would have had the effect of dissipating, instead of adding to, the gloomy fancies that now possess you."

"Good heavens!" cried George, "can you call them fancies, Mr. Chillingworth?"

"I do, indeed."

"Have you yet a doubt?"

"My young friend, I told you from the first, that I would not believe in your vampyre; and I tell you now, that if one was to come and lay hold of me by the throat, as long as I could at all gasp for breath I would tell him he was a d——d impostor."

"This is carrying incredulity to the verge of obstinacy."

"Far beyond it, if you please."

"You will not be convinced?" said Marchdale.

"I most decidedly, on this point, will not."

"Then you are one who would doubt a miracle, if you saw it with your own eyes."

"I would, because I do not believe in miracles. I should endeavor to find some rational and some scientific means of accounting for the phenomenon, and that's the very reason why we have no miracles now-a-days, between you and I, and no prophets and saints, and all that sort of thing."

"I would rather avoid such observations in such a place as this," said Marchdale.

"Nay, do not be the moral coward," cried Mr. Chillingworth, "to make your opinions, or the expression of them, dependent upon any certain locality."

"I know not what to think," said Henry; "I am bewildered quite. Let us now come away."

Mr. Marchdale replaced the lid of the coffin, and then the little party moved towards the staircase. Henry turned before he ascended, and glanced back into the vault.

"Oh," he said, "if I could but think there had been some mistake, some error of judgment, on which the mind could rest for hope."

"I deeply regret," said Marchdale, "that I so strenuously advised this expedition. I did hope that from it would have resulted much good."

"And you have every reason so to hope," said Chillingworth. "I advised it likewise, and I tell you that its result perfectly astonishes me, although I will not allow myself to embrace at once all the conclusions to which it would seem to lead me."

"I am satisfied," said Henry; "I know you both advised me for the best. The curse of Heaven seems now to have fallen upon me and my house."

"Oh, nonsense!" said Chillingworth. "What for?"

"Alas! I know not."

"Then you may depend that Heaven would never act so oddly. In the first place, Heaven don't curse anybody; and, in the second, it is too just to inflict pain where pain is not amply deserved."

They ascended the gloomy staircase of the vault. The countenances of both George and Henry were very much saddened, and it was quite evident that their thoughts were by far too busy to enable them to enter into any conversation. They did not, and particularly George, seem to hear all that was said to them. Their intellects seemed almost stunned by the unexpected circumstance of the disappearance of the body of their ancestor.

All along they had, although almost unknown to themselves, felt a sort of conviction that hey must find some remains of Marmaduke Bannerworth, which would render the supposition, even in the most superstition minds, that he was the vampyre, a thing totally and physically impossible.

But now the whole question assumed a far more bewildering shape. The body was not in its coffin — it had not there quietly slept the long sleep of death common to humanity. Where was it then? What had become of it? Where, how, and under what circumstances had it been removed? Had it itself burst the bands that held it, and hideously stalked forth into the world again to make one of its seeming inhabitants, and kept up for a hundred years a dreadful existence by such adventures as it had consummated at the hall, where, in the course of ordinary human life, it had once lived?

All these were questions which irresistibly pressed themselves upon the consideration of Henry and his brother. They were awful questions.

And yet, take any sober, sane, thinking, educated man, and show him all that they had seen, subject him to all which they had been subjected, and say if human reason, and all the arguments that the subtlest brain could back it with, would be able to hold out against such a vast accumulation of horrible evidences, and say, — "I don't believe it."

Mr. Chillingworth's was the only plan. He would not argue the question. He said at once, —

"I will not believe this thing — upon this point I will yield to no evidence whatever."

That was the only way of disposing of such a question; but there are not many who could so dispose of it, and not one so much interested in it as were the brothers Bannerworth, who could at all hope to get into such a state of mind.

The boards were laid carefully down again, and the screws replaced. Henry found himself unequal to the task, so it was done by Marchdale, who took pains to replace everything in the same state in which they had found it, even to laying the matting at the bottom of the pew.

Then they extinguished the light, and, with heavy hearts, they all walked towards the window, to leave the sacred edifice by the same means they had entered it.

"Shall we replace the pane of glass?" said Marchdale.

"Oh, it matters not — it matters not," said Henry, listlessly; "nothing matters now. I care not what becomes of me — am getting weary of a life which now must be one of misery and dread."

"You must not allow yourself to fall into such a state of mind as this," said the doctor, "or you will become a patient of mine very quickly."

"I cannot help it."

"Well, but be a man. If there are serious evils affecting you, fight out against them the best way you can."

"I cannot."

"Come, now, listen to me. We need not, I think, trouble ourselves about the pane of glass, so come along."

He took the arm of Henry and walked on with him a little in advance of the others.

"Henry," he said, "the best way, you may depend, of meeting evils, be they great or small, is to get up an obstinate feeling of defiance against them. Now, when anything occurs which is uncomfortable to me, I endeavor to convince myself, and I have no great difficulty in doing so, that I am a decidedly injured man."

"Indeed!"

"Yes; I get very angry, and that gets up a kind of obstinacy, which makes me not feel half so much mental misery as would be my portion if I were to succumb to the evil, and commence whining over it, as many people do, under the pretence of being resigned."

"But this family affliction of mine transcends anything that anybody else ever endured."

"I don't know that; but it is a view of the subject which, if I were you, would only make me more obstinate."

"What can I do?"

"In the first place, I would say to myself, 'There may or there may not be supernatural beings, who, from some physical derangement of the ordinary nature of things, make themselves obnoxious to living people; if there are, d — n them! There may be vampyres; and if there are, I defy them.' Let the imagination paint its very worst terrors; let fear do what it will and what it can in peopling the mind with horrors. Shrink from nothing, and even then I would defy them all."

"Is not that like defying Heaven?"

"Most certainly not; for in all we say and in all we do we act from the impulses of that mind which is given to us by Heaven itself. If Heaven creates an intellect and a mind of a certain order, Heaven will not quarrel that it does the work which it was adapted to do."

"I know these are your opinions. I have heard you mention them before."

"They are the opinions of every rational person, Henry Bannerworth, because they will stand the test of reason; and what I urge upon you is, not to allow yourself to be mentally prostrated, even if a vampyre had paid a visit to your house. Defy him, say I — fight him. Self-preservation is a great law of nature, implanted in all our hearts; do you summon it to your aid."

"I will endeavor to think as you would have me. I though more than once of summoning religion to my aid."

"Well, that is religion."

"Indeed!"

"I consider so, and the most rational religion of all. All that we read about religion that does not seem expressly to agree with it, you may consider as an allegory."

"But, Mr. Chillingworth, I cannot and will not renounce the sublime truths of Scripture. They may be incomprehensible; they may be inconsistent; and some of them may look ridiculous; but still they are sacred and sublime, and I will not renounce them although my reason may not accord with them, because they are the laws of Heaven."

No wonder this powerful argument silenced Mr. Chillingworth, who was one of those characters in society who hold most dreadful opinions, and who would destroy religious beliefs, and all the different sects of the world, if they could, and endeavor to introduce instead some horrible system of human reason and profound philosophy.

But how soon the religious man silences his opponent; and let it not be supposed that, because his opponent says no more upon the subject, he does so because he is disgusted with the stupidity of the other; no, it is because he is completely beaten, and has nothing more to say.

The distance now between the church and the hall was nearly traversed, and Mr. Chillingworth, who was a very good man, not withstanding his disbelief in certain things of course paved the way for him to hell, took a kind leave of Mr. Marchdale and the brothers, promising to call on the following morning and see Flora.

Henry and George then, in earnest conversation with Marchdale, proceeded homewards. It was evident that the scene in the vault had made a deep and saddening impression on them, and one which was not likely easily to be eradicated.

Chapter IX.

THE OCCURRENCES OF THE NIGHT AT THE HALL. – THE
SECOND APPEARANCE OF THE VAMPYRE, AND THE
PISTOL-SHOT.

*D*espite the full and free consent which Flora had given to her brothers to entrust her solely to the care of her mother and her own courage at the hall, she felt greater fear creep over her after they were gone than she chose to acknowledge.

A sort of presentiment appeared to come over her that some evil was about to occur, and more than once she caught herself almost in the act of saying, –

"I wish they had not gone."

Mrs. Bannerworth, too, could not be supposed to be entirely destitute of uncomfortable feelings, when she came to consider how poor a guard she was over her beautiful child, and how much terror might even deprive of the little power she had, should the dreadful visitor again make his appearance.

"But it is but for two hours," thought Flora, "and two hours will soon pass away."

There was, too, another feeling which gave her some degree of confidence, although it arose from a bad source, inasmuch as it was one which showed powerfully how much her mind was dwelling on the particulars of the horrible belief in the class of supernatural beings, one of whom she believed had visited her.

That consideration was this. The two hours of absence from the hall of its male inhabitants would be from nine o'clock until eleven, and those were not the two hours during which she felt that she would be most timid on account of the vampyre.

"It was after midnight before," she thought, "when it came, and perhaps it may not be able to come earlier. It may not have the power, until that time, to make its hideous visits, and, therefore, I will believe myself safe."

She had made up her mind not to go to bed until the return of her brothers, and she and her mother sat in a small room that was used as a breakfast-room, and which had a latticed window that opened on to the lawn.

This window had in the inside strong oaken shutters, which had been fastened as securely as their construction would admit of some time before the departure of the brothers and Mr. Marchdale on that melancholy expedition, the object of which, if it had been known to her, would have added so much to the terrors of poor Flora.

It was not even guessed at, however remotely, so that she had not the additional affliction of thinking, that while she was sitting there, a prey to all sorts of imaginative terrors, they were perhaps gathering fresh evidence, as, indeed, they were, of the dreadful reality of the appearance which, but for the collateral circumstances attendant upon its coming and its going, she would fain have persuaded herself was but the vision of a dream.

It was before nine that the brothers started, but in her own mind Flora gave them to eleven, and when she heard ten o'clock sound from a clock which stood in the hall, she felt pleased to think that in another hour they would surely be at home.

"My dear," said her mother, "you look more like yourself, now."

"Do I, mother?"

"Yes, you are well again."

"Ah, if I could forget —"

"Time, dear Flora, will enable you to do so, and all the rest of what made you so unwell will pass away. You will soon forget it all."

"I will hope to do so."

"Be assured that, some day or another, something will occur, as Henry says, to explain all that has happened, in some way consistent with reason and the ordinary nature of things, my dear Flora."

"Oh, I will cling to such a belief; I will get Henry, upon whose judgment I know I can rely, to tell me so, and each time that I hear such words from his lips, I will contrive to dismiss some portion of the terror which now, I cannot but confess, clings to my heart."

Flora laid her hand upon her mother's arm, and in a low, anxious tone of voice, said, — "Listen, mother."

Mrs. Bannerworth turned pale, as she said, — "Listen to what, dear?"

"Within these last ten minutes," said Flora, "I have thought three or four times that I heard a slight noise without. Nay, mother, do not tremble — it may be only fancy."

Flora herself trembled, and was of a death-like paleness; once or twice she passed her hand across her brow, and altogether she presented a picture of much mental suffering.

They now conversed in anxious whispers, and almost all they said consisted in anxious wishes for the return of the brothers and Mr. Marchdale.

"You will be happier and more assured, my dear, with some company," said Mrs. Bannerworth. "Shall I ring for the servants, and let them remain in the room with us, until they who are our best safeguards next to Heaven return?"

"Hush — hush — hush, mother!"

"What do you hear?"

"I thought — I heard a faint sound."

"I heard nothing, dear."

"Listen again, mother. Surely I could not be deceived so often. I have now, at least, six times heard a sound as if some one was outside by the windows."

"No, no, my darling, do not think; your imagination is active and in a state of excitement."

"It is, and yet —"

"Believe me, it deceives you."

"I hope to Heaven it does!"

There was a pause of some minutes' duration, and then Mrs. Bannerworth again urged slightly the calling of some of the servants, for she thought that their presence might have the effect of giving a different direction to her child's thoughts; but Flora saw her place her hand upon the bell, and she said, —

"No, mother, no — not yet, not yet. Perhaps I am deceived."

Mrs. Bannerworth upon this sat down, but no sooner had she done so than she heartily regretted she had not rung the bell, for, before another word could be spoken, there came too perceptibly upon their ears for there to be any mistake at all about it, a strange scratching noise upon the window outside.

A faint cry came from Flora's lips, as she exclaimed, in a voice of great agony, —

"Oh, God! — oh, God! It has come again!"

Mrs. Bannerworth became faint, and unable to move or speak at all; she could only sit like one paralyzed, and unable to do more than listen to and see what was going on.

The scratching noise continued for a few seconds, and then altogether ceased. Perhaps, under ordinary circumstances, such a sound outside the window would have scarcely afforded food for comment at all, or, if it had, it would have been attributed to some natural effect, or to the exertions of some bird or animal to obtain admittance to the house.

But there had occurred now enough in that family to make any little sound of wonderful importance, and these things which before would have passed completely unheeded, at all events without creating much alarm, were now invested with a fearful interest.

When the scratching noise ceased, Flora spoke in a low, anxious whisper, as she said, —

"Mother, you heard it then?"

Mrs. Bannerworth tried to speak, but she could not; and then suddenly, with a loud clash, the bar, which on the inside appeared to fasten the shutters strongly, fell as if by some invisible agency, and the shutters now, but for the intervention of the window, could be easily pushed open from without.

Mrs. Bannerworth covered her face with her hands, and, after rocking to and fro for a moment, she fell off her chair, having fainted with the excess of terror that came over her.

For about the space of time in which a fast speaker could count twelve, Flora thought her reason was leaving her, but it did not. She found herself recovering; and there she sat, with her eyes fixed upon the window, looking more like some exquisitely-chiseled statue of despair than a being of flesh and blood, expecting each moment to have its eyes blasted by some horrible appearance, such as might be supposed to drive her to madness.

And now again came the strange knocking or scratching against the pane of glass of the window.

This continued for some minutes, during which it appeared likewise to Flora that some confusion was going on at another part of the house, for she fancied she heard voices and the banging of doors.

It seemed to her as if she must have sat looking at the shutters of that window a long time before she saw them shake, and then one wide hinged portion of them slowly opened.

Once again horror appeared to be on the point of producing madness in her brain, and then, as before, a feeling of calmness rapidly ensued.

She was able to see plainly that something was by the window, but what it was she could not plainly discern, in consequence of the lights she had in the room. A few moments, however, sufficed to settle that mystery, for the window was opened and a figure stood before her.

One glance, one terrified glance, in which her whole soul was concentrated, sufficed to shew her who and what the figure was. There was a tall, gaunt form — there was the faded ancient apparel — the lustrous metallic-looking eyes — its half-opened mouth, exhibiting tusk-like teeth! It was — yes, it was — *the vampyre!*

It stood for a moment gazing at her, and then in the hideous way it had attempted before to speak, it apparently endeavored to utter some words which it could not make articulate to human ears. The pistols lay before Flora. Mechanically she raised one, and pointed it at the figure. It advanced a step, and then she pulled the trigger.

A stunning report followed. There was a loud cry of pain, and the vampyre fled. The smoke and confusion that was incidental to the spot prevented her from seeing if the figure walked or ran away. She thought he heard a crashing sound among the plants outside the window, as if it had fallen, but she did not feel quite sure.

It was no effort of any reflection, but a purely mechanical movement, that made her raise the other pistol, and discharge that likewise in the direction the vampyre had taken. Then casting the weapon away, she rose, and made a frantic rush from the room. She opened the door, and was dashing out, when she found herself caught in the circling arms of some one who either had been there waiting, or who had just at that moment got there.

The thought that it was the vampyre, who by some mysterious means had got there, and was about to make her his prey, now overcame her completely, and she sunk into a state of utter insensibility on the moment.

Chapter X.

THE RETURN FROM THE VAULT. – THE ALARM, AND THE SEARCH AROUND THE HALL.

*I*t so happened that George and Henry Bannerworth, along with Mr. Marchdale, had just reached the gate which conducted into the garden of the mansion when they all were alarmed by the report of a pistol. Amid the stillness of the night, it came upon them with so sudden a shock, that they involuntarily paused, and there came from the lips of each an expression of alarm.

"Good heavens!" cried George, "can that be Flora firing at any intruder?"

"It must be," cried Henry; "she has in her possession the only weapons in the house."

Mr. Marchdale turned very pale, and trembled slightly, but he did not speak.

"On, on," cried Henry; "for God's sake, let us hasten on."

As he spoke, he cleared the gate at a bound, and at a terrific pace he made towards the house, passing over beds, and plantations, and flowers heedlessly, so that he went the most direct way to it.

Before, however, it was possible for any human speed to accomplish even half of the distance, the report of the other shot came upon his ears, and he even fancied he heard the bullet whistle past his head in tolerably close proximity. This supposition gave him a clue to the direction at all events from whence the shots proceeded, otherwise he knew not from which window they were fired, because it had not occurred to him, previous to leaving home, to inquire in which room Flora and his mother were likely to be seated waiting his return.

He was right as regarded the bullet. It was that winged messenger of death which had passed his head in such very dangerous proximity, and consequently he made with tolerable accuracy towards the open window from whence the shots had been fired.

The night was not near so dark as it had been, although even yet it was very far from being a light one, and he was soon enabled to see that there was a room, the window of which was wide open, and lights burning on the table within. He made towards it in a moment, and entered it. To his astonishment, the first objects he beheld were Flora and a stranger, who was now supporting her in his arms. To grapple him by the throat was the work of a moment, but the stranger cried aloud in a voice which sounded familiar to Henry, —

"Good God, are you all mad?"

Henry relaxed his hold, and looked in his face.

"Gracious heavens, it is Mr. Holland!" he said.

"Yes; did you not know me?"

Henry was bewildered. He staggered to a seat, and, in doing so, he saw his mother stretched apparently lifeless upon the floor. To raise her was the work of a moment, and then Marchdale and George, who had followed him as fast as they could, appeared at the open window.

Such a strange scene as that small room now exhibited had never been equaled in Bannerworth Hall. There was young Mr. Holland, of whom mention has already been made, as the affianced lover of Flora, supporting her fainting form. There was Henry doing equal service to his mother; and on the floor lay the two pistols, and one of the candles which had been upset in the confusion: while the terrified attitudes of George and Mr. Marchdale at the window completed the strange-looking picture.

"What is this — oh! what has happened?" cried George.

"I know not — I know not," said Henry. "Some one summon the

servants; I am nearly mad."

Mr. Marchdale at once rung the bell, for George looked so faint and ill as to be incapable of doing so; and he rung it so loudly and so effectually, that the two servants who had been employed suddenly upon the others leaving came with much speed to know what was the matter.

"See to your mistress," said Henry. "She is dead, or has fainted. For God's sake, let who can give me some account of what has caused all this confusion here."

"Are you aware, Henry," said Marchdale, "that a stranger is present in the room?"

He pointed at Mr. Holland as he spoke, who, before Henry could reply, said, —

"Sir, I may be a stranger to you, as you are to me, and yet no stranger to those whose home this is."

"No, no," said Henry, "you are no stranger to us, Mr. Holland, but are thrice welcome — none can be more welcome. Mr. Marchdale, this is Mr. Holland, of whom you have heard me speak."

"I am proud to know you, sir," said Mr. Marchdale.

"Sir, I thank you," replied Holland, coldly.

It will so happen; but, at first sight, it appeared as if those two persons had some sort of antagonistic feeling towards each other, which threatened to prevent effectually their ever becoming intimate friends.

The appeal of Henry to the servants to know if they could tell him what had occurred was answered in the negative. All they knew was, that they had heard two shots fired, and that, since then, they had remained where they were, in a great fright, until the bell was rung violently. This was no news at all, and, therefore, the only chance was, to wait patiently for the recovery of the mother, or of Flora, from one or the other of whom surely some information could be at once then procured.

Mrs. Bannerworth was removed to her own room, and so would Flora have been; but Mr. Holland, who was supporting her in his arms, said, —

"I think the air from the open window is recovering her, and it is likely to do so. Oh, do not now take her from me, after so long an absence. Flora, Flora, look up; do you not know me? You have not yet given me one look of acknowledgement. Flora, dear Flora!"

The sound of his voice seemed to act as the most potent of charms in restoring her to consciousness; it broke through the death-like trance in which she lay, and, opening her beautiful eyes, she fixed them upon his face, saying, —

"Yes, yes; it is Charles — it is Charles."

She burst into a hysterical flood of tears, and clung to him like some terrified child to its only friend in the whole wide world.

"Oh, my dear friends," cried Charles Holland, "do not deceive me; has Flora been ill?"

"We have all been ill," said George.

"All ill?"

"Ay, and nearly mad," exclaimed Harry.

Holland looked from one to the other in surprise, as well he might, nor was that surprise at all lessened when Flora made an effort to extricate herself from his embrace, as she exclaimed, —

"You must leave me — you must leave me, Charles, for ever! Oh! never, never look upon my face again!"

"I — I am bewildered," said Charles.

"Leave me, now," continued Flora; "think me unworthy; think what you will, Charles, but I cannot, I dare not, now be yours."

"Is this a dream?"

"Oh, would it were. Charles, if we had never met, you would be happier — I could not be more wretched."

"Flora, Flora, do you say these words of so great cruelty to try my love?"

"No, as Heaven is my judge, I do not."

"Gracious Heaven, then, what do they mean?"

Flora shuddered, and Henry, coming up to her, took her hand in his tenderly, as he said, —

"Has it been again?"

"It has."

"You shot it?"

"I fired full upon it, Henry, but it fled."

"It did — fly?"

"It did, Henry, but it will come again — it will surely come again."

"You — you hit it with the bullet?" interposed Mr. Marchdale. "Perhaps you killed it?"

"I think I must have hit it, unless I am mad."

Charles Holland looked from one to the other with such a look of intense surprise, that George remarked it, and said at once to him, —

"Mr. Holland, a full explanation is due to you, and you shall have it."

"You seem to be the only rational person here," said Charles. "Pray what is it that everybody calls '*it?*'"

"Hush — hush!" said Henry; "you will soon hear, but not at present."

"Hear me, Charles," said Flora. "From this moment, mind, I do release you from every vow, from every promise made to me of constancy and love; and if you are wise, Charles, and will be advised, you will now this moment leave this house never to return to it."

"No," said Charles — "no; by Heaven I love you, Flora! I have come to say again all that in another clime I said with joy to you. When I forget you, let what trouble may oppress you, may God forget me, and my own right hand forget to do me honest service."

"Oh! no more — no more!" sobbed Flora.

"Yes, much more, if you will tell me of words which will be stronger than others in which to paint my love, my faith, and my constancy."

"Be prudent," said Henry. "Say no more."

"Nay, upon such a theme I could speak for ever. You may cast me off, Flora; but until you tell me you love another, I am yours till the death, and then with a sanguine hope at my heart that we shall meet again, never, dearest, to part."

Flora sobbed bitterly.

"Oh!" she said, "this is the unkindest blow of all — this is worse than all."

"Unkind!" echoed Holland.

"Heed her not," said Henry; "she means not you."

"Oh, no — no!" she cried. "Farewell, Charles — dear Charles."

"Oh, say that word again!" he exclaimed, with animation. "It is the first time such music has met my ears."

"It must be the last."

"No, no — oh, no."

"For your own sake I shall be able now, Charles, to show you that I really loved you."

"Not by casting me from you?"

"Yes, even so. That will be the way to show that I love you."

She held up her hands wildly, as she added, in an excited voice, —

"The curse of destiny is upon me! I am singled out as one lost and accursed. Oh, horror — horror! would that I were dead!"

Charles staggered back a pace or two until he came to a table, at which he clutched for support. He turned very pale as he said, in a faint voice, —

"Is — is she mad, or am I?"

"Tell him that I am mad, Henry," cried Flora. "Do not, oh, do not make his lonely thoughts terrible with more than that. Tell him I am mad."

"Come with me," whispered Henry to Holland. "I pray you come with me at once, and you shall know all."

"I — will."

"George, stay with Flora for a time. Come, come, Mr. Holland, you ought, and you shall know all; then you can come to a judgment for yourself. This way, sir. You cannot, in the wildest freak of your imagination, guess that I have now to tell you."

Never was mortal man so utterly bewildered by the events of the last hour of his existence as was now Charles Holland, and truly he might well be so. He had arrived in England, and made what speed he could to the house of a family whom he admired for their intelligence, their high culture, and in one member of which his whole thoughts of domestic happiness in this world were centered, and he found nothing but confusion, incoherence, mystery, and the wildest dismay.

Well might he doubt if he were sleeping or waking — well might he ask if he or they were mad.

And now, as, after a long, lingering look of affection upon the pale, suffering form of Flora, he followed Henry from the room, his thoughts were busy in fancying a thousand vague and wild imaginations with respect to the communication which was promised to be made to him.

But, as Henry had truly said to him, not in the wildest freak of his imagination could he conceive of anything near the terrible strangeness and horror of that which he had to tell him, and consequently he found himself closeted with Henry in a small private room, removed from the domestic part of the hall, to the full in as bewildered a state as he had been from the first.

Chapter XI.

THE COMMUNICATION TO THE LOVER. — THE HEART'S DESPAIR.

*C*onsternation is sympathetic, and any one who had looked upon the features of Charles Holland, now that he was seated with Henry Bannerworth, in expectation of a communication which his fears told him was to blast all the dearest and most fondly cherished hopes for ever, would scarcely have recognized in him the same young man who, one short hour before, had knocked so loudly, and so full of joyful hope and expectation, at the door of the hall.

But so it was. He knew Henry Bannerworth too well to suppose that any unreal cause could blanch his cheek. He knew Flora too well to imagine for one moment that caprice had dictated the, to him, fearful words of dismissal she had uttered to him.

Happier would it at that time have been to Charles Holland had she acted capriciously towards him, and convinced him that his true heart's devotion had been cast at the feet of one unworthy of so really noble a gift. Pride would then have enabled him, no doubt, successfully to resist the blow. A feeling of honest and proper indignation at having his feelings trifled with, would, no doubt, have sustained him; but, alas! the case seemed to be widely different.

True, she implored him to think of her no more — no longer to cherish in his breast the fond dream of affection which had been its guest so long; but the manner in which she did so brought along with it an irresistible conviction, that she was making a noble sacrifice of her own feelings for him, from some cause which was involved in the profoundest mystery.

But now he was to hear all. Henry had promised to tell him, and as he looked into his pale, but handsomely intellectual face, he half dreaded the disclosure he yet panted to hear.

"Tell me all, Henry — tell me all," he said. "Upon the words that come from your lips I know I can rely."

"I will have no reservations with you," said Henry, sadly. "You ought to know all, and you shall. Prepare yourself for the strangest revelation you ever heard."

"Indeed!"

"Ay. One which in hearing you may well doubt; and one which, I hope you will never find opportunity of verifying."

"You speak in riddles."

"And yet speak truly, Charles. You heard with what a frantic vehemence Flora desired you to think no more of her?"

"I did — I did."

"She was right. She is a noble-hearted girl for uttering those words. A dreadful incident in our family has occurred, which might well induce you to pause before uniting your fate with that of any member of it."

"Impossible. Nothing can possibly subdue the feelings of affection I entertain for Flora. She is worthy of any one, and, as such, amid all changes — all mutations of fortune, she shall be mine."

"Do not suppose that any change of fortune has produced the scene you were witness to."

"Then, what else?"

"I will tell you, Holland. In all your travels, and in all your reading, did you ever come across anything about vampyres?"

"About what?" cried Charles, drawing his chair forward a little. "About what?"

"You may well doubt the evidence of your own ears, Charles Holland, and wish me to repeat what I said. I say, do you know anything about vampyres?"

Charles Holland looked curiously in Henry's face, and the latter immediately added, —

"I can guess what is passing in your mind at present, and I do not wonder at it. You think I must be mad."

"Well, really, Henry, your extraordinary question —"

"I knew it. Were I you, I should hesitate to believe the tale; but the fact is, we have every reason to believe that one member of our own family is one of those horrible preternatural beings called vampyres."

"Good God, Henry, can you allow your judgment for a moment to stoop to such a superstition?"

"That's what I have asked myself a hundred times; but, Charles Holland, the judgment, the feelings, and all the prejudices, natural and acquired, must succumb to actual ocular demonstration. Listen to me, and do not interrupt me. You shall know all, and you shall know it circumstantially."

Henry then related to the astonished Charles Holland all that had occurred, from the first alarm of Flora, up to that period when he, Holland, caught her in his arms as she was about to leave the room.

"And now," he said in conclusion, "I cannot tell what opinion you may come to as regards these most singular events. You will recollect that here is the unbiased evidence of four or five people to the facts, and, beyond that, the servants, who have seen something of the horrible visitor."

"You bewilder me, utterly," said Charles Holland.

"As we are all bewildered."

"But — but, gracious Heaven! it cannot be."

"It is."

"No — no. There is — there must be yet some dreadful mistake."

"Can you start any supposition by which we can otherwise explain any of the phenomena I have described to you? If you can, for Heaven's sake do so, and you will find no one who will cling to it with more tenacity than I."

"Any other species or kind of supernatural appearance might admit of argument; but this, to my perception, is too wildly improbable — too much at variance with all we see and know of the operations of nature."

"It is so. All that we have told ourselves repeatedly, and yet is all human reason at once struck down by the few brief words of — 'We have seen it.'"

"I would doubt my eyesight."

"One might; but many cannot be laboring under the same delusion."

"My friend, I pray you, do not make me shudder at the supposition that such a dreadful thing as this is possible."

"I am, believe me, Charles, most unwilling to oppress any one with the knowledge of these evils; but you will clearly understand that you may, with perfect honor, now consider yourself free from all engagements you have entered into with Flora."

"No, no! By Heaven, no!"

"Yes, Charles. Reflect upon the consequences now of a union with such a family."

"Oh, Henry Bannerworth, can you suppose me so dead to all good feeling, so utterly lost to honorable impulses, as to eject from my heart her who has possession of it entirely, on such a ground as this?"

"You would be justified."

"Coldly justified in prudence I might be. There are a thousand circumstances in which a man may be justified in a particular course of action, and that course yet may be neither honorable nor just. I love Flora; and were she tormented by the whole of the supernatural world, I should still love her. Nay, it becomes, then, a higher and a nobler duty on my part to stand between her and those evils, if possible."

"Charles — Charles," said Henry, "I cannot of course refuse you my need of praise and admiration for your generosity of feeling; but, remember, if we are compelled, despite all our feelings and all our predilections to the contrary, to give in to a belief in the existence of vampyres, why may we not at once receive as the truth all that is recorded of them?"

"To what do you allude?"

"To this. That one who has been visited by a vampyre, and whose blood has formed a horrible repast for such a being, becomes, after death, one of the dreadful race, and visits others in the same way."

"Now this must be insanity," cried Charles.

"It bears the aspect of it, indeed," said Henry; "oh that you could by some means satisfy yourself that I am mad."

"There may be insanity in this family," thought Charles, with such an exquisite pang of misery that he groaned aloud.

"Already," added Henry, mournfully, "already the blighting influence of the dreadful tale is upon you, Charles. Oh, let me add my advice to Flora's entreaties. She loves you, and we all esteem you; fly, then, from us, and leave us to encounter our miseries alone. Fly from us, Charles Holland, and take with you our best wishes for happiness which you cannot know here."

"Never," cried Charles; "I devote my existence to Flora. I will not play the coward, and fly from one whom I love, on such grounds. I devote my life to her."

Henry could not speak for emotion for several minutes, and when at length, in a faltering voice, he could utter some words, he said, —

"God of heaven, what happiness is marred by these horrible events? What have we all done to be the victims of such a dreadful act of vengeance?"

"Henry, do not talk in that way," cried Charles. "Rather let us bend all our energies to overcoming the evil, than spend any time in useless lamentations. I cannot even yet give in to a belief in the existence of such a being as you say visited Flora."

"But the evidences."

"Look you here, Henry: until I am convinced that some things have happened which it is totally impossible could happen by any human means whatever, I will not ascribe them to supernatural influence."

"But what human means, Charles, could produce what I have now narrated to you?"

"I do not know, just at present, but I will give the subject the most attentive consideration. Will you accommodate me here for a time?"

"You know you are welcome here as if the house were your own, and all that it contains."

"I believe so, most truly. You have no objection, I presume, to my conversing with Flora upon this strange subject?"

"Certainly not. Of course you will be careful to say nothing which can add to her fears."

"I shall be most guarded, believe me. You say that your brother George, Mr. Chillingworth, yourself, and this Mr. Marchdale, have all been cognizant of the circumstances."

"Yes — yes."

"Then with the whole of them you permit me to hold free communication upon the subject?"

"Most certainly."

"I will do so then. Keep up good heart, Henry, and this affair, which looks so full of terror at first sight, may yet be divested of some of its hideous aspect."

"I am rejoiced, if anything can rejoice me now," said Henry, "to see you view the subject with so much philosophy."

"Why," said Charles, "you made a remark of your own, which enabled me, viewing the matter in its very worst and most hideous aspect, to gather hope."

"What was that?"

"You said, properly and naturally enough, that if ever we felt that there was such a weight of evidence in favor of a belief in the existence of vampyres that we are compelled to succumb to it, we might as well receive all the popular feelings and superstitions concerning them likewise."

"I did. Where is the mind to pause, when once we open it to the reception of such things?"

"Well, then, if that be the case, we will watch this vampyre and catch it."

"Catch it?"

"Yes; surely it can be caught; as I understand, this species of being is not like an apparition, that may be composed of thin air, and utterly impalpable to the human touch, but it consists of a revivified corpse."

"Yes, yes."

"Then it is tangible and destructible. By Heaven! if ever I catch a glimpse of any such thing, it shall drag me to its home, be that where it may, or I will make it prisoner."

"Oh, Charles! you know not the feeling of horror that will come across you when you do. You have no idea of how the warm blood will seem to curdle in your veins, and how you will be paralyzed in every limb."

"Did you feel so?"

"I did."

"I will endeavor to make head against such feelings. The love of Flora shall enable me to vanquish them. Think you it will come again tomorrow?"

"I can have no thought one way or the other."

"It may. We must arrange among us all, Henry, some plan of watching which, without completely prostrating our health and strength, will always provide that some one shall be up all night and on the alert."

"It must be done."

"Flora ought to sleep with the consciousness now that she has ever at hand some intrepid and well-armed protector, who is not only himself prepared to defend her, but who can in a moment give an alarm to us all, in case of necessity requiring it."

"It would be a dreadful capture to make to seize a vampyre," said Henry.

"Not at all; it would be a very desirable one. Being a corpse revivified, it is capable of complete destruction, so as to render it no longer a scourge to any one."

"Charles, Charles, are you jesting with me, or do you really give any credence to the story?"

"My dear friend, I always make it a rule to take things at their worst, and then I cannot be disappointed. I am content to reason upon this matter as if the fact of the existence of a vampyre were thoroughly established, and then to think upon what is best to be done about it."

"You are right."

"If it should turn out then that there is an error in the fact, well and good — we are all the better off; but if otherwise, we are prepared, and armed at all points."

"Let it be so, then. It strikes me, Charles, that you will be the coolest and the calmest among us all on the emergency; but the hour now waxes late, I will get them to prepare a chamber for you, and at least tonight, after what has occurred already, I should think we can be under no apprehension."

"Probably not. But, Henry, if you would allow me to sleep in that room where the portrait hangs of him whom you suppose to be the vampyre, I should prefer it."

"Prefer it!"

"Yes; I am not one who courts danger for danger's sake, but I would rather occupy that room, to see if the vampyre, who perhaps has a partiality for it, will pay me a visit."

"As you please, Charles. You can have the apartment. It is in the same state as when occupied by Flora. Nothing has been, I believe, removed from it."

"You will let me, then, while I remain here, call it my room?"

"Assuredly."

This arrangement was accordingly made to the surprise of all the household, not one of whom would, indeed, have slept, or attempted to sleep there for any amount of reward. But Charles Holland had his own reasons for preferring that chamber, and he was conducted to it in the course of half an hour by Henry, who looked around it with a shudder, as he bade his young friend good night.

Chapter XII.

CHARLES HOLLAND'S SAD FEELINGS. – THE PORTRAIT. – THE OCCURRENCE OF THE NIGHT AT THE HALL.

*C*harles Holland wished to be alone, if ever any human being had wished fervently to be so. His thoughts were most fearfully oppressive. The communication that had been made to him by Henry Bannerworth, had about it too many strange, confirmatory circumstances to enable him to treat it, in his own mind, with the disrespect that some mere freak of a distracted and weak imagination would, most probably, received from him.

He had found Flora in a state of excitement which could arise only from some such terrible cause as had been mentioned by her brother, and then he was, from an occurrence which certainly never could have entered into his calculations, asked to forego the bright dream of happiness which he had held so long and so rapturously to his heart.

How truly he found that the course of true love ran not smooth; and yet how little would any one have suspected that from such a cause as that which now oppressed his mind, any obstruction would arise.

Flora might have been fickle and false; he might have seen some other fairer face, which might have enchained his fancy, and woven for him a new heart's chain; death might have stepped between him and the realization of his fondest hopes; loss of fortune might have made love cruel which would have yoked to its distresses a young and beautiful girl, reared in the lap of luxury, and who was not, even by those who loved her, suffered to feel, even in later years, any of the pinching necessities of the family.

All these things were possible — some of them were probable; and yet none of them had occurred. She loved him still; and he, although he had looked on many a fair face, and basked in the sunny smile of beauty, had never for a moment forgotten her faith, or lost his devotion to his own dear English girl.

Fortune he had enough for both; death had not even threatened to rob him of the prize of such a noble and faithful heart which he had won. But a horrible superstition had arisen, which seemed to place at once an impassable abyss between them, and to say to him, in a voice of thundering denunciation, —

"Charles Holland, will you have a vampyre for your bride?"

The thought was terrific. He paced the gloomy chamber to and fro with rapid strides, until the idea came across his mind that by so doing he might not only be proclaiming to his kind entertainers how much he was mentally distracted, but he likewise might be seriously distracting them.

The moment this occurred to him he sat down, and was profoundly still for some time. He then glanced at the light which had been given to him, and he found himself almost unconsciously engaged in a mental calculation as to how long it would last him in the night.

Half ashamed, then, of such terrors, as such a consideration would seem to indicate, he was on the point of hastily extinguishing it, when he happened to cast his eyes on the now mysterious and highly interesting portrait in the panel.

The picture, as a picture, was well done, whether it was a correct likeness or not of the party whom it represented. It was one of those kind of portraits that seem so lifelike, that, as you look at them, they seem to return your gaze fully, and even to follow you with their eyes from place to place.

By candlelight such an effect is more likely to become striking and remarkable than by daylight; and now, as Charles Holland shaded his eyes from the light, so as to cast its full radiance upon the portrait, he felt wonderfully interested in its life-like appearance.

"Here is true skill," he said; "such as I have not before seen. How strangely this likeness of a man whom I never saw seems to gaze upon me."

Unconsciously, too, he aided the effect, which he justly enough called life-like, by a slight movement of the candle, such as any one not blessed with nerves of iron would be sure to make, and such a movement made the face look as if it was inspired with vitality.

Charles remained looking at the portrait for a considerable period of time. He found a kind of fascination in it which prevented him from drawing his eyes away from it. It was not fear which induced him to continue gazing on it, but the circumstance that it was a likeness of the man who, after death, was supposed to have borrowed so new and so hideous an existence, combined with its artistic merits, chained him to the spot.

"I shall now," he said, "know that face again, let me see it where I may, or under what circumstances I may. Each feature is now indelibly fixed upon my memory — I can never mistake it."

He turned aside as he uttered these words, and as he did so his eyes fell upon a part of the ornamental frame which composed the edge of the panel, and which seemed to him to be of a different color from the surrounding portion.

Curiosity and increased interest prompted him at once to make a closer inquiry into the matter; and by a careful and diligent scrutiny, he was almost induced to come to the positive opinion, that at no very distant period in time past, the portrait had been removed from the place it occupied.

When once this idea, even vague and indistinct as it was, in consequence of the slight grounds he had formed it on, had got possession of his mind, he felt most anxious to prove its verification or its fallacy.

He held the candle in a variety of situations, so that its light fell in different ways on the picture; and the more he examined it, the more he felt convinced that it must have been moved lately.

It would appear as if, in its removal, a piece of the old oaken carved framework of the panel had been accidentally broken off, which caused the new look of the fracture, and that this accident, from the nature of the broken bit of framing, could have occurred in any other way than from an actual or attempted removal of the picture, he felt was extremely unlikely.

He set down the candle on a chair near at hand, and tried if the panel was fast in its place. Upon the very first touch, he felt convinced it was not so, and that it was easily moved. How to get it out, though, presented a difficulty, and to get it out was tempting.

"Who knows," he said to himself, "what may be behind it? This is an old baronial sort of hall, and the greater portion of it was, no doubt, built at a time when the construction of such places as hidden chambers and intricate staircases were, in all buildings of importance, considered desiderata."

That he should make some discovery behind the portrait, now became an idea that possessed him strongly, although he certainly had no definite grounds for really supposing that he should do so.

Perhaps the wish was more father to the thought than he, in the partial state of excitement he was in, really imagined; but so it was. He felt convinced that he should not be satisfied until he had removed that panel from the wall, and seen what was immediately behind it.

After the panel containing the picture had been placed where it was, it appeared that pieces of molding had been inserted all around, which had had the effect of keeping it in its place, and it was a fracture of one of these pieces which had first called Charles Holland's attention to the probability of the picture having been removed. That he should have to get two, at least, of the pieces of molding away, before he could hope to remove the picture, was to him quite apparent, and he was considering how he should accomplish such a result, when he was suddenly startled by a knock at his chamber door.

Until that sudden demand for admission at his door came, he scarcely knew to what a nervous state he had worked himself up. It was an odd sort of tap — one only — a single tap, as if some one demanded admittance, and wished to awaken his attention with the least possible chance of disturbing any one else.

"Come in," said Charles, for he knew he had not fastened his door; "come in."

There was no reply, but after a moment's pause, the same sort of low tap came again.

Again he cried "come in," but, whoever it was, seemed determined that the door should be opened for him, and no movement was made from the outside. A third time the tap came, and Charles was very close to the door when he heard it, for with a noiseless step he had approached it intending to open it. The instant this third mysterious demand for admission came, he did open it wide. There was no one there! In an instant he crossed the threshold into the corridor, which ran right and left. A window at one end of it now sent in the moon's rays, so that it was tolerably light, but he could see no one. Indeed, to look for any one, he felt sure was needless, for he had opened his chamber-door almost simultaneously with the last knock for admission.

"It is strange," he said, as he lingered on the threshold of his room door for some moments; "my imagination could not so completely deceive me. There was most certainly a demand for admission."

Slowly, then, he returned to his room again, and closed the door behind him.

"One thing is evident," he said, "that if I am in this apartment and to be subjected to these annoyances, I shall get no rest, which will soon exhaust me."

This thought was a very provoking one, and the more he thought that he should ultimately find a necessity for giving up that chamber he had himself asked as a special favor to be allowed to occupy, the more vexed he became to think what construction might be put upon his conduct for so doing.

"They will fancy me a coward," he thought, "and that I dare not sleep here. They may not, of course, say so, but they will think that my appearing so bold was one of those acts of bravado which I have not courage to carry fairly out."

Taking this view of the matter was just the way to enlist a young man's pride in staying, under all circumstances, where he was, and, with a slight accession of color, which, even although he was alone, would visit his cheeks, Charles Holland said aloud, —

"I will remain the occupant of this room come what may, happen what may. No terrors, real or unsubstantial, shall drive me from it: I will brave them all, and remain here to brave them."

Tap came the knock at the door again, and now, with more an air of vexation than fear, Charles turned again towards it, and listened. Tap in another minute again succeeded, and most annoyed, he walked close to the door, and laid his hand upon the lock, ready to open it at the precise moment of another demand for admission being made.

He had not to wait long. In about half a minute it came again, and, simultaneously with the sound, the door flew open. There was no one to be seen; but, as he opened the door, he heard a strange sound in the corridor — a sound which scarcely could be called a groan, and scarcely a sigh, but seemed a compound of both, having the agony of the one combined with the sadness of the other. From what direction it came he could not at the moment decide, but he called out, —

"Who's there? who's there?"

The echo of his own voice alone answered him for a few moments, and then he heard a door open, and a voice, which he knew to be Henry's, cried, —

"What is it? who speaks?"

"Henry," said Charles.

"Yes — yes — yes."

"I fear I have disturbed you."

"You have been disturbed yourself, or you would not have done so. I shall be with you in a moment."

Henry closed his door before Charles Holland could tell him not to come to him, as he intended to do, for he felt ashamed to have, in a manner of speaking, summoned assistance for so trifling a cause of alarm as that to which he had been subjected. However, he could not go to Henry's chamber to forbid him from coming to his, and, more vexed than before, he retired to his room again to await his coming.

He left the door open now, so that Henry Bannerworth, when he had got on some articles of dress, walked in at once, saying, —

"What has happened, Charles?"

"A mere trifle, Henry, concerning which I am ashamed you should have been at all disturbed."

"Never mind that, I was wakeful."

"Did you hear me open my door?"

"I heard a door open, which kept me listening, but I could not decide which door it was till I heard your voice in the corridor."

"Well, it was this door; and I opened it twice in consequence of the repeated taps for admission that came to it; some one had been knocking at it, and, when I go to it, lo! I can see nobody."

"Indeed!"

"Such is the case."

"You surprise me."

"I am very sorry to have disturbed you, because, upon such a ground, I do not feel that I ought to have done so; and, when I called out in the corridor, I assure you it was with no such intention."

"Do not regret it for a moment," said Henry; "you were quite justified in making an alarm on such an occasion."

"It's strange enough, but still it may arise from some accidental cause; admitting, if we did but know it, of some ready enough explanation."

"It may, certainly, but, after what has happened already, we may well suppose a mysterious connection between any unusual sight or sound, and the fearful ones we have already seen."

"Certainly we may."

"How earnestly that strange portrait seems to look upon us, Charles."

"It does, and I have been examining it carefully. It seems to have been removed lately."

"Removed!"

"Yes, I think as far as I can judge, that it has been taken from its frame; I mean, that the panel on which it is painted has been taken out."

"Indeed!"

"If you touch it you will find it loose, and, upon a close examination, you will perceive that a piece of the molding which holds it in its place has been chipped off, which is done in such a place what I think it could only have arisen during the removal of the picture."

"You must be mistaken."

"I cannot, of course, take upon myself, Henry, to say precisely such is the case," said Charles.

"But there is no one here to do so."

"That I cannot say. Will you permit me and assist me to remove it? I have a great curiosity to know what is behind it."

"If you have, I certainly will do so. We thought of taking it away altogether, but when Flora left this room the idea was given up as useless. Remain here a few moments, and I will endeavor to find something which shall assist us in its removal."

Henry left the mysterious chamber in order to search in his own for some means of removing the frame-work of the picture, so that the panel would slip easily out, and while he was gone, Charles Holland continued gazing upon it with greater interest, if possible, than before.

In a few minutes Henry returned, and although what he had succeeded in finding were very inefficient implements for the purpose, yet with this aid the two young men set about the task.

It is said, and said truly enough, that "where there is a will there is a way," and although the young men had no tools at all adapted for the purpose, they did succeed in removing the molding from the sides of the panel, and then by a little tapping at one end of it, and using a knife as a lever at the other end of the panel, they got it fairly out.

Disappointment was all they got for their pains. On the other side there was nothing but a rough wooded wall, against which the finer and more nicely finished oak paneling of the chamber rested.

"There is no mystery here," said Henry.

"None whatever," said Charles, as he tapped the wall with his knuckles, and found all hard and sound. "We are foiled."

"We are indeed."

"I had a strange presentiment, now," added Charles, "that we should make some discovery that would repay us for our trouble. It appears, however, that such is not to be the case; for you see nothing presents itself to us but the most ordinary appearances."

"I perceive as much; and the panel itself, although of more than ordinary thickness, is, after all, but a bit of planed oak, and apparently fashioned for no other object than to paint the portrait on."

"True. Shall we replace it?"

Charles reluctantly assented, and the picture was replaced in its original position. We say Charles reluctantly assented, because, although he had now had ocular demonstration that there was really nothing behind the panel but the ordinary woodwork which might have been expected from the construction of the old house, but he could not, even with such a fact staring him in the face, get rid entirely of the feeling that had come across him, to the effect that the picture had some mystery or another.

"You are not yet satisfied," said Henry, as he observed the doubtful look of Charles Holland's face.

"My dear friend," said Charles, "I will not deceive you. I am much disappointed that we have made no discovery behind that picture."

"Heaven knows we have mysteries enough in our family," said Henry.

Even as he spoke they were both startled by a strange clattering noise at the window, which was accompanied by a shrill, odd kind of shriek, which sounded fearful and preternatural on the night air.

"What is that?" said Charles.

"God only knows," said Henry.

The two young men naturally turned their earnest gaze in the direction of the window, which we have before remarked was one unprovided with shutters, and there, to their intense surprise, they saw, slowly rising up from the lower part of it, what appeared to be a human form. Henry would have dashed forward, but Charles restrained him, and drawing quickly from its case a large holster pistol, he leveled it carefully at the figure, saying in a whisper, —

"Henry, if I don't hit it, I will consent to forfeit my head."

He pulled the trigger — a loud report followed — the room was filled with smoke, and then all was still. A circumstance, however, had occurred, as a consequence of the concussion of the air produced by the discharge of the pistol, which neither of the young men had for the moment calculated upon, and that was the putting out of the only light they there had.

In spite of this circumstance, Charles, the moment he had discharged the pistol, dropped it and sprung forward to the window. But here he was perplexed, for he could not find the old fashioned, intricate fastening which held it shut, and he had to call to Henry, —

"Henry! For God's sake open the window for me, Henry! The fastening of the window is known to you, but not to me. Open it for me."

Thus called upon, Henry sprung forward, and by this time the report of the pistol had effectually alarmed the whole household. The flashing of lights from the corridor came into the room, and in another minute, just as Henry succeeded in getting the window wide open, and Charles Holland had made his way on to the balcony, both George Bannerworth and Mr. Marchdale entered the chamber, eager to know what had occurred. To their eager questions Henry replied, —

"Ask me not now;" and then calling to Charles, he said, — "Remain where you are, Charles, while I run down to the garden immediately beneath the balcony."

"Yes — yes," said Charles.

Henry made prodigious haste, and was in the garden immediately below the bay window in a wonderfully short space of time. He spoke to Charles, saying, —

"Will you now descend? I can see nothing here; but we will both make a search."

George and Mr. Marchdale were both now in the balcony, and they would have descended likewise, but Henry said, —

"Do not all leave the house. God only knows, now, situated as we are, what might happen."

"I will remain, then," said George. "I have been sitting up tonight as the guard, and, therefore, may as well continue to do so."

Marchdale and Charles Holland clambered over the balcony, and easily, from its insignificant height, dropped into the garden. The night was beautiful, and profoundly still. There was not a breath of air sufficient to stir a leaf on a tree, and the very flame of the candle which Charles had left burning in the balcony burnt clearly and steadily, being perfectly unruffled by any wind.

It cast a sufficient light close to the window to make everything very plainly visible, and it was evident at a glance that no object was there, although had that figure, which Charles had shot at, and no doubt hit, been flesh and blood, it must have dropped immediately below.

As they looked up for a moment after a cursory examination of the ground, Charles exclaimed, —

"Look at the window! As the light is now situated, you can see the hole made in one of the panes of glass by the passage of the bullet from my pistol."

They did look, and there the clear, round hole, without any starring, which a bullet discharged close to a pane of glass will make in it, was clearly and plainly discernible.

"You must have hit him," said Henry.

"One would think so," said Charles; "for that was the exact place where the figure was."

"And there is nothing here," added Marchdale. "What can we think of these events — what resource has the mind against the most dreadful suppositions concerning them?"

Charles and Henry both were silent; in truth, they knew not what to think and the words uttered by Marchdale were too strikingly true to dispute for a moment. They were lost in wonder.

"Human means against such an appearance as we saw tonight," said Charles, "are evidently useless."

"My dear young friend," said Marchdale, with much emotion, as he grasped Henry Bannerworth's hand, and the tears stood in his eyes as he did so, — "my dear young friend, these constant alarms will kill you. They will drive you, and all whose happiness you hold dear, distracted. You must control these dreadful feelings, and there is but one chance that I can see of getting the better of these."

"What is that?"

"By leaving this place for ever."

"Alas! am I to be driven from the home of my ancestors from such a cause as this? And whither am I to fly? Where are we to find a refuge? To leave here will be at once to break up the establishment which is now held together, certainly upon the sufferance of creditors, but still to their advantage, inasmuch as I am doing what no one else would do, namely, paying away to within the scantiest pittance the whole proceeds of the estate which spreads around me."

"Heed nothing but an escape from such horrors as seem to be accumulating now around you."

"If I were sure that such a removal would bring with it such a corresponding advantage, I might, indeed, be induced to risk all to accomplish it."

"As regards poor dear Flora," said Mr. Marchdale, "I know not what to say, or what to think; she has been attacked by a vampyre, and after this mortal life shall have ended, it is dreadful to think there may be a possibility that she, with all her beauty, all her excellence and purity of mind, and all those virtues and qualities which should make her the beloved of all, and which do, indeed, attach all hearts towards her, should become one of that dreadful tribe of beings who cling to existence by feeding, in the most dreadful manner, upon the life blood of others — oh, it is dreadful to contemplate! Too horrible — too horrible!"

"Then wherefore speak of it?" said Charles, with some asperity. "Now, by the great God of Heaven, who sees all our hearts, I will not give in to such a horrible doctrine! I will not believe it; and were death itself my portion for my want of faith, I would this moment die in my disbelief of anything so truly fearful!"

"Oh, my young friend," added Marchdale, "if anything could add to the pangs which all who love, and admire, and respect Flora Banner-worth must feel at the unhappy condition in which she is placed, it would be the noble nature of you, who, under happier auspices, would have been her guide through life, and the happy partner of her destiny."

"As I will be still."

"May Heaven forbid it! We are now among ourselves, and can talk freely upon such a subject. Mr. Charles Holland, if you wed, you would look forward to being blessed with children — those sweet ties which bind the sternest hearts to life with so exquisite a bondage. Oh, fancy, then, for a moment, the mother of your babes coming at the still hour of midnight to drain from their veins the very lifeblood she gave to them. To drive you and them mad with the expected horror of such visitations — to make your nights hideous — your days but so many hours of melancholy retrospection. Oh, you know not the world of terror, on the awful brink of which you stand, when you talk of making

Flora Bannerworth a wife."

"Peace! oh, peace!" said Henry.

"Nay, I know my words are unwelcome," continued Mr. Marchdale. "It happens, unfortunately for human nature, that truth and some of our best and holiest feelings are too often at variance, and hold a sad contest —"

"I will hear no more of this," cried Charles Holland, — "I will hear no more!"

"I have done," said Mr. Marchdale.

"And 'twere well you had not begun."

"Nay, say not so. I have but done what I considered a solemn duty."

"Under that assumption of doing duty — a solemn duty — heedless of the feelings and the opinions of others," said Charles, sarcastically, "more mischief is produced — more heart-burnings and anxieties caused, than by any other two causes of such mischievous results combined. I wish to hear no more of this."

"Do not be angered with Mr. Marchdale, Charles," said Henry. "He can have no motive but our welfare in what he said. We should not condemn a speaker because his words may not sound pleasant to our ears."

"By Heaven!" said Charles, with animation, "I meant not to be illiberal; but I will not, because I cannot see a man's motives for active interference in the affairs of others, always be ready, merely on account of such ignorance, to jump to a conclusion that they must be estimable."

"Tomorrow, I leave this house," said Marchdale.

"Leave us?" exclaimed Henry.

"Ay, for ever."

"Nay, now, Mr. Marchdale, is this generous?"

"Am I treated generously by one who is your own guest, and towards whom I was willing to hold out the honest right hand of friendship?"

Henry turned to Charles Holland, saying, —

"Charles, I know your generous nature. Say you meant no offence to my mother's old friend."

"If to say I meant no offence," said Charles, "is to say I meant no insult, I say it freely."

"Enough," cried Marchdale; "I am satisfied."

"But do not," added Charles, "draw me any more such pictures as the one you have already presented to my imagination, I beg of you. From the storehouse of my own fancy I can find quite enough to make me wretched, if I choose to be so; but again and again do I say I will not allow this monstrous superstition to tread me down, like the tread of a giant on a broken reed. I will contend against it while I have life to do so."

"Bravely spoken."

"And when I desert Flora Bannerworth, may Heaven from that moment desert me!"

"Charles!" cried Henry, with emotion, "dear Charles, my more than friend — brother of my heart — noble Charles!"

"Nay, Henry, I am not entitled to your praises. I were base indeed to be other than that which I purpose to be. Come weal or woe — come what may, I am the affianced husband of your sister, and she, and she only, can break asunder the tie that binds me to her."

Chapter *XIII.*

THE OFFER FOR THE HALL. – THE VISIT TO SIR FRANCIS VARNEY. – THE STRANGE RESEMBLANCE. – A DREADFUL SUGGESTION.

*T*he party made a strict search through every nook and corner of the garden, but it proved to be a fruitless one: not the least trace of any one could be found. There was only one circumstance, which was pondered over deeply by them all, and that was that, beneath the window of the room in which Flora and her mother sat while the brothers were on their visit to the vault of their ancestors, were visible marks of blood to a considerable extent.

It will be remembered that Flora had fired a pistol at the spectral appearance, and that immediately upon that it had disappeared, after uttering a sound which might well be construed into a cry of pain from a wound.

That a wound then had been inflicted upon some one, the blood beneath the window now abundantly testified; and when it was discovered, Henry and Charles made a very close examination indeed of the garden, to discover what direction the wounded figure, be it man or vampyre, had taken.

But the closest scrutiny did not reveal to them a single spot of blood, beyond the space immediately beneath the window; — there the apparition seemed to have received its wound, and then, by some mysterious means, to have disappeared.

At length, wearied with the continued excitement, combined with want of sleep, to which they had been subjected, they returned to the hall.

Flora, with the exception of the alarm she experienced from the firing of the pistol, had met with no disturbance, and that, in order to spare her painful reflections, they told her was merely done as a precautionary measure, to proclaim to any one who might be lurking in the garden that the inmates of the house were ready to defend themselves against any aggression.

Whether or not she believed this kind deceit they knew not. She only sighed deeply, and wept. The probability is, that she more than suspected the vampyre had made another visit, but they forbore to press the point; and, leaving her with her mother, Henry and George went from her chamber again — the former to endeavor to seek some repose, as it would be his turn to watch on the succeeding night, and the latter to resume his station in a small room close to Flora's chamber, where it had been agreed watch and ward should be kept by turns while the alarm lasted.

At length, the morning again dawned upon that unhappy family, and to none were its beams more welcome.

The birds sang their pleasant carols beneath the window. The sweet, deep-colored autumnal sun shone upon all objects with a golden luster; and to look abroad, upon the beaming face of nature, no one could for a moment suppose, except from sad experience, that there were such things as gloom, misery, and crime, upon the earth.

"And must I," said Henry, as he gazed from a window of the hall upon the undulating park, the majestic trees, the flowers, the shrubs, and the many natural beauties with which the place was full, — "must I be chased from this spot, the home of my self and my kindred, by a phantom — must I indeed seek refuge elsewhere, because my own home has become hideous?"

It was indeed a cruel and a painful thought! It was one he yet would not, could not be convinced was absolutely necessary. But now the sun was shining: it was morning; and the feelings, which found a home in his breast amid the darkness, the stillness, and the uncertainty of night, were chased away by those glorious beams of sunlight, that fell upon hill, valley, and stream, and the thousand sweet sounds of life and animation that filled that sunny air!

Such a revulsion of feeling was natural enough. Many of the distresses and mental anxieties of night vanish with the night, and those which oppressed the heart of Henry Bannerworth were considerably modified.

He was engaged in these reflections when he heard the sound of the lodge bell, and as a visitor was now somewhat rare at this establishment, he waited with some anxiety to see to whom he was indebted for so early a call.

In the course of a few minutes, one of the servants came to him with a letter in her hand.

It bore a large handsome seal, and, from its appearance, would seem to have come from some personage of consequence. A second glance at it shewed him the name of "Varney" in the corner, and, with some degree of vexation, he muttered to himself,

"Another condoling epistle from the troublesome neighbor whom I have not yet seen."

"If you please, sir," said the servant who had brought him the letter, "as I'm here, and you are here, perhaps you'll have no objection to give me what I'm to have for the day and two nights as I've been here, cos I can't stay in the family as is so familiar with all sorts o' ghostesses: I ain't used to such company."

"What do you mean?" said Henry.

The question was a superfluous one: too well he knew what the woman meant, and the conviction came across his mind strongly that no domestic would consent to live long in a house which was subject to such dreadful visitations.

"What does I mean!" said the woman, — "why, sir, if it's all the same to you, I don't myself come of a wampyre family, and I don't choose to remain in a house where there is sich things encouraged. That's what I means, sir."

"What wages are owning to you?" said Henry.

"Why, as to wages, I only comed here by the day."

"Go, then, and settle with my mother. The sooner you leave this house, the better."

"Oh, indeed, I'm sure I don't want to stay."

This woman was one of these who were always armed at all points for a row, and she had no notion of concluding any engagement, of any character whatever, without some disturbance; therefore to see Henry take what she said with such provoking calmness was aggravating in the extreme; but there was no help for such a source of vexation. She could find no other ground of quarrel than what was connected with the vampyre, and, as Henry would not quarrel with her on such a score, she was compelled to give it up in despair.

When Henry found himself alone, and free from the annoyance of this woman, he turned his attention to the letter he held in his hand, and which, from the autograph in the corner, he knew came from his new neighbor, Sir Francis Varney, whom, by some chance or another, he had never yet seen.

To his great surprise, he found that the letter contained the following words: —

Dear Sir, —

"As a neighbor, by purchase of an estate contiguous to your own, I am quite sure you have excused, and taken in good part, the cordial offer I made to you of friendship and service some short time since; but now, in addressing to you a distinct proposition, I trust I shall meet with an indulgent consideration, whether such a proposition be accordant with your views or not.

"What I have heard from common report induces me to believe that Bannerworth Hall cannot be a desirable residence for yourself, or your amiable sister. If I am right in that conjecture, and you have any serious thought of leaving the place, I would earnestly recommend you, as one having some experience in such descriptions of property, to sell it at once.

"Now the proposition with which I conclude this letter is, I know, of a character to make you doubt the disinterestedness of such advice; but that it is disinterested, nevertheless, is a fact of which I can assure my own heart, and of which I beg to assure you. I propose, then, should you, upon consideration, decide upon such a course of proceeding, to purchase of you the Hall. I do not ask for a bargain on account of any extraneous circumstances which may at the present time depreciate the value of the property, but I am willing to give a fair price for it. Under these circumstances, I trust, sir, that you will give a kindly consideration to my offer, and even if you reject it, I hope that, as neighbors, we may live on in peace and amity, and in the interchange of those good offices which should subsist between us. Awaiting your reply,

"Believe me to be, dear sir,
"Your very obedient servant,
"FRANCIS VARNEY.
"To Henry Bannerworth, Esq."

Henry, after having read this most unobjectionable letter through, folded it up again, and placed it in his pocket. Clasping his hands, then, behind his back, a favorite attitude of his when he was in deep contemplation, he paced to and fro in the garden for some time in deep thought.

"How strange," he muttered. "It seems that every circumstance combines to induce me to leave my old ancestral home. It appears as if everything now that happened had that direct tendency. What can be the meaning of all this? 'Tis very strange — amazingly strange. Here arise circumstances which are enough to induce any man to leave a particular place. Then a friend, in whose single-mindedness and judgment I know I can rely, advised that step, and immediately upon the back of that comes a fair and candid offer."

There was an apparent connection between all these circumstances which much puzzled Henry. He walked to and fro for nearly an hour, until he heard a hasty footstep approaching him and upon looking in the direction from whence it came, he saw Mr. Marchdale.

"I will seek Marchdale's advice," he said, "upon this matter. I will hear what he says concerning it."

"Henry," said Marchdale, when he came sufficiently near to him for conversation, "why do you remain here alone?"

"I have received a communication from our neighbor, Sir Francis Varney," said Henry.

"Indeed!"

"It is here. Peruse it for yourself, and then tell me, Marchdale, candidly what you think of it."

"I suppose," said Marchdale, as he opened the letter, "it is another friendly note of condolence on the state of your domestic affairs, which, I grieve to say, from the prattling of domestics, whose tongues it is quite impossible to silence, have become the food for gossip all over the neighboring villages and estates."

"If anything could add another pang to those I have already been made to suffer," said Henry, "it would certainly arise from being made the food of vulgar gossip. But read the letter, Marchdale. You will find its contents of a more important character than you anticipate."

"Indeed!" said Marchdale, as he ran his eyes eagerly over the note. When he had finished it he glanced at Henry, who then said, —

"Well, what is your opinion?"

"I know not what to say, Henry. You know that my own advice to you had been to get rid of this place."

"It has."

"With the hope that the disagreeable affair connected with it now may remain connected with it as a house, and not with you and yours as a family."

"It may be so."

"There appears to me every likelihood of it."

"I do not know," said Henry, with a shudder. "I must confess, Marchdale, that to my own perceptions it seems more probably that the infliction we have experienced from the strange visitor, who seems now resolved to pester us with visits, will rather attach to a family than to a house. The vampyre may follow us."

"If so, of course the parting with the Hall would be a great pity, and no gain."

"None in the least."

"Henry, a thought has struck me."

"Let's hear it, Marchdale."

"It is this: — Suppose you were to try the experiment of leaving the Hall without selling it. Suppose for one year you were to let it to someone, Henry."

"It might be done."

"Ay, and it might, with very great promise and candor, be proposed to this very gentleman, Sir Francis Varney, to take it for one year, to see how he likes it before becoming the possessor of it. Then if he found himself tormented by the vampyre, he need not complete the purchase, or if you found that the apparition followed you from hence, you might yourself return, feeling that perhaps here, in the spots familiar to your youth, you might be most happy, even under such circumstances as at present oppress you."

"Most happy!" ejaculated Henry.

"Perhaps I should not have used that word."

"I am sure you should not," said Henry, "when you speak of me."

"Well — well; let us hope that the time may not be very far distant when I may use the term happy, as applied to you in the most conclusive and the strongest manner it can be used."

"Oh," said Henry, "I will hope; but do not mock me with it now, Marchdale, I pray you."

"Heaven forbid that I should mock you!"

"Well — well; I do not believe you are the man to do so to any one. But about the affair of the house."

"Distinctly, then, if I were you, I would call upon Sir Francis Varney, and make him an offer to become a tenant of the hall for twelve months, during which time you could go where you please, and test the fact of absence ridding you or not ridding you of the dreadful visitant who makes the night here truly hideous."

"I will speak to my mother, to George, and to my sister of the matter. They shall decide."

Mr. Marchdale now strove in every possible manner to raise the spirits of Henry Bannerworth, by painting to him the future in far more radiant colors than the present, and endeavoring to induce a belief in his mind that a short period of time might after all replace in his mind, and the minds of those who were naturally so dear to him, all their wonted serenity.

Henry, although he felt not much comfort from these kindly efforts, yet could feel gratitude to him who made them; and after expressing such a feeling to Marchdale, in strong terms, he repaired to the house, in order to hold a solemn consultation with those whom he felt ought to be consulted as well as himself as to what steps should be taken with regard to the Hall.

The proposition, or rather the suggestion, which had been made by Marchdale upon the proposition of Sir Francis Varney, was in every respect so reasonable and just, that it met, as was to be expected, with the concurrence of every member of the family.

Flora's cheeks almost resumed some of their wonted color at the mere thought now of leaving that home to which she had been at one time so much attached.

"Yes, dear Henry," she said, "let us leave here if you are agreeable so to do, and in leaving this house, we will believe that we leave behind us a world of terror."

"Flora," remarked Henry, in a tone of slight reproach, "if you were so anxious to leave Bannerworth Hall, why did you not say so before this proposition came from other mouths? You know your feelings upon such a subject would have been laws to me."

"I knew you were attached to the old house," said Flora; "and, besides, events have come upon us all with such fearful rapidity, there has scarcely been time to think."

"True — true."

"And you will leave, Henry?"

"I will call upon Sir Francis Varney myself, and speak to him upon the subject."

A new impetus to existence appeared now to come over the whole family, at the idea of leaving a place which always would be now associated in their minds with so much terror. Each member of the family felt happier, and breathed more freely than before, so that the change which had come over them seemed almost magical. And Charles Holland, too, was much better pleased, and he whispered to Flora, —

"Dear Flora, you will now surely no longer talk of driving from you the honest heart that loves you?"

"Hush, Charles, hush!" she said; "meet me in an hour hence in the garden, and we will talk of this."

"That hour will seem an age," he said.

Henry, now, having made a determination to see Sir Francis Varney, lost no time in putting it into execution. At Mr. Marchdale's own request, he took him with him, as it was desirable to have a third person present in the sort of business negotiation which was going on. The estate which had been so recently entered upon by the person calling himself Sir Francis Varney, and which common report said he had purchased, was a small, but complete property, and situated so close to the grounds connected with Bannerworth Hall, that a short walk soon placed Henry and Mr. Marchdale before the residence of this gentleman, who had shown so kindly a feeling towards the Bannerworth family.

"Have you seen Sir Francis Varney?" asked Henry of Mr. Marchdale, as he rung the gate-bell.

"I have not. Have you?"

"No; I never saw him. It is rather awkward our both being absolute strangers to his person."

"We can but send in our names, however; and, from the great vein of courtesy that runs through his letter, I have no doubt but we shall receive the most gentlemanly reception from him."

A servant in handsome livery appeared at the iron-gates, which opened upon a lawn in the front of Sir Francis Varney's house, and to this domestic Henry Bannerworth handed his card, on which he had written, in pencil, likewise the name of Mr. Marchdale.

"If your master," he said, "is within, we shall be glad to see him."

"Sir Francis is at home, sir," was the reply, "although not very well. If you will be pleased to walk in, I will announce you to him."

Henry and Marchdale followed the man into a handsome enough reception room where they were desired to wait while their names were announced.

"Do you know if this gentleman be a baronet," said Henry, "or a knight merely?"

"I really do not; I never saw him in my life, or heard of him before he came into this neighborhood."

"And I have been too much occupied with the painful occurrences of this hall to know anything of our neighbors. I dare say Mr. Chillingworth, if we had thought to ask him, would have known something concerning him."

"No doubt."

This brief colloquy was put an end to by the servant, who said, —

"My master, gentlemen, is not very well; but he begs me to present his best compliments, and to say he is much gratified with your visit, and will be happy to see you in his study."

Henry and Marchdale followed the man up a flight of stone stairs, and then they were conducted through a large apartment into a smaller one. There was very little light in this small room; but at the moment of their entrance a tall man, who was seated, rose, and, touching the spring of a blind that was to the window, it was up in a moment, admitting a broad glare of light. A cry of surprise, mingled with terror, came from Henry Bannerworth's lip. *The original of the portrait on the panel stood before him!* There was the lofty stature, the long, sallow face, the slightly projecting teeth, the dark, lustrous, although somewhat somber eyes; the expression of the features — all were alike.

"Are you unwell, sir?" said Sir Francis Varney, in soft, mellow accents, as he handed a chair to the bewildered Henry.

"God of Heaven!" said Henry; "how like!"

"You seem surprised, sir. Have you ever seen me before?"

Sir Francis drew himself up to his full height, and cast a strange glance upon Henry, whose eyes were riveted upon his face, as if with a species of fascination which he could not resist.

"Marchdale," Henry gasped; "Marchdale, my friend, Marchdale. I — I am surely mad."

"Hush! be calm," whispered Marchdale.

"Calm — calm — can you not see? Marchdale, is this a dream? Look — look — oh! look."

"For God's sake, Henry, compose yourself."

"Is your friend often thus?" said Sir Francis Varney, with the same mellifluous tone which seemed habitual with him.

"No, sir, he is not; but recent circumstances have shattered his nerves; and, to tell the truth, you bear so strong a resemblance to an old portrait, in his house, that I do not wonder so much as I otherwise should at his agitation."

"Indeed."

"A resemblance!" said Henry; "a resemblance! God of Heaven! it is the face itself."

"You much surprise me," said Sir Francis.

Henry sunk into the chair which was near him, and he trembled violently. The rush of painful thoughts and conjectures that came through his mind was enough to make any one tremble. "Is this the vampyre?" was the horrible question that seemed impressed upon his very brain, in letters of flame. "Is this the vampyre?"

"Are you better, sir?" said Sir Francis Varney, in his bland, musical voice. "Shall I order refreshment for you?"

"No — no," gasped Henry; "for the love of truth tell me! Is — is your name really Varney?"

"Sir?"

"Have you no other name to which, perhaps, a better title you could urge?"

"Mr. Bannerworth, I can assure you that I am too proud of the name of the family to which I belong to exchange it for any other, be it what it may."

"How wonderfully like!"

"I grieve to see you so much distressed, Mr. Bannerworth. I presume ill health has thus shattered your nerves?"

"No; ill health has not done the work. I know not what to say, Sir Francis Varney, to you; but recent events in my family have made the sight of you full of horrible conjectures."

"What mean you, sir?"

"You know, from common report, that we have had a fearful visitor at our house."

"A vampyre, I have heard," said Sir Francis Varney, with a bland, and almost beautiful smile, which displayed his white, glistening teeth to perfection.

"Yes; a vampyre, and — and —"

"I pray you go on, sir; you surely are above the vulgar superstition of believing in such matters?"

"My judgment is assailed in too many ways and shapes for it to hold out probably as it ought to do against so hideous a belief, but never was it so much bewildered as now."

"Why so?"

"Because —"

"Nay, Henry," whispered Mr. Marchdale, "it is scarcely civil to tell Sir Francis to his face, that he resembles a vampyre."

"I must, I must."

"Pray, sir," interrupted Varney to Marchdale, "permit Mr. Bannerworth to speak here freely. There is nothing in the whole world I so much admire as candor."

"Then you so much resemble the vampyre," added Henry, "that — that I know not what to think."

"Is it possible?" said Varney.

"It is a damning fact."

"Well, it's unfortunate for me, I presume? Ah!"

Varney gave a twinge of pain, as if some sudden bodily ailment had attacked him severely.

"You are unwell, sir?" said Marchdale.

"No, no — no," he said; "I — hurt my arm, and happened accidentally to touch the arm of this chair with it."

"A hurt?" said Henry.

"Yes, Mr. Bannerworth."

"A — a wound?"

"Yes, a wound, but not much more than skin deep. In fact, little beyond an abrasion of the skin."

"May I inquire how you came by it?"

"Oh, yes. A slight fall."

"Indeed."

"Remarkable, is it not? Very remarkable. We never know a moment when, from some most trifling cause, we may receive some serious bodily hurt. How true it is, Mr. Bannerworth, that in the midst of life we are in death."

"And equally true, perhaps," said Henry, "that in the midst of death there may be found a horrible life."

"Well, I should not wonder. There are really so many strange things in this world, that I have left off wondering at anything now."

"There are strange things," said Henry. "You wish to purchase of me the Hall, sir?"

"If you wish to sell."

"You — you are perhaps attached to the place? Perhaps you recollected it, sir, long ago?"

"Not very long," smiled Sir Francis Varney. "It seems a nice comfortable old house; and the grounds, too, appear to be amazingly well wooded, which, to one of rather a romantic temperament like myself, is always an additional charm to a place. I was extremely pleased with it the first time I beheld it, and a desire to call myself the owner of it took possession of my mind. The scenery is remarkable for its beauty, and, from what I have seen of it, it is rarely to be excelled. No doubt you are greatly attached to it."

"It has been my home from infancy," returned Henry, "and being also the residence of my ancestors for centuries, it is natural that I should be so."

"True — true."

"The house, no doubt, has suffered much," said Henry, "within the last hundred years."

"No doubt it has. A hundred years is a tolerable long space of time, you know."

"It is, indeed. Oh, how any human life which is spun out to such an extent, must lose its charms, by losing all its fondest and dearest associations."

"Ah, how true," said Sir Francis Varney.

He had some minutes previously touched a bell, and at this moment a servant brought in on a tray some wine and refreshments.

Chapter XIV.

HENRY'S AGREEMENT WITH SIR FRANCIS VARNEY. — THE SUDDEN ARRIVAL AT THE HALL. — FLORA'S ALARM.

On the tray which the servant brought into the room, were refreshments of different kinds, including wine, and after waving his hand for the domestic to retire, Sir Francis Varney said, —

"You will be better, Mr. Bannerworth, for a glass of wind after your walk, and you too, sir. I am ashamed to say, I have quite forgotten your name."

"Marchdale."

"Mr. Marchdale. Ay, Marchdale. Pray, sir, help yourself."

"You take nothing yourself?" said Henry.

"I am under a strict regimen," replied Varney. "The simplest diet alone does for me, and I have accustomed myself to long abstinence."

"He will not eat or drink," muttered Henry, abstractedly.

"Will you sell me the Hall?" said Sir Francis Varney.

Henry looked in his face again, from which he had only momentarily withdrawn his eyes, and he was then more struck than ever with the resemblance between him and the portrait on the panel of what had been Flora's chamber. What made that resemblance, too, one about which there could scarcely be two opinions, was the mark or cicatrix of a wound in the forehead, which the painter had slightly indented in the portrait, but which was much more plainly visible on the forehead of Sir Francis Varney. Now that Henry observed the distinctive mark, which he had not done before, he could feel no doubt, and a sickening sensation came over him at the thought that he was actually now in the presence of one of those terrible creatures, vampyres.

"You do not drink," said Varney. "Most young men are not so modest with a decanter of unimpeachable wine before them. Pray help yourself."

"I cannot."

Henry rose as he spoke, and turning to Marchdale, he said, in addition, —

"Will you come away?"

"If you please," said Marchdale, rising.

"But you have not, my dear sir," said Varney, "given me yet an answer about the Hall?"

"I cannot yet," answered Henry, "I will think. My present impression is, to let you have it on whatever terms you may yourself propose, always provided you consent to one of mine."

"Name it."

"That you never show yourself in my family."

"How very unkind. I understand you have a charming sister, young, beautiful, and accomplished. Shall I confess, now, that I had hopes of making myself agreeable to her?"

"You make yourself agreeable to her? The sight of you would blast her for ever, and drive her to madness."

"Am I so hideous?"

"No, but — you are —"

"Hush, Henry, hush," cried Marchdale. "Remember you are in this gentleman's house."

"True, true. Why does he tempt me to say these dreadful things? I do not want to say them."

"Come away, then — come away at once. Sir Francis Varney, my friend, Mr. Bannerworth, will think over your offer, and let you know. I think you may consider that your wish to become the purchaser of the Hall will be complied with."

"I wish to have it," said Varney, "and I can only say, that if I am master of it, I shall be very happy to see any of the family on a visit at any time."

"A visit!" said Henry, with a shudder. "A visit to the tomb were far more desirable. Farewell, sir."

"Adieu," said Sir Francis Varney, and he made one of the most elegant bows in the world, while there came over his face a peculiarity of expression that was strange, if not painful, to contemplate. In another minute Henry and Marchdale were clear of the house, and with feelings of bewilderment and horror, which beggar all description, poor Henry allowed himself to be led by the arm by Marchdale to some distance, without uttering a word. When he did speak, he said, —

"Marchdale, it would be charity of some one to kill me."

"To kill you?"

"Yes, for I am certain otherwise that I must go mad."

"Nay, nay; rouse yourself."

"This man, Varney, is a vampyre."

"Hush! hush!"

"I tell you, Marchdale," cried Henry, in a wild, excited manner, "he is a vampyre. He is the dreadful being who visited Flora at the still hour of midnight, and drained the life-blood from her veins. He is a vampyre. There are such things. I cannot doubt now. Oh, God, I wish now that your lightnings would blast me, as here I stand, for ever into annihilation, for I am going mad to be compelled to feel that such horrors can really have existence."

"Henry — Henry."

"Nay, talk not to me. What can I do? Shall I kill him? Is it not a sacred duty to destroy such a thing? Oh, horror — horror. He must be killed — destroyed — burnt, and the very dust to which he is consumed must be scattered to the winds of Heaven. It would be a deed well done, Marchdale."

"Hush! hush! These words are dangerous."

"I care not."

"What if they were overheard now by unfriendly ears? What might not be the uncomfortable results? I pray you be more cautious what you say of this strange man."

"I must destroy him."

"And wherefore?"

"Can you ask? Is he not a vampyre?"

"Yes; but reflect, Henry, for a moment upon the length to which you might carry out so dangerous an argument. It is said that vampyres are made by vampyres sucking the blood of those who, but for that circumstance, would have died and gone to decay in the tomb along with ordinary mortals; but that being so attacked during life by a vampyre, they themselves, after death, become such."

"Well — well, what is that to me?"

"Have you forgotten Flora?"

A cry of despair came from poor Henry's lips, and in a moment he seemed completely, mentally and physically, prostrated.

"God of Heaven!" he moaned, "I had forgotten her!"

"I thought you had."

"Oh, if the sacrifice of my own life would suffice to put an end to all this accumulating horror, how gladly would I lay it down. Ay, in any way — in any way. No mode of death should appall me. No amount of pain make me shrink. I could smile then upon the destroyer, and say, 'welcome — welcome — most welcome.'"

"Rather, Henry, seek to live for those whom you love than die for them. Your death would leave them desolate. In life you may ward off many a blow of fate from them."

"I may endeavor so to do."

"Consider that Flora may be wholly dependent upon such kindness as you may be able to bestow upon her."

"Charles clings to her."

"Humph!"

"You do not doubt him?"

"My dear friend, Henry Bannerworth, although I am not an old man, yet I am so much older than you that I have seen a great deal of the world, and am, perhaps, far better able to come to accurate judgments with regard to individuals."

"No doubt — no doubt; but yet —"

"Nay, hear me out. Such judgments, founded upon experience, when uttered have all the character of prophecy about them. I, therefore, now prophecy to you that Charles Holland will yet be so stung with horror at the circumstance of a vampyre visiting Flora, that he will never make her his wife."

"Marchdale, I differ from you most completely," said Henry. "I know that Charles Holland is the very soul of honor."

"I cannot argue the matter with you. It has not become a thing of fact. I have only sincerely to hope that I am wrong."

"You are, you may depend, entirely wrong. I cannot be deceived in Charles. From you such words produce no effect but one of regret that you should so much err in your estimate of any one. From any one but yourself they would have produced in me a feeling of anger I might have found it difficult to smother."

"It has often been my misfortune through life," said Mr. Marchdale, sadly, "to give the greatest offence where I feel the truest friendship, because it is in such quarters that I am always tempted to speak too freely."

"Nay, no offence," said Henry. "I am distracted, and scarcely know what I say. Marchdale, I know that you are my sincere friend; but, I tell you, I am nearly mad."

"My dear Henry, be calmer. Consider upon what is to be said concerning this interview at home."

"Ay; that is a consideration."

"I should not think it advisable to mention the disagreeable fact, that in your neighbor you think you have found out the nocturnal disturber of your family."

"No — no."

"I would say nothing of it. It is not at all probable that, after what you have said to him, this Sir Francis Varney, or whatever his real name may be, will obtrude himself upon you."

"If he should he surely dies."

"He will, perhaps, consider that such a step would be dangerous to him."

"It would be fatal, so help me, Heaven; and then would I take especial care that no power of resuscitation should ever enable that man again to walk the earth."

"They say the only way of destroying a vampyre is to fix him to the earth with a stake, so that he cannot move, and then, of course, decomposition will take its course, as in ordinary cases."

"Fire would consume him, and be a quicker process," said Henry. "But these are fearful reflections, and, for the present, we will not pursue them. Now to play the hypocrite, and endeavor to look composed and serene to my mother, and to Flora, while my heart is breaking."

The two friends had by this time reached the hall, and leaving his friend Marchdale, Henry Bannerworth, with feelings of the most unenviable description, slowly made his way to the apartment occupied by his mother and sister.

Chapter XV.

THE OLD ADMIRAL AND HIS SERVANT. – THE
COMMUNICATION FROM THE LANDLORD OF THE
NELSON'S ARMS.

While those matters of most grave and serious import were going on at the Hall, while each day, and almost each hour in each day, was producing more and more conclusive evidence upon a matter which at first had seemed too monstrous to be at all credited, it may well be supposed what a wonderful sensation was produced among the gossip-mongers of the neighborhood by the exaggerated reports that had reached them.

The servants, who had left the Hall on no other account, as they declare, but sheer fright at the awful visits of the vampyre, spread the news far and wide, so that in the adjoining villages and market-towns the vampyre of Bannerworth Hall became quite a staple article of conversation.

Such a positive godsend for the lovers of the marvelous had not appeared in the country side within the memory of that sapient individual – the oldest inhabitant.

And, moreover, there was one thing which staggered some people of better education and maturer judgments, and that was, that the more they took pains to inquire into the matter, in order, if possible, to put an end to what they considered a gross lie from the commencement, the more evidence they found to stagger their own senses upon the subject.

Everywhere then, in every house, public as well as private, something was being continually said of the vampyre. Nursery maids began to think a vampyre vastly superior to "old scratch and old bogie" as a means of terrifying their infant charges into quietness, if not to sleep, until they themselves became too much afraid upon the subject to mention it.

But nowhere was gossiping carried on upon the subject with more systematic fervor than at an inn called the Nelson's Arms, which was in the high street of the nearest market town to the Hall.

There, it seemed as if the lovers of the horrible made a point of holding their head quarters, and so thirsty did the numerous discussions make the guests, that the landlord was heard to declare that he, from his heart, really considered a vampyre as very nearly equal to a contested election.

It was towards evening on the same day that Marchdale and Henry made their visit to Sir Francis Varney, that a postchaise drew up to the inn we have mentioned. In the vehicle were two persons of exceedingly dissimilar appearance and general aspect.

One of these people was a man who seemed fast verging upon seventy years of age, although, from his still ruddy and embrowned complexion and stentorian voice, it was quite evident he intended yet to keep time at arm's-length for many years to come.

He was attired in ample and expensive clothing, but every article had a naval animus about it, if we may be allowed such an expression with regard to clothing. On his buttons was an anchor, and the general assortment and color of the clothing as nearly assimilated as possible to the undress naval uniform of an officer of high rank some fifty or sixty years ago.

His companion was a younger man, and about his appearance there was no secret at all. He was a genuine sailor, and he wore the shore costume of one. He was hearty looking, and well dressed, and evidently well fed.

As the chaise drove up to the door of the inn, this man made an observation to the other to the following effect, —

"A-hoy!"

"Well, you lubber, what now?" cried the other.

"They call this the Nelson's Arms; and you know, shiver me, that for the best half of his life he had but one."

"D — n you!" was the only rejoinder he got for his observation; but, with that, he seemed very well satisfied.

"Heave to!" he then shouted to the postillion, who was about to drive the chaise into the yard. "Heave to, you lubberly son of a gun! we don't want to go into the dock."

"Ah!" said the old man, "let's get out, Jack. This is the port; and, do you hear, and be cursed to you, let's have no swearing, d — n you, nor bad language, you lazy swab."

"Aye, aye," cried Jack; "I've not been ashore now a matter o' ten years, and not larnt a little shore-going politeness, admiral, I ain't been your *walley de sham* without larning a little about land reckonings. Nobody would take me for a sailor now, I'm thinking, admiral."

"Hold your noise!"

"Aye, aye, sir."

Jack, as he was called, bundled out of the chaise when the door was opened, with a movement so closely resembling what would have ensued had he been dragged out by the collar, that one was tempted almost to believe that such a feat must have been accomplished by some invisible agency.

He then assisted the old gentleman to alight, and the landlord of the inn commenced the usual profusion of bows with which a passenger by a postchaise is usually welcomed in preference to one by a stagecoach.

"Be quiet, will you!" shouted the admiral, for such indeed he was. "Be quiet."

"Best accommodations, sir — good wine — well-aired beds — good attendance — fine air —"

"Belay there," said Jack; and he gave the landlord what he considered a gentle admonition, but which consisted of such a dig in the ribs, that he made as many evolutions as the clown in a pantomime when he vociferated hot codlings.

"Now, Jack, where's the sailing instructions?" said his master.

"Here, sir, in the locker," said Jack, as he took from his pocket a letter, which he handed to the admiral.

"Won't you step in, sir?" said the landlord, who had begun now to recover a little from the dig in the ribs.

"What's the use of coming into port and paying harbor dues, and all that sort of thing, till we know if it's the right, you lubber, eh?"

"No; oh, dear me, sir, of course — God bless me, what can the old gentleman mean?"

The admiral opened the letter, and read: —

"If you stop at the Nelson's Arms at Uxotter, you will hear of me, and I can be sent for, when I will tell you more.

"Yours, very obediently and humbly,

"JOSIAH CRINKLES."

"Who the deuce is he?"

"This is Uxotter, sir," said the landlord; "and here you are, sir, at the Nelson's Arms. Good beds — good wine — good —"

"Silence!"

"Yes, sir, — oh, of course."

"Who the devil is Josiah Crinkles?"

"Ha! ha! ha! ha! Makes me laugh, sir. Who the devil indeed! They do say the devil and lawyers, sir, know something of each other — makes me smile."

"I'll make you smile out of the other side of that d——d great hatchway of a mouth of yours in a minute. Who is Crinkles?"

"Oh, Mr. Crinkles, sir, everybody knows. A most respectable attorney, sir, indeed, a highly respectable man, sir."

"A lawyer?"

"Yes, sir, a lawyer."

"Well, I'm d——d!"

Jack gave a long whistle, and both master and man looked at each other aghast.

"Now, hang me!" cried the admiral, "if ever I was so taken in all my life."

"Ay, ay, sir," said Jack.

"To come a hundred and seventy miles to see a d——d swab of a rascally lawyer."

"Ay, ay, sir."

"I'll smash him — Jack!"

"Yer honor?"

"Get into the chaise again."

"Well, but where's Master Charles? Lawyers, in course, sir, is all blessed rogues; but howsomedever, he may have for once in his life this here one of 'em have told us of the right channel, and if so be as he has, don't be the Yankee to leave him among the pirates. I'm ashamed of you."

"You infernal scoundrel; how dare you preach to me in such a way, you lubberly rascal?"

"Cos you desarves it."

"Mutiny — mutiny — by Jove! Jack, I'll have you put in irons — you're a scoundrel, and no seaman."

"No seaman! — no seaman!"

"Not a bit of one."

"Very good. It's time, then, as I was off the purser's books. Good bye to you; I only hopes as you may get a better seaman to stick to you and be your *walley de sham* nor Jack Pringle, that's all the harm I wish you. You didn't call me no seaman in the Bay of Corfu, when the bullets were scuttling our nobs."

"Jack, you rascal, give us your fin. Come here, you d——d villain. You'll leave me, will you?"

"Not if I know it."

"Come in, then."

"Don't tell me I'm no seaman. Call me a wagabone if you like, but don't hurt my feelins. There I'm as tender as a baby, I am. — Don't do it."

"Confound you, who is doing it?"

"The devil."

"Who is?"

"Don't, then."

Thus wrangling, they entered the inn, to the great amusement of several bystanders, who had collected to hear the altercation between them.

"Would you like a private room, sir?" said the landlord.

"What's that to you?" said Jack.

"Hold your noise, will you?" cried his master. "Yes, I should like a private room, and some grog."

"Strong as the devil!" put in Jack.

"Yes, sir — yes, sir. Good wines — good beds — good —"

"You said all that before, you know," remarked Jack, as he bestowed upon the landlord another terrific dig in the ribs.

"Hilloa!" cried the admiral, "you can send for that infernal lawyer, Mister Landlord."

"Mr. Crinkles, sir?"

"Yes, yes."

"Who may I have the honor to say, sir, wants to see him?"

"Admiral Bell."

"Certainly, admiral, certainly. You'll find him a very conversable, nice, gentlemanly little man, sir."

"And tell him Jack Pringle is here, too," cried the seaman.

"Oh, yes, yes — of course," said the landlord, who was in such a state of confusion from the digs in the ribs he had received, and the noise his guests had already made in his house, that, had he been suddenly put upon his oath, he would scarcely have liked to say which was the master and which was the man.

"The idea, now, Jack," said the admiral, "of coming all this way to see a lawyer."

"Ay, ay, sir."

"If he's said he was a lawyer, we would have known what to do. But it's a take in, Jack."

"So I think. Howsomedever, we'll serve him out when we catch him, you know."

"Good — so we will."

"And, then, again, he may know something about Master Charles, sir, you know. Lord love him, don't you remember when he came aboard to see you once at Portsmouth?"

"Ah! I do indeed."

"And how he said he hated the French, and quite a baby, too. What perseverance and sense. 'Uncle,' says he to you, 'when I'm a big man, I'll go in a ship, and fight all the French in a heap,' says he. 'And beat 'em, my boy, too,' says you; cos you thought he'd forgot that; and then he says, 'what's the use of saying that, stupid? — don't we always beat 'em?'"

The admiral laughed and rubbed his hands, as he cried aloud, —

"I remember, Jack — I remember him. I was stupid to make such a remark."

"I know you was — a d——d old fool I thought you."

"Come, come. Hilloa, there!"

"Well, then, what do you call me no seaman for?"

"Why, Jack, you bear malice like a marine."

"There you go again. Good-bye. Do you remember when we were yardarm to yard arm with those two Yankee frigates, and took 'em both? You didn't call me a marine then, when the scuppers were running with blood. Was I a seaman then?"

"You were, Jack — you were; and you saved my life."

"I didn't."

"You did."

"I say I didn't — it was a marline-spike."

"But I say you did, you rascally scoundrel. I say you did, and I won't be contradicted in my own ship."

"Call this your ship?"

"No, d — n it, — I —"

"Mr. Crinkles," said the landlord, flinging the door wide open, and so at once putting an end to the discussion which always apparently had a tendency to wax exceedingly warm.

"The shark, by G-d!" said Jack.

A little, neatly dressed man made his appearance, and advanced rather timidly into the room. Perhaps he had heard from the landlord that the parties who had sent for him were of rather a violent sort.

"So you are Crinkles, are you?" cried the admiral. "Sit down, though you are a lawyer."

"Thank you, sir. I am an attorney, certainly and my name is certainly Crinkles."

"Look at that."

The admiral placed the letter in the little lawyer's hands, who said, —

"Am I to read it?"

"Yes, to be sure."

"Aloud?"

"Read it to the devil, of you like, in a pig's whisper, or a West India hurricane."

"Oh, very good, sir. I — I am willing to be agreeable, so I'll read it aloud, if it's all the same to you."

He then opened the letter and read as follows: —

"To Admiral Bell.

"Admiral, — Being, from various circumstances, aware that you take a warm and a praiseworthy interest in your nephew Charles Holland, I venture to write to you concerning a matter in which your immediate and active cooperation with others may rescue him from a condition which will prove, if allowed to continue, very much to his detriment, and ultimate unhappiness.

"You are, then, hereby informed, that he, Charles Holland, has, much earlier than he ought to have done, returned to England, and that the object of his return is to contract a marriage into a family in every way objectionable, and with a girl who is highly objectionable.

"You, admiral, are his nearest and almost his only relative in the world; you are the guardian of his property, and, therefore, it becomes a duty on your part to interfere to save him from the ruinous consequences of a marriage, which is sure to bring ruin and distress upon himself and all who take an interest in his welfare.

"The family he wishes to marry into is named Bannerworth, and the young lady's name is Flora Bannerworth. When, however, I inform you that a *vampyre* is in that family, and that if he married into it, he marries a vampyre, and will have vampyres for children, I trust I have said enough to warn you upon the subject, and to induce you to lose no time in repairing to the spot.

"If you stop at the Nelson's Arms in Uxotter, you will hear of me. I can be sent for, when I will tell you more.

"Yours, very obediently and humbly,

                    "JOSIAH CRINKLES."

P.S. I enclose you Dr. Johnson's definition of a vampyre, which is as follows:

"VAMPYRE (a German blood-sucker) — by which you perceive how many vampyres, from time immemorial, must have been well entertained at the expense of John Bull, at the court of St. James, where nothing hardly is to be met with but German blood-suckers."

The lawyer ceased to read, and the amazed look with which he glanced at the face of Admiral Bell would, under any other circumstances, have much amused him. His mind, however, was by far too much engrossed with a consideration of the danger of Charles Holland, his nephew, to be amused at anything; so, when he found that the little lawyer said nothing, he bellowed out, —

"Well, sir?"

"We-we-well," said the attorney.

"I've sent for you, and here you are, and here I am, and here's Jack Pringle. What have you got to say?"

"Just this much," said Mr. Crinkles, recovering himself a little, "just this much, sir, that I never saw that letter before in all my life."

"You — never — saw — it?"

"Never."

"Didn't write it?"

"On my solemn word of honor, sir, I did not."

Jack Pringle whistled, and the admiral looked puzzled. Like the admiral in the song, too, he "grew paler," and then Mr. Crinkles added, —

"Who has forged my name to a letter such as this, I cannot imagine. As for writing to you, sir, I never heard of your existence, except publicly, as one of those gallant officers who have spent a long life in nobly fighting their country's battles, and who are entitled to the admiration and the applause of every Englishman."

Jack and the admiral looked at each other in amazement, and then the latter exclaimed, —

"What! This from a lawyer?"

"A lawyer, sir," said Crinkles, "may know how to appreciate the deeds of gallant men, although he many not be able to imitate them. That letter, sir, is a forgery, and I now leave you, only much gratified at the incident which has procured me the honor of an interview with a gentleman, whose name will live in the history of his country. Good day, sir! Good day!"

"No. I'm d——d if you go like that," said Jack, as he sprang to the door, and put his back against it. "You shall take a glass with me in honor of the wooden walls of Old England, d — e, if you was twenty lawyers."

"That's right, Jack," said the admiral. "Come, Mr. Crinkles, I'll think, for your sake, there may be two decent lawyers in the world, and you one of them. We must have a bottle of the best wine the ship — I mean the house — can afford together."

"If it is your command, admiral, I obey with pleasure," said the attorney; "and although I assure you, on my honor, I did not write that letter, yet some of the matters mentioned in it are so generally notorious here, that I can afford you some information concerning them."

"Can you?"

"I regret to say I can, for I respect the parties."

"Sit down, then — sit down. Jack, run to the steward's room and get the wine. We will go into it now starboard and larboard. Who the deuce could have written that letter?"

"I have not the least idea, sir."

"Well — well, never mind; it has brought me here, that's something, so I won't grumble much at it. I didn't know my nephew was in England, and I dare say he didn't know I was; but here we both are, and I won't rest till I've seen him, and ascertained how the what's-its-name —"

"The vampyre."

"Ah! the vampyre."

"Shiver my timbers!" said Jack Pringle, who now brought in some wine much against the remonstrances of the waiters of the establishment, who considered that he was treading upon their vested interests by so doing. — "Shiver my timbers, if I knows what a *wamphigher* is, unless he's some distant relation to Davy Jones!"

"Hold your ignorant tongue," said the admiral; "nobody wants you to make a remark, you great lubber!"

"Very good," said Jack, and he sat down the wine on the table, and then retired to the other end of the room, remarking to himself that he was not called a great lubber on a certain occasion, when bullets were scuttling their nobs, and they were yard arm to yard arm with God knows who.

"Now, mister lawyer," said Admiral Bell, who had about him a large share of the habits of a rough sailor. "Now, mister lawyer, here is a glass first to our better acquaintance, for d – e, if I don't like you!"

"You are very good, sir."

"Not at all. There was a time, when I'd just as soon have thought of asking a young shark to supper with me in my own cabin as a lawyer, but I begin to see that there may be such a thing as a decent, good sort of fellow seen in the law; so here's good luck to you, and you shall never want a friend or a bottle while Admiral Bell has a shot in the locker."

"Gammon," said Jack.

"D – n you, what do you mean by that?" roared the admiral, in a furious tone.

"I wasn't speaking to you," shouted Jack, about two octaves higher. "It's two boys in the street as is pretending they're a going to fight, and I know d—d well they won't."

"Hold your noise."

"I'm going. I wasn't told to hold my noise, when our nobs were being scuttled off Beyrout."

"Never mind him, mister lawyer," added the admiral. "He don't know what he's talking about. Never mind him. You go on and tell me all you know about the – the —"

"The vampyre!"

"Ah! I always forget the names of strange fish. I suppose, after all, it's something of the mermaid order?"

"That I cannot say, sir; but certainly the story, in all its painful particulars, has made a great sensation all over the country."

"Indeed!"

"Yes, sir. You shall hear how it occurred. It appears that one night Miss Flora Bannerworth, a young lady of great beauty, and respected and admired by all who knew her was visited by a strange being who came in at the window."

"My eye," said Jack, "if it waren't me, I wish it had a been."

"So petrified by fear was she, that she had only time to creep half out of the bed, and to utter one cry of alarm, when the strange visitor seized her in his grasp."

"D – n my pig tail," said Jack, "what a squall there must have been, to be sure."

"Do you see this bottle?" roared the admiral.

"To be sure, I does; I think as it's time I seed another."

"You scoundrel, I'll make you feel it against that d——d stupid head of yours, if your interrupt this gentleman again."

"Don't be violent."

"Well, as I was saying," continued the attorney, "she did, by great good fortune, manage to scream, which had the effect of alarming the whole house. The door of her chamber, which was fast, was broken open."

"Yes, yes –"

"Ah," cried Jack.

"You may imagine the horror and the consternation of those who entered the room to find her in the grasp of a fiend-like figure, whose teeth were fastened on her neck and who was actually draining her veins of blood."

"The devil!"

"Before any one could lay hands sufficiently upon the figure to detain it, it had fled precipitately from its dreadful repast. Shots were fired after it in vain."

"And they let it go?"

"They followed it, I understand, as well as they were able, and saw it scale the garden wall of the premises; there it escaped, leaving, as you may well imagine, on all their minds, a sensation of horror difficult to describe."

"Well, I never did hear anything the equal of that. Jack, what do you think of it?"

"I haven't begun to think, yet," said Jack.

"But what about my nephew, Charles?" added the admiral.

"Of him I know nothing."

"Nothing?"

"Not a word, admiral. I was not aware you had a nephew, or that any gentleman bearing that, or any other relationship to you, had any sort of connection with these mysterious and most unaccountable circumstances. I tell you all I have gathered from common report about this vampyre business. Further I know not, I assure you."

"Well, a man can't tell what he don't know. It puzzles me to think who could possibly have written me this letter."

"That I am completely at a loss to imagine," said Crinkles. "I assure you, my gallant sir, that I am much hurt at the circumstance of any one using my name in such a way. But, nevertheless, as you are here, permit me to say, that it will be my pride, my pleasure, and the boast of the remainder of my existence, to be of some service to so gallant a defender of my country, and one whose name, along with the memory of his deeds, is engraved upon the heart of every Briton."

"Quite ekal to a book, he talks," said Jack. "I never could read one myself, on account o' not knowing how, but I've heard 'em read, and that's just the sort o' incomprehensible gammon."

"We don't want any of your ignorant remarks," said the admiral, "so you be quiet."

"Ay, ay, sir."

"Now, Mister Lawyer, you are an honest fellow, and an honest fellow is generally a sensible fellow."

"Sir, I thank you."

"If so be as what this letter says it true, my nephew Charles has got a liking for this girl, who has had her neck bitten by a vampyre, you see."

"I perceive, sir."

"Now what would you do?"

"One of the most difficult, as well, perhaps, as one of the most ungracious of tasks," said the attorney, "is to interfere with family affairs. The cold and steady eye of reason generally sees things in such very different lights to what they appear to those whose feelings and whose affections are much compromised in their results."

"Very true. Go on."

"Taking, my dear sir, what in my humble judgment appears a reasonable view of this subject, I should say it would be a dreadful thing for your nephew to marry into a family any member of which was liable to the visitations of a vampyre."

"It wouldn't be pleasant."

"The young lady might have children."

"Oh, lots," cried Jack.

"Hold your noise, Jack."

"Ay, ay, sir."

"And she might herself actually, when after death she became a vampyre, come and feed on her own children."

"Become a vampyre! What, is she going to be a vampyre too?"

"My dear sir, don't you know that it is a remarkable fact, as regards the physiology of vampyres, that whoever is bitten by one of these dreadful beings, becomes a vampyre?"

"The devil!"

"It is a fact, sir."

"Whew!" whistled Jack; "she might bite us all, and we should be a whole ship's crew o' *wamphigaers*. There would be a confounded go!"

"It's not pleasant," said the admiral, as he rose from his chair, and paced to and fro in the room, "it's not pleasant. Hang me up at my own yardarm if it is."

"Who said it was?" cried Jack.

"Who asked you, you brute?"

"Well, sir," added Mr. Crinkles, "I have given you all the information I can; and I can only repeat what I before had the honor of saying more at large, namely, that I am your humble servant to command, and that I shall be happy to attend upon you at any time."

"Thank ye — thank ye, Mr. — a — a —"

"Crinkles."

"Ah, Crinkles. You shall hear from me again, sir, shortly. Now that I am down here, I will see to the very bottom of this affair, were it deeper than fathom ever sounded. Charles Holland was my poor sister's son; he's the only relative I have in the wide world, and his happiness is dearer to my heart than my own."

Crinkles turned aside, and, by the twinkle of his eyes, one might premise that the honest little lawyer was much affected.

"God bless you, sir," he said; "farewell."

"Good day to you."

"Good-bye, lawyer," cried Jack. "Mind how you go. D — n me, if you don't seem a decent sort of fellow, and, after all, you may give the devil a clear berth, and get into heaven's straits, with a flowing sheet, provided you don't, towards the end of the voyage, make any lubberly blunders."

The old admiral threw himself into a chair with a deep sigh.

"Jack," said he.

"Aye, aye, sir."

"What's to be done now?"

Jack opened the window to discharge the superfluous moisture from an enormous quid he had indulged himself with while the lawyer was telling about the vampyre, and then again turning his face towards his master, he said, —

"Do? What shall we do? Why, go at once and find out Charles, our *nevy*, and ask him all about it, and see the young lady, too, and lay hold o' the *wamphigher* if we can, as well, and go at the whole affair broadside to broadside, till we make a prize of all the particulars, arter which we can turn it over in our minds agin, and see what's to be done."

"Jack, you are right. Come along."

"I knows I am. Do you know now which way to steer?"

"Of course not. I never was in this latitude before, and the channel looks intricate. We will hail a pilot, Jack, and then we shall be all right, and if we strike it will be his fault."

"Which is a mighty great consolation," said Jack. "Come along."

Chapter XVI.

THE MEETING OF THE LOVERS IN THE GARDEN. – AN
AFFECTING SCENE. – THE SUDDEN APPEARANCE OF SIR
FRANCIS VARNEY.

Our readers will recollect that Flora Bannerworth had made an appointment with Charles Holland in the garden of the hall. This meeting was looked forward to by the young man with a variety of conflicting feelings, and he passed the intermediate time in a most painful state of doubt as to what would be its result.

The thought that he should be much urged by Flora to give up all thoughts of making her his, was a most bitter one to him, who loved her with so much truth and constancy, and that she would say all she could to induce such a resolution in his mind he felt certain. But to him the idea of now abandoning her presented itself in the worst of aspects.

"Shall I," he said, "sink so low in my own estimation, as well as in hers, and in that of all honorable-minded persons, as to desert her now in the hour of affliction? Dare I be so base as actually or virtually to say to her, 'Flora, when your beauty was undimmed by sorrow – when all around you seemed life and joy, I loved you selfishly for the increased happiness which you might bestow upon me; but now the hand of misfortune presses heavily upon you – you are not what you were, and I desert you?' Never – never – never!"

Charles Holland, it will be seen by some of our more philosophic neighbors, felt more acutely than he reasoned; but let his errors of argumentation be what they may, can we do other than admire the nobility of soul which dictated such a self denying generous course as that he was pursuing?

As for Flora, Heaven only knows if at that precise time her intellect had completely stood the test of the trying events which had nearly overwhelmed it.

The two grand feelings that seemed to possess her mind were fear of the renewed visits of the vampyre, and an earnest desire to release Charles Holland from his repeated vows of constancy towards her.

Feeling, generosity, and judgment, all revolted holding a young man to such a destiny as hers. To link him to her fate, would be to make him to a real extent a sharer in it, and the more she heard fall from his lips in the way of generous feelings of continued attachment to her, the more severely did she feel that he would suffer most acutely if united to her.

And she was right. The very generosity of feeling which would have now prompted Charles Holland to lead Flora Bannerworth to the altar, even with the marks of the vampyre's teeth upon her throat, gave an assurance of the depth of feeling which would have made him an ample haven in all her miseries, in all her distresses and afflictions.

What was familiarly in the family at the Hall called the garden, was a semicircular piece of ground shaded in several directions by trees, and which was exclusively devoted to the growth of flowers. The piece of ground was nearly hidden from the view of the house, and in its center was a summerhouse, which at the usual season of the year was covered with all kinds of creeping plants of exquisite perfumes, and rare beauty. All around, too, bloomed the fairest and sweetest of flowers, which a rich soil and a sheltered situation could produce.

Alas! though, of late many weeds had straggled up among their more estimable floral culture, for the decayed fortunes of the family had prevented them from keeping the necessary servants, to place the Hall and its grounds in a state of neatness, such as it had once been the pride of the inhabitants of the place to see them. It was then in this flower garden that Charles and Flora used to meet.

As may be supposed, he was on the spot before the appointed hour, anxiously expecting the appearance of her who was so really and truly dear to him. What to him were the sweet flowers that there grew in such happy luxuriance and heedless beauty? Alas, the flower that to his mind was fairer than them all, was blighted, and in the wan cheek of her whom he loved, he sighed to see the lily usurping the place of the radiant rose.

"Dear, dear Flora," he ejaculated, "you must indeed be taken from this place, which is so full of the most painful remembrances now. I cannot think that Mr. Marchdale somehow is a friend to me, but that conviction, or rather impression, does not paralyze my judgment sufficiently to induce me not to acknowledge that his advice is good. He might have couched it in pleasanter words — words that would not, like daggers, each have brought a deadly pang home to my heart, but still I do think that in his conclusion he was right."

A light sound, as of some fairy footstep among the flowers, came upon his ears, and turning instantly to the direction from whence the sound proceeded, he saw what his heart had previously assured him of, namely that it was his Flora that was coming.

Yes, it was she; but, ah, how pale, how wan — how languid and full of the evidences of much mental suffering was she. Where now was the elasticity of that youthful step? Where now was that lustrous beaming beauty of mirthfulness, which was wont to dawn in those eyes?

Alas, all was changed. The exquisite beauty of form was there, but the light of joy which had lent its most transcendent charms to that heavenly face, was gone. Charles was by her side in a moment. He had her hand clasped in his, while his disengaged one was wound tenderly around her taper waist.

"Flora, dear, dear Flora," he said, "you are better. Tell me that you feel the gentle air revives you?"

She could not speak. Her heart was too full of woe.

"Oh; Flora, my own, my beautiful," he added, in those tones which come so direct from the heart, and which are so different from any assumption of tenderness. "Speak to me, dear, dear Flora — speak to me if it be but a word."

"Charles," was all she could say, and then she burst into a flood of tears, and leant so heavily upon his arm, that it was evident but for that support she must have fallen.

Charles Holland welcomed those, although they grieved him so much that he could have accompanied them with his own, but then he knew that she would be soon now more composed, and they would relieve the heart whose sorrows had called them into existence.

He forbore to speak to her until he felt this sudden gush of feeling was subsiding into sobs, and then in low, soft accents, he again endeavored to breathe comfort to her afflicted and terrified spirit.

"My dear Flora," he said, "remember that there are warm hearts that love you. Remember that neither time nor circumstance can change such endearing affection as mine. Ah, Flora, what evil is there in the whole world that love may not conquer, and in the height of its noble feelings laugh to scorn."

"Oh, hush, hush, Charles, hush."

"Wherefore, Flora, would you still the voice of pure affection? I love you surely, as few have ever loved. Ah, why would you forbid me to give such utterance as I may to those feelings which fill up my whole heart?"

"No — no — no."

"Flora, Flora, wherefore do you say no?"

"Do not, Charles, now speak to me of affection or love. Do not tell me you love me now."

"Not tell you I love you! Ah, Flora, if my tongue, with its poor eloquence to give utterance to such a sentiment, were to do its office, each feature of my face would tell the tale. Each action would show to all the world how much I loved you."

"I must not now hear this. Great God of Heaven give me strength to carry out the purpose of my soul."

"What purpose is it, Flora, that you have to pray thus fervently for strength to execute? Oh, if it savor aught of reason against love's majesty, forget it. Love is a gift from Heaven. The greatest and the most glorious gift it ever bestowed upon its creatures. Heaven will not aid you in repudiating that which is the one grand redeeming feature that rescues human nature from a world of reproach."

Flora wrung her hands despairingly as she said, —

"Charles, I know I cannot reason with you. I know I have not power of language, aptitude of illustration, nor depth of thought to hold a mental contention with you."

"Flora, for what do I contend?"

"You, you speak of love."

"And I have, ere this, spoken to you of love unchecked."

"Yes, yes. Before this."

"And now, wherefore not now? Do not tell me you are changed."

"I am changed, Charles. Fearfully changed. The curse of God has fallen upon me, I know not why. I know not that in word or in thought I have done evil, except perchance unwittingly, and yet — the vampyre."

"Let not that affright you."

"Affright me! It has killed me."

"Nay, Flora, you think too much of what I still hope to be susceptible of far more rational explanation."

"By your own words, then, Charles, I must convict you. I cannot, I dare not be yours, while such a dreadful circumstance is hanging over me, Charles; if a more rational explanation than the hideous one which my own fancy gives to the form that visits me can be found, find it, and rescue me from despair and from madness."

They had now reached the summerhouse, and as Flora uttered these words she threw herself on to a seat, and covering her beautiful face with her hands, she sobbed convulsively.

"You have spoken," said Charles, dejectedly. "I have heard that which you wished to say to me."

"No, no. Not all, Charles."

"I will be patient, then, although what more you may have to add should tear my very heart-strings."

"I — I have to add, Charles," she said, in a tremulous voice, "that justice, religion, mercy — every human attribute which bears the name of virtue, calls loudly upon me no longer to hold you to vows made under different auspices."

"Go on, Flora."

"I then implore you, Charles, finding me what I am, to leave me to the fate which it has pleased Heaven to cast upon me. I do not ask you, Charles, not to love me."

"'Tis well. Go on, Flora."

"Because I should like to think that, although I might never see you more, you loved me still. But you must think seldom of me, and you must endeavor to be happy with some other —"

"You cannot, Flora, pursue the picture you yourself would draw. These words come not from your heart."

"Yes — yes — yes."

"Did you ever love me?"

"Charles, Charles, why will you add another pang to those you know must already rend my heart?"

"No, Flora, I would tear my own heart from my bosom ere I would add one pang to yours. Well I know that gentle maiden modesty would seal your lips to the soft confession that you love me. I could not hope the joy of hearing you utter these words. The tender devoted lover is content to see the truthful passion in the speaking eyes of beauty. Content is he to translate it from a thousand acts, which, to eyes that look not so acutely as a lover's, bear no signification; but when you tell me to seek happiness with another, well may the anxious question burst from my throbbing heart of, 'Did you ever love me, Flora?'"

Her senses hung entranced upon his words. Oh, what a witchery is in the tongue of love. Some even of the former color of her cheek returned as, forgetting all for the moment but that she was listening to the voice of him, the thoughts of whom had made up the day dream of her happiness, she gazed upon his face.

His voice ceased. To her it seemed as if some music had suddenly left off in its most exquisite passage. She clung to his arm — she looked imploringly up to him. Her head sunk upon his breast as she cried,

"Charles, Charles, I did love you. I do love you now."

"Then let sorrow and misfortune shake their grisly locks in vain," he cried. "Heart to heart — hand to hand with me, defy them."

He lifted up his arms towards Heaven as he spoke, and at the moment came such a rattling peal of thunder, that the very earth seemed to shake upon its axis.

A half scream of terror burst from the lips of Flora, as she cried, —

"What was that?"

"Only thunder," said Charles, calmly.

"'Twas an awful sound."

"A natural one."

"But at such a moment, when you were defying Fate to injure us. Oh!

Charles, is it ominous?"

"Flora, can you really give way to such idle fancies?"

"The sun is obscured."

"Ay, but it will shine all the brighter for its temporary eclipse. The thunderstorm will clear the air of many noxious vapors; the forked lightning has its uses as well as its powers of mischief. Hark! there it is again."

Another peal, of almost equal intensity to the other, shook the firmament. Flora trembled.

"Charles," she said, "this is the voice of Heaven. We must part — we must part forever. I cannot be yours."

"Flora, this is madness. Think again, dear Flora. Misfortunes for a time will hover over the best and most fortunate of us; but, like the clouds that now obscure the sweet sunshine, will pass away, and leave no trace behind them. The sunshine of joy will shine on you again."

There was a small break in the clouds, like a window looking into Heaven. From it streamed one beam of sunlight, so bright, so dazzling, and so beautiful, that it was a sight of wonder to look upon. It fell upon the face of Flora; it warmed her cheek; it lent luster to her pale lips and tearful eyes; it illuminated that little summerhouse as if it had been the shrine of some saint.

"Behold!" cried Charles, "where is your omen now?"

"God of Heaven!" cried Flora; and she stretched out her arms.

"The clouds that hover over your spirit now," said Charles, "shall pass away. Accept this beam of sunlight as a promise from God."

"I will — I will. It is going."

"It has done its office."

The clouds closed over the small orifice, and all was gloom again as before.

"Flora," said Charles, "you will not ask me now to leave you?"

She allowed him to clasp her to his heart. It was beating for her, and for her only.

"You will let me, Flora, love you still?"

Her voice, as she answered him, was like the murmur of some distant melody the ears can scarcely translate to the heart.

"Charles, we will live, love, and die together."

And now there was a rapt stillness in that summerhouse for many minutes — a trance of joy. They did not speak, but now and then she would look into his face with an old familiar smile, and the joy of his heart was near to bursting in tears from his eyes.

A shriek burst from Flora's lips — as shriek so wild and shrill that it awakened echoes far and near. Charles staggered back a step, as if shot, and then in such agonised accents as he was long indeed in banishing the remembrance of, she cried, —

"The vampyre! the vampyre!"

Chapter *XVII.*

THE EXPLANATION. — THE ARRIVAL OF THE ADMIRAL AT THE HOUSE. — A SCENE OF CONFUSION, AND SOME OF ITS RESULTS.

So sudden and so utterly unexpected a cry of alarm from Flora, at such a time might well have the effect of astounding the nerves of any one, and no wonder that Charles was for a few seconds absolutely petrified and almost unable to think.

Mechanically, then, he turned his eyes towards the door of the summer-house, and there he saw a tall, thin man, rather elegantly dressed, whose countenance certainly, in its wonderful resemblance to the portrait on the panel, might well appall any one.

The stranger stood in the irresolute attitude on the threshold of the summer-house of one who did not wish to intrude, but who found it as awkward, if not more so now, to retreat than to advance.

Before Charles Holland could summon any words to his head, or think of freeing himself from the clinging grasp of Flora, which was wound around him, the stranger made a very low and courtly bow, after which he said, in winning accents, —

"I very much fear that I am an intruder here. Allow me to offer my warmest apologies, and to assure, sir, and you, madam, that I had no idea any one was in the arbour. You perceive the rain is falling smartly, and I made towards here, seeing it was likely to shelter me from the shower."

These words were spoken in such a plausible and courtly tone of voice, that they might well have become any drawing room in the kingdom.

Flora kept her eyes fixed upon him during the utterance of these words, and as she convulsively clutched the arm of Charles, she kept on whispering —

"The vampyre! the vampyre!"

"I much fear," added the stranger, in the same bland tones, "that I have been the cause of some alarm to the young lady!"

"Release me," whispered Charles to Flora. "Release me; I will follow him at once."

"No, no — do not leave me — do not leave me. The vampyre — the dreadful vampyre!"

"But, Flora —"

"Hush — hush — hush! It speaks again."

"Perhaps I ought to account for my appearance in the garden at all," added the insinuating stranger. "The fact is, I came on a visit —"

Flora shuddered.

"To Mr. Henry Bannerworth," continued the stranger; "and finding the garden-gate open, I came in without troubling the servants, which I much regret, as I can perceive I have alarmed and annoyed the lady. Madam, pray accept of my apologies."

"In the name of God, who are you?" said Charles.

"My name is Varney."

"Oh, yes. You are the Sir Francis Varney, residing close by, who bears so fearful a resemblance to —"

"Pray go on, sir. I am all attention."

"To a portrait here."

"Indeed! Now I reflect a moment, Mr. Henry Bannerworth did incidentally mention something of the sort. It's a most singular coincidence."

The sound of approaching footsteps was now plainly heard, and in a few moments Henry and George, along with Mr. Marchdale, reached the spot. Their appearance showed that they had made haste, and Henry at once exclaimed, —

"We heard, or fancied we heard, a cry of alarm."

"You did hear it," said Charles Holland. "Do you know this gentleman?"

"It is Sir Francis Varney."

"Indeed!"

Varney bowed to the new comers, and was altogether as much at his ease as everybody else seemed quite the contrary. Even Charles Holland found the difficulty of going up to such a well-bred, gentlemanly man, and saying, "Sir, we believe you to be a vampyre" — to be almost, if not insurmountable.

"I cannot do it," he thought, "but I will watch him."

"Take me away," whispered Flora. "'Tis he — 'tis he. Oh, take me away, Charles."

"Hush, Flora, hush. You are in some error; the accidental resemblance should not make us be rude to this gentleman."

"The vampyre! — it is the vampyre!"

"Are you sure, Flora?"

"Do I know your features — my own — my brother's? Do not ask me to doubt — I cannot. I am quite sure. Take me from his hideous presence, Charles."

"The young lady, I fear, is very much indisposed," remarked Sir Francis Varney, in a sympathetic tone of voice. "If she will take my arm, I shall esteem it a great honor."

"No — no — no! — God! no," cried Flora.

"Madam, I will not press you."

He bowed, and Charles led Flora from the summerhouse towards the hall.

"Flora," he said, "I am bewildered — I know not what to think. That man most certainly has been fashioned after the portrait which is on the panel in the room you formerly occupied; or it has been painted from him."

"He is my midnight visitor!" exclaimed Flora. "He is the vampyre; — this Sir Francis Varney is the vampyre."

"Good God! What can be done?"

"I know not. I am nearly distracted."

"Be calm, Flora. If this man be really what you name him, we now know from what quarter the mischief comes, which is, at all events, a point gained. Be assured we shall place a watch upon him."

"Oh, it is terrible to meet him here."

"And he is so wonderfully anxious, too, to possess the Hall."

"He is — he is."

"It looks strange, the whole affair. But, Flora, be assured of one thing, and that is, for your own safety."

"Can I be assured of that?"

"Most certainly. Go to your mother now. Here we are, you see, fairly within doors. Go to your mother, dear Flora, and keep yourself quiet. I will return to this mysterious man now with a cooler judgment than I left him."

"You will watch him, Charles?"

"I will, indeed."

"And you will not let him approach the house here alone?"

"I will not."

"Oh, that the Almighty should allow such beings to haunt the earth!"

"Hush, Flora, hush! we cannot judge of his all wise purpose."

"'Tis hard that the innocent should be inflicted with its presence."

Charles bowed his head in mournful assent.

"Is it not very, very dreadful?"

"Hush — hush! Calm yourself, dearest, calm yourself. Recollect that all we have to go upon in this matter is a resemblance, which, after all, may be accidental. But leave it all to me, and be assured that now I have some clues to this affair, I will not lose sight of it, or of Sir Francis Varney."

So saying, Charles surrendered Flora to the care of their mother, and then was hastening back to the summer-house, when he met the whole party coming towards the Hall, for the rain was each moment increasing in intensity.

"We are returning," remarked Sir Francis Varney, with a half bow and a smile, to Charles.

"Allow me," said Henry, "to introduce you, Mr. Holland, to our neighbor, Sir Francis Varney."

Charles felt himself compelled to behave with courtesy, although his mind was so full of conflicting feelings as regarded Varney; but there was no avoiding, without such brutal rudeness as was inconsistent with all his pursuits and habits, replying in something like the same strain to the extreme courtly politeness of the supposed vampyre.

"I will watch him closely," thought Charles. "I can do no more than watch him closely."

Sir Francis Varney seemed to be a man of the most general and discursive information. He talked fluently and pleasantly upon all sorts of topics, and notwithstanding he could not but have heard what Flora had said of him, he asked no question whatever upon that subject.

This silence as regarded a matter which would at once have induced some sort of inquiry from any other man, Charles felt told much against him, and he trembled to believe for a moment that, after all, it really might be true.

"Is he a vampyre?" he asked himself. "Are there vampyres, and is this man of fashion — this courtly, talented, educated gentleman one?" It was a perfectly hideous question.

"You are charmingly situated here," remarked Varney, as, after ascending the few steps that led to the hall door, he turned and looked at the view from that slight altitude.

"The place has been much esteemed," said Henry, "for its picturesque beauties of scenery."

"And well it may be. I trust, Mr. Holland, the young lady is much better?"

"She is, sir," said Charles.

"I was not honored by an introduction."

"It was my fault," said Henry, who spoke to his extraordinary guest with an air of forced hilarity. "It was my fault for not introducing you to my sister."

"And that was your sister?"

"It was, sir."

"Report has not belied her — she is beautiful. But she looks rather pale, I thought. Has she bad health?"

"The best of health."

"Indeed! Perhaps the little disagreeable circumstance, which is made so much food for gossip in the neighborhood, has affected her spirits?"

"It has."

"You allude to the supposed visit here of a vampyre?" said Charles, as he fixed his eyes upon Varney's face.

"Yes, I allude to the supposed appearance of the supposed vampyre in this family," said Sir Francis Varney, as he returned the earnest gaze of Charles, with such unshrinking assurance, that the young man was compelled, after about a minute, nearly to withdraw his own eyes.

"He will not be cowed," thought Charles. "Use has made him familiar to such cross-questioning."

It appeared now suddenly to occur to Henry that he had said something at Varney's own house which should have prevented him from coming to the Hall, and he now remarked, —

"We scarcely expected the pleasure of your company here, Sir Francis Varney."

"Oh, my dear sir, I am aware of that; but you roused my curiosity. You mentioned to me that there was a portrait here amazingly like me."

"Did I?"

"Indeed you did, or how could I know it? I wanted to see if the resemblance was so perfect."

"Did you hear, sir," added Henry, "that my sister was alarmed at your likeness to the portrait?"

"No, really."

"I pray you walk in, and we will talk more at large upon that matter."

"With great pleasure. One leads a monotonous life in the country, when compared with the brilliancy of a court existence. Just now I have no particular engagement. As we are near neighbors I see no reason why we should not be good friends, and often interchange such civilities as make up the amenities of existence, and which, in the country, more particularly, are valuable."

Henry could not be hypocrite enough to assent to this; but still, under the present aspect of affairs, it was impossible to return any but a civil reply; so he said, —

"Oh, yes, of course — certainly. My time is very much occupied, and my sister and mother see no company."

"Oh, now, how wrong."

"Wrong, sir?"

"Yes, surely. If anything more than another tends to harmonize individuals, it is the society of that fairer half of the creation which we love for their very foibles. I am much attached to the softer sex — to young persons of health. I like to see the rosy cheeks, where the warm blood mantles in the superficial veins, and all is loveliness and life."

Charles shrank back, and the word "Demon" unconsciously escaped his lips.

Sir Francis took no manner of notice of the expression, but went on talking, as if he had been on the very happiest terms with every one present.

"Will you follow me, at once, to the chamber where the portrait hangs," said Henry, "or will you partake of some refreshment first?"

"No refreshment for me," said Varney. "My dear friend, if you will permit me to call you such, this is a time of the day at which I never do take any refreshment."

"Nor at any other," thought Henry.

They all went to the chamber where Charles had passed one very disagreeable night, and when they arrived, Henry pointed to the portrait on the panel, saying —

"There, Sir Francis Varney, is your likeness."

He looked, and, having walked up to it, in an under tone, rather as if he were conversing with himself than making a remark, for anyone else to hear, he said —

"It is wonderfully like."

"It is, indeed," said Charles.

"If I stand beside it, thus," said Varney, placing himself in a favorable attitude for comparing the two faces, "I dare say you will be more struck with the likeness than before."

So accurate was it now, that the same light fell upon his face as that under which the painter had executed the portrait, that all started back a step or two.

"Some artists," remarked Varney, "have the sense to ask where a portrait is to be hung before they paint it, and then they adapt their lights and shadows to those which would fall upon the original, were it similarly situated."

"I cannot stand this," said Charles to Henry; "I must question him farther."

"As you please, but do not insult him."

"I will not."

"He is beneath my roof now, and, after all, it is but a hideous suspicion we have of him."

"Rely upon me."

Charles stepped forward, and once again confronting Varney, with an earnest gaze, he said —

"Do you know, sir, that Miss Bannerworth declares the vampyre she fancies to have visited this chamber to be, in features, the exact counterpart of this portrait?"

"Does she indeed?"

"She does, indeed."

"And perhaps, then, that accounts for her thinking that I am the vampyre, because I bear a strong resemblance to the portrait."

"I should not be surprised," said Charles.

"How very odd."

"Very."

"And yet entertaining. I am rather amused than otherwise. The idea of being a vampyre. Ha! ha! If ever I go to a masquerade again, I shall certainly assume the character of a vampyre."

"You would do it well."

"I dare say, now, I should make quite a sensation."

"I am certain you would. Do you not think, gentlemen, that Sir Francis Varney would enact the character to the very life? By Heavens, he would do it so well that one might, without much difficulty, really imagine him a vampyre."

"Bravo — bravo," said Varney, as he gently folded his hands together, with that genteel applause that may even be indulged in in a box at the opera itself. "Bravo. I like to see young persons enthusiastic; it looks as if they had some of the real fire of genius in their composition. Bravo — bravo."

This was, Charles thought, the very height and acme of impudence, and yet what could he do? What could he say? He was foiled by the downright coolness of Varney.

As for Henry, George, and Mr. Marchdale, they had listened to what was passing between Sir Francis and Charles in silence. They feared to diminish the effect of anything Charles might say, by adding a word of their own; and, likewise, they did not wish to lose one observation that might come from the lips of Varney.

But now Charles appeared to have said all he had to say, be turned to the window and looked out. He seemed like a man who had made up his mind, for a time, to give up some contest in which he had been engaged.

And, perhaps, not so much did he give it up from any feeling or consciousness of being beaten, as from a conviction that it could be the more effectually, at some other and far more eligible opportunity, renewed.

Varney now addressed Henry, saying, — "I presume the subject of our conference, when you did me the honor of a call, is no secret to any one here?"

"None whatever," said Henry.

"Then, perhaps, I am too early in asking you if you have made up your mind?"

"I have scarcely, certainly, had time to think."

"My dear sir, do not let me hurry you; I much regret, indeed, the intrusion."

"You seem anxious to possess the Hall," remarked Mr. Marchdale, to Varney.

"I am."

"Is it new to you?"

"Not quite. I have some boyish recollections connected with this neighborhood, among which Bannerworth Hall stands sufficiently prominent."

"May I ask how long ago that was?" said Charles Holland, rather abruptly.

"I do not recollect, my enthusiastic young friend," said Varney. "How old are you?"

"Just about twenty-one."

"You are, then, for your age, quite a model of discretion."

It would have been difficult for the most accurate observer of human nature to have decided whether this was said truthfully or ironically, so Charles made no reply to it whatever.

"I trust," said Henry, "we shall induce you, as this is your first visit, Sir Francis Varney, to the Hall, to partake of something."

"Well, well, a cup of wine —"

"Is at your service."

Henry now led the way to a small parlor, which, although by no means one of the showiest rooms of the house, was, from the care and exquisite carving with which it abounded, much more to the taste of any who possessed an accurate judgment in such works of art.

Then wine was ordered, and Charles took an opportunity of whispering to Henry, —

"Notice well if he drinks."

"I will."

"Do you see that beneath his coat there is a raised place, as if his arm was bound up?"

"I do."

"There, then, was where the bullet from the pistol fired by Flora, when we were at the church, hit him."

"Hush! for God's sake, hush! you are getting into a dreadful state of excitement, Charles; hush! hush!"

"And can you blame —"

"No, no; but what can we do?"

"You are right. Nothing we can do at present. We have a clue now, and be it our mutual inclination, as well as a duty, to follow it. Oh, you shall see how calm I will be!

"For heaven's sake, be so. I have noted that his eyes flash upon yours with no friendly feeling."

"His friendship were a curse."

"Hush! he drinks!"

"Watch him."

"I will."

"Gentlemen all," said Sir Francis Varney, in such soft, dulcet tones, that it was quite a fascination to hear him speak; "gentlemen all, being as I am, much delighted with your company, do not accuse me of presumption, if I drink now, poor drinker that I am, to our future merry meetings."

He raised the wine to his lips, and seemed to drink, after which he replaced the glass upon the table.

Charles glanced at it, it was still full.

"You have not drank, Sir Francis Varney," he said.

"Pardon me, enthusiastic young sir," said Varney, "perhaps you will have the liberality to allow me to take my wine how I please and when I please."

"Your glass is full."

"Well, sir?"

"Will you drink it?"

"Not at any man's bidding, most certainly. If the fair Flora Bannerworth would grace the board with her sweet presence, methinks I could then drink on, on, on."

"Hark you, sir," cried Charles, "I can bear no more of this. We have had in this house most horrible and damning evidence that there are such things as vampyres."

"Have you really? I suppose you eat raw pork at supper, and so had the nightmare?"

"A jest is welcome in its place, but pray hear me out, sir, if it suit your lofty courtesy to do so."

"Oh, certainly."

"Then I say we believe, as far as human judgment has a right to go, that a vampyre has been here."

"Go on, it's interesting. I always was a lover of the wild and the wonderful."

"We have, too," continued Charles, "some reason to believe that you are the man."

Varney tapped his forehead as he glanced at Henry, and said, —

"Oh, dear, I did not know. You should have told me he was a little wrong about the brain; I might have quarreled with the lad. Dear me, how lamentable for his poor mother."

"This will not do, Sir Francis Varney *alias* Bannerworth."

"Oh — oh! Be calm — be calm."

"I defy you to your teeth, sir! No, God, no! Your teeth!"

"Poor lad! Poor lad!"

"You are a cowardly demon, and here I swear to devote myself to your destruction."

Sir Francis Varney drew himself up to his full height, and that was immense, as he said to Henry, —

"I pray you, Mr. Bannerworth, since I am thus grievously insulted beneath your roof, to tell me if your friend here be mad or sane?"

"He's not mad."

"Then —"

"Hold, sir! The quarrel shall be mine. In the name of my persecuted sister — in the name of Heaven, Sir Francis Varney, I defy you."

Sir Francis, in spite of his impenetrable calmness, appeared somewhat moved, as he said, —

"I have endured insult sufficient — I will endure no more. If there are weapons at hand —"

"My young friend," interrupted Mr. Marchdale, stepping between the excited men, "is carried away by his feelings, and knows not what he says. You will look upon it in that light, Sir Francis."

"We need no interference," exclaimed Varney, his hitherto bland voice changing to one of fury. "The hot blooded fool wishes to fight, and he shall — to the death — to the death."

"And I say he shall not," exclaimed Mr. Marchdale, taking Henry by the arm. "George," he added, turning to the young man, "assist me in persuading your brother to leave the room. Conceive the agony of your sister and mother if anything should happen to him."

Varney smiled with a devilish sneer, as he listened to these words, and then he said, —

"As you will — as you will. There will be plenty of time, and perhaps better opportunity, gentlemen. I bid you good day."

And with provoking coolness, he then moved towards the door, and quitted the room.

"Remain here," said Mr. Marchdale; "I will follow him, and see that he quits the premises."

He did so, and the young men, from the window, beheld Sir Francis walking slowly across the garden, and then saw Mr. Marchdale follow on his track.

While they were thus occupied, a tremendous ringing came at the gate, but their attention was so riveted to what was passing in the garden, that they paid not the least attention to it.

Chapter *XVIII*.

THE ADMIRAL'S ADVICE. — THE CHALLENGE TO THE
VAMPYRE. — THE NEW SERVANT AT THE HALL.

*T*he violent ringing of the bell continued uninterruptedly until at
length George volunteered to answer it. The fact was, that now there was
no servant at all in the place for, after the one who had recently
demanded of Henry her dismissal had left, the other was terrified to
remain alone, and had precipitately gone from the house, without even
going through the ceremony of announcing her intention to do so. To
be sure she sent a boy for her money afterwards, which may be considered as a great act of condescension.

Suspecting, then, this state of things, George himself hastened to the
gate, and, being not over well pleased at the continuous and unnecessary
ringing which was kept up at it, he opened it quickly, and cried, with
more impatience, by a vast amount, than was usual with him.

"Who is so impatient that he cannot wait a seasonable time for the
door to be opened?"

"And who the d — l are you?" cried one who was immediately outside.

"Who do you want?" cried George.

"Shiver my timbers!" cried Admiral Bell, for it was no other than
that personage. "What's it to you?"

"Ay, ay," added Jack, "answer that if you can, you shore-going-looking
swab."

"Two madmen, I suppose," ejaculated George, and he would have
closed the gate upon them; but Jack introduced between it and the post
the end of a thick stick, saying, —

"Avast there! None of that; we have had trouble enough to get in. If
you are the family lawyer, or the chaplain, perhaps you'll tell us where
Mister Charley is."

"Once more I demand of you who you want?" said George, who was now perhaps a little amused at the conduct of the impatient visitors.

"We want the admiral's *nevey*," said Jack.

"But how do I know who is the admiral's *nevey*, as you call him."

"Why, Charles Holland, to be sure. Have you got him aboard or not?"

"Mr. Charles Holland is certainly here; and, if you had said at once, and explicitly, that you wished to see him, I could have given you a direct answer."

"He is here?" cried the admiral.

"Most certainly."

"Come along, then; yet, stop a bit. I say, young fellow, just before we go any further, tell us if he has maimed the vampyre?"

"The what?"

"The *wamphigher*," said Jack, by way of being, as he considered, a little more explanatory than the admiral.

"I do not know what you mean," said George; "if you wish to see Mr. Charles Holland walk in and see him. He is in this house; but, for myself, as you are strangers to me, I decline answering any questions, let their import be what they may."

"Hilloa! who are they?" suddenly cried Jack, as he pointed to two figures some distance off in the meadows, who appeared to be angrily conversing.

George glanced in the direction towards which Jack pointed, and there he saw Sir Francis Varney and Mr. Marchdale standing within a few paces of each other, and apparently engaged in some angry discussion.

His first impulse was to go immediately towards them; but before he could execute even that suggestion of his mind, he saw Varney strike Marchdale, and the latter fell to the ground.

"Allow me to pass," cried George, as he endeavored to get by the rather unwieldy form of the admiral. But, before he could accomplish this, for the gate was narrow, he saw Varney, with great swiftness, make off, and Marchdale, rising to his feet, came towards the Hall.

When Marchdale got near enough to the garden-gate to see George, he motioned to him to remain where he was, and then, by quickening his pace, he soon came up to the spot.

"Marchdale," cried George, "you have had an encounter with Sir Francis Varney."

"I have," said Marchdale, in an excited manner. "I threatened to follow him, but he struck me to the earth as easily as I could a child. His strength is superhuman."

"I saw you fall."

"I believe, but that he was observed, he would have murdered me."

"Indeed!"

"What, do you mean to say that lanky, horse-marine looking fellow is as bad as that?" said the admiral.

Marchdale now turned his attention to the two new comers, upon whom he looked with some surprise, and then, turning to George, he said, —

"Is this gentleman a visitor?"

"To Mr. Holland, I believe he is," said George; "but I have not the pleasure of knowing his name."

"Oh, you may know my name as soon as you like," cried the admiral. "The enemies of old England know it, and I don't care if all the world knows it. I'm old Admiral Bell, something of a hulk now, but still able to head a quarter-deck if there was any need to do so."

"Ay, ay," cried Jack, and taking from his pocket a boatswain's whistle, he blew a blast, so long, and loud, and shrill, that George was fain to cover his ears with his hands to shut out the brain-piercing, and, to him, unusual sound.

"And are you, then, a relative," said Marchdale, "of Mr. Holland's, sir, may I ask?"

"I'm his uncle, and be d——d to him, if you must know, and some one has told me that the young scamp thinks of marrying a mermaid, or a ghost or a vampyre, or some such thing, so, for the sake of the memory of his poor mother, I've come to say no to the bargain, and d — n me, who cares."

"Come in, sir," said George, "I will conduct you to Mr. Holland. I presume this is your servant?"

"Why, not exactly. That's Jack Pringle, he was my boatswain, you see, and now he's a kind o' something betwixt and between. Not exactly a servant."

"Ay, ay, sir," said Jack. "Have it all your own way, though we is paid off."

"Hold your tongue, you audacious scoundrel, will you."

"Oh, I forgot, you don't like anything said about paying off, cos it puts you in mind of —"

"Now, d — n you, I'll have you strung up to the yard-arm, you dog, if you don't belay there."

"I'm done. All's right."

By this time the party, including the admiral, Jack, George Bannerworth, and Marchdale, had got more than halfway across the garden, and were observed by Charles Holland and Henry, who had come to the steps of the hall to see what was going on. The moment Charles saw the admiral a change of color came over his face, as he exclaimed, —

"By all that's surprising, there is my uncle!"

"Your uncle!" said Henry.

"Yes, as good a hearted man as ever drew breath, and yet, withal, as full of prejudices, and as ignorant of life, as a child."

Without waiting for any reply from Henry, Charles Holland rushed forward, and seizing his uncle by the hand, he cried, in tones of genuine affection, —

"Uncle, dear uncle, how came you to find me out?"

"Charley, my boy," cried the old man, "bless you; I mean, confound your d——d impudence; you rascal, I'm glad to see you; no, I ain't, you young mutineer. What do you mean by it, you ugly, ill looking, d——d fine fellow — my dear boy. Oh, you infernal scoundrel."

All this accompanied by a shaking of the hand, which was enough to dislocate anybody's shoulder, and which Charles was compelled to bear as well as he could.

It quite prevented him from speaking, however, for a few moments, for it nearly shook the breath out of him. When, then, he could get in a word, he said, —

"Uncle, I dare say you are surprised."

"Surprised! D — n me, I am surprised."

"Well, I shall be able to explain all to your satisfaction, I am sure. Allow me now to introduce you to my friends."

Turning then to Henry, Charles said, —

"This is Mr. Henry Bannerworth, uncle; and this is Mr. George Bannerworth, both good friends of mine; and this is Mr. Marchdale, a friend of theirs, uncle."

"Oh, indeed!"

"And here you see Admiral Bell, my most worthy, but rather eccentric uncle."

"Confound your impudence."

"What brought him here I cannot tell; but he is a brave officer, and a gentleman."

"None of your nonsense," said the admiral.

"And here you see Jack Pringle," said that individual, introducing himself, since no one appeared inclined to do that office for him, "a tar for all weathers. One who hates the French, and is never so happy as when he's alongside o' some o' those lubberly craft blazing away."

"That's uncommonly true," remarked the admiral.

"Will you walk in, sir?" said Henry, courteously. "Any friend of Charles Holland is most welcome here. You will have much to excuse us for, because we are deficient in servants at present, in consequence of some occurrences in our family, which your nephew has our full permission to explain to you in full."

"Oh, very good, I tell you what it is, all of you, what I've seen of you, d — e, I like, so here goes. Come along, Jack."

The admiral walked into the house, and as he went, Charles Holland said to him, —

"How came you to know I was here, uncle?"

"Some fellow wrote me a dispatch."

"Indeed!"

"Yes, saying as you was a going to marry some odd sort of fish as it wasn't at all the thing to introduce into the family."

"Was — was a vampyre mentioned?"

"That's the very thing."

"Hush, uncle — hush."

"What for?"

"Do not, I implore, hint at such at thing before these kind friends of mine. I will take an opportunity within the next hour of explaining all to you, and you shall form your own kind and generous judgment upon circumstances in which my honor and my happiness are so nearly concerned."

"Gammon," said the admiral.

"What, uncle?"

"Oh, I know you want to palaver me into saying it's all right. I suppose if my judgment and generosity don't like it, I shall be an old fool, and a cursed goose?"

"Now, uncle."

"Now, *nevey.*"

"Well, well — no more at present. We will talk over this at leisure. You promise me to say nothing about it until you have heard my explanation, uncle?"

"Very good. Make it as soon as you can, and as short as you can, that's all I ask of you."

"I will, I will."

Charles was to the full as anxious as his uncle could be to enter upon the subject, some remote information of which, he felt convinced, had brought the old man down to the Hall. Who it could have been that so far intermeddled with his affairs as to write to him, he could not possibly conceive.

A very few words will suffice to explain the precise position in which Charles Holland was. A considerable sum of money had been left to him, but it was saddled with the condition that he should not come into possession of it until he was one year beyond the age which is usually denominated that of discretion, namely, twenty-one. His uncle, the admiral, was the trustee of his fortune, and he, with rare discretion, had got the active and zealous assistance of a professional gentleman of great honor and eminence to conduct the business for him.

This gentleman had advised that for the two years between the ages of twenty and twenty-two, Charles Holland should travel, inasmuch as in English society he would find himself in an awkward position, being for one whole year of age, and yet waiting for his property.

Under such circumstances, reasoned the lawyer, a young man, unless he is possessed of a very rare discretion indeed, is almost sure to get fearfully involved with moneylenders. Being of age, his notes, and bills, and bonds would all be good, and he would be in a ten times worse situation than a wealthy minor.

All this was duly explained to Charles, who, rather eagerly than otherwise, caught at the idea of a two years wander on the continent, where he could visit so many places, which to a well read young man like himself, and one of a lively imagination, were full of the most delightful associations.

But the acquaintance with Flora Bannerworth effected a great revolution in his feelings. The dearest, sweetest spot on earth became that which she inhabited. When the Bannerworths left him abroad, he knew not what to do with himself. Everything, and every pursuit in which he had before taken a delight, became most distasteful to him. He was, in fact, in a short time, completely "used up," and then he determined upon returning to England, and finding out the dear object of his attachment at once. This resolution was no sooner taken, than his health and spirits returned to him, and with what rapidity he could, he now made his way to his native shores.

The two years were so nearly expired, that he made up his mind he would not communicate either with his uncle, the admiral, or the professional gentleman upon whose judgment he set so high and so just a value. And at the Hall he considered he was in perfect security from any interruption, and so he would have been, but for that letter which was written to Admiral Bell, and signed Josiah Crinkles, but which Josiah Crinkles so emphatically denied all knowledge of. Who wrote it, remains at present one of those mysteries which time, in the progress of our narrative, will clear up.

The opportune, or rather the painful juncture at which Charles Holland had arrived at Bannerworth Hall, we are well cognizant of. Where he expected to find smiles he found tears, and the family with whom he had fondly hoped he should pass a time of uninterrupted happiness, he found plunged in the gloom incidental to an occurrence of the most painful character.

Our readers will perceive, too, that coming as he did with an utter disbelief in the vampyre, Charles had been compelled, in some measure, to yield to the overwhelming weight of evidence which had been brought to bear upon the subject, and although he could not exactly be said to believe in the existence and the appearance of the vampyre at Bannerworth Hall, he was upon the subject in a most painful state of doubt and indecision.

Charles now took an opportunity to speak to Henry privately, and inform him exactly how he stood with his uncle, adding —

"Now, my dear friend, if you forbid me, I will not tell my uncle of this sad affair, but I must own I would rather do so fully and freely, and trust to his own judgment upon it."

"I implore you to do so," said Henry. "Conceal nothing. Let him know the precise situation and circumstances of the family by all means. There is nothing so mischievous as secrecy: I have the greatest dislike of it. I beg you tell him all."

"I will; and with it, Henry, I will tell him that my heart is irrevocably Flora's."

"Your generous clinging to one whom your heart saw and loved, under very different auspices," said Henry, "believe me, Charles, sinks deep into my heart. She has related to me something of a meeting she had with you."

"Oh, Henry, she may tell you what I said; but there are no words which can express the depth of my tenderness. 'Tis only time which can prove how much I love her."

"Go to your uncle," said Henry, in a voice of emotion. "God bless you, Charles. It is true you would have been fully justified in leaving my sister; but the nobler and the more generous path you have chosen has endeared you to us all."

"Where is Flora now?" said Charles.

"She is in her own room. I have persuaded her, by some occupation, to withdraw her mind from a too close and consequently painful contemplation of the distressing circumstances in which she feels herself placed."

"You are right. What occupation best pleases her?"

"The pages of a romance once had charms for her gentle spirit."

"Then come with me, and, from among the few articles I brought with me here, I can find some papers which may help her to pass some merry hours."

Charles took Henry to his room, and, unstrapping a small valise, he took from it some manuscript paper, one of which he handed to Henry, saying, —

"Give that to her: it contains an account of a wild adventure, and shows that human nature may suffer much more — and that wrongfully too — than came ever under our present mysterious affliction."

"I will," said Henry; "and, coming from you, I am sure it will have a more than ordinary value in her eyes."

"I will now," said Charles, "seek my uncle. I will tell him how I love her; and at the end of my narration, if he should not object, I would fain introduce her to him, that he might himself see that, let what beauty may have met his gaze, her peer he never yet met with, and may in vain hope to do so."

"You are partial, Charles."

"Not so. 'Tis true I look upon her with a lover's eyes, but I look still with those of truthful observation."

"Well, I will speak to her about seeing your uncle, and let you know. No doubt, he will not be at all averse to an interview with any one who stands high in your esteem."

The young men now separated — Henry, to seek his beautiful sister; and Charles, to communicate to his uncle the strange particulars connected with Varney, the Vampyre.

Chapter XIX.

FLORA IN HER CHAMBER. — HER FEARS. — THE MANUSCRIPT. — AN ADVENTURE.

*H*enry found Flora in her chamber. She was in deep thought when he tapped at the door of the room, and such was the state of nervous excitement in which she was that even the demand for admission made by him to the room was sufficient to produce from her a sudden cry of alarm.

"Who — who is there?" she then said, in accents full of terror.

"'Tis I, dear Flora," said Henry.

She opened the door in an instant, and, with a feeling of grateful relief, exclaimed, —

"Oh, Henry, is it only you?"

"Who did you suppose it was, Flora?"

She shuddered.

"I — I — do not know; but I am so foolish now, and so weak-spirited, that the slightest noise is enough to alarm me."

"You must, dear Flora, fight up, as I had hoped you were doing, against this nervousness."

"I will endeavor. Did not some strangers come a short time since, brother?"

"Strangers to us, Flora, but not to Charles Holland. A relative of his

— an uncle whom he much respects, has found him out here, and has now come to see him."

"And to advise him," said Flora as she sunk into a chair, and wept bitterly; "to advise him, of course, to desert, as he would a pestilence, a vampyre bride."

"Hush, hush! for the sake of Heaven, never make use of such a phrase, Flora. You know not what a pang it brings to my heart to hear you."

"Oh, forgive me, brother."

"Say no more of it, Flora. Heed it not. It may be possible — in fact, it may well be supposed as more than probable — that the relative of Charles Holland may shrink from sanctioning the alliance, but do you rest securely in the possession of the heart which I feel convinced is wholly yours, and which, I am sure, would break ere it surrendered you."

A smile of joy came across Flora's pale but beautiful face, as she cried, —

"And you, dear brother — you think so much of Charles's faith?"

"As heaven is my judge, I do."

"Then I will bear up with what strength God may give me against all things that seek to depress me; I will not be conquered."

"You are right, Flora; I rejoice to find in you such a disposition. Here is some manuscript which Charles thinks will amuse you, and he bade me ask you if you would be introduced to his uncle."

"Yes, yes — willingly."

"I will tell him so; I know he wishes it, and I will tell him so. Be patient, dear Flora, and all may yet be well."

"But, brother, on your sacred word, tell me do you not think this Sir Francis Varney is the vampyre?"

"I know not what to think, and do not press me for a judgment now. He shall be watched."

Henry left his sister, and she sat for some moments in silence with the papers before her that Charles had sent her.

"Yes," she then said, gently, "he loves me — Charles loves me; I ought to be very, very happy. He loves me. In those words are concentrated a whole world of joy — Charles loves me — he will not forsake me. Oh, was there ever such dear love — such fond devotion? — never, never. Dear Charles. He loves me — he loves me!"

The very repetition of these words had a charm for Flora — a charm which was sufficient to banish much sorrow; even the much-dreaded vampyre was forgotten while the light of love was beaming up on her, and she told herself, —

"He is mine! — he is mine! He loves me truly."

After a time, she turned to the manuscript which her brother had brought her, and, with a far greater concentration of mind than she had thought it possible she could bring to it, considering the many painful subjects of contemplation that she might have occupied herself with, she read the pages with very great pleasure and interest.

The tale was one which chained her attention both by its incidents and the manner of its recital. It commenced as follows, and was titled, "Hugo de Verole; or, the Double Plot."

In a very mountainous part of Hungary lived a nobleman whose paternal estates covered many a mile of rock and mountain land, as well as some fertile valleys, in which reposed a hardy and contented peasantry.

The old Count Hugo de Verole had quitted life early, and had left his only son, the then Count Hugo de Verole, a boy of scarcely ten years, under the guardianship of his mother, an arbitrary and unscrupulous woman.

The count, her husband, had been one of those quiet, even-tempered men, who have no desire to step beyond the sphere in which they are placed; he had no cares, save those included in the management of his estate, the prosperity of his serfs, and the happiness of those around him.

His death caused much lamentation throughout his domains, it was so sudden and unexpected, being in the enjoyment of his health and strength until a few hours previous, and then his energies became prostrated by pain and disease. There was a splendid funeral ceremony, which, according the usages of his house, took place by torchlight.

So great and rapid were the ravages of disease, that the count's body quickly became a mass of corruption. All were amazed at the phenomena, and were heartily glad when the body was disposed of in the place prepared for its reception in the vaults of his own castle. The guests who came to witness the funeral, and attend the count's obsequies, and to condole with the widow on the loss she had sustained, were entertained sumptuously for many days.

The widow sustained her part well. She was inconsolable for the loss of her husband, and mourned his death bitterly. Her grief appeared profound, but she, with difficulty, subdued it to within decent bounds, that she might not offend any of her numerous guests.

However, they left her with the assurances of their profound regard, and then when they were gone, when the last guest had departed, and were no longer visible to the eye of the countess, as she gazed from the battlements, then her behavior changed totally.

She descended from the battlements, and then with an imperious gesture she gave her orders that all the gates of the castle should be closed, and a watch set.

All signs of mourning she ordered to be laid on one side save her own, which she wore, and then she retired to her own apartment, where she remained unseen.

Here the countess remained in profound meditation for nearly two days, during which time the attendants believed she was praying for the welfare of the soul of their deceased master, and they feared she would starve herself to death if she remained any longer.

Just as they had assembled together for the purpose of either recalling her from her vigils or breaking open the door, they were amazed to see the countess open the room-door, and stand in the midst of them.

"What do you here?" she demanded, in a stern voice.

"We came, my lady, to see — see — if — if you are well."

"And why?"

"Because we hadn't seen your ladyship these two days, and we thought that your grief was so excessive that we feared some harm might befall you."

The countess's brows contracted for a few seconds, and she was about to make a hasty reply, but she conquered the desire to do so, and merely said, —

"I am not well, I am faint; but, had I been dying, I should not have thanked you for interfering to prevent me; however, you acted for the best, but do so no more. Now prepare me some food."

The servants, thus dismissed, repaired to their stations, but with such degree of alacrity, that they sufficiently showed how much they feared their mistress.

The young count, who was only in his sixth year, knew little about the loss he had sustained; but after a day or two's grief, there was an end of his sorrow for the time.

That night there came to the castle-gate a man dressed in a black cloak, attended by a servant. They were both mounted on good horses, and they demanded to be admitted to the presence of the Countess de Hugo de Verole.

The message was carried to the countess, who started, but said, —

"Admit the stranger."

Accordingly the stranger was admitted, and shown into the apartment where the countess was sitting.

At a signal the servants retired, leaving the countess and the stranger alone. It was some moments ere they spoke, and then the countess said in a low tone, —

"You are come?"

"I am come."

"You cannot now, you see, perform your threat. My husband, the count, caught a putrid disease, and he is no more."

"I cannot indeed do what I intended, inform your husband of your amours; but I can do something as good, and which will give you as much annoyance."

"Indeed."

"Aye, more, if will cause you to be hated. I can spread reports."

"You can."

"And these may ruin you."

"They may."

"What do you intend to do? Do you intend that I shall be an enemy or a friend? I can be either, according to my will."

"What, do you desire to be either?" inquired the countess, with a careless tone.

"If you refuse my terms, you can make me an implacable enemy, and if you grant them, you can make me a useful friend and auxiliary," said the stranger.

"What would you do if you were my enemy?" inquired the countess.

"It is hardly my place," said the stranger, "to furnish you with a knowledge of my intentions, but I will say this much, that the bankrupt Count of Morven is your lover."

"Well?"

"And in the second place, that you were the cause of the death of your husband."

"How dare you, sir —"

"I dare say so much, and I dare say, also, that the Count of Morven bought you the drug of me, and that he gave it to you, and that you gave it to the count your husband."

"And what could you do if you were my friend?" inquired the countess, in the same tone, and without emotion.

"I should abstain from doing all this; I should be able to put any one else out of your way for you, when you get rid of this Count of Morven, as you assuredly will; for I know him too well not to be sure of that."

"Get rid of him!"

"Exactly, in the same manner you got rid of the old count."

"Then I accept your terms."

"It is agreed, then?"

"Yes, quite."

"Well, then, you must order me some rooms in a tower, where I can pursue my studies in quiet."

"You will be seen and noticed — all will be discovered."

"No, indeed, I will take care of that. I can so far disguise myself that he will not recognize me, and you can give out I am a philosopher or necromancer, or what you will; no one will come to me — they will be terrified."

"Very well."

"And the gold?"

"Shall be forthcoming as soon as I can get it. The count has placed all his gold in safe keeping, and all I can seize are the rents as they become due."

"Very well; but let me have them. In the meantime you must provide for me, as I have come here with the full intention of staying here, or in some neighboring town."

"Indeed!"

"Yes; and my servant must be discharged, as I want none here."

The countess called to an attendant and gave the necessary orders, and afterwards remained some time with the stranger, who had thus so unceremoniously thrust himself upon her, and insisted upon staying under such strange and awful circumstances.

*T*he Count of Morven came a few weeks after, and remained some days with the countess. They were ceremonious and polite until they had a moment to retire from before people, when the countess changed her cold disdain to a cordial and familiar address.

"And now, my dear Morven," she exclaimed, as soon as they were unobserved — "and now, my dear Morven, that we are not seen, tell me, what have you been doing with yourself?"

"Why, I have been in some trouble. I never had gold that would stay by me. You know my hand was always open."

"The old complaint again."

"No; but having come to the end of my store, I began to grow serious."

"Ah, Morven!" said the countess, reproachfully.

"Well, never mind; when my purse is low my spirits sink, as the mercury does with the cold. You used to say my spirits were mercurial — I think they were."

"Well, what did you do?"

"Oh, nothing."

"Was that what you were about to tell me?" inquired the countess.

"Oh, dear, no. You recollect the Italian quack of whom I bought the drug you gave to the count, and which put an end to his days — he wanted more money. Well, as I had no more to spare, I could spare no more to him, and he turned vicious, and threatened. I threatened, too, and he knew I was fully able and willing to perform any promise I might make to him on that score. I endeavored to catch him, as he had already began to set people off on the suspicious and marvelous concerning me, and if I could have come across him, I would have laid him very low indeed."

"And you could not find him?"

"No, I could not."

"Well, then, I will tell you where he is at this present moment."

"You?"

"Yes, I."

"I can scarcely credit my senses at what you say," said Count Morven. "My worthy doctor, you are little better than a candidate for divine honors. But where is he?"

"Will you promise to be guided by me?" said the countess.

"If you make it a condition upon which you grant the information, I must."

"Well, then, I take that as a promise."

"You may. Where — oh, where is he?"

"Remember your promise. Your doctor is at this moment in this castle."

"This castle?"

"Yes, this castle."

"Surely there must be some mistake; it is too much fortune at once."

"He came here for the same purpose he went to you."

"Indeed!"

"Yes, to get more money by extortion and a promise to poison anybody I liked."

"D — n! it is the offer he made to me, and he named you."

"He named you to me, and said I should be soon tired of you."

"You have caged him?"

"Oh, dear, no; he has a suite of apartments in the eastern tower, where he passes for a philosopher, or a wizard, as people like best."

"How?"

"I have given him leave there."

"Indeed!"

"Yes; and what is more amazing is, that he is to aid me in poisoning you when I have become tired of you."

"This is a riddle I cannot unravel; tell me the solution."

"Well, dear, listen, — he came to me and told me of something I already knew, and demanded money and a residence for his convenience, and I have granted him the asylum."

"You have?"

"I have."

"I see; I will give him an inch or two of my Andrea Ferrara."

"No — no."

"Do you countenance him?"

"For a time. Listen — we want men in the mines; my late husband sent very few men to them in late years, and therefore they are getting short of men there."

"Aye, aye."

"The thing will be for you to feign ignorance of the man, and then you will be able to get him seized, and placed in the mines, for such men as he are dangerous, and carry poisoned weapons."

"Would he not be better out of the world at once; there would be no escape, and no future contingencies?"

"No — no. I will have no more lives taken; and he will be made useful; and, moreover, he will have time to reflect upon the mistake he had made in threatening me."

"He was paid for the job, and he had no future claim. But what about the child?"

"Oh, he may remain for some time longer here with us."

"It will be dangerous to do so," said the count; "he is now ten years old, and there is no knowing what may be done for him by his relatives."

"They dare not enter the gates of this castle Morven."

"Well, well; but you know he might have traveled the same road as his father, and all would be settled."

"No more lives, as I told you; but we can easily secure him in some other way, and we shall be equally as free from him and them."

"That is enough — there are dungeons, I know, in this castle, and he can be kept there safe enough."

"He can; but that is not what I propose. We can put him in the mines and confine him as a lunatic."

"Excellent!"

"You see, we must make those mines more productive somehow or other; they would be so, but the count would not hear of it; he said it was so inhuman, they were so destructive of life."

"Psha! what were the mines intended for if not for use?"

"Exactly — I often said so, but he always put a negative to it."

"We'll make use of an affirmative, my dear countess, and see what will be the result in a change of policy. By the way, when will our marriage be celebrated?"

"Not for some months."

"How, so long? I am impatient."

"You must restrain your impatience — but we must have the boy settled first, and the count will have been dead a longer time then, and we shall not give so much scandal to the weak-minded fools that were his friends, for it will be dangerous to have so many events happen about the same period."

"You shall act as you think proper — but the first thing to be done will be, to get this cunning doctor quietly out of the way."

"Yes."

"I must contrive to have him seized, and carried to the mines."

"Beneath the tower in which he lives is a trap-door and a vault, from which, by means of another trap and vault, is a long subterranean passage that leads to a door that opens into one end of the mines; near this end live several men whom you must give some reward to, and they will, by concert, seize him, and set him to work."

"And if he will not work?"

"Why, they will scourge him in such a manner, that he would be afraid even of a threat of repetition of the same treatment."

"That will do. But I think the worthy doctor will split himself with rage and malice, he will be like a caged tiger."

"But he will be denuded of his teeth and claws," replied the countess, smiling; "therefore he will have leisure to repent of having threatened his employers."

Some weeks passed over, and the Count of Morven contrived to become acquainted with the doctor. They appeared to be utter strangers to each other, though each knew the other; the doctor having disguised himself, he believed the disguise impenetrable, and therefore sat at ease.

"Worthy doctor," said the count to him, one day; "you have, no doubt, in your studies, become acquainted with many of the secrets of science."

"I have, my lord count; I may say there are few that are not known to Father Aldrovani. I have spent many years in research."

"Indeed!"

"Yes; the midnight lamp has burned till the glorious sun has reached the horizon, and brings back the day, and yet have I been found beside my books."

"'Tis well; men like you should well know the value of the purest and most valuable metals the earth produces?"

"I know of but one — that is gold!"

"'Tis what I mean."

"But 'tis hard to procure from the bowels of the earth — from the heart of these mountains by which we are surrounded."

"Yes, that is true. But know you not the owners of this castle and territory possess these mines and work them?"

"I believe they do; but I thought they had discontinued working them some years."

"Oh, no! that was given out to deceive the government, who claimed so much out of its products."

"Oh! ah! aye, I see now."

"And ever since they have been working it privately, and storing bars of gold up in the vaults of this —"

"Here, in this castle?"

"Yes, beneath this very tower — it being the least frequented — the strongest, and perfectly inaccessible from all sides, save the castle — it was placed there for the safest deposit."

"I see; and there is much gold deposited in the vaults?"

"I believe there is an immense quantity in the vaults."

"And what is your motive for telling me of this hoard of the precious metal?"

"Why, doctor, I thought that you or I could use a few bars; and that, if we acted in concert, we might be able to take away, at various times, and secrete, in some place or other, enough to make us rich men for all our lives."

"I should like to see this gold before I said anything about it," replied the doctor, thoughtfully.

"As you please; do you find a lamp that will not go out by the sudden draughts of air, or have the means of relighting it, and I will accompany you."

"When?"

"This very night, good doctor, when you shall see such a golden harvest you never yet hoped for, or even believed in."

"Tonight be it, then," replied the doctor. "I will have a lamp that will answer our purpose, and some other matters."

"Do, good doctor," and the count left the philosopher's cell.

*T*he plan takes," said the count to the countess, "give me the keys, and the worthy man will be in safety before daylight."

"Is he not suspicious?"

"Not at all."

*T*hat night, about an hour before midnight, the Count Morven stole towards the philosopher's room. He tapped at the door.

"Enter," said the philosopher.

The count entered, and saw the philosopher seated, and by him a lamp of peculiar construction, and incased in gauze wire, and a cloak.

"Are you ready?" inquired the count.

"Quite," he replied.

"Is that your lamp?"

"It is."

"Follow me, then, and hold the lamp tolerably high, as the way is strange, and the steps steep."

"Lead on."

"You have made up your mind, I dare say, as to what share of the undertaking you will accept of with me."

"And what if I will not?" said the philosopher, coolly.

"It falls to the ground, and I return the keys to their place."

"I dare say I shall not refuse, if you have not deceived me as to the quantity and purity of the metal they have stored up."

"I am no judge of these metals, doctor. I am no assayest; but I believe you will find what I have to show you will far exceed your expectations on that head."

"'Tis well; proceed."

They had now got to the first vault, in which stood the first door, and, with some difficulty, they opened the vault door.

"It has not been opened for some time," said the philosopher.

"I dare say not, they seldom used to go here, from what I can learn, though it is kept a great secret."

"And we can keep it so, likewise."

"True."

They now entered the vault, and came to the second door, which opened into a kind of flight of steps, cut out of the solid rock, and then along a passage cut out of the mountain, of some kind of stone, but not so hard as the rock itself.

"You see," said the count, "what care has been taken to isolate the place, and detach it from the castle, so that it should not be dependent upon the possessor of the castle. This is the last door but one, and now prepare yourself for a surprise, doctor, this will be an extraordinary one."

So saying, the count opened the door, and stepped on one side, when the doctor approached the place, and was immediately thrust forward by the count and he rolled down some steps into the mine, and was immediately seized by some of the miners, who had been stationed there for that purpose, and carried to a distant part of the mine, there to work for the remainder of his life.

The count, seeing all secure, refastened the doors, and returned to the castle. A few weeks after this the body of a youth, mangled and disfigure, was brought to the castle, which the countess said was her son's body.

The count had immediately secured the real heir, and thrust him into the mines, there to pass a life of labor and hopeless misery.

*T*here was a high feast held. The castle gates were thrown open, and everybody who came were entertained without question.

This was on the occasion of the count's and countess's marriage. It seemed many months after the death of her son, whom she affected to mourn for a long time.

However, the marriage took place, and in all magnificence and splendor. The countess again appeared arrayed in splendor and beauty: she was proud and haughty, and the count was imperious.

In the mean time, the young Count de Hugo de Verole was confined in the mines, and the doctor with him.

By a strange coincidence, the doctor and the young count became companions, and the former, meditating projects of revenge, educated the young count as well as he was able for several years in the mines, and cherished in the young man a spirit of revenge. They finally escaped together, and proceeded to Leyden, where the doctor had friends, and where he placed his pupil at the university, and thus made him a most efficient means of revenge, because the education of the count gave him a means of appreciating the splendor and rank he had been deprived of. He, therefore, determined to remain at Leyden until he was of age, and then apply to his father's friends, and then to his sovereign, to dispossess and punish them both for their double crimes.

The count and countess lived on in a state of regal splendor. The immense revenue of his territory, and the treasure the late count had amassed, as well as the revenue that the mines brought in, would have supported a much larger expenditure than even their tastes disposed them to enjoy.

They had heard nothing of the escape of the doctor and the young count. Indeed, those who knew of it held their peace and said nothing about it, for they feared the consequences of their negligence. The first intimation they received was at the hands of a state messenger, summoning them to deliver up the castle revenues and treasure of the late count.

This was astonishing to them, and they refused to do so, but were soon after seized upon by a regiment of cuirassiers sent to take them, and they were accused of the crime of murder at the instance of the doctor.

They were arraigned and found guilty, and, as they were of the patrician order, their execution was delayed, and they were committed to exile. This was done out of favor to the young count, who did not wish to have his family name tainted by a public execution, or their being confined like convicts.

The count and countess quitted Hungary, and settled in Italy, where they lived upon the remains of the Count of Morven's property, shorn of all their splendor but enough to keep them from being compelled to do any menial office.

The young count took possession of his patrimony and his treasure at last, such as was left by his mother and her paramour.

The doctor continued to hide his crimes from the young count, and the perpetrators denying all knowledge of it, he escaped; but he returned to his native place, Leyden, with a reward for his services from the young count.

Flora rose from her perusal of the manuscript, which here ended, and even as she did so, she heard a footstep approaching her chamber door.

Chapter XX.

THE DREADFUL MISTAKE. – THE TERRIFIC INTERVIEW IN
THE CHAMBER. – THE ATTACK OF THE VAMPYRE.

*T*he footstep which Flora, upon the close of the tale she had been
reading, heard approaching her apartment, came rapidly along the
corridor.

"It is Henry, returned to conduct me to an interview with Charles's
uncle," she said. "I wonder, now, what manner of man he is. He should
in some respect resemble Charles; and if he do so, I shall bestow upon
him some affection for that alone."

Tap – tap came upon the chamber door.

Flora was not at all alarmed now, as she had been when Henry
brought her the manuscript. From some strange action of the nervous
system, she felt quite confident, and resolved to brave everything. But
then she felt quite sure that it was Henry, and before the knocking had
taken her by surprise.

"Come in," she said, in a cheerful voice. "Come in."

The door opened with wonderful swiftness – a figure stepped into
the room, and then closed it as rapidly, and stood against it. Flora tried
to scream, but her tongue refused its office; a confused whirl of sensations passed through her brain – she trembled, and an icy coldness came
over her. It was Sir Francis Varney, the vampyre!

He had drawn up his tall, gaunt frame to its full height, and crossed
his arms upon his breast; there was a hideous smile upon his sallow
countenance, and his voice was deep and sepulchral, as he said, –

"Flora Bannerworth, hear that which I have to say, and hear it calmly.
You need have nothing to fear. Make an alarm – scream, or shout for
help, and, by the hell beneath us, you are lost!"

There was a death-like, cold, passionless manner about the utterance
of these words, as if they were spoken mechanically, and came from no

human lips.

Flora heard them, and yet scarcely comprehended them; she stepped slowly back till she reached a chair, and there she held for support. The only part of the address of Varney that thoroughly reached her ears, was that if she gave any alarm some dreadful consequences were to ensue. But it was not on account of these words that she really gave no alarm; it was because she was utterly unable to do so.

"Answer me," said Varney. "Promise that you will hear that which I have to say. In so promising you commit yourself to no evil, and you shall hear that which shall give you much peace."

It was in vain she tried to speak; her lips moved, but she uttered no sound.

"You are terrified," said Varney, "and yet I know not why. I do not come to do you harm, although harm have you done me. Girl, I come to rescue you from a thralldom of the soul under which you now labor."

There was a pause of some moments' duration, and then, faintly, Flora managed to say, —

"Help! help! Oh, help me, Heaven!"

Varney made a gesture of impatience, as he said, —

"Heaven works no special matters now. Flora Bannerworth, if you have as much intellect as your nobility and beauty would warrant the world in supposing, you will listen to me."

"I — I hear," said Flora, as she still, dragging the chair with her, increased the distance between them.

"'Tis well. You are now more composed."

She fixed her eyes upon the face of Varney with a shudder. There could be no mistake. It was the same which, with the strange, glassy looking eyes, had glared upon her on that awful night of the storm, when she was visited by the vampyre. And Varney returned that gaze unflinchingly. There was a hideous and strange contortion of his face now as he said, —

"You are beautiful. The most cunning statuary might well model some rare work of art from those rounded limbs, that were surely made to bewitch the gazer. Your skin rivals the driven snow — what a face of loveliness, and what a form of enchantment."

She did not speak, but a thought came across her mind, which at once crimsoned her cheek — she knew she had fainted on the first visit of the vampyre, and now he, with a hideous reverence, praised beauties which he might have cast his demonic eyes over at such a time.

"You understand me," he said. "Well, let that pass. I am something allied to humanity yet."

"Speak your errand," gasped Flora, "or come what may, I scream for help to those who will not be slow to render it."

"I know it."

"You know I will scream?"

"No; you will hear me. I know they would not be slow to render help to you, but you will not call for it; I will present to you no necessity."

"Say on — say on."

"You perceive I do not attempt to approach you; my errand is one of peace."

"Peace from you! Horrible being, if you be really what even now my appalled imagination shrinks from naming you, would not even to you absolute annihilation be a blessing?"

"Peace, peace. I came not here to talk on such a subject. I must be brief, Flora Bannerworth, for time presses. I do not hate you. Wherefore should I? You are young, and you are beautiful, and you bear a name which should command, and does command, some portion of my best regard."

"There is a portrait," said Flora, "in this house."

"No more — no more. I know what you would say."

"It is yours."

"The house, and all within, I covet," he said, uneasily. "Let that suffice. I have quarreled with your brother — I have quarreled with one who just now fancies he loves you."

"Charles Holland loves me truly."

"It does not suit me now to dispute that point with you. I have the means of knowing more of the secrets of the human heart than common men. I tell you, Flora Bannerworth, that he who talks to you of love, loves you not but with the fleeting fancy of a boy; and there is one who hides deep in his heart a world of passion, one who has never spoken to you of love, and yet who loves you with a love as afar surpassing the evanescent fancy of this boy Holland, as does the mighty ocean the most placid lake that ever basked in idleness beneath a summer's sun."

There was a wonderful fascination in the manner now of Varney. His voice sounded like music itself. His words flowed from his tongue, each gently and properly accented, with all the charm of eloquence.

Despite her trembling horror of that man — despite her fearful opinion, which might be said to amount to a conviction of what he really was, Flora felt an irresistible wish to hear him speak on. Ay, despite, too, the ungrateful theme to her heart which he had now chosen as the subject of his discourse, she felt her fear of him gradually dissipating, and now when he made a pause, she said, —

"You are much mistaken. On the constancy and truth of Charles Holland, I would stake my life."

"No doubt, no doubt."

"Have you spoken now that which you had to say?"

"No, no. I tell you I covet this place, I would purchase it, but having with your bad-tempered brothers quarreled, they will hold no further converse with me."

"And well they may refuse."

"Be that as it may, sweet lady, I come to you to be my mediator. In the shadows of the future I can see many events which are to come."

"Indeed."

"It is so. Borrowing some wisdom from the past, and some from resources I would not detail to you, I know that if I have inflicted much misery upon you, I can spare you much more. Your brother or your lover will challenge me."

"Oh, no, no."

"I say such will happen, and I can kill either. My skill as well as my strength is superhuman."

"Mercy! mercy!" gasped Flora.

"I will spare either or both on a condition."

"What fearful condition?"

"It is not a fearful one. Your terrors go far beyond the fact. All I wish, maiden, of you is to induce these imperious brothers of yours to sell or let the Hall to me."

"Is that all?"

"It is. I ask no more, and, in return, I promise you not only that I will not fight with them, but that you shall never see me again. Rest securely, maiden, you will be undisturbed by me."

"Oh, God! that were indeed an assurance worth the striving for," said Flora.

"It is one you may have. But —"

"Oh, I knew — my heart told me there was yet some fearful condition to come."

"You are wrong again. I only ask of you that you keep this meeting a secret."

"No, no, no — I cannot."

"Nay, what so easy?"

"I will not; I have no secrets from those I love."

"Indeed, you will find soon the expediency of a few at least; but if you will not, I cannot urge it longer. Do as your wayward woman's nature prompts you."

There was a slight, but a very slight, tone of aggravation in these words, and the manner in which they were uttered.

As he spoke, he moved from the door towards the window, which opened into a kitchen garden. Flora shrunk as far from him as possible, and for a few minutes they regarded each other in silence.

"Young blood," said Varney, "mantles in your veins."

She shuddered with terror.

"Be mindful of the condition I have proposed to you. I covet Bannerworth Hall."

"I — I hear."

"And I must have it. I will have it, although my path to it be through a sea of blood. You understand me, maiden? Repeat what has passed between us or not, as you please. I say, beware of me, if you keep not the condition I have proposed."

"Heaven knows that this place is becoming daily more hateful to us all," said Flora.

"Indeed!"

"You well might know so much. It is no sacrifice to urge it now. I will urge my brothers."

"Thanks — a thousand thanks. You many not live to regret having made a friend of Varney —"

"The vampyre!" said Flora.

He advanced towards her a step, and she involuntarily uttered a scream of terror.

In an instant his hand clasped her waist with the power of an iron vice; she felt his hot breath flushing on her cheek. Her senses reeled, and she found herself sinking. She gathered all her breath and all her energies into one piercing shriek, and then she fell to the floor. There was a sudden crash of broken glass, and then all was still.

Chapter XXI.

THE CONFERENCE BETWEEN THE UNCLE AND NEPHEW, AND THE ALARM.

*M*eanwhile Charles Holland had taken his uncle by the arm, and led him into a private room.

"Dear uncle," he said, "be seated, and I will explain everything without reserve."

"Seated! — nonsense! I'll walk about," said the admiral. "D — n me! I've no patience to be seated, and very seldom had or have. Go on now, you young scamp."

"Well — well; you abuse me, but I am quite sure, had you been in my situation, you would have acted precisely as I have done."

"No, I shouldn't."

"Well, but, uncle —"

"Don't think to come over me by calling me uncle. Hark you, Charles — from this moment I won't be your uncle any more."

"Very well, sir."

"It ain't very well. And how dare you, you buccaneer, call me sir, eh? I say, how dare you?"

"I will call you anything I like."

"But I won't be called anything I like. You might as well call me at once Morgan the Pirate, for he was called anything he liked. Hilloa, sir! how dare you laugh, eh? I'll teach you to laugh at me. I wish I had you on board ship — that's all, you young rascal. I'd soon teach you to laugh at your superior officer, I would."

"Oh, uncle, I did not laugh at you."

"What did you laugh at, then?"

"At the joke."

"Joke. D — n me, there was no joke at all!"

"Oh, very good."

"And it ain't very good."

Charles knew very well that, this sort of humor, in which was the old admiral, would soon pass away, and then that he would listen to him comfortably enough; so he would not allow the least exhibition of petulance or mere impatience to escape himself, but contented himself by waiting until the ebullition of feeling fairly worked itself out.

"Well, well," at length said the old man, "you have dragged me here, into a very small and very dull room, under pretence of having something to tell me, and I have heard nothing yet."

"Then I will now tell you," said Charles. "I fell in love —"

"Bah!"

"With Flora Bannerworth, abroad; she is not only the most beautiful of created beings —"

"Bah!"

"But her mind is of the highest order of intelligence, honor, candor, and all amiable feelings —"

"Bah!"

"Really, uncle, if you say 'Bah!' to everything, I cannot go on."

"And what the deuce difference, sir, does it make to you, whether I say 'Bah!' or not?"

"Well, I love her. She came to England, and, as I could not exist, but was getting ill, and should, no doubt, have died if I had not done so, I came to England."

"But d — e, I want to know about the mermaid."

"The vampyre, you mean, sir."

"Well, well, the vampyre."

"Then, uncle, all I can tell you is, that it is supposed a vampyre came one night and inflicted a wound upon Flora's neck with his teeth, and that he is still endeavoring to renew his horrible existence from the young, pure blood that flows through her veins."

"The devil he is!"

"Yes. I am bewildered, I must confess, by the mass of circumstances that have combined to give the affair a horrible truthfulness. Poor Flora is much injured in health and spirits; and when I came home, she, at once, implored me to give her up, and think of her no more, for she could not think of allowing me to unite my fate with hers, under such circumstances."

"She did?"

"Such were her words, uncle. She implored me — she used the word 'implore' — to fly from her, to leave her to her fate, to endeavor to find happiness with some one else."

"Well?"

"But I saw her heart was breaking."

"What o' that?"

"Much of that, uncle. I told her that when I deserted her in the hour of misfortune that I hoped Heaven would desert me. I told her that if her happiness was wrecked, to cling yet to me, and that with what power and what strength God had given me, I would stand between her and all ill."

"And what then?"

"She — she fell upon my breast and wept and blessed me. Could I desert her — could I say to her, 'My dear girl, when you were full of health and beauty, I loved you, but now that sadness is at your heart I leave you?' Could I tell her that, uncle, and yet call myself a man?"

"No!" reared the old admiral, in a voice that made the room echo again; "and I tell you what, if you had done so, d — n you, you puppy, I'd have braced you, and — and married the girl myself. I would, d — e, but I would."

"Dear uncle!"

"Don't dear me, sir. Talk of deserting a girl when the signal of distress, in the shape of a tear, is in her eye?"

"But I —"

"You are a wretch — a confounded lubberly boy — a swab — a d——d bad grampus."

"You mistake, uncle."

"No, I don't. God bless you, Charles, you shall have her — if a whole ship's crew of vampyres said no, you shall have her. Let me see her —

just let me see her."

The admiral gave his lips a vigorous wipe with his sleeve, and Charles said hastily, —

"My dear uncle, you will recollect that Miss Bannerworth is quite a young lady."

"I suppose she is."

"Well, then, for God's sake, don't attempt to kiss her."

"Not kiss her! d — e, they like it. Not kiss her, because she's a young lady! D — e, do you think I'd kiss a corporal of marines?"

"No, uncle; but you know young ladies are very delicate."

"And ain't I delicate — shiver my timbers, ain't I delicate? Where is she? that's what I want to know."

"Then you approve of what I have done?"

"You are a young scamp, but you have got some of the old admiral's family blood in you, so don't take any credit for acting like an honest man — you couldn't help it."

"But if I had not so acted," said Charles, with a smile, "what would have become of the family blood, then?"

"What's that to you? I would have disowned you, because that very thing would have convinced me you were an impostor, and did not belong to the family at all."

"Well, that would have been one way of getting over the difficulty."

"No difficulty at all. The man who deserts the good ship that carries him through the waves, or the girl that trusts her heart to him, ought to be chopped up into meat for wild monkeys."

"Well, I think so too."

"Of course you do."

"Why, of course?"

"Because it's so d——d reasonable that, being a nephew of mine, you can't possibly help it."

"Bravo, uncle! I had no idea you were so argumentative."

"Hadn't you a spooney; you'd be an ornament to the gun-room, you would; but where's the 'young lady' who is so infernal delicate — where is she, I say?"

"I will fetch her, uncle."

"Ah, do; I'll be bound, now, she's one of the right build — a good figure-head, and don't make too much stern-way."

"Well, well, whatever you do, now don't pay her any compliments, for your efforts in that line are of such a very doubtful order, that I shall dread to hear you."

"You be off, and mind your own business; I haven't been at sea forty years without picking up some out-and-out delicate compliments to say to a young lady."

"But do you really imagine, now, that the deck of a man-of-war is a nice place to pick up courtly compliments in?"

"Of course I do. There you hear the best of language, d − e! You don't know what you are talking about, you fellows that have stuck on shore all your lives; it's we seamen who learn life."

"Well, well − hark!"

"What's that?"

"A cry − did you not hear a cry?"

"A signal of distress, by G − d!"

In their efforts to leave the room, the uncle and nephew for about a minute actually blocked up the doorway, but the superior bulk of the admiral prevailed, and after nearly squeezing poor Charles flat, he got out first.

But this did not avail him, for he knew not where to go. Now, the second scream which Flora had uttered when the vampyre had clasped her waist came upon their ears, and, as they were outside the room, it acted well as a guide in which direction to come.

Charles fancied correctly enough at once that it proceeded from the room which was called "Flora's own room," and thitherward accordingly he dashed at tremendous speed.

Henry, however, happened to be nearer at hand, and, moreover, he did not hesitate a moment, because he knew that Flora was in her own room; so he reached it first, and Charles saw him rush in a few moments before he could reach the room.

The difference of time, however, was very slight, and Henry had only just raised Flora from the floor as Charles appeared.

"God of Heaven!" cried the latter, "what has happened?"

"I know not," said Henry; "as God is my judge, I know not. Flora, Flora, speak to us! Flora! Flora!"

"She has fainted!" cried Charles. "Some water may restore her. Oh, Henry, Henry, is not this horrible?"

"Courage! courage!" said Henry, although his voice betrayed what a terrible state of anxiety he was himself in; "you will find water in that decanter, Charles. Here is my mother, too! Another visit! God help us!"

Mrs. Bannerworth sat down on the edge of the sofa which was in the room, and could only wring her hands and weep.

"Avast!" cried the admiral, making his appearance. "Where's the enemy, lads?"

"Uncle," said Charles, "uncle, uncle, the vampyre has been here again − the dreadful vampyre!"

"D − n me, and he's gone, too, and carried half the window with him. Look there!"

It was literally true; the window, which was a long latticed one, was smashed through.

"Help! oh, help!" said Flora, as the water that was dashed in her face began to recover her.

"You are safe!" cried Henry, "you are safe!"

"Flora," said Charles; "you know my voice, dear Flora? Look up, and you will see there are none here but those who love you."

Flora opened her eyes timidly as she said, —

"Has it gone?"

"Yes, yes, dear," said Charles. "Look around you; here are none but true friends."

"And tried friends, my dear," said Admiral Bell, "excepting me; and whenever you like to try me, afloat or ashore, d — n me, shew me Old Nick himself, and I won't shrink — yard arm and yard arm — grapnel to grapnel — pitch pots and grenades!"

"This is my uncle, Flora," said Charles.

"I thank you, sir," said Flora, faintly.

"All right!" whispered the admiral to Charles; "what a figure-head to be sure! Poll at Swansea would have made just about four of her, but she wasn't so delicate, d — n me!"

"I should think not."

"You are right for once in a way, Charley."

"What was it that alarmed you?" said Charles, tenderly, as he now took one of Flora's hands in his.

"Varney — Varney, the vampyre."

"Varney!" exclaimed Henry; "Varney here!"

"Yes, he came in at that door; and when I screamed, I suppose — for I hardly was conscious — he darted out through the window."

"This," said Henry, "is beyond all human patience. By Heaven! I cannot and will not endure it."

"It shall be my quarrel," said Charles; "I shall go at once and defy him. He shall meet me."

"Oh, no, no, no," said Flora, as she clung convulsively to Charles. "No, no; there is a better way."

"What way?"

"The place has become full of terrors. Let us leave it. Let him, as he wishes, have it."

"Let *him* have it?"

"Yes, yes, God knows, if it purchase an immunity from these visits, we may well be overjoyed. Remember that we have ample reasons to believe him more than human. Why should you allow yourselves to risk a personal encounter with such a man, who might be glad to kill you that he might have an opportunity of replenishing his own hideous existence from your best heart's blood?"

The young men looked aghast.

"Besides," added Flora, "you cannot tell what dreadful powers of mischief he may have, against which human courage might be of no avail."

"There is truth and reason," said Mr. Marchdale, stepping forward, "in what Flora says."

"Only let me come across him, that's all," said Admiral Bell, "and I'll soon find out what he is. I suppose he's some long slab of a lubber after all, ain't he, with no strength."

"His strength is immense," said Marchdale. "I tried to seize him, and I fell beneath his arm as if I had been struck by the hammer of a Cyclops."

"A what?" cried the admiral.

"A Cyclops."

"D — n me, I served aboard the Cyclops eleven years, and never saw a very big hammer aboard of her."

"What on earth is to be done?" said Henry.

"Oh," chimed in the admiral, "there's always a bother about what's to be done on earth. Now, at sea, I could soon tell you what was to be done."

"We must hold a solemn consultation over this matter," said Henry. "You are safe now, Flora."

"Oh, be ruled by me. Give up the Hall."

"You tremble."

"I do tremble, brother, for what may yet ensue. I implore you to give up the Hall. It is but a terror to us now — give it up. Have no more to do with it. Let us make terms with Sir Francis Varney. Remember, we dare not kill him."

"He ought to be smothered," said the admiral.

"It is true," remarked Henry, "we dare not, even holding all the terrible suspicions we do, take his life."

"By foul means certainly not," said Charles, "were he ten times a vampyre. I cannot, however, believe that he is so invulnerable as he is represented."

"No one represents him here," said Marchdale. "I speak, sir, because I saw you glance at me. I only know that, having made two unsuccessful attempts so to seize him, he eluded me, once by leaving in my grasp a piece of his coat, and the next time he struck me down, and I feel yet the effects of the terrific blow."

"You hear?" said Flora.

"Yes, I hear," said Charles.

"For some reason," added Marchdale, in a tone of emotion, "what I say seems to fall always badly upon Mr. Holland's ear. I know not why; but if it will give him any satisfaction, I will leave Bannerworth Hall tonight."

"No, no, no," said Henry; "for the love of Heaven, do not let us quarrel."

"Hear, hear," cried the admiral. "We can never fight the enemy well if the ship's crew are on bad terms. Come now, you Charles, this appears to be an honest, gentlemanly fellow — give him your hand."

"If Mr. Charles Holland," said Marchdale, "knows aught to my prejudice in any way, however slight, I here beg of him to declare it at once, and openly."

"I cannot assert that I do," said Charles.

"Then what the deuce do you make yourself so disagreeable for, eh?" cried the admiral.

"One cannot help one's impression and feelings," said Charles; "but I am willing to take Mr. Marchdale's hand."

"And I yours, young sir," said Marchdale, "in all sincerity of spirit, and with good will towards you."

They shook hands; but it required no conjuror to perceive that it was not done willingly or cordially. It was a hand shaking of that character which seemed to imply on each side, "I don't like you, but I don't know positively any harm of you."

"There now," said the admiral, "that's better."

"Now, let us hold counsel about this Varney," said Henry. "Come to the parlor all of you, and we will endeavor to come to some decided arrangement."

"Do not weep, mother," said Flora. "All may yet be well. We will leave this place."

"We will consider that question, Flora," said Henry; "and believe me your wishes will go a long way with all of us, as you may well suppose they always would."

They left Mrs. Bannerworth with Flora, and proceeded to the small oaken parlor, in which were the elaborate and beautiful carvings which have been before mentioned.

Henry's countenance, perhaps, wore the most determined expression of all. He appeared now as if he had thoroughly made up his mind to do something which should have a decided tendency to put a stop to the terrible scenes which were now day by day taking place beneath that roof.

Charles Holland looked serious and thoughtful, as if he were revolving some course of action in his mind concerning which he was not quite clear.

Mr. Marchdale was more sad and depressed, to all appearance, than any of them.

As for the admiral, he was evidently in a state of amazement, and knew not what to think. He was anxious to do something, and yet what that was to be he had not the most remote idea, any more than as if he was not at all cognizant of any of those circumstances, every one of which was so completely out of the line of his former life and experience.

George had gone to call on Mr. Chillingworth, so he was not present at the first part of this serious council of war.

Chapter *XXII.*

THE CONSULTATION. – THE DETERMINATION TO LEAVE THE HALL.

*T*his was certainly the most seriously reasonable meeting which had been held at Bannerworth Hall on the subject of the much dreaded vampyre. The absolute necessity for doing something of a decisive character was abundantly apparent, and when Henry promised Flora that her earnest wish to leave the house should not be forgotten as an element in the discussion which was about to ensue, it was with a rapidly growing feeling on his own part, to the effect that that house, associated even as it was with many endearing recollections, was no home for him.

Hence he was the more inclined to propose a departure from the Hall if it could possibly be arranged satisfactorily in a pecuniary point of view. The pecuniary point of view, however, in which Henry was compelled to look at the subject, was an important and a troublesome one.

We have already hinted at the very peculiar state of the finances of the family; and, in fact, although the income derivable from various sources ought to have been amply sufficient to provide Henry, and those who were dependent upon him, with a respectable livelihood, yet it was nearly all swallowed up by the payment of regular installments upon family debts incurred by his father. And the creditors took great credit to themselves that they allowed of such an arrangement, instead of sweeping off all before them, and leaving the family to starve.

The question, therefore, or, at all events, one of the questions, now was, how far would a departure from the Hall of him, Henry, and the other branches of the family, act upon that arrangement?

During a very few minutes' consideration, Henry, with the frank and candid disposition which was so strong a characteristic of his character, made up his mind to explain all this fully to Charles Holland and his uncle.

When once he formed such a determination he was not likely to be slow in carrying it into effect, and no sooner, then, were the whole of them seated in the small oaken parlor than he made an explicit statement of his circumstances.

"But," said Mr. Marchdale, when he had done, "I cannot see what right your creditors have to complain of where you live, so long as you perform your contract to them."

"True; but they always expected me, I know, to remain at the Hall, and if they chose, why, of course, at any time, they could sell off the whole property for what it would fetch, and pay themselves as far as the proceeds would go. At all events, I am quite certain there could be nothing at all left for me."

"I cannot imagine," added Mr. Marchdale, "that any men could be so unreasonable."

"It is scarcely to be borne," remarked Charles Holland, with more impatience than he usually displayed, "that a whole family are to be put to the necessity of leaving their home for no other reason than the being pestered by such a neighbor as Sir Francis Varney. It makes one impatient and angry to reflect upon such a state of things."

"And yet they are lamentably true," said Henry. "What can we do?"

"Surely there must be some sort of remedy."

"There is but one that I can imagine, and that is one we all alike revolt from. We might kill him."

"That is out of the question."

"Of course my impression is that he bears the same name really as myself, and that he is my ancestor, from whom was painted the portrait on the panel."

"Have circumstances really so far pressed upon you," said Charles Holland, "as at length to convince you that this man is really the horrible creature we surmise he may be?"

"Dare we longer doubt it?" cried Henry, in a tone of excitement. "He is the vampyre."

"I'll be hanged if I believe it," said Admiral Bell! "Stuff and nonsense! Vampyre, indeed! Bother the vampyre."

"Sir," said Henry, "you have not had brought before you, painfully, as we have, all the circumstances upon which we, in a manner, feel compelled to found this horrible belief. At first incredulity was a natural thing. We had no idea that ever we would be brought to believe in such a thing."

"That is the case," added Marchdale. "But, step by step, we have been driven from utter disbelief in this phenomenon to a trembling conviction that it must be true."

"Unless we admit that, simultaneously, the senses of a number of persons have been deceived."

"That is scarcely possible."

"Then do you mean really to say there are such fish?" said the admiral.

"We think so."

"Well, I'm d——d! I have heard all sorts of yarns about what fellows have seen in one ocean or another; but this does beat them all to nothing."

"It is monstrous," exclaimed Charles.

There was a pause of some few moments' duration, and then Mr. Marchdale said, in a low voice, —

"Perhaps I ought not to propose any course of action until you, Henry, have yourself done so; but even at the risk of being presumptuous, I will say that I am firmly of the opinion that you ought to leave the Hall."

"I am inclined to think so, too," said Henry.

"But the creditors?" interposed Charles.

"I think they might be consulted on the matter beforehand," added Marchdale, "when no doubt they would acquiesce in an arrangement which could do them no harm."

"Certainly, no harm," said Henry, "for I cannot take the estate with me, as they well know."

"Precisely. If you do not like to sell it, you can let it."

"To whom?"

"Why, under the existing circumstances, it is not likely you would get any tenant for it than the one who has offered himself."

"Sir Francis Varney?"

"Yes. It seems to be a great object with him to live here, and it appears to me, that notwithstanding all that has occurred, it is most decidedly the best policy to let him."

Nobody could really deny the reasonableness of this advice, although it seemed strange, and was repugnant to the feelings of them all, as they heard it. There was a pause of some seconds' duration, and then Henry said, —

"It does, indeed seem singular, to surrender one's house to such a being."

"Especially," said Charles, "after what has occurred."

"True."

"Well," said Mr. Marchdale, "if any better plan of proceeding, taking the whole case into consideration, can be devised, I shall be most happy."

"Will you consent to put off all proceedings for three days?" said

Charles Holland, suddenly.

"Have you any plan, my dear sir?" said Mr. Marchdale.

"I have, but it is one which I would rather say nothing about for the present."

"I have no objection," said Henry, "I do not know that three days can make any difference in the state of affairs. Let it be so, if you wish, Charles."

"Then I am satisfied," said Charles. "I cannot but feel that, situated as I am regarding Flora, this is almost more my affair than even yours, Henry."

"I cannot see that," said Henry. "Why should you take upon yourself more of the responsibility of these affairs than I, Charles? You induce in my mind a suspicion that you have some desperate project in your imagination, which by such a proposition you would seek to reconcile us to."

Charles was silent, and Henry then added, —

"Now, Charles, I am quite convinced that what I have hinted at is the fact. You have conceived some scheme which you fancy would be much opposed by us?"

"I will not deny that I have," said Charles. "It is one, however, which you must allow me for the present to keep locked in my own breast."

"Why will you not trust us?"

"For two reasons."

"Indeed!"

"The one is, that I have not yet thoroughly determined upon the course I project; and the other is, that it is one in which I am not justified in involving anyone else."

"Charles, Charles," said Henry, despondingly; "only consider for a moment into what new misery you may plunge poor Flora, who is, Heaven knows, already sufficiently afflicted, by attempting an enterprise which even we, who are your friends, may unwittingly cross you in the performance of."

"This is one in which I fear no such result. It cannot so happen. Do not urge me."

"Can't you say at once what you think of doing?" said the old admiral. "What do you mean by turning your sails in all sorts of directions so oddly? You sneak, why don't you be what do you call it — explicit?"

"I cannot, uncle."

"What, are you tongue-tied?"

"All here know well," said Charles, "that if I do not unfold my mind fully, it is not that I fear to trust any one present, but from some other most special reason."

"Charles, I forbear to urge you further," said Henry, "and only implore you to be careful."

At this moment the room door opened, and George Bannerworth, accompanied by Mr. Chillingworth, came in.

"Do not let me intrude," said the surgeon; "I fear, as I see you seated, gentlemen, that my presence must be a rudeness and a disturbance to some family consultation among yourselves?"

"Not at all, Mr. Chillingworth," said Henry. "Pray be seated; we are very glad indeed to see you. Admiral Bell, this is a friend on whom we can rely — Mr. Chillingworth."

"And one of the right sort, I can see," said the admiral, as he shook Mr. Chillingworth by the hand.

"Sir, you do me much honor," said the doctor.

"None at all, none at all; I suppose you know all about this infernal odd vampyre business?"

"I believe I do, sir."

"And what do you think of it?"

"I think time will develop the circumstances sufficiently to convince us all that such things cannot be."

"D — n me, you are the most sensible fellow, then, that I have yet met with since I have been in this neighborhood; for everybody else is so convinced about the vampyre, that they are ready to swear by him."

"It would take much more to convince me. I was coming over here when I met Mr. George Bannerworth coming to my house."

"Yes," said George, "and Mr. Chillingworth has something to tell us of a nature confirmatory of our own suspicions."

"It is strange," said Henry; "but any piece of news, come it from what quarter it may, seems to be confirmatory, in some degree or another, of that dreadful belief in vampyres."

"Why," said the doctor, "when Mr. George says that my news is of such a character, I think he goes a little too far. What I have to tell you, I do not conceive has anything whatever to do with the fact, or one fact of there being vampyres."

"Let us hear it," said Henry.

"It is simply this, that I was sent for by Sir Francis Varney myself."

"You sent for?"

"Yes; he sent for me by a special messenger to come to him, and when I went, which, under the circumstances, you may well guess, I did with all the celerity possible, I found it was to consult me about a flesh wound in his arm, which was showing some angry symptoms."

"Indeed."

"Yes, it was so. When I was introduced to him I found him lying on a couch, and looking pale and unwell. In the most respectful manner, he asked me to be seated, and when I had taken a chair, he added, —

"'Mr. Chillingworth, I have sent for you in consequence of a slight accident which has happened to my arm. I was incautiously loading some firearms, and discharged a pistol so close to me that the bullet inflicted a wound on my arm.'

"'If you will allow me,' said I, 'to see the wound, I will give you my opinion.'

"He then showed me a jagged wound, which had evidently been caused by the passage of a bullet, which, had it gone a little deeper, must have inflicted a serious injury. As it was, the wound was trifling.

"He had evidently been attempting to dress it himself, but finding some considerable inflammation, he very likely got a little alarmed."

"You dressed the wound?"

"I did."

"And what do you think of Sir Francis Varney, now that you have had so capital an opportunity," said Henry, "of a close observation of him?"

"Why, there is certainly something odd about him which I cannot well define, but, take him altogether, he can be a very gentlemanly man indeed."

"So he can."

"His manners are easy and polished; he has evidently mixed in good society, and I never, in all my life, heard such a sweet, soft, winning voice."

"That is strictly him. You noticed, I presume, his great likeness to the portrait on the panel?"

"I did. At some moments, and viewing his face in some particular lights, it showed much more strongly than at others. My impression was that he could, when he liked, look much more like the portrait on the panel than when he allowed his face to assume its ordinary appearance."

"Probably such an impression would be produced upon your mind," said Charles, "by some accidental expression of the countenance which even he was not aware of, and which often occurs in families."

"It may be so."

"Of course you did not hint, sir, at what has passed here with regard to him?" said Henry.

"I did not. Being, you see, called in professionally, I had no right to take advantage of that circumstance to make any remarks to him about his private affairs."

"Certainly not."

"It was all one to me whether he was a vampyre or not, professionally, and however deeply I might feel, personally, interested in the matter, I said nothing to him about it, because, you see, if I had, he would have had a fair opportunity of saying at once, 'Pray, sir, what is that to you?' and I should have been at a loss what to reply."

"Can we doubt," said Henry, "but that this very wound has been inflicted upon Sir Francis Varney, by the pistol-bullet which was discharged at him by Flora?"

"Everything leads to such an assumption certainly," said Charles Holland.

"And yet you cannot even deduce from that the absolute fact of Sir Francis Varney's being a vampyre?"

"I do not think, Mr. Chillingworth," said Marchdale, "anything would convince you but a visit from him, and an actual attempt to fasten upon some of your own veins."

"That would not convince me," said Chillingworth.

"Then you will not be convinced?"

"I certainly will not. I mean to hold out to the last. I said at the first, and I say so still, that I never will give way to this most outrageous superstition."

"I wish I could think with you," said Marchdale, with a shudder; "but there may be something in the very atmosphere of this house which has been rendered hideous by the awful visits that have been made to it, which forbids me to disbelieve in those things which others more happily situated can hold at arm's length, and utterly repudiate."

"There may be," said Henry; "but as to that, I think, after the very strongly expressed wish of Flora, I will decide upon leaving the house."

"Will you sell it or let it?"

"The latter I should much prefer," was the reply.

"But who will take it now, except Sir Francis Varney? Why not at once let him have it? I am well aware that this does sound odd advice, but remember, we are all the creatures of circumstance, and that, in some cases where we least like it, we must swim with the stream."

"That you will not decide upon, however, at present," said Charles Holland, as he rose.

"Certainly not; a few days can make no difference."

"None for the worse, certainly, and possibly much for the better."

"Be it so; we will wait."

"Uncle," said Charles, "Will you spare me half an hour of your company?"

"An hour, my boy, if you want it," said the admiral, rising from his chair.

"Then this consultation is over," said Henry, "and we quite understand that to leave the Hall is a matter determined on, and that in a few days a decision shall come as to whether Varney the Vampyre shall be its tenant or not."

Chapter XXIII.

THE ADMIRAL'S ADVICE TO CHARLES HOLLAND. – THE CHALLENGE TO THE VAMPYRE.

When Charles Holland got his uncle into a room by themselves, he said, –

"Uncle, you are a seaman, and accustomed to decide upon matters of honor. I look upon myself as having been most grievously insulted by this Sir Francis Varney. All accounts agree in representing him as a gentleman. He goes openly by a title, which, if it were not his, could easily be contradicted; therefore, on the score of position in life, there is no fault to find with him. What would you do if you were insulted by this gentleman?"

The old admiral's eyes sparkled, and he looked comically in the face of Charles, as he said, –

"I know now where you are steering."

"What would you do, uncle?"

"Fight him!"

"I knew you would say so, and that's just what I want to do as regards Sir Francis Varney."

"Well, my boy, I don't know that you can do better. He must be a thundering rascal, whether he is a vampyre or not; so if you feel that he has insulted you, fight him by all means, Charles."

"I am much pleased, uncle, to find that you take my view of the subject," said Charles. "I knew that if I mentioned such a thing to the Bannerworths, they would endeavor all in their power to persuade me against it."

"Yes, no doubt; because they are all impressed with a strange fear of this fellow's vampyre powers. Besides, if a man is going to fight, the fewer people he mentions it to the most decidedly the better, Charles."

"I believe that is the fact, uncle. Should I overcome Varney, there will most likely be at once an end to the numerous and uncomfortable perplexities of the Bannerworths as regards him; and if he overcome me, why, then, at all events, I shall have made an effort to rescue Flora from the dread of this man."

"And then he shall fight me," added the admiral, "so he shall have two chances, at all events, Charles."

"Nay, uncle, that would, you know, scarcely be fair. Besides, if I should fall, I solemnly bequeath Flora Bannerworth to your good offices. I much fear that the pecuniary affairs of poor Henry, — from no fault of his, Heaven knows, — are in a very bad state, and that Flora may yet live to want some kind and able friend."

"Never fear, Charles. The young creature shall never want while the old admiral has got a shot in the locker."

"Thank you, uncle, thank you. I have ample cause to know, and to be able to rely upon your kind and generous nature. And now about the challenge?"

"You write it, boy, and I'll take it."

"Will you second me, uncle?"

"To be sure I will. I wouldn't trust anybody else to do so on any account. You leave all the arrangements with me, and I'll second you as you ought to be seconded."

"Then I will write it at once, for I have received injuries at the hands of that man, or devil, be he what he may, that I cannot put up with. His visit to the chamber of her whom I love would alone constitute ample ground of action."

"I should say it rather would, my boy."

"And after this corroborative story of the wound, I cannot for a moment doubt that Sir Francis Varney is the vampyre, or the personifier of the vampyre."

"That's clear enough, Charles, Come, just you write your challenge, my boy, at once, and let me have it."

"I will, uncle."

Charles was a little astonished, although pleased, at his uncle's ready acquiescence in his fighting a vampyre, but that circumstance he ascribed to the old man's habits of life, which made him so familiar with strife and personal contentions of all sorts, that he did not ascribe to it that amount of importance which more peaceable people did. Had he, while he was writing the note to Sir Francis Varney, seen the old admiral's face, and the exceedingly cunning look it wore, he might have suspected that the acquiescence in the duel was but a seeming acquiescence. This, however, escaped him, and in a few moments he read to his uncle the following note: —

"TO SIR FRANCIS VARNEY.

"Sir, — The expressions made use of towards me by you, as well as general circumstances, which I need not further allude to here, induce me to demand of you that satisfaction due from one gentleman to another. My uncle, Admiral Bell, is the bearer of this note, and will arrange preliminaries with any friend you may choose to appoint to act in your behalf. I am, sir, yours, &c.
                    "CHARLES HOLLAND."

"Will that do?" said Charles.

"Capital!" said the admiral.

"I am glad you like it."

"Oh, I could not help liking it. The least said and the most to the purpose, always pleases me best; and this explains nothing and demands all you want — which is a fight; so it's all right, you see, and nothing can possibly be better."

Charles did glance in his uncle's face, for he suspected, from the manner in which these words were uttered, that the old man was amusing himself a little at his expense. The admiral, however, looked so supernaturally serious that Charles was foiled.

"I repeat, it's a capital letter," he said.

"Yes, you said so."

"Well, what are you staring at?"

"Oh, nothing."

"Do you doubt my word?"

"Not at all, uncle; only I thought there was a degree of irony in the manner in which you spoke."

"Not at all, my boy. I never was more serious in all my life."

"Very good. Then you will remember that I leave my honor in this affair completely in your hands."

"Depend upon me, my boy."

"I will, and do."

"I'll be off and see the fellow at once."

"The admiral bustled out of the room, and in a few moments Charles heard him calling loudly, —

"Jack — Jack Pringle, you lubber, where are you? — Jack Pringle, I say."

"Ay, ay, sir," said Jack, emerging from the kitchen, where he had been making himself generally useful in assisting Mrs. Bannerworth, there being no servant in the house, to cook some dinner for the family.

"Come on, you rascal, we are going for a walk."

"The rations will be served out soon," growled Jack.

"We shall be back in time, you cormorant, never fear. You are always thinking of eating and drinking, you are, Jack; and I'll be hanged if I think you ever think of anything else. Come on, will you; I'm going on rather a particular cruise just now, so mind what you are about."

"Aye, aye, sir," said the tar, and these two originals, who so perfectly understood each other, walked away, conversing as they went, and their different voices coming upon the ear of Charles, until distance obliterated all impression of the sound.

Charles paced to and fro in the room where he had held this brief and conclusive conversation with his uncle. He was thoughtful, as any one might well be who knew not but that the next four-and-twenty hours would be the limit of his sojourn in this world.

"Oh, Flora — Flora!" he at length said, "how happy we might to have been! but all is past now, and there seems nothing left us and that is in my killing this fearful man who is invested with so dreadful an existence. And if I do kill him in fair and in open fight, I will take care that his mortal frame has no power again to revisit the glimpses of the moon."

It was strange to imagine that such was the force of many concurrent circumstances, that a young man like Charles Holland, of first-rate abilities and education, should find it necessary to give in so far to a belief which was repugnant to all his best feelings and habits of thought, as to be reasoning with himself upon the best means of preventing the resuscitation of the corpse of a vampyre. But so it was. His imagination had yielded to a succession of events which very few persons indeed could have held out against.

"I have heard and read," he said, as he continued his agitated and uneasy walk, "of how these dreadful beings are to be kept in their graves. I have heard of stakes being driven through the body so as to pin it to the earth until the gradual progress of decay has rendered its revivification a thing of utter and total impossibility. Then, again," he added, after a slight pause, "I have heard of their being burned, and the ashes scattered to the winds of Heaven to prevent them from ever again uniting or assuming human form."

These were disagreeable and strange fancies, and he shuddered while he indulged in them. He felt a kind of trembling horror come over him even at the thought of engaging in conflict with a being who, perhaps, had lived more than a hundred years.

"That portrait," he thought, "on the panel, is the portrait of a man in the prime of life. If it be the portrait of Sir Francis Varney, by the date which the family ascribe to it he must be nearly one hundred and fifty years of age now."

This was a supposition which carried the imagination to a vast amount of strange conjectures.

"What changes he must have witnessed about him in that time," thought Charles. "How he must have seen kingdoms totter and fall, and how many changes of habits, of manners, and of custom must he have become a spectator of. Renewing too, ever and anon, his fearful existence by such fearful means."

This was a wide field of conjecture for a fertile imagination, and now that he was on the eve of engaging with such a being in mortal combat, on behalf of her he loved, the thoughts it gave rise to came more strongly and thickly upon him than ever they had done before.

"But I will fight him," he suddenly said, "for Flora's sake, were he a hundred times more hideous a being than so many evidences tend to prove him. I will fight with him, and it may be my fate to rid the world of such a monster in human form."

Charles worked himself up to a kind of enthusiasm by which he almost succeeded in convincing himself that, in attempting the destruction of Sir Francis Varney, he was the champion of human nature.

It would be aside from the object of these pages, which is to record facts as they occurred, to enter into the metaphysical course of reasoning which came across Charles's mind; suffice it to say that he felt nothing shaken as regarded his resolve to meet Varney the Vampyre, and that he made up his mind the conflict should be one of life or death.

"It must be so," he said. "It must be so. Either he or I must fall in the fight which shall surely be."

He now sought Flora, for how soon might he now be torn from her forever by the irresistible hand of death. He felt that, during the few brief hours which now would only elapse previous to his meeting with Sir Francis Varney, he could not enjoy too much of the society of her who reigned supreme in his heart, and held in her own keeping his best affections.

But while Charles is thus employed, let us follow his uncle and Jack Pringle to the residence of Varney, which, as the reader is aware, was so near at hand that it required not many minutes' sharp walking to reach it.

The admiral knew well he could trust Jack with any secret, for long habits of discipline and deference to the orders of superiors takes off the propensity to blabbering which, among civilians who are not accustomed to discipline, is so very prevalent. The old man therefore explained to Jack what he meant to do, and it received Jack's full approval; but as in the enforced detail of other matters it must come out, we will not here prematurely enter into the admiral's plans.

When they reached the residence of Sir Francis Varney, they were received courteously enough, and the admiral desired Jack to wait for him the handsome hall of the house, while he was shewn up stairs to the private room of the vampyre.

"Confound the fellow!" muttered the old admiral, "he is well lodged at all events. I should say he was not one of those vampyres who have nowhere to go to but their own coffins when the evening comes."

The room into which the admiral was shewn had green blinds to it, and they were all drawn down. It is true that the sun was shining brightly outside, although transiently, but still a strange green tinge was thrown over everything in the room, and more particularly did it appear to fall upon the face of Varney, converting his usually sallow countenance into a still more hideous and strange color. He was sitting upon a couch, and, when the admiral came in, he rose, and said, in a deep-toned voice, extremely different to that he usually spoke in, —

"My humble home is much honored, sir, by your presence in it."

"Good morning," said the admiral. "I have come to speak to you, sir, rather seriously."

"However abrupt this announcement may sound to me," said Varney, "I am quite sure I shall always hear, with the most profound respect, whatever Admiral Bell may have to say."

"There is no respect required," said the admiral, "but only a little attention."

Sir Francis bowed in a stately manner, saying, —

"I shall be quite unhappy if you will not be seated, Admiral Bell."

"Oh, never mind that, Sir Francis Varney, if you be Sir Francis Varney; for you may be the devil himself, for all I know. My nephew, Charles Holland, considers that, one way and another, he has a very tolerable quarrel with you."

"I much grieve to hear it."

"Do you?"

"Believe me, I do. I am most scrupulous in what I say; and an assertion that I am grieved, you may thoroughly and entirely depend upon."

"Well, well, never mind that; Charles Holland is a young man just entering into life. He loves a girl who is, I think, every way worthy of him."

"Oh, what a felicitous prospect!"

"Just hear me out, if you please."

"With pleasure, sir — with pleasure."

"Well, then, when a young, hot-headed fellow thinks he has a good ground of quarrel with anybody, you will not be surprised at his wanting to fight it out."

"Not at all."

"Well, then, to come to the point, my nephew, Charles Holland, has a fancy for fighting with you."

"Ah!"

"You take it d——d easy."

"My dear sir, why should I be uneasy? He is not my nephew, you know. I shall have no particular cause, beyond those feelings of common compassion which I hope inhabit my breast as well as every one else's."

"What do you mean?"

"Why, he is a young man just, as you say, entering into life, and I cannot help thinking it would be a pity to cut him off like a flower in the bud, so very soon."

"Oh, you make quite sure, then, of settling him, do you?"

"My dear sir, only consider; he might be very troublesome, indeed; you know young men are hot-headed and troublesome. Even if I were only to maim him, he might be a continual and never-ceasing annoyance to me. I think I should be absolutely, in a manner of speaking, compelled to cut him off."

"The devil you do!"

"As you say, sir."

"D — n your assurance, Mr. Vampyre, or whatever odd fish you may be."

"Admiral Bell, I never called upon you and received a courteous reception, and then insulted you."

"Then why do you talk of cutting off a better man than yourself? D — n it, what would you say to him cutting you off?"

"Oh, as for me, my good sir, that's quite another thing. Cutting me off is very doubtful."

Sir Francis Varney gave a strange smile as he spoke, and shook his head, as if some most extraordinary and extravagant proposition had been mooted, which it was scarcely worth the while of anybody possessed of common sense to set about expecting.

Admiral Bell felt strongly inclined to get into a rage, but he repressed the idea as much as he could, although, but for the curious faint green light that came through the blinds, his heightened color would have sufficiently proclaimed what state of mind he was in.

"Mr. Varney," he said, "all this is quite beside the question; but at all events, if it have any weight at all, it could to have a considerable influence in deciding you to accept the terms I propose."

"What are they, sir?"

"Why, that you permit me to espouse my nephew Charles's quarrel, and meet you instead of him."

"You meet me?"

"Yes; I've met a better man more than once before. It can make no difference to you."

"I don't know that, Admiral Bell. One generally likes, in a duel, to face him with whom one has had the misunderstanding, be it on what grounds it may."

"There's some reason, I know, in what you say; but, surely, if I am willing, you need not object."

"And is your nephew willing thus to shift the danger and the job of resenting his own quarrels on to your shoulders?"

"No; he knows nothing about it. He has written you a challenge, of which I am the bearer, but I voluntarily, and of my own accord, wish to meet you instead."

"This is a strange mode of proceeding."

"If you will not accede to it, and fight him first, and any harm comes to him, you shall fight me afterwards."

"Indeed."

"Yes, indeed you shall, however surprised you may look."

"As this appears to be a family affair, then," said Sir Francis Varney, "it certainly does appear immaterial which of you I fight with first."

"Quite so; now you take a sensible view of the question. Will you meet me?"

"I have no particular objection. Have you settled all your affairs, and made your will?"

"What's that to you?"

"Oh, I only asked, because there is generally so much food for litigation if a man dies intestate, and is worth any money."

"You make devilish sure," said the admiral, "of being the victor. Have you made your will?"

"Oh, my will," smiled Sir Francis; "that, my good sir, is quite an indifferent affair."

"Well, make it or not, as you like. I am old, I know, but I can pull a trigger as well as any one."

"Do what?"

"Pull a trigger."

"Why, you don't suppose I resort to any such barbarous modes of fighting?"

"Barbarous! Why, how do you fight then?"

"As a gentleman, with my sword."

"Swords! Oh, nonsense! nobody fights with swords now a days. That's all exploded."

"I cling to the customs and the fashions of my youth," said Varney. "I have been, years ago, accustomed always to wear a sword, and to be without one now vexes me."

"Pray, how many years ago?"

"I am older than I look, but that is not the question. I am willing to meet you with swords if you like. You are no doubt aware that, as the challenged party, I am entitled to the choice of weapons."

"I am."

"Then you cannot object to my availing myself of the one in the use of which I am perfectly unequalled."

"Indeed."

"Yes, I am, I think, the first swordsman in Europe; I have had immense practice."

"Well, sir, you have certainly made a most unexpected choice of weapons. I can use a sword still, but am by no means I master of fencing.

However, it shall not be said that I went back from my word, and let the chances be as desperate as they may, I will meet you."

"Very good."

"With swords?"

"Ay, with swords; but I must have everything properly arranged, so that no blame can rest on me, you know. As you will be killed, you are safe from all consequences, but I shall be in a very different position; so, if you please, I must have this meeting got up in such a manner as shall enable me to prove, to whoever may question me on the subject, that you had fair play."

"Oh, never fear that."

"But I do fear it. The world, my good sir, is censorious, and you cannot stop people from saying extremely ill-natured things."

"What is it that you require, then?"

"I require that you send me a friend with a formal challenge."

"Well?"

"Then I shall refer him to a friend of mine, and they two must settle everything between them."

"Is that all?"

"Not quite. I will have a surgeon on the ground, in case, when I pink you, there should be a chance of saving your life. It always looks humane."

"When you pink me?"

"Precisely."

"Upon my word, you take these affairs easy. I suppose you have had a few of them?"

"Oh, a good number. People like yourself worry me into them. I don't like the trouble, I assure you; it is no amusement to me. I would rather, by a great deal, make some concession than fight, because I will fight with swords, and the result is then so certain that there is no danger in the matter to me."

"Hark you, Sir Francis Varney. You are either a very clever actor, or a man, as you say, of such skill with your sword, that you can make sure of the result of a duel. You know, therefore, that it is not fair play on your part to fight a duel with that weapon."

"Oh, I beg your pardon there. I never challenge anybody, and when foolish people call me out, contrary to my inclination, I think I am bound to take what care of myself I can."

"D — n me, there's some reason in that, too," said the admiral; "but why do you insult people?"

"People insult me first."

"Oh, nonsense!"

"How should you like to be called a vampyre, and stared at as if you were some hideous natural phenomenon?"

"Well, but —"

"I say, Admiral Bell, how should you like it? I am a harmless country gentleman, and because, in the heated imagination of some member of a crack-brained family, some housebreaker has been converted into a vampyre, I am to be pitched upon as the man, and insulted and persecuted accordingly."

"But you forget the proofs."

"What proofs?"

"The portrait, for one."

"What! Because there is an accidental likeness between me and an old picture, am I to be set down as a vampyre? Why, when I was in Austria last, I saw an old portrait of a celebrated court fool, and you so strongly resemble it, that I was quite struck when I first saw you with the likeness; but I was not so unpolite as to tell you that I considered you were the court fool turned vampyre."

"D — n your assurance!"

"And d — n yours, if you come to that."

The admiral was fairly beaten. Sir Francis Varney was by far too long-headed and witty for him. After now in vain endeavoring to find something to say, the old man buttoned up his coat in a great passion, and looking fiercely at Varney, he said, —

"I don't pretend to a gift of the gab. D — n me, it ain't one of my peculiarities; but though you may talk me down, you shan't keep me down."

"Very good, sir."

"It is not very good. You shall hear from me."

"I am willing."

"I don't care whether you are willing or not. You shall find that when once I begin to tackle an enemy, I don't so easily leave him. One or both of us, sir, is sure to sink."

"Agreed."

"So say I. You shall find that I'm a tar for all weathers, and if you were hundred and fifty vampyres all rolled into one, I'd tackle you somehow."

The admiral walked to the door in high dudgeon; when he was near to it, Varney said, in some of his most winning and gentle accents, —

"Will you not take some refreshment, sir, before you go from my humble house?"

"No!" roared the admiral.

"Something cooling?"

"No!"

"Very good, sir. A hospitable host can do no more that offer to entertain his guests."

Admiral Bell turned at the door, and said, with some degree of intense bitterness, "You look rather poorly. I suppose, tonight, you will go and suck somebody's blood, you shark — you confounded vampyre! You ought to be made to swallow a red-hot brick, and then let dance about till it digests."

Varney smiled as he rang the bell, and said to a servant, —

"Show my very excellent friend Admiral Bell out. He will not take any refreshments."

The servant bowed, and preceded the admiral down the staircase; but, to his great surprise, instead of a compliment in the shape of a shilling or half-a-crown for his pains, he received a tremendous kick behind, with a request to go and take it to his master, with his compliments.

The fume that the old admiral was in beggars all description. He walked to Bannerworth Hall at such a rapid pace, that Jack Pringle had the greatest difficulty in the world to keep up with him, so as to be at all within speaking distance.

"Hilloa, Jack," cried the old man, when they were close to the Hall. "Did you see me kick that fellow?"

"Ay, ay, sir."

"Well, that's some consolation, at any rate, if somebody saw it. It ought to have been his master, that's all I can say to it, and I wish it had."

"How have you settled it, sir?"

"Settled what?"

"The fight, sir."

"D — n me, Jack, I haven't settled it at all."

"That's bad, sir."

"I know it is; but it shall be settled for all that, I can tell him, let him vapor as much as he may about pinking me, and one thing and another."

"Pinking you, sir?"

"Yes. He wants to fight with cutlasses, or toasting-forks, d — n me, I don't know exactly which, and then he must have a surgeon on the ground, for fear when he pinks me I shouldn't slip my cable in a regular way, and he should be blamed."

Jack gave a long whistle, as he replied, —

"Going to do it, sir?"

"I don't know what I'm going to do. Mind, Jack, mum's the word."

"Ay, ay, sir."

"I'll turn the matter over in my mind, and then decide upon what had best be done. If he pinks me, I'll take d——d good care he don't pink Charles."

"No, sir, don't let him do that. A *wamphigher*, sir, ain't no good opponent to anybody. I never seed one afore, but it strikes me as the best way to settle him, would be to shut him up in some little bit of a cabin, and then smoke him with brimstone, sir."

"Well, well, I'll consider, Jack, I'll consider. Something must be done, and that quickly too. Zounds, here's Charles — what the deuce shall I say to him, by way of an excuse, I wonder, for not arranging his affair with Varney? Hang me, if I ain't taken aback now, and don't know where to place a hand."

Chapter *XXIV.*

THE LETTER TO CHARLES. — THE QUARREL. — THE ADMIRAL'S NARRATIVE. — THE MIDNIGHT MEETING

*I*t was Charles Holland who now advanced hurriedly to meet the admiral. The young man's manner was anxious. He was evidently most intent upon knowing what answer could be sent by Sir Francis Varney to his challenge.

"Uncle," he said, "tell me at once, will he meet me? You can talk of particulars afterwards, but now tell me at once if he will meet me?"

"Why, as to that," said the admiral, with a great deal of fidgety hesitation, "you see, I can't exactly say."

"Not say!"

"No. He's a very odd fish. Don't you think he's a very odd fish, Jack Pringle?"

"Ay, ay, sir."

"There, you hear, Charles, that Jack is of my opinion that your opponent is an odd fish."

"But, uncle, why trifle with my impatience thus? Have you seen Sir Francis Varney?"

"Seen him. Oh, yes."

"And what did he say?"

"Why, to tell the truth, my lad, I advise you not to fight with him at all."

"Uncle, is this like you? This advice from you, to compromise my honor, after sending a man a challenge?"

"D – n it all, Jack, I don't know how to get out of it," said the admiral. "I tell you what it is, Charles, he wants to fight with swords; and what on earth is the use of your engaging with a fellow who has been practicing at his weapon for more than a hundred years?"

"Well, uncle, if any one had told me that you would be terrified by this Sir Francis Varney into advising me not to fight, I should have had no hesitation whatever in saying such a thing was impossible."

"I terrified?"

"Why, you advise me not to meet this man, even after I have challenged him."

"Jack," said the admiral, "I can't carry it on, you see. I never could go on with anything that was not as plain as an anchor, and quite straightforward. I must just tell all that has occurred."

"Ay, ay, sir. The best way."

"You think so, Jack?"

"I know it is, sir, always axing pardon for having a opinion at all, excepting when it happens to be the same as yourn, sir."

"Hold your tongue, you libelous villain! Now, listen to me, Charles. I got up a scheme of my own."

Charles gave a groan, for he had a very tolerable appreciation of his uncle's amount of skill in getting up a scheme of any kind of description.

"Now here am I," continued the admiral, "an old hulk, and not fit for use any more. What's the use of me, I should like to know? Well, that's settled. But you are young and hearty, and have a long life before you. Why should you throw away your life upon a lubberly vampyre?"

"I begin to perceive now, uncle," said Charles, reproachfully, "why you, with such apparent readiness, agreed to this duel taking place."

"Well I intended to fight the fellow myself, that's the long and short of it, boy."

"How could you treat me so?"

"No nonsense, Charles. I tell you it was all in the family. I intended to fight him myself. What was the odds whether I slipped my cable with his assistance, or in the regular course a little after this? That's the way to argufy the subject; so, as I tell you, I made up my mind to fight him myself."

Charles looked despairingly, but said, –

"What was the result?"

"Oh, the result! D – n me, I suppose that's to come. The vagabond won't fight like a Christian. He says he's quite willing to fight anybody that calls him out, provided it's all regular."

"Well – well."

"And he, being the party challenged – for he says he never himself challenges anybody, as he is quite tired of it — must have his choice of weapons."

"He is entitled to that; but it is generally understood now-a-days that pistols are the weapons in use among gentlemen for such purposes."

"Ah, but he won't understand any such thing, I tell you. He will fight with swords."

"I suppose he is, then, an adept at the use of the sword?"

"He says he is."

"No doubt — no doubt. I cannot blame a man for choosing, when he has the liberty of choice, that weapon in the use of which he most particularly, from practice, excels."

"Yes; but if he be one half the swordsman he has had time enough, according to all accounts, to be, what sort of chance have you with him?"

"Do I hear you reasoning thus?"

"Yes, to be sure you do. I have turned wonderfully prudent, you see: so I mean to fight him myself, and mind, now, you have nothing whatever to do with it."

"An effort of prudence that, certainly."

"Well, didn't I say so?"

"Come — come, uncle, this won't do. I have challenged Sir Francis Varney, and I must meet him with any weapon he may, as the challenged party, choose to select. Besides, you are not, I dare say, aware that I am a very good fencer, and probably stand as fair a chance as Varney in a contest with swords."

"Indeed!"

"Yes, uncle. I could not be so long on the continent as I have been without picking up a good knowledge of the sword, which is so popular all over Germany."

"Humph! but only consider, this d——d fellow is no less than a hundred and fifty years old."

"I care not."

"Yes, but I do."

"Uncle, uncle, I tell you I will fight with him; and if you do not arrange matters for me so that I can have the meeting with this man, which I have myself sought, and cannot, even if I wished, now recede from with honor, I must seek some other less scrupulous friend to do so."

"Give me an hour or two to think of it, Charles," said the admiral. "Don't speak to any one else, but give me a little time. You shall have no cause of complaint. Your honor cannot suffer in my hands."

"I will wait your leisure, uncle; but remember that such affairs as these, when once broached, had always better be concluded with all convenient dispatch."

"I know that, boy — I know that."

The admiral walked away, and Charles, who really felt much fretted at the delay which had taken place, returned to the house.

He had not been there long, when a lad, who had been temporarily hired during the morning by Henry to answer the gate, brought him a note saying, —

"A servant, sir, left this for you just now."

"For me?" said Charles as he glanced at the direction. "This is strange, for I have no acquaintance about here. Does any one wait?"

"No, sir."

The note was properly directed to him, therefore Charles Holland at once opened it. A glance at the bottom of the page told him that it came from his enemy, Sir Francis Varney, and then he read it with much eagerness. It ran thus: —

"SIR, — Your uncle, as he stated himself to be, Admiral Bell, was the bearer to me, as I understood him this day, of a challenge from you. Owing to some unaccountable hallucination of intellect, he seemed to imagine that I intended to set myself up as a sort of animated target, for any one to shoot at who might have a fancy so to do.

"According to this eccentric view of the case, the admiral had the kindness to offer to fight me first, when, should he not have the good fortune to put me out of the world, you were to try your skill, doubtless.

"I need scarcely say that I object to these family arrangements. You have challenged me, and fancying the offence sufficient, you defy me to mortal combat. If, therefore, I fight with any one at all, it must be with you.

"You will clearly understand me, sir, that I do not accuse you of being at all privy to this freak of intellect of your uncle's. He, no doubt, alone conceived it, with a laudable desire on his part of serving you. If, however, you have any inclination to meet me, do so tonight, in the middle of the park surrounding your own friends' estate.

"There is a pollard oak growing close to a small pool; you, no doubt, have noticed the spot often. Meet me there, if you please, and any satisfaction you like I will give you, at twelve o'clock this night.

"Come alone, or you will not see me. It shall be at your own option entirely, to convert the meeting to a hostile one or not. You need send me no answer to this. If you are at the place I mention at the time I have named, well and good. If you are not, I can only, if I please, imagine that you shrink from a meeting with

"FRANCIS VARNEY."

Charles Holland read this letter twice over carefully, and then folding it up, and placing it in his pocket, he said, —

"Yes, I will meet him; he may be assured that I do not shrink from Francis Varney. In the name of honor, love, virtue, and Heaven, I will meet this man, and it shall go hard with me but I will this night wring from him the secret of what he really is. For the sake of her who is so dear to me — for her sake, I will meet this man, or monster, be he what he may."

It would have been far more prudent had Charles informed Henry Bannerworth or George of his determination to meet the vampyre that evening, but he did not do so. Somehow he fancied it would be some reproach against his courage if he did not go, and go alone, too, for he could not help suspecting that, from the conduct of his uncle, Sir Francis Varney might have got up an opinion inimical to his courage.

With all the eager excitement of youth, there was nothing that arrayed itself to his mind in such melancholy and uncomfortable colors as an imputation upon his courage.

"I will show this vampyre, if he be such," he said, "that I am not afraid to meet him, and alone, too, at his own hour — at midnight, even when, if his preternatural powers be of more avail to him than at any other time, he can attempt, if he dare, to use them."

Charles resolved upon going armed, and with the greatest care he loaded his pistols, and placed them aside ready for action, when the time should come to set out to meet the vampyre at the spot in the park which had been particularly alluded to in his letter.

This spot was perfectly well known to Charles; indeed, no one could be a single day at Bannerworth Hall without noticing it, so prominent an object was that pollard oak, standing, as it did, alone, with the beautiful green sward all around it. Near it was the pool which had been mentioned, which was, in reality, a fishpond, and some little distance off commenced the thick plantation, among the intricacies of which Sir Francis Varney, or the vampyre, had been supposed to disappear, after the revivification of his body at the full of the moon.

This spot was in view of several of the windows of the house, so that if the night should happen to be a very light one, and any of the inhabitants of the Hall should happen to have the curiosity to look from those particular windows, no doubt the meeting between Charles Holland and the vampyre would be seen.

This, however, was a contingency which was nothing to Charles, whatever it might be to Sir Francis Varney, and he scarcely at all considered it was worth consideration. He felt more happy and comfortable now that everything seemed to be definitely arranged by which he could come to some sort of explanation with that mysterious being who had so effectually, as yet, succeeded in destroying his peace of mind and his prospects of happiness.

"I will this night force him to declare himself," thought Charles. "He shall tell me who and what he really is, and by some means I will endeavor to put an end to those frightful persecutions which Flora has suffered."

This was a thought which considerably raised Charles's spirits, and when he sought Flora again, which he now did, she was surprised to see him so much more easy and composed in his mind, which was sufficiently shown by his manner, than he had been but so short a time before.

"Charles," she said, "what has happened to give such an impetus to your spirits?"

"Nothing, dear Flora, nothing; but I have been endeavoring to throw from my mind all gloomy thoughts, and to convince myself that in the future you and I, dearest, may yet be very happy."

"Oh, Charles, if I could but think so."

"Endeavor, Flora, to think so. Remember how much our happiness is always in our own power, Flora, and that, let fate do her worst, so long as we are true to each other, we have a recompense for every ill."

"Oh, indeed, Charles, that is a dear recompense."

"And it is well that no force of circumstances short of death itself can divide us."

"True, Charles, true, and I am more than ever now bound to look upon you with a loving heart; for have you not clung to me generously under circumstances which, if any at all could have justified you in rending asunder every tie which bound us together, surely would have done so most fully."

"It is misfortune and distress that tries love," said Charles. "It is thus that the touchstone is applied to see if it be current gold indeed, or some base metal, which by a superficial glitter imitates it."

"And your love is indeed true gold."

"I am unworthy of one glance from those dear eyes if it were not."

"Oh, if we could but go from here, I think then we might be happy. A strong impression is upon my mind, and has been so for some time, that these persecutions to which I have been subjected are peculiar to this house."

"Think you so?"

"I do, indeed!"

"It may be so, Flora. You are aware that your brother has made up his mind that he will leave the Hall."

"Yes, yes."

"And that only in deference to an expressed wish of mine he put off the carrying such a resolve into effect for a few days."

"He said so much."

"Do not, however, imagine, dearest Flora, that those few days will be idly spent."

"Nay, Charles, I could not imagine so."

"Believe me, I have some hopes that in that short space of time I shall be able to accomplish yet something which shall have a material effect upon the present posture of affairs."

"Do not run into danger, Charles."

"I will not. Believe me, Flora, I have too much appreciation of the value of an existence which is blessed by your love, to encounter any needless risks."

"You say needless. Why do you not confide in me, and tell me if the object you have in view to accomplish in the few days delay is a dangerous one at all."

"Will you forgive me, Flora, if for once I keep a secret from you?"

"Then, Charles, along with the forgiveness I must conjure up a host of apprehensions."

"Nay, why so?"

"You would tell me if there were no circumstances that you feared would fill me with alarm."

"Now, Flora, your fears and not your judgment condemn me. Surely you cannot think me so utterly heedless as to court danger for danger's sake."

"No, not so——"

"You pause."

"And yet you have a sense of what you call honor, which, I fear, would lead you into much risk."

"I have a sense of honor; but not that foolish one which hangs far more upon the opinions of others than my own. If I thought a course of honor lay before me, and all the world, in a mistaken judgment, were to condemn it as wrong, I would follow it."

"You are right, Charles, you are right. Let me pray of you to be careful, and, at all events, to interpose no more delay to our leaving this house than you shall feel convinced is absolutely necessary for some object of real and permanent importance."

Charles promised Flora Bannerworth that for her sake, as well as his own, he would be most specially careful of his safety; and then in such endearing conversation as may well be supposed to be dictated by such hearts as theirs another happy hour was passed away.

They pictured to themselves the scene where first they met, and with a world of interest hanging on every word they uttered, they told each other of the first delightful dawnings of that affection which had sprung up between them, and which they fondly believed neither time nor circumstance would have the power to change or subvert.

In the meantime the old admiral was surprised that Charles was so patient, and had not been to him to demand the result of his deliberation.

But he knew not on what rapid pinions time flies, when in the presence of those whom we love. What was an actual hour, was but a fleeting minute to Charles Holland, as he sat with Flora's hand clasped in his, and looking at her sweet face.

At length a clock striking reminded him of his engagement with his uncle, and he reluctantly rose.

"Dear Flora," he said, "I am going to sit up to watch tonight, so be under no sort of apprehension."

"I will feel doubly safe," she said.

"I have now something to talk to my uncle about, and must leave you."

Flora smiled, and held out her hand to him. He pressed it to his heart. He knew not what impulse came over him, but for the first time he kissed the cheek of the beautiful girl.

With a heightened color she gently repulsed him. He took a long lingering look at her as he passed out of the room, and when the door was closed between them, the sensation he experienced was as if some sudden cloud has swept across the face of the sun, dimming to a vast extent its precious luster.

A strange heaviness came across his spirits, which before had been so unaccountably raised. He felt as if the shadow of some coming evil was resting on his soul — as if some momentous calamity was preparing for him, which would almost be enough to drive him to madness, and irredeemable despair.

"What can this be," he exclaimed, "that thus oppressed me? What feeling is this that seems to tell me, I shall never again see Flora Bannerworth?"

Unconsciously he uttered these words, which betrayed the nature of his worst forebodings.

"Oh, this is weakness," he then added. "I must fight out against this; it is mere nervousness. I must not endure it, I will not suffer myself thus to become the sport of imagination. Courage, courage, Charles Holland. There are real evils enough, without your adding to them by those of a disordered fancy. Courage, courage, courage."

Chapter XXV.

THE ADMIRAL'S OPINION. – THE REQUEST OF CHARLES.

Charles then sought the admiral, whom he found with his hands behind him, pacing to and fro in one of the long walks of the garden, evidently in a very unsettled state of mind. When Charles appeared, he quickened his pace, and looked in such a state of unusual perplexity that it was quite ridiculous to observe him.

"I suppose, uncle, you have made up your mind thoroughly by this time?"

"Well, I don't know that."

"Why, you have had long enough surely to think over it. I have not troubled you soon."

"Well, I cannot exactly say you have, but, somehow or another, I don't think very fast, and I have an unfortunate propensity after a time of coming exactly round to where I began."

"Then, to tell the truth, uncle, you can come to no sort of conclusion."

"Only one."

"And what may that be?"

"Why, that you are right in one thing, Charles, which is, that having sent a challenge to this fellow of a vampyre, you must fight him."

"I suspect that that is a conclusion you had from the first, uncle?"

"Why so?"

"Because it is an obvious and a natural one. All your doubts, and trouble, and perplexities, have been to try and find some excuse for not entertaining that opinion, and now that you really find it in vain to make it, I trust that you will accede as you first promised to do, and not seek by any means to thwart me."

"I will not thwart you, my boy, although in my opinion you ought not to fight with a vampyre."

"Never mind that. We cannot urge that as a valid excuse, so long as he chooses to deny being one. And after all, if he be really wrongfully suspected, you must admit that he is a very injured man."

"Injured! — nonsense. If he is not a vampyre, he's some other out-of-the-way sort of fish, you may depend. He's the oddest-looking fellow ever I came across in all my born days, ashore or afloat."

"Is he?"

"Yes, he is: and yet, when I come to look at the thing again, in my mind, some droll sights that I have seen come across my memory. The sea is a place for wonders and for mysteries. Why, we see more in a day and a night there, than you landsmen could contrive to make a whole twelvemonth's wonder of."

"But you never saw a vampyre, uncle?"

"Well, I don't know that. I didn't know anything about vampyres till I came here, but that was my ignorance, you know. There might have been lots of vampyres where I've been, for all I know."

"Oh, certainly, but as regards this duel, will you wait now until tomorrow morning, before you take any further steps in the matter?"

"Till tomorrow morning?"

"Yes, uncle."

"Why, only a little while ago, you were all eagerness to have something done off-hand."

"Just so; but now I have a particular reason for waiting until tomorrow morning."

"Have you? Well, as you please, boy — as you please. Have everything your own way."

"You are very kind, uncle; and now I have another favor to ask of you."

"What is it!"

"Why, you know that Henry Bannerworth receives but a very small sum out of the whole proceeds of the estate here, which ought, but for his father's extravagance, to be wholly at his disposal."

"So I have heard."

"I am certain he is at present distressed for money, and I have not much. Will you lend me fifty pounds, uncle, until my own affairs are sufficiently arranged to enable you to pay yourself again?"

"Will I! of course I will."

"I wish to offer that sum as an accommodation to Henry. From me, I dare say he will receive it freely, because he must be convinced how freely it is offered; and, besides, they look upon me now almost as a member of the family, in consequence of my engagement with Flora."

"Certainly, and quite correct too; there's a fifty-pound note, my boy; take it, and do what you like with it, and when you want any more, come to me for it."

"I know I could trespass thus far on your kindness, uncle."

"Trespass! It's no trespass at all."

"Well, we will not fall out about the terms in which I cannot help expressing my gratitude to you for many favors. Tomorrow, you will arrange the duel for me."

"As you please. I don't altogether like going to that fellow's house again."

"Well, then, we can manage, I dare say, by note."

"Very good. Do so. He puts me in mind altogether of a circumstance that happened a good while ago, when I was at sea, and not so old a man as I am now."

"Puts you in mind of a circumstance, uncle?"

"Yes; he's something like a fellow that figured in an affair that I know a good deal about; only I do think as my chap was more mysterious by a d——d sight than this one."

"Indeed!"

"Oh, dear, yes. When anything happens in an odd way at sea, it is as odd again as anything that occurs on land, my boy, you may depend."

"Oh, you only fancy that, uncle, because you have spent so long a time at sea."

"No, I don't imagine it, you rascal. What can you have on shore equal to what we have at sea? Why, the sights that come before us would make you landsmen's hairs stand up on end, and never come down again."

"In the ocean, do you mean, that you see those sights, uncle?"

"To be sure. I was once in the southern ocean, in a small frigate, looking out for a seventy-four we were to join company with, when a man at the mast-head sung out that he saw her on the larboard bow. Well, we thought it all right enough, and made away that quarter, when what do you think it turned out to be?"

"I really cannot say."

"The head of a fish."

"A fish!"

"Yes! a d——d deal bigger than the hull of a vessel. He was swimming along with his head just what I dare say he considered a shaving or so out of the water."

"But where were the sails, uncle?"

"The sails?"

"Yes; your man at the mast-head must have been a poor seaman not to have missed the sails."

"Ah, that's one of your shore-going ideas, now. You know nothing whatever about it. I'll tell you where the sails were, master Charley."

"Well, I should like to know."

"The spray, then, that he dashed up with a pair of fins that were close to his head, was in such a quantity, and so white, that they looked just like sails."

"Oh!"

"Ah! you may say 'oh!' but we all saw him — the whole ship's crew; and we sailed alongside of him for some time, till he got tired of us, and suddenly dived down, making such a vortex in the water, that the ship shook again, and seemed for about a minute as if she was inclined to follow him to the bottom of the sea."

"And what do you suppose it was, uncle?"

"How should I know?"

"Did you ever see it again?"

"Never; though others have caught a glimpse of him now and then in the same ocean, but never came so near him as we did, that ever I heard of, at all events. They may have done so."

"It is singular!"

"Singular or not, it's a fool to what I can tell you. Why I've seen things that if I were to set about describing them to you, you would say I was making up a romance."

"Oh, now; it's quite impossible, uncle, anyone could ever suspect you of such a thing."

"You'd believe me, would you?"

"Of course I would."

"Then here goes. I'll just tell you now of a circumstance that I haven't liked to mention to anybody yet."

"Indeed! why so?"

"Because I didn't want to be continually fighting people for not believing it; but here you have it: —

We were outward bound; a good ship, a good captain, and good messmates, you know, go far toward making a prosperous voyage a pleasant and happy one, and on this occasion we had every reasonable prospect of all.

Our hands were all tried men — they had been sailors from infancy; none of your French craft, that serve an apprenticeship and then become landlubbers again. Oh, no, they were stanch and true, and loved the sea as the sluggard loves his bed, or the lover his mistress.

Ay, and for the matter of that, the love was a more enduring and a more healthy love, for it increased with years, and made men love one another, and they would stand by each other while they had a limb to life — while they were able to chew a quid or wink an eye, leave alone wag a pigtail.

We were outward bound for Ceylon, with cargo, and were to bring spices and other matters home from the Indian market. The ship was new and good — a pretty craft; she sat like a duck upon the water, and a stiff breeze carried her along the surface of the waves without your rocking, and pitching, and tossing, like an old wash-tub at a mill-tail, as I have had the misfortune to sail in more than once afore.

No, no, we were well laden, and well pleased, and weighed anchor with light hears and a hearty cheer.

Away we went down the river, and soon rounded the North Foreland, and stood out in the Channel. The breeze was a steady and stiff one, and carried us through the water as though it had been made for us.

"Jack," said I to a messmate of mine, as he stood looking at the skies, then at the sails, and finally at the water, with a graver air than I thought was at all consistent with the occasion or circumstances.

"Well," he replied.

"What ails you? You seem as melancholy as if we were about to cast lots who should be eaten first. Are you well enough?"

"I am hearty enough, thank Heaven," he said, "but I don't like this breeze."

"Don't like the breeze!" said I; "why, mate, it is as good and kind a breeze as ever filled a sail. What would you have, a gale?"

"No, no; I fear that."

"With such a ship, and such a set of hearty able seamen, I think we could manage to weather out the stiffest gale that ever whistled through a yard."

"That may be; I hope it is, and I really believe and think so."

"Then what makes you so infernally mopish and melancholy?"

"I don't know, but can't help it. It seems to me as though there was something hanging over us, and I can't tell what."

"Yes, there are the colors, Jack, at the masthead they are flying over us with a hearty breeze."

"Ah! ah!" said Jack, looking up at the colors, and then went away without saying anything more, for he had some piece of duty to perform.

I thought my messmate had something on his mind that caused him to feel sad and uncomfortable, and I took no more notice of it; indeed, in the course of a day or two he was as merry as any of the rest, and had no more melancholy that I could perceive, but was as comfortable as anybody.

We had a gale off the coast of Biscay, and rode it out without the loss of a spar or a yard; indeed, without the slightest accident or rent of any kind.

"Now, Jack, what do you think of our vessel?" said I.

"She's like a duck upon water, rises and falls with the waves, and doesn't tumble up and down like a hoop over stones."

"No, no; she goes smoothly and sweetly; she is a gallant craft, and this is her first voyage, and I predict a prosperous one."

"I hope so," he said.

Well, we went on prosperously enough for about three weeks; the ocean was as calm and as smooth as a meadow, the breeze light but good, and we stemmed along majestically over the deep blue waters, and passed coast after coast, though all around was nothing but the apparently pathless main in sight.

"A better sailor I never stepped into," said the captain one day; "it would be a pleasure to live and die in such a vessel."

Well, as I said, we had been three weeks or thereabouts, when one morning, after the sun was up and the decks washed, we saw a strange man sitting on one of the water-casks that were on deck, for, being full, we were compelled to stow some of them on deck.

You may guess those on deck did a little more than stare at this strange and unexpected apparition. By jingo, I never saw men open their eyes wider in all my life, nor was I any exception to the rule. I stared, as well I might; but we said nothing for some minutes, and the stranger looked calmly on us, and then cocked his eye with a nautical air up at the sky, as if he expected to receive a two-penny-post letter from St. Michael, or a *billet doux* from the Virgin Mary.

"Where has he come from?" said one of the men in a low tone to his companion, who was standing by him at that moment.

"How can I tell?" replied his companion. "He may have dropped from the clouds; he seems to be examining the road; perhaps he is going back."

The stranger sat all this time with the most extreme and provoking coolness and unconcern; he deigned us but a passing notice, but it was very slight.

He was a tall, spare man — what is termed long and lathy — but he was evidently a powerful man. He had a broad chest, and long, sinewy arms, a hooked nose, and a black, eagle eye. His hair was curly, but frosted by age; it seemed as though it had been tinged with white at the extremities, but he was hale and active otherwise to judge from appearances.

Notwithstanding all this, there was a singular repulsiveness about him that I could not imagine the cause, or describe; at the same time there was an air of determination in his wild and singular-looking eyes, and over their whole there was decidedly an air and an appearance so sinister as to be positively disagreeable.

"Well," said I, after we had stood some minutes, "where did you come from, shipmate?"

He looked at me and then up at the sky, in a knowing manner.

"Come, come, that won't do; you have none of Peter Wilkins's wings, and couldn't come on the aerial dodge; it won't do; how did you get here?"

He gave me an awful wink, and made a sort of involuntary movement, which jumped him up a few inches, and he bumped down again on the water-cask.

"That's as much as to say," thought I, "that he's sat himself on it."

"I'll go and inform the captain," says I, "of this affair; he'll hardly believe me when I tell him, I am sure."

So saying, I left the deck and went to the cabin, where the captain was at breakfast, and related to him what I had seen respecting the stranger. The captain looked at me with an air of disbelief, and said, —

"What? — do you mean to say there's a man on board we haven't seen before?"

"Yes, I do, Captain, I never saw him afore, and he's sitting beating his heels on the water-cask on deck."

"The devil!"

"He is, I assure you, sir; and he won't answer any questions."

"I'll see to that. I'll see if I can't make the lubber say something, providing his tongue's not cut out. But how came he on board? Confound it, he can't be the devil, and dropped from the moon."

"Don't know, captain," said I. "He is evil-looking enough, to my mind, to be the father of evil, but it's ill bespeaking attentions from that quarter at any time."

"Go on, lad: I'll come up after you."

I left the cabin, and I heard the captain coming up after me. When I got on deck, I saw he had not moved from the place where I left him. There was a general commotion among the crew when they heard of the occurrence, and all crowded round him, save the man at the helm who had to remain at his post.

The captain now came forward, and the men fell a little back as he approached.

For a moment the captain stood silent, attentively examining the stranger, who was excessively cool, and stood the scrutiny with the same unconcern that he would had the captain been looking at his watch.

"Well, my man," said the captain, "how did you come here?"

"I'm part of the cargo," he said, with an indescribable leer.

"Part of the cargo be d——d!" said the captain, in sudden rage, for he thought the stranger was coming his jokes too strong, "I know you are not in the bills of lading."

"I'm contraband," replied the stranger; "and my uncle's the great cham of Tartary."

The captain stared, as well he might, and did not speak for some minutes; all the while the stranger kept kicking his heels against the water-casks and squinting up at the skies; it made us feel very queer.

"Well, I must confess you are not in the regular way of trading."

"Oh, no," said the stranger; "I am contraband — entirely contraband."

"And how did you come on board?"

At this question the stranger again looked curiously up at the skies, and continued to do so for more than a minute; he then turned his gaze upon the captain.

"No, no," said the captain: "Eloquent dumb show won't do with me; you didn't come, like Mother Shipton, upon a birch broom. How did you come on board my vessel?"

"I walked on board," said the stranger.

"You walked on board; and where did you conceal yourself?"

"Below."

"Very good; and why didn't you stay below altogether?"

"Because I wanted fresh air. I'm in a delicate state of health, you see; it doesn't do to stay in a confined place too long."

"Confound the binnacle!" said the captain; it was his usual oath when anything bothered him, and he could not make it out. "Confound the binnacle! — what a delicate-looking animal you are. I wish you had stayed where you were; your delicacy would have been all the same to me. Delicate, indeed!"

"Yes, very," said the stranger, coolly.

There was something so comic in the assertion of his delicateness of health, that we should have all laughed; but we were somewhat scared, and had not the inclination.

"How have you lived since you came on board?" inquired the captain.

"Very indifferently."

"But how? What have you eaten? and what have you drank?"

"Nothing; I assure you. All I did while I was below was —"

"What?"

"Why, I sucked my thumbs like a polar bear in its winter quarters."

And as he spoke the stranger put his two thumbs into his mouth, and extraordinary thumbs they were, too, for each would have filled an ordinary man's mouth.

"These," said the stranger, pulling them out, and gazing at them wistfully, and with a deep sigh he continued, —

"These were thumbs at one time; but they are nothing now to what they were."

"Confound the binnacle!" muttered the captain to himself, and then he added, aloud, —

"It's cheap living, however, but where are you going to, and why did you come aboard?"

"I wanted a cheap cruise, and I am gong there and back."

"Why, that's where we are going," said the captain.

"Then we are brothers," exclaimed the stranger, hopping off the water cask like a kangaroo, and bounding toward the captain, holding out his hand as though he would have shaken hands with him.

"No, no," said the captain; "I can't do it."

"Can't do it!" exclaimed the stranger, angrily. "What do you mean?"

"That I can't have anything to do with contraband articles; I am a fair trader, and do all above board. I haven't a chaplain on board, or he should offer up prayers for your preservation, and the recovery of your health, which seems so delicate."

"That be —"

"The strange didn't finish the sentence; he merely screwed his mouth up into an incomprehensible shape, and puffed out a lot of breath, with some force, and which sounded very much like a whistle; but, oh, what thick breath he had, it was as much like smoke as anything I ever saw, and so my shipmate said.

"I say, captain," said the stranger, as he saws him pacing the deck.

"Well."

"Just send me up some beef and biscuit, and some coffee royal — be sure it's royal, do you hear, because I'm partial to brandy, it's the only good thing there is on earth."

I shall not easily forget the captain's look as he turned towards the stranger, and gave his huge shoulders a shrug, as much as to say, —

"Well, I can't help it now; he's here, and I can't throw him overboard."

The coffee, beef, and biscuit were sent him, and the stranger seemed to eat them with great *gout*, and drank the coffee with much relish, and returned the things saying,

"Your captain is an excellent cook; give him my compliments."

I thought the captain would think that was but a left-handed compliment, and look more angry than pleased, but no notice was taken of it.

It was strange, but this man had impressed upon all in the vessel some singular notion of his being more than he should be — more than a mere mortal, and not one endeavored to interfere with him; the captain was a stout and dare devil a fellow as you would well meet with, yet he seemed tacitly to acknowledge more than he would say, for he never after took any further notice of the stranger nor he of him.

They had barely any conversation, simply a civil word when they first met, and so forth; but there was little or no conversation of any kind between them.

The stranger slept upon deck, and lived upon deck entirely; he never once went below after we saw him, and his own account of being below so long.

This was very well, but the night watch did not enjoy his society, and would have willingly dispensed with it at that hour so particularly lonely and dejected upon the broad ocean, and perhaps a thousand miles away from the nearest point of land.

At this dread and lonely hour, when no sound reaches the ear and disturbs the rapt stillness of the night, save the whistling of the wind through the cordage, or an occasional dash of water against the vessel's side, the thoughts of the sailor are fixed on far distant objects — his own native land and the friends and loved ones he has left behind him.

He then thinks of the wilderness before, behind, and around him; of the immense body of water, almost in places bottomless; gazing upon such a scene, and with thoughts as strange and indefinite as the very boundless expanse before him it is no wonder if he should become superstitious; the time and place would indeed unbidden, conjure up thoughts and feelings of a fearful character and intensity.

The stranger at such times would occupy his favorite seat upon the water cask and looking up at the sky and then on the ocean, and between whiles he would whistle a strange, wild, unknown melody.

The flesh of the sailors used to creep up in knots and bumps when they heard it; the wind used to whistle as an accompaniment and pronounce fearful sounds to their ears.

The wind had been highly favorable from the first, and since the stranger had been discovered it had blown fresh, and we went along at a rapid rate, stemming the water, and dashing the spray off from the bows, and cutting the water like a shark.

This was very singular to us, we couldn't understand it, neither could the captain, and we looked very suspiciously at the stranger, and wished him at the bottom, for the freshness of the wind now became a gale, and yet the ship came through the water steadily, and away we went before the wind, as if the devil drove us; and mind I don't mean to say he didn't.

The gale increased to a hurricane, and though we had not a stitch of canvass out, yet we drove before the gale as if we had been shot out of the mouth of a gun.

The stranger still sat on the water casks, and all night long he kept up his infernal whistle. Now, sailors don't like to hear any one whistle when there's such a gale blowing over their heads — it's like asking for more; but he would persist, and the louder and stronger the wind blew, the louder he whistled.

At length there came a storm of rain, lightning, and wind. We were tossed mountains high, and the foam rose over the vessel, and often entirely over our heads, and the men were lashed to their posts to prevent being washed way.

But the stranger still lay on the water casks, kicking his heels and whistling his infernal tune, always the same. He wasn't washed away nor moved by the action of the water; indeed, we heartily hoped and expected to see both him and the water cask floated overboard at every minute; but, as the captain said, —

"Confound the binnacle! the old water tub seems as if it were screwed on to the deck, and won't move off and he on the top of it."

There was a strong inclination to throw him overboard, and the men conversed in low whispers, and came round the captain, saying, —

"We have come, captain, to ask you what you think of this strange man who has come so mysteriously on board?"

"I can't tell you what to think, lads; he's past thinking about — he's something above my comprehension altogether, I promise you."

"Well, then, we are thinking much of the same thing, captain."

"What do you mean?"

"That he ain't exactly one of our sort."

"No, he's no sailor, certainly; and yet, for a land lubber, he's about as rum a customer as ever I met with."

"So he is, sir."

"He stands salt water well; and I must say that I couldn't lay a top of those water casks in that style very well."

"Nor nobody amongst us, sir."

"Well, then, he's in nobody's way, is he? — nobody wants to take his berth, I suppose?"

The men looked at each other somewhat blank; they didn't understand the meaning at all — far from it; and the idea of any one's wanting to take the stranger's place on the water casks was so outrageously ludicrous that at any other time they would have considered it a devilish good joke and have never ceased laughing at it.

He paused some minutes, and then one of them said, —

"It isn't that we envy him his berth, captain, 'cause nobody else could live there for a moment. Any one amongst us that had been there would have been washed overboard a thousand times over."

"So they would," said the captain.

"Well, sir, he's more than us."

"Very likely; but how can I help that?"

"We think he's the main cause of all this racket in the heavens — the storm and hurricane; and that, in short, if he remains much longer we shall all sink."

"I am sorry for it. I don't think we are in any danger, and had the strange being any power to prevent it, he would assuredly do so, lest he got drowned."

"But we think if he were thrown over board all would be well."

"Indeed!"

"Yes, captain, you may depend upon it he's the cause of all the mischief. Throw him over board and that's all we want."

"I shall not throw him overboard, even if I could do such a thing; and I am by no means sure of anything of the kind."

"We do not ask it, sir."

"What do you desire?"

"Leave to throw him over board — it is to save our own lives."

"I can't let you do any such thing; he's in nobody's way."

"But he's always a whistling. Only hark now, and in such a hurricane as this, it is dreadful to think of it. What else can we do, sir? — he's not human."

At this moment, the stranger's whistling came clear upon their ears; there was the same wild, unearthly notes as before, but the cadences were stronger, and there was a supernatural clearness in all the tones.

"There now," said another, "he's kicking the water cask with his heels."

"Confound the binnacle!" said the captain; "it sounds like short peals of thunder. Go and talk to him, lads."

"And if that won't do, sir, may we —"

"Don't ask me any questions. I don't think a score of the best men that were ever born could move him."

"I don't mind trying," said one.

Upon this the whole of the men moved to the spot where the water casks were standing and the stranger lay.

There he was, whistling like fury, and, at the same time, beating his heels to the tune against the empty casks. We came up to him, and he took no notice of us at all, but kept on in the same way.

"Hilloa!" shouted one.

"Hilloa!" shouted another.

No notice, however, was taken of us, and one of our number, a big, Herculean fellow, an Irishman, seized him by the leg, either to make him get up, or, as we thought, to give him a lift over our heads into the sea. However, he had scarcely got his fingers round the calf of the leg, when the stranger pinched his leg so tight against the water cask, that he could not move, and was as effectually pinned as if he had been nailed there. The stranger, after he had finished a bar of the music, rose gradually to a sitting posture, and without the aid of his hands, and looking the unlucky fellow in the face, he said, —

"Well, what do you want?"

"My hand," said the fellow.

"Take it then," he said.

He did take it, and we saw that there was blood on it.

The stranger stretched out his left hand, and taking him by the breech, he lifted him, without any effort, upon the water-cask beside him.

We all stared at this, and couldn't help it; and we were quite convinced we could not throw him over board but he would probably have no difficulty in throwing us over board.

"Well, what do you want?" he again exclaimed to us all.

We looked at one another, and had scarce courage to speak; at length I said, —

"We wish you to leave off whistling."

"Leave off whistling!" he said. "And why should I do anything of the kind?"

"Because it brings the wind."

"Ha! ha! why that's the very reason I am whistling, to bring the wind."

"But we don't want so much."

"Pho! pho! you don't know what's good for you — it's a beautiful breeze, and not a bit too stiff."

"It's a hurricane."

"Nonsense."

"But it is."

"Now you see how I'll prove you are wrong in a minute. You see my hair, don't you?" he said, after he took off his cap. "Very well, look now."

He got up on the water-cask, and stood bolt upright; and running his fingers through his hair, made it all stand straight on end.

"Confound the binnacle!" said the captain, "if ever I saw the like."

"There," said the stranger, triumphantly, "don't tell me there's any wind to signify; don't you see, it doesn't even move one of my grey hairs; and if it blew as hard as you say, I am certain it would move a hair."

"Confound the binnacle!" muttered the captain as he walked away. "D — n the caboose, if he ain't older than I am — he's too many for me and everybody else."

"Are you satisfied?"

What could we say? — we turned away and left the place, and stood at our quarters — there was no help for it — we were compelled to grin and abide by it.

As soon as we had left the place he put his cap on again and sat down on the water casks, and then took leave of his prisoner, whom he set free, and there lay at full length on his back, with his legs hanging down. Once more he began to whistle most furiously, and beat time with his feet.

For full three weeks did he continue at this game night and day, without any interruption, save such as he required to consume enough coffee royal, junk and biscuit, as would have served three hearty men.

Well, about that time, one night the whistling ceased and he began to sing — oh! it was singing — such a voice! Gog and Magog in Guildhall, London, when they spoke were nothing to him — it was awful; but the wind calmed down to a fresh and stiff breeze. He continued at this game for three whole days and nights, and on the fourth it ceased, and when we went to take his coffee royal to him he was gone.

We hunted about everywhere, but he was entirely gone, and in three weeks after we safely cast anchor, having performed our voyage in a good month under the usual time; and had it been an old vessel she would have leaked and started like a tub from the straining; however, we were glad enough to get in, and were curiously inquisitive as to what was put in our vessel to come back with, for as the captain said, —

"Confound the binnacle! I'll have no more contraband articles if I can help it."

Chapter *XXVI.*

THE MEETING AT MOONLIGHT IN THE PARK. – THE TURRET WINDOW IN THE HALL. – THE LETTERS.

*T*he old admiral showed such a strong disposition to take offence at Charles if he should presume, for a moment, to doubt the truth of the narrative than was thus communicated to him, that the latter would not anger him by so doing, but confined his observations upon it to saying that he considered it was very wonderful, and very extraordinary, and so on, which very well satisfied the old man.

The day was now, however, getting far advanced, and Charles Holland began to think of his engagement with the vampyre. He read and read the letter over and over again, but he could not come to a correct conclusion as to whether it intended to imply that he, Sir Francis Varney, would wish to fight him at the hour and place mentioned, or merely give him a meeting as a preliminary step.

He was rather, on the whole, inclined to think that some explanation would be offered by Varney, but at all events he persevered in his determination of going well armed, lest anything in the shape of treachery should be intended.

As nothing of any importance occurred now in the interval of time till nearly midnight, we will at once step to that time, and our readers will suppose it to be a quarter to twelve o'clock at night, and young Charles Holland on the point of leaving the house, to keep his appointment by the pollard oak, with the mysterious Sir Francis Varney.

He placed his loaded pistols conveniently in his pocket, so that at a moment's notice he could lay hands on them, and then wrapping himself up in a traveling cloak he had brought with him to Bannerworth

Hall, he prepared to leave his chamber.

The moon still shone, although now somewhat on the wane, and although there were certainly many clouds in the sky they were but of a light fleecy character, and very little interrupted the rays of light that came from the nearly full disc of the moon.

From his window he could not perceive the spot in the park where he was to meet Varney, because the room in which he was occupied not a sufficiently high place in the house to enable him to look over a belt of trees that stopped the view. From almost any of the upper windows the pollard oak could be seen.

It so happened now that the admiral had been placed in a room immediately above the one occupied by his nephew, and, as his mind was full of how he should manage with regard to arranging the preliminaries of the duel between Charles and Varney on the morrow, he found it difficult to sleep; and after remaining in bed about twenty minutes, and finding that each moment he was only getting more and more restless, he adopted a course which he always did under such circumstances.

He rose and dressed himself again, intending to sit up for an hour and then turn into bed and try a second time to get to sleep. But he had no means of getting a light, so he drew the heavy curtain from before the window, and let in as much of the moonlight as he could.

This window commanded a most beautiful and extensive view, for from it the eye could carry completely over the tops of the tallest trees, so that there was no interruption whatever to the prospect, which was as extensive as it was delightful.

Even the admiral, who never would confess to seeing much beauty in scenery where water formed not a large portion of it, could not resist opening his window and looking out, with a considerable degree of admiration, upon wood and dale, as they were illuminated by the moon's rays, softened, and rendered, if anything, more beautiful by the light vapors, though which they had to struggle to make their way.

Charles Holland, in order to avoid the likelihood of meeting with any one who would question him as to where he was going, determined upon leaving his room by the balcony, which, as we are aware, presented ample facilities for his so doing.

He cast a glance at the portrait in the panel before he left the apartment, and then saying —

"For you, dear Flora, for you I essay this meeting with the fearful original of that portrait," he immediately opened his window, and stepped out on to the balcony.

Young and active as was Charles Holland, to descend from that balcony presented to him no difficulty whatever, and he was, in a very few moments, safe in the garden of Bannerworth Hall.

He never thought, for a moment, to look up, or he would, in an instant, have seen the white head of his old uncle, as it was projected over the sill of the window of his chamber.

The drop of Charles from the balcony of his window, just made sufficient noise to attract the admiral's attention, and, then, before he could think of making any alarm, he saw Charles walking hastily across a grass plot, which was sufficiently in the light of the moon to enable the admiral at once to recognize him, and leave no sort of doubt as to his positive identity.

Of course, upon discovering that it was Charles, the necessity for making an alarm no longer existed, and, indeed, not knowing what it was that had induced him to leave his chamber, a moment's reflection suggested to him the propriety of not even calling to Charles, lest he should defeat some discovery which he might be about to make.

"He has heard something, or seen something," thought the admiral, "and is gone to find out what it is. I only wish I was with him; but up here I can do nothing at all, that's quite clear."

Charles, he saw, walked very rapidly, and like a man who has some fixed destination which he wishes to reach as quickly as possible.

When he dived among the trees which skirted one side of the flower gardens, the admiral was more puzzled than ever, and he said —

"Now where on earth is he off to? He is fully dressed and has his cloak about him."

After a few moments' reflection he decided that, having seen something suspicious, Charles must have got up, and dressed himself, to fathom it.

The moment this idea became fairly impressed upon his mind, he left his bedroom, and descended to where one of the brothers he knew was sitting up, keeping watch during the night. It was Henry who was so on guard; and when the admiral came into the room, he uttered an expression of surprise to find him up, for it was now some time past twelve o'clock.

"I have come to tell you that Charles has left the house," said the admiral.

"Left the house?"

"Yes; I saw him just now go across the garden."

"And you are sure it was he?"

"Quite sure. I saw him by the moonlight cross the green plot."

"Then you may depend he has seen or heard something, and gone alone to find out what it is rather than give any alarm."

"That is just what I think."

"It must be so. I will follow him, if you can show me exactly which way he went."

"That I can easily. And in case I should have made any mistake, which it is not at all likely, we can go to his room first and see if it is empty."

"A good thought, certainly, that will at once put an end to all doubt upon the question."

They both immediately proceeded to Charles's room, and then the admiral's accuracy of identification of his nephew was immediately proved by finding that Charles was not there, and that the window was wide open.

"You see I am right," said the admiral.

"You are," cried Henry; "but what have we here?"

"Where?"

"Here on the dressing-table. Here are no less than three letters, all laid as if on purpose to catch the eye of the first one who might enter the room."

"Indeed!"

"You perceive them?"

Henry held them to the light, and after a moment's inspection of them, he said, in a voice of much surprise, —

"Good God! what is the meaning of this?"

"The meaning of what?"

"The letters are addressed to parties in the house here. Do you not see?"

"To whom?"

"One to Admiral Bell —"

"The deuce!"

"Another to me, and the third to my sister Flora. There is some new mystery here."

The admiral looked at the superscription of one of the letters which was handed to him in silent amazement. Then he cried, —

"Set down the light, and let us read them."

Henry did so, and then they simultaneously opened the epistles which were severally addressed to them. There was a silence, as of the very grave, for some moments, and then the old admiral staggered to a seat, as he exclaimed, —

"Am I dreaming — am I dreaming?"

"Is this possible?" said Henry, in a voice of deep emotion, as he allowed the note addressed to him to drop on to the floor.

"D — n it, what does yours say?" cried the old admiral in a louder tone.

"Read it — what says yours?"

"Read it — I am amazed."

The letters were exchanged, and read by each with the same breathless attention they had bestowed upon their own; after which, they both looked at each other in silence, pictures of amazement, and the most absolute state of bewilderment.

Not to keep our readers in suspense, we at once transcribe each of these letters.

The one to the admiral contained these words, —

"MY DEAR UNCLE,

"Of course you will perceive the prudence of keeping this letter to yourself, but the fact is, I have now made up my mind to leave Bannerworth Hall.

"Flora Bannerworth is not now the person she was when first I knew her and loved her. Such being the case, and she having altered, not I, she cannot accuse me of fickleness.

"I still love the Flora Bannerworth I first knew, but I cannot make my wife one who is subject to the visitations of a vampyre.

"I have remained here long enough now to satisfy myself that this vampyre business is no delusion. I am quite convinced that it is a positive fact, and that, after death, Flora will herself become one of the horrible existences known by that name.

"I will communicate to you from the first large city on the continent whither I am going, at which I make any stay, and in the meantime, make what excuses you like at Bannerworth Hall, which I advise you to leave as quickly as you can, and believe me to be, my dear uncle, yours truly,

"CHARLES HOLLAND"

Henry's letter was this: —

"MY DEAR SIR,

"If you calmly and dispassionately consider the painful and distressing circumstances in which your family are placed, I am sure that, far from blaming me for the step which this note will announce to you I have taken, you will be the first to give me credit for acting with an amount of prudence and foresight which was highly necessary under the circumstances.

"If the supposed visits of the vampyre to your sister Flora had turned out, as at first I hoped they would, a delusion, and been in any satisfactory manner explained away I should certainly have felt pride and pleasure in fulfilling my engagement to that young lady.

"You must, however, yourself feel that the amount of evidence in favor of a belief that an actual vampyre has visited Flora, enforces a conviction of its truth.

"I cannot, therefore, make her my wife under such very singular circumstances.

"Perhaps you may blame me for not taking at once advantage

of the permission given me to forego my engagement when first I came to your house; but the fact is, I did not then in the least believe in the existence of the vampyre, but since a positive conviction of that most painful fact has now forced itself upon me, I beg to decline the honor of an alliance which I had at one time looked forward to with the most considerable satisfaction.

"I shall be on the continent as fast as conveyances can take me, therefore, should you entertain any romantic notions of calling me to an account for a course of proceeding I think perfectly and fully justifiable, you will not find me.

"Accept my assurances of my respect of yourself and pity for your sister, and believe me to be, my dear sir, your sincere friend,

"CHARLES HOLLAND."

These two letters might well make the admiral stare at Henry Bannerworth, and Henry stare at him.

An occurrence so utterly and entirely unexpected by both of them, was enough to make them doubt the evidence of their own senses. But there were the letters, as a damning evidence of the outrageous fact, and Charles Holland was gone.

It was the admiral who first recovered from the stunning effect of the epistles, and he, with a gesture of perfect fury, exclaimed, —

"The scoundrel! — the cold-blooded villain! I renounce him forever! he is no nephew of mine; he is some d——d imposter! Nobody with a dash of my family blood in his veins would have acted so to save himself from a thousand deaths."

"Who shall we trust now," said Henry, "when those whom we take to our inmost hearts deceive us thus? This is the greatest shock I have yet received. If there be a pang greater than another, surely it is to be found in the faithlessness and heartlessness of one we loved and trusted."

"He is a scoundrel!" roared the admiral. "D — n him, he'll die on a dunghill, and that's too good a place for him. I cast him off — I'll find him out, and old as I am, I'll fight him — I'll wring his neck, the rascal, and as for poor dear Miss Flora, God bless her! I'll — I'll marry her myself and make her an admiral. — I'll marry her myself. Oh, that I should be uncle to such a rascal!"

"Calm yourself," said Henry, "no one can blame you."

"Yes, you can; I had no right to be his uncle, and I was an old fool to love him."

The old man sat down, and his voice became broken with emotion as he said, —

"Sir, I tell you I would have died willingly rather than this should have happened. This will kill me now, — I shall die now of shame and grief."

Tears gushed from the admiral's eyes, and the sight of the noble old man's emotion did much to calm the anger of Henry, which, although he said but little, was boiling at his heart like a volcano.

"Admiral Bell," he said, "you have nothing to do with this business; we cannot blame you for the heartlessness of another. I have but one favor to ask of you."

"What — what can I do?"

"Say no more about him at all."

"I can't help saying something about him. You ought to turn me out of the house."

"Heaven forbid! What for?"

"Because I'm his uncle — his d——d old fool of an uncle, that has always thought so much of him."

"Nay, my good sir, that was a fault on the right side, and cannot discredit you. I though him the most perfect of human beings."

"Oh, if I could but have guessed this."

"It was impossible. Such duplicity never was equaled in this world — it was impossible to foresee it."

"Hold — hold! did he give you fifty pounds?"

"What?"

"Did he give you fifty pounds?"

"Give me fifty pounds! Most decidedly not; what made you think of such a thing?"

"Because today he borrowed fifty pounds of me, he said, to lend to you."

"I never heard of the transaction until this moment."

"The villain!"

"No doubt, sir, he wanted that amount to expedite his progress abroad."

"Well, now, damme, if an angel had come to me and said 'Hiloa! Admiral Bell, your nephew, Charles Holland, is a thundering rogue,' I should have said 'You're a liar!'"

"This is fighting against facts, my dear sir. He is gone — mention him no more; forget him, as I shall endeavor myself to do, and persuade my poor sister to do."

"Poor girl! what can we say to her?"

"Nothing, but give her all the letters, and let her be at once satisfied of the worthlessness of him she loved."

"The best way. Her woman's pride will then come to her help."

"I hope it will. She is of an honorable race, and I am sure she will not condescend to shed a tear for such a man as Charles Holland has proved himself to be."

"D — n him, I'll find him out, and make him fight you. He shall give you satisfaction."

"No, no."

"No? But he shall."

"I cannot fight with him."

"You cannot?"

"Certainly not. He is too far beneath me now. I cannot fight on honorable terms with one whom I despise as too dishonorable to contend with. I have nothing now but silence and contempt."

"I have though, for I'll break his neck when I see him, or he shall break mine. The villain! I'm ashamed to stay here, my young friend."

"How mistaken a view you take of this matter, my dear sir. As Admiral Bell, a gentleman, a brave officer, and a man of the purest and most unblemished honor, you confer a distinction upon us by your presence here."

The admiral wrung Henry by the hand, as he said, —

"Tomorrow — wait until tomorrow; we will talk over this matter tomorrow — I cannot tonight, I have not patience; but tomorrow, my dear boy, we will have it all out. God bless you. Good night.

Chapter XXVII.

THE NOBLE CONFIDENCE OF FLORA BANNERWORTH IN HER LOVER. — HER OPINION OF THE THREE LETTERS. — THE ADMIRAL'S ADMIRATION.

*T*o describe the feelings of Henry Bannerworth on the occasion of this apparent defalcation from the path of rectitude and honor by his friend, as he had fondly imagined Charles Holland to be, would be next to impossible.

If, as we have taken occasion to say, it be a positive fact, that a noble and a generous mind feels more acutely any heartlessness of this description from one on whom it has placed implicit confidence, than the most deliberate and wicked of injuries from absolute strangers, we can easily conceive that Henry Bannerworth was precisely the person to feel most acutely the conduct whence all circumstances appeared to fix upon Charles Holland, upon whose faith, truth, and honor, he would have staked his very existence but a few short hours before.

With such a bewildered sensation that he scarcely knew where he walked or whither to betake himself, did he repair to his own chamber, and there he strove, with what energy he was able to bring to the task, to find out some excuse, if he could, for Charles's conduct. But he could find none. View it in what light he would, it presented by a picture of the most heartless selfishness it had ever been his lot to encounter.

The tone of the letters, too, which Charles had written, materially aggravated the moral delinquency of which he had been guilty; better, far better, had he not attempted an excuse at all than have attempted such excuses as were there put down in those epistles.

A more cold-blooded, dishonorable proceeding could not possibly be conceived.

It would appear, that while he entertained a doubt with regard to the reality of the visitation of the vampyre to Flora Bannerworth, he had been willing to take to himself abundance of credit for the most honorable feelings, and to induce a belief in the minds of all that an exalted feeling of honor, as well as a true affection that would know no change, kept him at the feet of her whom he loved.

Like some braggart, who, when there is no danger, is a very hero, but who, the moment he feels convinced he will be actually and truly called upon for an exhibition of his much-vaunted prowess, had Charles Holland deserted the beautiful girl, who, if anything, had now certainly, in her misfortunes, a far higher claim upon his kindly feeling than before.

Henry could not sleep, although, at the request of George, who offered to keep watch for him the remainder of the night, he attempted to do so.

He in vain said to himself, "I will banish from my mind this most unworthy subject. I have told Admiral Bell that contempt is the only feeling I can now have for his nephew, and yet I now find myself dwelling upon him, and upon his conduct, with a perseverance which is a foe to my repose."

At length came the welcome and beautiful light of day, and Henry rose fevered and unrefreshed.

His first impulse now was to hold a consultation with his brother George, as to what was to be done, and George advised that Mr. Marchdale, who as yet knew nothing of the matter, should be immediately informed of it, and consulted, as being probably better qualified than either of them to come to a just, a cool, and a reasonable opinion upon the painful circumstance, which it could not be expected that either of them would be able to view calmly.

"Let it be so, then," said Henry; "Mr. Marchdale shall decide for us."

They at once sought this friend of the family, who was in his own bed-room, and when Henry knocked at the door, Marchdale opened it hurriedly, eagerly inquiring what was the matter.

"There is no alarm," said Henry. "We have only come to tell you of a circumstance which has occurred during the night, and which will somewhat surprise you."

"Nothing calamitous, I hope?"

"Vexatious; and yet, I think it is a matter upon which we ought almost to congratulate ourselves. Read those two letters, and give us your candid opinion upon them."

Henry placed in Mr. Marchdale's hands the letter addressed to himself, as well as that to the admiral.

Marchdale read them both with marked attention, but he did not exhibit in his countenance so much surprise as regret.

When he had finished, Henry said to him, —

"Well, Marchdale, what think you of this new and extraordinary episode in our affairs?"

"My dear young friends," said Marchdale, in a voice of great emotion, "I know not what to say to you. I have no doubt but that you are both of you much astonished at the receipt of these letters, and equally so at the sudden absence of Charles Holland."

"And are not you?"

"Not so much as you, doubtless, are. The fact is, I never did entertain a favorable opinion of the young man, and he knew it. I have been accustomed to the study of human nature under a variety of aspects; I have made it a matter of deep, and I may add, sorrowful, contemplation, to study and remark those minor shades of character which commonly escape observation wholly. And, I repeat, I always had a bad opinion of Charles Holland, which he guessed, and hence he conceived a hatred to me, which more than once, as you cannot but remember, showed itself in little acts of opposition and hostility."

"You much surprise me."

"I expected to do so. But you cannot help remembering that at one time I was on the point of leaving here solely on his account."

"You were so."

"Indeed I should have done so, but that I reasoned with myself upon the subject, and subdued the impulse of the anger which some years ago, when I had not seen so much of the world, would have guided me."

"But why did you not impart to us your suspicions? We should at least, then, have been prepared for such a contingency as has occurred."

"Place yourself in my position, and then ask yourself what you would have done. Suspicion is one of those hideous things which all men would be most specially careful not only how they entertain at all, but how they give expression to. Besides, whatever may be the amount of one's own internal conviction with regard to the character of any one, there is just a possibility that one may be wrong."

"True, true."

"That possibility ought to keep any one silent who has nothing but suspicion to go upon, however cautious it may make him, as regards his dealings with the individual. I only suspected from little minute shades of character, that would peep out in spite of him, that Charles Holland was not the honorable man he would fain have had everybody believe him to be."

"And had you from the first such a feeling?"

"I had."

"It is very strange."

"Yes; and what is more strange still, is that he from the first seemed to know it; and despite a caution which I could see he always kept uppermost in his thought, he could not help speaking tartly to me at times."

"I have noticed that," said George.

"You may depend it is a fact," added Marchdale, "that nothing so much excites the deadly and desperate hatred of a man who is acting a hypocritical part, as the suspicion, well grounded or not, that another sees and understands the secret impulses of his dishonorable heart."

"I cannot blame you, or any one else, Mr. Marchdale," said Henry, "that you did not give utterance to your secret thought, but I do wish that you had done so."

"Nay, dear Henry," replied Mr. Marchdale, "believe me, I have made this matter a subject of deep thought, and have abundance of reasons why I ought not to have spoken to you upon the subject."

"Indeed!"

"Indeed I have, and not among the least important is the one, that if I had acquainted you with my suspicions, you would have found yourself in the painful position of acting a hypocritical part yourself towards this Charles Holland, for you must either have kept the secret that he was suspected, or you must have shewn it to him by your behavior."

"Well, well, I dare say, Marchdale, you acted for the best. What shall we do now?"

"Can you doubt?"

"I was thinking of letting Flora at once know the absolute and complete worthlessness of her lover, so that she could have no difficulty in at once tearing herself from him by the assistance of the natural pride which would surely come to her aid, upon finding herself so much deceived."

"The test may be possible."

"You think so?"

"I do, indeed."

"Here is a letter, which of course remains unopened, addressed to Flora by Charles Holland. The admiral rather thought it would hurt her feelings to deliver her such an epistle, but I must confess I am of the contrary opinion upon that point, and think now the more evidence she has of the utter worthlessness of him who professed to love her with so much disinterested affection, the better it will be for her."

"You could not, possibly, Henry, have taken a more sensible view of the subject."

"I am glad you agree with me."

"No reasonable man could do otherwise, and from what I have seen of Admiral Bell, I am sure, upon reflection, he will be of the same opinion."

"Then it shall be so. The first shock to poor Flora may be severe, but we shall then have the consolation of knowing that it is the only one, and that in knowing the very worst, she has no more on that score to apprehend. Alas, alas! the hand of misfortune now appears to have pressed heavily upon us indeed. What in the name of all that is unlucky and disastrous, will happen next, I wonder?"

"What can happen?" said Marchdale; "I think you have now got rid of the greatest evil of all — a false friend."

"We have, indeed."

"Go, then, to Flora; assure her that in the affection of others who know no falsehood, she will find a solace from every ill. Assure her that there are hearts that will place themselves between her and every misfortune."

Mr. Marchdale was much affected as he spoke. Probably he felt deeper than he chose to express the misfortunes of that family for whom he entertained so much friendship. He turned aside his head to hide the traces of emotion which, despite even his great powers of self-command, would shew themselves upon his handsome and intelligent countenance. Then it appeared as if his noble indignation had got, for a few brief moments, the better of all prudence, and he exclaimed, —

"The villain! the worse than villain! who would, with a thousand artifices, make himself beloved by a young, unsuspecting, and beautiful girl, but then to leave her to the bitterness of regret, than she had ever given such a man a place in her esteem. The heartless ruffian!"

"Be calm, Mr. Marchdale, I pray you be calm," said George; "I never saw you so much moved."

"Excuse me," he said, "excuse me; I am much moved, and I am human. I cannot always, let me strive my utmost, place a curb upon my feelings."

"They are feelings which do you honor."

"Nay, nay, I am foolish to have suffered myself to be led away into such a hasty expression of them. I am accustomed to feel acutely and to feel deeply, but it is seldom I am so much overcome as this."

"Will you accompany us to the breakfast-room at once, Mr. Marchdale, where we will make this communication to Flora; you will then be able to judge by her manner of receiving it, what it will be best to say to her."

"Come, then, and pray be calm. The least that is said upon this painful and harassing subject, after this morning, will be the best."

"You are right — you are right."

Mr. Marchdale hastily put on his coat. He was dressed, with the exception of that one article of apparel, when the brothers came to his chamber, and then he came to the breakfast-parlor where the painful communication was to be made to Flora of her lover's faithlessness.

Flora was already seated in that apartment. Indeed, she had been accustomed to meet Charles Holland there before others of the family made their appearance, but, alas! this morning the kind and tender lover was not there.

The expression that sat upon the countenances of her brothers, and of Mr. Marchdale, was quite sufficient to convince her that something more serious than usual had occurred, and she at the moment turned very pale. Marchdale observed this change of countenance in her, and he advanced towards her, saying, —

"Calm yourself, Flora, we have something to communicate to you, but it is a something which should excite indignation, and no other feeling, in your breast."

"Brother, what is the meaning of this?" said Flora, turning aside from Marchdale, and withdrawing the hand which he would have taken.

"I would rather have Admiral Bell here before I say anything," said Henry, "regarding a matter in which he cannot but feel much interested personally."

"Here he is," said the admiral, who at that moment had opened the door of the breakfast room. "Here he is, so now fire away and don't spare the enemy."

"And Charles?" said Flora, "where is Charles?"

"D — n Charles!" cried the admiral, who had not been much accustomed to control his feelings.

"Hush! hush!" said Henry; "my dear sir, hush! do not indulge now in any invectives. Flora, here are three letters; you will see that the one which is unopened is addressed to yourself. However, we wish you to read the whole three of them, and then to form your own free and unbiased opinion."

Flora looked as pale as a marble statue, when she took the letters into her hands. She let the two that were open fall on the table before her, while she eagerly broke the seal of that which was addressed to herself.

Henry, with an instinctive delicacy, beckoned every one present to the window, so that Flora had not the pain of feeling that any eyes were fixed upon her but those of her mother, who had just come into the room, while she was perusing those documents which told such a tale of heartless dissimulation.

"My dear child," said Mrs. Bannerworth, "you are ill."

"Hush! mother — hush!" said Flora; "let me know all."

She read the whole of the letters through, and then, as the last one dropped from her grasp, she exclaimed, —

"Oh, God! oh, God! what is all that has occurred compared to this? Charles — Charles — Charles!"

"Flora!" exclaimed Henry, suddenly turning from the window. "Flora, is this worthy of you?"

"Heaven now support me!"

"Is this worthy of the name you bear, Flora? I should have thought, and I did hope, that woman's pride would have supported you."

"Let me implore you," added Marchdale, "to summon indignation to your aid, Miss Bannerworth."

"Charles — Charles — Charles!" she again exclaimed, as she wrung her hands despairingly.

"Flora, if anything could add a sting to my already irritated feelings," said Henry, "this conduct of yours would."

"Henry — brother, what mean you? Are you mad?"

"Are you, Flora?"

"God, I wish now that I was."

"You have read those letters, and yet you call upon the name of him who wrote them with frantic tenderness."

"Yes, yes," she cried; "frantic tenderness is the word. It is with frantic tenderness I call upon his name, and ever will. — Charles! Charles! — dear Charles!"

"This surpasses all belief," said Marchdale.

"It is the frenzy of grief," added George; "but I did not expect it of her. Flora — Flora, think again."

"Think — think — the rush of thought distracts. Whence came these letters? — where did you find these most disgraceful forgeries?"

"Forgeries!" exclaimed Henry; and he staggered back, as if some one had struck him a blow.

"Yes, forgeries!" screamed Flora. "What has become of Charles Holland? Has he been murdered by some secret enemy, and then these most vile fabrications made up in his name? Oh, Charles, Charles, are you lost to me for ever?"

"Good God!" said Henry; "I did not think of that."

"Madness! – madness!" cried Marchdale.

"Hold!" shouted the admiral. "Let me speak to her."

He pushed every one aside, and advanced to Flora. He seized both her hands in his own, and in a tone of voice that was struggling with feeling, he cried, –

"Look at me, my dear; I'm an old man – old enough to be your grandfather, so you needn't mind looking at me steadily in the face. Look at me, I want to ask you a question."

Flora raised her beautiful eyes, and looked the old weather-beaten admiral full in the face.

Oh! what a striking contrast did those two persons present to each other. That young and beautiful girl, with her small, delicate, childlike hands clasped, and completely hidden in the huge ones of the old sailor, the white, smooth skin contrasted with his wrinkled, hardened features.

"My dear," he cried, "you have read those – those d——d letters, my dear?"

"I have, sir."

"And what do you think of them?"

"They were not written by Charles Holland, your nephew."

A choking sensation seemed to come over the old man, and he tried to speak, but in vain. He shook the hands of the young girl violently, until he saw that he was hurting her, and then, before she could be aware of what he was about, he gave her a kiss on the cheek, as he cried, –

"God bless you – God bless you! You are the sweetest, dearest little creature that ever was, or that ever will be, and I'm a d——d old fool, that's what I am. These letters were not written by my nephew, Charles. He is incapable of writing them, and, d – n me, I shall take shame to myself as long as I live for ever thinking so."

"Dear sir," said Flora, who somehow or another did not seem at all offended at the kiss which the old man had given her; "dear sir, how could you believe, for one moment, that they came from him? There has been some desperate villainy on foot. Where is he? – oh, find him, if he be yet alive. If they who have thus striven to steal from him that honor, which is the jewel of his heart, have murdered him, seek them out, sir, in the sacred name of justice, I implore you."

"I will – I will. I don't renounce him; he is my nephew still – Charles Holland – my own dear sister's son; and you are the best girl, God bless you, that ever breathed. He loved you – he loves you still; and if he's above ground, poor fellow, he shall yet tell you himself he never saw those infamous letters."

"You – you will seek for him?" sobbed Flora, and the tears gushed from her eyes. "Upon you, sir, who, as I do, feel assured of his innocence, I alone rely. If all the world say he is guilty, we will not think so."

"I'm d—d if we do."

Henry had sat down by the table, and, with his hands clasped together, seemed in an agony of thought.

He was now roused by a thump on the back by the admiral, who cried, —

"What do you think, now, old fellow? D — n it, things look a little different now."

"As God is my judge," said Henry, holding up his hands, "I know not what to think, but my heart and feeling all go with you and with Flora, in your opinion of the innocence of Charles Holland."

"I knew you would say that, because you could not possibly help it, my dear boy. Now we are all right again, and all we have got to do is to find out which way the enemy has gone, and then give chase to him."

"Mr. Marchdale, what do you think of this new suggestion," said George to that gentleman.

"Pray, excuse me," was his reply; "I would much rather not be called upon to give an opinion."

"Why, what do you mean by that?" said the admiral.

"Precisely what I say, sir."

"D — n me, we had a fellow once in the combined fleets, who never had an opinion till after something had happened, and then he always said that was just what he thought."

"I was never in the combined, or any other fleet, sir," said Marchdale coldly.

"Who the devil said you were?" roared the admiral.

Marchdale merely hawed.

"However," added the admiral, "I don't care, and never did, for anybody's opinion, when I know I am right. I'd back this dear girl here for opinions, and good feelings, and courage to express them, against all the world, I would, any day. If I was not the old hulk I am, I would take a cruise in any latitude under the sun, if it was only for the chance of meeting with just such another."

"Oh, lose no time!" said Flora. "If Charles is not to be found in the house, lose no time in searching for him, I pray you; seek him, wherever there is the remotest probability he may chance to be. Do not let him think he is deserted."

"Not a bit of it," cried the admiral. "You make your mind easy, then, my dear. If he's above ground, we shall find him out, you may depend upon it. Come along master Henry, you and I will consider what had best be done in this uncommonly ugly matter."

Henry and George followed the admiral from the breakfast-room, leaving Marchdale there, who looked serious and full of melancholy thought.

It was quite clear that he considered Flora had spoken from the generous warmth of her affection as regarded Charles Holland, and not from the conviction which reason would have enforced her to feel.

When he was now alone with her and Mrs. Bannerworth, he spoke in a feeling and affectionate tone regarding the painful and inexplicable events which had transpired.

Chapter XXVIII.

MR. MARCHDALE'S EXCULPATION OF HIMSELF. – THE SEARCH THROUGH THE GARDENS. – THE SPOT OF THE DEADLY STRUGGLE. – THE MYSTERIOUS PAPER.

*I*t was, perhaps, very natural that, with her feelings towards Charles Holland, Flora should shrink from every one who seemed to be of a directly contrary impression, and when Mr. Marchdale now spoke, she showed but little inclination to hear what he had to say in explanation.

The genuine and unaffected manner, however, in which he spoke, could not but have its effect upon her, and she found herself compelled to listen, as well as, to a great extent, approve of the sentiments that fell from his lips.

"Flora," he said, "I beg that you will here, in the presence of your mother, give me a patient hearing. You fancy that, because I cannot join so glibly as the admiral in believing that these letters are forgeries, I must be your enemy."

"Those letters," said Flora, "were not written by Charles Holland."

"That is your opinion."

"It is more than an opinion. He could not write them."

"Well, then, of course, if I felt inclined, which Heaven alone knows I do not, I could not hope successfully to argue against such a conviction. But I do not wish to do so. All I want to impress upon you is, that I am not to be blamed for doubting his innocence; and, at the same time, I wish to assure you that no one in this house would feel more exquisite satisfaction than I in seeing it established."

"I thank you for so much," said Flora; "but as, to my mind, his innocence has never been doubted, it needs to me no establishing."

"Very good. You believe these letters forgeries."

"I do."

"And that the disappearance of Charles Holland is enforced, and not of his own free will?"

"I do."

"Then you may rely upon my unremitting exertions night and day to find him; and any suggestions you can make, which is likely to aid in the search shall, I pledge myself, be fully carried out."

"I thank you, Mr. Marchdale."

"My dear," said the mother, "rely on Mr. Marchdale."

"I will rely on any one who believes Charles Holland innocent of writing those odious letters, mother — I rely upon the admiral. He will aid me heart and hand."

"And so will Mr. Marchdale."

"I am glad to hear it."

"And yet doubt it, Flora," said Marchdale, dejectedly. "I am very sorry that such should be the case; I will not, however, trouble you any further, nor, give me leave to assure you, will I relax in my honest endeavors to clear up this mystery."

So saying, Mr. Marchdale bowed, and left the room, apparently more vexed than he cared to express at the misconstruction which had been put upon his conduct and motives. He at once sought Henry and the admiral, to whom he expressed his most earnest desire to aid in attempting to unravel the mysterious circumstances which had occurred.

"This strongly-expressed opinion of Flora," he remarked, "is of course amply sufficient to induce us to pause before we say one word more that shall in any way sound like a condemnation of Mr. Holland. Heaven forbid that it should."

"No," said the admiral; "don't."

"I do not intend."

"I would not advise anybody."

"Sir, if you use that as a threat —"

"A threat?"

"Yes; I must say, it sounded marvelously like one."

"Oh, dear, no — quite a mistake. I consider that every man has a fair right to the enjoyment of his opinion. All I have to remark is, that I shall, after what has occurred, feel myself called upon to fight anybody who says those letters were written by my nephew."

"Indeed, sir."

"Ah, indeed."

"You will permit me to say such is a strange mode of allowing every one the free enjoyment of his opinion."

"Not at all."

"Whatever pains and penalties may be the result, Admiral Bell, of differing with so infallible authority as yourself, I shall do so whenever my judgment induces me."

"You will?"

"Indeed I will."

"Very good. You know all the consequences."

"As to fighting you, I should refuse to do so."

"Refuse?"

"Yes; most certainly."

"Upon what ground?"

"Upon the ground that you were a madman."

"Come," now interposed Henry, "let me hope that, for my sake as well as for Flora's, this dispute will proceed no further."

"I have not courted it," said Marchdale. "I have much temper, but I am not a stick or a stone."

"D – e, if I don't think," said the admiral, "you are a bit of both."

"Mr. Henry Bannerworth," said Marchdale, "I am your guest, and but for the duty I feel in assisting in the search for Mr. Charles Holland, I should at once leave your house."

"You need not trouble yourself on my account," said the admiral; "if I find no clue to him in the neighborhood for two or three days, I shall be off myself."

"I am going," said Henry, rising, "to search the garden and adjoining meadows; if you two gentlemen choose to come with me, I shall of course be happy of your company; if, however, you prefer remaining here to wrangle, you can do so."

This had the effect, at all events, of putting a stop to the dispute for the present, and both the admiral and Mr. Marchdale accompanied Henry on his search. The search was commenced immediately under the balcony of Charles Holland's window, from which the admiral had seen him emerge.

There was nothing particular found there, or in the garden. Admiral Bell pointed out accurately the route he had seen Charles take across the grass plot just before he himself left his chamber to seek Henry.

Accordingly, this route was now taken, and it led to a low part of the garden wall, which any one of ordinary vigor could easily have surmounted.

"My impression is," said the admiral, "that he got over here."

"The ivy appears to be disturbed," remarked Henry.

"Suppose we mark the spot, and then go round to the other side?" suggested George.

This was agreed to; for, although the young might have chosen rather to clamber over the wall than go round, it was doubtful if the old admiral could accomplish such a feat.

The distance round, however, was not great, and as they had cast over the wall a handful of flowers from the garden to mark the precise spot, it was easily discoverable.

The moment they reached it, they were panic-stricken by the appearances which it presented. The grass was for some yards round about completely trodden up, and converted into mud. There were deep indentations of feet-marks in all directions, and such abundance of evidence that some most desperate struggle had recently taken place there, that the most skeptical person in the world could not have entertained any doubt upon the subject.

Henry was the first to break the silence with which they each regarded the broken ground.

"This is conclusive to my mind," he said, with a deep sigh. "Here has poor Charles been attacked."

"God keep him!" exclaimed Marchdale, "and pardon me my doubts — I am now convinced."

The old admiral gazed about him like one distracted. Suddenly he cried —

"They have murdered him. Some fiends in the shape of men have murdered him, and Heaven only knows for what."

"It seems but too probably," said Henry. "Let us endeavor to trace the footsteps. Oh! Flora, Flora, what terrible news this will be to you."

"A horrible supposition comes across my mind," said George. "What if he met the vampyre?"

"It may have been so," said Marchdale, with a shudder. "It is a point which we could endeavor to ascertain, and I think we may do so."

"How?"

"By some inquiry as to whether Sir Francis Varney was from home at midnight last night."

"True; that might be done."

"The question, suddenly put to one of his servants, would, most probably, be answered as a thing of course."

"It would."

"Then it shall be decided upon. And now, my friend, since you have some of you thought me lukewarm in this business, I pledge myself that, should it be ascertained that Varney was from home at midnight last evening, I will defy him personally, and meet him hand to hand."

"Nay, nay," said Henry, "leave that course to younger hands."

"Why so?"

"It more befits me to be his challenger."

"No, Henry. You are differently situated to what I am."

"How so?"

"Remember, that I am in the world a lone man; without ties or connections. If I lose my life, I compromise no one by my death; but you have a mother and a bereaved sister to look to who will deserve your care."

"Hilloa," cried the admiral, "what's this?"

"What?" cried each, eagerly, and they pressed forward to where the admiral was stooping to the ground to pick up something which was nearly completely trodden into the grass.

He with some difficulty raised it. It was a small slip of paper, on which was some writing, but it was so much covered with mud as not to be legible.

"If this be washed," said Henry, "I think we shall be able to read it clearly."

"We can soon try that experiment," said George. "And as the footsteps, by some mysterious means, show themselves nowhere else but in this one particular spot, any further pursuit of inquiry about here appears useless."

"Then we will return to the house," said Henry, "and wash the mud from this paper."

"There is one important point," remarked Marchdale, "which appears to me we have all overlooked."

"Indeed!"

"Yes."

"What may that be?"

"It is this. Is any one here sufficiently acquainted with the handwriting of Mr. Charles Holland to come to an opinion upon the letters?"

"I have some letters from him," said Henry, "which we received while on the continent, and I dare say Flora has likewise."

"Then they should be compared with the alleged forgeries."

"I know his handwriting well," said the admiral. "The letters bear so strong a resemblance to it that they would deceive anybody."

"Then you may depend," remarked Henry, "some most deep-laid and desperate plot is going on."

"I begin," added Marchdale, "to dread that such must be the case. What say you to claiming the assistance of the authorities, as well as offering a large reward for any information regarding Mr. Charles Holland?"

"No plan shall be left untried, you may depend."

They had now reached the house, and Henry having procured some clean water, carefully washed the paper which had been found among the trodden grass. When freed from the mixture of clay and mud which had obscured it, they made out the following words, —

"— it be so well. At the next full moon seek a convenient spot, and it can be done. The signature is, to my apprehension, perfect. The money which I hold, in my opinion, is much more in amount than you imagine, must be ours; and as for —"

Here the paper was torn across, and no further words were visible upon it.

Mystery seemed now to be accumulating upon mystery; each one, as it showed itself darkly, seeming to bear some remote relation to what preceded it; and yet only confusing it the more.

That this apparent scrap of a letter had dropped from some one's pocket during the fearful struggle, of which there were such ample evidences, was extremely probably; but what it related to, by whom it was written, or by whom dropped, were unfathomable mysteries.

In fact, no one could give an opinion upon these matters at all; and after a further series of conjectures, it could only be decided, that unimportant as the scrap of paper appeared now to be, it should be preserved in case it should, as there was a dim possibility that it might, become a connecting link in some chain of evidence at another time.

"And here we are," said Henry, "completely at fault, and knowing not what to do."

"Well, it is a hard case," said the admiral, "that, with all the will in the world to be up and doing something, we are lying here like a fleet of ships in a calm, as idle as possible."

"You perceive we have no evidence to connect Sir Francis Varney with this affair, either nearly or remotely," said Marchdale.

"Certainly not," replied Henry.

"But yet, I hope you will not lose sight of the suggestion I proposed, to the effect of ascertaining if he were from home last night."

"But how is that to be carried out?"

"Boldly."

"How boldly?"

"By going at once, I should advise, to his house, and asking the first one of his domestics you may happen to see."

"I will go over," cried George; "on such occasions as these one cannot act upon ceremony."

He seized his hat, and without waiting for a word from any one approving or condemning his going, off he went.

"If," said Henry, "we find that Varney has nothing to do with the matter, we are completely at fault."

"Completely," echoed Marchdale.

"In that case, admiral, I think we ought to defer to your feelings upon the subject and do whatever you suggest should be done."

"I shall offer a hundred pound reward to any one who can and will bring any news of Charles."

"A hundred pounds is too much," said Marchdale.

"Not at all; and while I am about it, since the amount is made a subject of discussion, I shall make it two hundred, and that may benefit some rascal who is not so well paid for keeping the secret as I will pay him for disclosing it."

"Perhaps you are right," said Marchdale.

"I know I am, as I always am."

Marchdale could not forbear a smile at the opinionated old man, who thought no one's opinion upon any subject at all equal to his own; but he made no remark and only waited, as did Henry, with evident anxiety for the return of George.

The distance was not great, and George certainly performed his errand quickly, for he was back in less time than they had thought he could return in. The moment he came into the room, he said, without waiting for any inquiry to be made of him, —

"We are at fault again. I am assured that Sir Francis Varney never stirred from home after eight o'clock last evening."

"D — n it, then," said the admiral, "let us give the devil his due. He could not have had any hand in this business."

"Certainly not."

"From whom, George, did you get your information?" asked Henry, in a desponding tone.

"From, first of all, one of his servants, whom I met away from the house, and then from one whom I saw at the house."

"There can be no mistake, then?"

"Certainly none. The servants answered me at once, and so frankly that I cannot doubt it."

The door of the room was slowly opened, and Flora came in. She looked almost the shadow of what she had been but a few weeks before. She was beautiful, but she almost realized the poet's description of one who had suffered much, and was sinking into an early grave, the victim of a broken heart: —

"She was more beautiful than death,
And yet as sad to look upon."

Her face was of a marble paleness, and as she clasped her hands, and glanced from face to face, to see if she could gather hope and consolation from the expression of any one, she might have been taken for some exquisite statue of despair.

"Have you found him?" she said. "Have you found Charles?"

"Flora, Flora," said Henry, as he approached her.

"Nay, answer me; have you found him? You went to seek him. Dead of alive, have you found him?"

"We have not, Flora."

"Then I must seek him myself. None will search for him as I will search; I must myself seek him. 'Tis true affection that can alone be successful in such a search."

"Believe me, dear Flora, that all has been done which the shortness of the time that has elapsed would permit. Further measures will now immediately be taken. Rest assured, dear sister, that all will be done that the utmost zeal can suggest."

"They have killed him! they have killed him!" she said mournfully. "Oh, God, they have killed him! I am not now mad, but the time will come when I must surely be maddened. The vampyre has killed Charles Holland — the dreadful vampyre!"

"Nay, now, Flora, this is frenzy."

"Because he loved me has he been destroyed. I know it, I know it. The vampyre has doomed me to destruction. I am lost, and all who loved me will be involved in one common ruin on my account. Leave me all of you to perish. If, for iniquities done in our family, some one must suffer to appease the divine vengeance, let that one be me, and only me."

"Hush, sister, hush!" cried Henry. "I expected not this from you. The expressions you use are not your expressions. I know you better. There is abundance of divine mercy, but no divine vengeance. Be calm, I pray you."

"Calm! calm!"

"Yes. Make an exertion of that intellect we all know you to possess. It is too common a thing with human nature, when misfortune over-takes it, to imagine that such a state of things is specially arranged. We quarrel with Providence because it does not interfere with some special miracle in our favor; forgetting that, being denizens of this earth, and members of a great social system, we must be subject occasionally to the accidents which will disturb its efficient working."

"Oh, brother, brother!" she exclaimed, as she dropped into a seat, "you have never loved."

"Indeed!"

"No; you have never felt what it was to hold your being upon the breath of another. You can reason calmly, because you cannot know the extent of feeling you are vainly endeavoring to combat."

"Flora, you do me less than justice. All I wish to impress upon your mind is, that you are not in any way picked out by Providence to be specially unhappy — that there is no perversion of nature on your account."

"Call you that hideous vampyre form that haunts me no perversion of ordinary nature?"

"What is is natural," said Marchdale.

"Cold reasoning to one who suffers as I suffer. I cannot argue with you; I can only know that I am most unhappy — most miserable."

"But that will pass away, sister, and the sun of your happiness may smile again."

"Oh, if I could but hope!"

"And wherefore should you deprive yourself of that poorest privilege of the most unhappy?"

"Because my heart tells me to despair."

"Tell it you won't, then," cried Admiral Bell. "If you had been at sea as long as I have, Miss Bannerworth, you would never despair of anything at all."

"Providence guarded you," said Marchdale.

"Yes, that's true enough, I dare say. I was in a storm once off Cape Ushant, and it was only through Providence, and cutting away the mainmast myself, that we succeeded in getting into port."

"You have one hope," said Marchdale to Flora, as he looked in her wan face.

"One hope?"

"Yes. Recollect you have one hope."

"What is that?"

"You think that, by removing from this place, you may find that peace which is here denied you."

"No, no, no."

"Indeed. I thought that such was your firm conviction."

"It was; but circumstances have altered."

"How?"

"Charles Holland has disappeared here, and here must I remain to seek for him."

"True he may have disappeared here," remarked Marchdale; "and yet that may be no argument for supposing him still here."

"Where, then, is he?"

"God knows how rejoiced I should be if I were able to answer your question."

"I must seek him, dead or alive! I must see him before I bid adieu to this world, which has now lost all its charms for me."

"Do not despair," said Henry; "I will go to the town now at once, to make known our suspicions that he has met with some foul play. I will set every means in operation that I possibly can to discover him. Mr. Chillingworth will aid me, too; and I hope that not many days will elapse, Flora, before some intelligence of a most satisfactory nature shall be brought to you on Charles Holland's account."

"Go, go, brother; go at once."

"I go now at once."

"Shall I accompany you?" said Marchdale.

"No. Remain here to keep watch over Flora's safety while I am gone; I can alone do all that can be done."

"And don't forget to offer the two hundred pounds reward," said the admiral, "to any one who can bring us news of Charles, on which we can rely."

"I will not."

"Surely — surely something must result from that," said Flora, as she looked in the admiral's face, as if to gather encouragement in her dawning hopes from its expression.

"Of course it will, my dear," he said. "Don't you be downhearted; you and I are of one mind in this affair, and of one mind we will keep. We won't give up our opinions for anybody."

"Our opinions," she said, "of the honor and honesty of Charles Holland. That is what we will adhere to."

"Of course we will."

"Ah, sir, it joys me, even in the midst of this, my affliction, to find one at least who is determined to do him full justice. We cannot find such contradictions in nature as that mind, full of noble impulses, should stoop to such a sudden act of selfishness as those letters would attribute to Charles Holland. It cannot — cannot be."

"You are right, my dear. And now, Master Henry, you be off, will you, if you please."

"I am off now. Farewell, Flora, for a brief space."

"Farewell, brother; and Heaven speed you on your errand."

"Amen to that," cried the admiral; "and now, my dear, if you have got half an hour to spare, just tuck your arm under mine, and take a walk with me in the garden, for I want to say something to you."

"Most willingly," said Flora.

"I would not advise you to stray far from the house, Miss Bannerworth," said Marchdale.

"Nobody asked you for advice," said the admiral. "D — e, do you want to make out that I ain't capable of taking care of her?"

"No, no; but —"

"Oh, nonsense! Come along, my dear; and if all the vampyres and odd fish that were ever created were to come across our path, we would settle them somehow or another. Come along, and don't listen to anybody's croaking."

Chapter *XXIX*.

A PEEP THOROUGH AN IRON GRATING. – THE LONELY
PRISONER IN HIS DUNGEON. – THE MYSTERY.

Without forestalling the interest of our story, or recording a fact
in its wrong place, we now call our readers' attention to a circumstance
which may, at all events, afford some food for conjecture.

Some distance from the Hall, which, from time immemorial, had
been the home and the property of the Bannerworth family, was an
ancient ruin known by the name of Monks' Hall.

It was conjectured that this ruin was the remains of some one of those
half monastic, half military buildings which, during the middle ages,
were so common in almost every commanding situation in every county
of England.

At a period of history when the church arrogated to itself an amount
of political power which the intelligence of the spirit of the age now
denies to it, and when its members were quite ready to assert at any time
the truth of their doctrines by the strong arm of power, such buildings
as the one, the old grey ruins of which were situated near Bannerworth
Hall, were erected.

Ostensibly for religious purposes, but really as a stronghold for
defense, as well as for aggression, this Monks' Hall, as it was called,
partook quite as much of the character of a fortress, as of an ecclesiastical
building.

The ruins covered a considerable extent of ground, but the only part
which seemed successfully to have resisted the encroaches of time, at
least to a considerable extent, was a long hall in which the jolly monks
no doubt feasted and caroused.

Adjoining to this hall, were the walls of other parts of the building,
and at several places there were small, low, mysterious-looking doors
that led, heaven knows where, into some intricacies and labyrinths

beneath the building, which no one had, within the memory of man, been content to run the risk of losing himself in.

It was related that among these subterranean passages and arches there were pitfalls and pools of water; and whether such a statement was true or not, it certainly acted as a considerable damper upon the vigor of curiosity.

This ruin was so well known in the neighborhood, and had become from earliest childhood so familiar to the inhabitants of Bannerworth Hall, that one would as soon expect an old inhabitant of Ludgate-hill to make some remark about St. Paul's, as any of them to allude to the ruins of Monks' Hall.

They never now thought of going near to it, for in infancy they had sported among its ruins, and it had become one of those familiar objects which, almost, from that very familiarity, cease to hold a place in the memories of those who know it so well.

It is, however, to this ruin we would now conduct our readers, premising that what we have to say concerning it now, is not precisely in the form of a connected portion of our narrative.

*I*t is evening — the evening of that first day of heart loneliness to poor Flora Bannerworth. The lingering rays of the setting sun are gilding the old ruins with a wondrous beauty. The edges of the decayed stones seem now to be tipped with gold, and as the rich golden refulgence of light gleams upon the painted glass which still adorned a large window of the hall, a flood of many-colored beautiful light was cast within, making the old flag-stones, with which the interior was paved, look more like some rich tapestry, laid down to do honor to a monarch.

So picturesque and so beautiful an aspect did the ancient ruin wear, that to one with a soul to appreciate the romantic and the beautiful, it would have amply repaid the fatigue of a long journey now to see it.

And as the sun sank to rest, the gorgeous colors that it cast upon the moldering wall, deepened from an appearance of burnished gold to a crimson hue, and from that again the color changed to a shifting purple, mingling with the shadows of the evening, and so gradually fading away into absolute darkness.

The place is as silent as the tomb — a silence far more solemn than could have existed, had there been no remains of a human habitation; because even these timeworn walls were suggestive of what once had been; and the rapt stillness which now pervaded them brought with them a melancholy feeling for the past.

There was not even the low hum of insect life to break the stillness of these ancient ruins.

And now the last rays of the sun are gradually fading away. In a short time all will be darkness. A low gentle wind is getting up, and beginning slightly to stir the tall blades of grass that have shot up between some of the old stones. The silence is broken, awfully broken, by a sudden cry of despair; such a cry as might come from some imprisoned spirit, doomed to waste an age of horror in a tomb.

And yet it was scarcely to be called a scream, and not all a groan. It might have come from some one on the moment of some dreadful sacrifice, when the judgment had not sufficient time to call courage to its aid, but involuntarily had induced that sound which might not be repeated.

A few startled birds flew from odd holes and corners about the ruins, to seek some other place of rest. The owl hooted from a corner of what had once been a belfry, and a dreamy-looking bat flew out from a cranny and struck itself headlong against a projection.

Then all was still again. Silence resumed its reign, and if there had been a mortal ear to drink in that sudden sound, the mind might well have doubted if fancy had not more to do with the matter than reality.

From out a portion of the ruins that was enveloped in the deepest gloom, there now glides a figure. It is of gigantic height, and it moves along with a slow and measured tread. An ample mantle envelopes the form, which might well have been taken for the spirit of one of the monks who, centuries since, had made that place their home.

It walked the whole length of the ample hall we have alluded to, and then, at the window from which had streamed the long flood of many colored light, it paused.

For more than ten minutes this mysterious looking figure there stood.

At length there passed something on the outside of the window, that looked like the shadow of a human form.

Then the tall, mysterious, apparition-looking man turned, and sought a side entrance to the hall.

Then he paused, and, in about a minute, he was joined by another who must have been he who had so recently passed the stained glass window on the outer side.

There was a friendly salutation between these two beings, and they walked to the center of the hall, where they remained for some time in animated conversation.

From the gestures they used, it was evident that the subject of their discourse was one of deep and absorbing interest to both. It was one, too, upon which, after a time, they seemed a little to differ, and more than once they each assumed attitudes of mutual defiance.

This continued until the sun had so completely sunk, that twilight was beginning sensibly to wane, and then gradually the two men appeared to have come to a better understanding, and whatever might be the subject of their discourse, there was some positive result evidently arrived at now.

They spoke in lower tones. They used less animated gestures than before; and, after a time, they both walked slowly down the hall towards the dark spot from whence the first tall figure had so mysteriously emerged.

*T*here is a dungeon — damp and full of the most unwholesome exhalations — deep under ground it seems, and, in its excavations, it would appear as if some small land springs had been liberated, for the earthen floor was one continued extent of moisture.

From the roof, too, came perpetually the dripping of water, which fell with sullen, startling splashes in the pool below.

At one end, and near to the roof, — so near that to reach it, without the most efficient means from the inside, was a matter of positive impossibility — is a small iron grating, and not much larger than might be entirely obscured by any human face than might be close to it from the outside of the dungeon.

That dreadful abode is tenanted. In one corner, on a heap of straw, which appears freshly to have been cast into the place, lies a hopeless prisoner.

It is no great stretch of fancy to suppose, that it is from his lips came the sound of terror and of woe that had disturbed the repose of that lonely spot.

The prisoner is lying on his back; a rude bandage round his head, on which were numerous spots of blood, would seem to indicate that he had suffered personal injury in some recent struggle. His eyes were open. They were fixed despairingly, perhaps unconsciously, upon that small grating which looked into the upper world.

That grating slants upwards, and looks to the west, so that any one confined in that dreary dungeon might be tantalized, on a sweet summer's day, by seeing the sweet blue sky, and occasionally the white clouds flitting by in that freedom which he cannot hope for.

The carol of a bird, too, might reach him there. Alas! sad remembrance of life, and joy, and liberty.

But now all is deepening gloom. The prisoner sees nothing — hears nothing; and the sky is not quite dark. That small grating looks like a strange light-patch in the dungeon wall.

Hark! some footstep sounds upon his ear. The creaking of a door follows — a gleam of light shines into the dungeon, and the tall mysterious-looking figure in the cloak stands before the occupant of that wretched place.

Then comes in the other man, and he carries in his hand writing materials. He stoops to the stone couch on which the prisoner lies, and offers him a pen, as he raises him partially from the miserable damp pallet.

But there is no speculation in the eyes of that oppressed man. In vain the pen is repeatedly placed in his grip, and a document of some length, written on parchment, is spread out before him to sign. In vain is he held up now by both of the men, who have thus mysteriously sought him in his dungeon; he has not power to do as they would wish him. The pen falls from his nerveless grasp, and, with a deep sigh, when they cease to hold him up, he falls heavily back upon the stone couch.

Then the two men looked at each other for about a minute silently; after which he who was the shorter of the two raised one hand, and, in a voice of such concentrated hatred and passion as was horrible to hear, he said, —

"D — n!"

The reply of the other was a laugh; and then he took the light from the floor, and motioned the one who seemed so little able to control his feelings of bitterness and disappointment to leave the place with him.

With a haste and vehemence, then, which showed how much angered he was, the shorter man of the two now rolled up the parchment, and placed it in a breast pocket of his coat.

He cast a withering look of intense hatred on the form of the nearly unconscious prisoner, and then prepared to follow the other.

But when they reached the door of the dungeon, the taller man of the two paused, and appeared for a moment or two to be in deep thought; after which he handed the lamp he carried to his companion, and approached the pallet of the prisoner.

He took from his pocket a small bottle, and, raising the head of the feeble and wounded man, he poured some portion of the contents into his mouth, and watched him swallow it.

The other looked on in silence, and then they both slowly left the dreary dungeon.

*T*he wind rose, and the night had deepened into the utmost darkness. The blackness of a night, unilluminated by the moon, which would not now rise for some hours, was upon the ancient ruins. All was calm and still, and no one would have supposed that aught human was within those ancient, dreary looking walls.

Time will show who it was who lay in that unwholesome dungeon, as well as who were they who visited him so mysteriously, and retired again with feelings of such evident disappointment with the document it seemed of such importance, at least to one of them, to get that unconscious man to sign.

Chapter *XXX*.

THE VISIT OF FLORA TO THE VAMPYRE. – THE OFFER. – THE SOLEMN ASSEVERATION.

Admiral Bell had, of course, nothing particular to communicate to Flora in the walk he induced her to take with him in the gardens of Bannerworth Hall, but he could talk to her upon a subject which was sure to be a welcome one, namely, Charles Holland.

And not only could he talk to her of Charles, but he was willing to talk of him in the style of enthusiastic commendation which assimilated best with her own feelings. No one but the honest old admiral, who was as violent in his likes and his dislikes as any one could possibly be, could just then have conversed with Flora Bannerworth to her satisfaction of Charles Holland.

He expressed no doubts whatever concerning Charles's faith, and to his mind, now that he had got that opinion firmly fixed in his mind, everybody that held a contrary one he at once denounced as a fool or a rogue.

"Never you mind, Miss Flora," he said; "you will find, I dare say, that all will come right eventually. D — n me! the only thing that provokes me in the whole business is, that I should have been such an old fool as for a moment to doubt Charles."

"You should have known him better, sir."

"I should, my dear, but I was taken by surprise, you see, and that was wrong, too, for a man who has held a responsible command."

"But the circumstances, dear sir, were of a nature to take everyone by surprise."

"They were, they were. But now, candidly speaking, and I know I can speak candidly to you; do you really think this Varney is the vampyre?"

"I do."

"You do? Well, then, somebody must tackle him, that's quite clear; we can't put up with his fancies always."

"What can be done?"

"Ah, that I don't know, but something must be done, you know. He wants this place; Heaven only knows why or wherefore he has taken such a fancy to it; but he has done so, that is quite clear. If it had a good sea view, I should not be so much surprised; but there's nothing of the sort, so it's no way at all better than any other shore-going stupid sort of house, that you can see nothing but land from."

"Oh, if my brother would but make some compromise with him to restore Charles to us and take the house, me might yet be happy."

"D — n it! then you still think that he has a hand in spiriting away Charles?"

"Who else could do so?"

"I'll be hanged if I know. I do feel tolerably sure, and I have good deal of reliance upon your opinion, my dear; I say, I do feel tolerably sure: but, if I was d—d sure, now, I'd soon have it out of him."

"For my sake, Admiral Bell, I wish now to extract one promise from you."

"Say your say, my dear, and I'll promise you."

"You will not then expose yourself to the danger of any personal conflict with that most dreadful man, whose powers of mischief we do not know, and therefore cannot well meet or appreciate."

"Whew! is that what you mean?"

"Yes; you will, I am sure, promise me so much."

"Why, my dear, you see the case is this. In affairs of fighting, the less ladies interfere the better."

"Nay, why so?"

"Because — because, you see, a lady has no reputation for courage to keep up. Indeed, it's rather the other way, for we dislike a bold woman as much as we hold in contempt a cowardly man."

"But if you grant to us females that in consequence of our affections, we are not courageous, you must likewise grant how much we are doomed to suffer from the dangers of those whom we esteem."

"You would be the last person in the world to esteem a coward."

"Certainly. But there is more true courage often in not fighting than in entering into a contest."

"You are right enough there, my dear."

"Under ordinary circumstances, I should not oppose your carrying out the dictates of your honor, but now, let me entreat you not to meet this dreadful man, if man he can be called, when you know not how unfair the contest may be."

"Unfair?"

"Yes. May he not have some means of preventing you from injuring him, and of overcoming you, which no mortal possesses?"

"He may."

"Then the supposition of such a case ought to be sufficient ground for at once inducing you to abandon all idea of meeting with him."

"My dear, I'll consider of this matter."

"Do so."

"There is another thing, however, which now you will permit me to ask of you as a favor."

"It is granted ere it is spoken."

"Very good. Now you must not be offended with what I am going to say, because, however it may touch that very proper pride which you, and such as you, are always sure to possess, you are fortunately at all times able to call sufficient judgment to your aid to enable you to see what is really offensive and what is not."

"You alarm me by such a preface."

"Do I? then here goes at once. Your brother Henry, poor fellow, has enough to do, has he not, to make all ends meet."

A flush of excitement came over Flora's cheek as the old admiral thus bluntly broached a subject of which she already knew the bitterness to such a spirit as her brother's.

"You are silent," continued the old man; "by that I guess I am not wrong in my supposition; indeed it is hardly a supposition at all, for Master Charles told me as much, and no doubt he had it from a correct quarter."

"I cannot deny it, sir."

"Then don't. It ain't worth denying, my dear. Poverty is no crime, but, like being born a Frenchman, it's a d——d misfortune."

Flora could scarcely refuse a smile, as the nationality of the old admiral peeped out even in the midst of his most liberal and best feelings.

"Well," he continued, "I don't intend that he shall have so much trouble as he has had. The enemies of his king and his country shall free him from his embarrassments."

"The enemies?"

"Yes; who else?"

"You speak in riddles, sir."

"Do I? Then I'll soon make the riddles plain. When I went to sea I was worth nothing — as poor as a ship's cat after the crew had been paid off for a month. Well, I began fighting away as hard and fast as I could, and the more I fought, and the more hard knocks I gave and took, the more money I got."

"Indeed!"

"Yes; prize after prize we hauled into port, and at last the French vessels wouldn't come out of their harbors."

"What did you do then?"

"What did we do then? Why what was the most natural thing in the whole world for us to do, we did."

"I cannot guess."

"Well, I am surprised at that. Try again."

"Oh, yes; I can guess now. How could I have been so dull? You went and took them out."

"To be sure we did — to be sure we did, my dear; that's how we managed them. And, do you see, at the end of the war I found myself with lots of prize money, all wrung from old England's enemies, and I intend that some of it shall find its way to your brother's pocket; and you see that will bear out just what I said, that the enemies of his king and his country shall free him from his difficulties — don't you see?"

"I see your noble generosity, admiral."

"Noble fiddlesticks! Now I have mentioned this matter to you, my dear, and I don't so much mind talking to you about such matters as I should to your brother, I want you to do me the favor of managing it all for me."

"How, sir?"

"Why, just this way. You must find out how much money will free your brother just now from a parcel of botherations that beset him, and then I will give it to you, and you can hand it to him, you see, so I need not say anything about it; and if he speaks to me on the subject at all, I can put him down at once by saying, 'avast there, it's no business of mine.'"

"And can you, dear admiral, imagine that I could conceal the generous source from where so much assistance came?"

"Of course; it will come from you. I take a fancy to make you a present of a sum of money; you do with it as you please — it's yours, and I have no right and no inclination to ask you what use you put it to."

Tears gushed from the eyes of Flora as she tried to utter some word, but could not. The admiral swore rather fearfully, and pretended to wonder much what on earth she could be crying for. At length, after the first gush of feeling was over, she said, —

"I cannot accept of so much generosity, sir — I dare not."

"Dare not!"

"No; I should think meanly of myself were I to take advantage of the boundless munificence of your nature."

"Take advantage! I should like to see anybody take advantage of me, that's all."

"I ought not to take the money of you. I will speak to my brother, and well I know how much he will appreciate the noble, generous offer, my dear sir."

"Well, settle it your own way, only remember I have a right to do what I like with my own money."

"Undoubtedly."

"Very good. Then as that is undoubted, whatever I lend to him, mind I give to you, so it's as broad as it's long, as the Dutchman said, when he looked at the new ship that was built for him, and you may as well take it yourself you see, and make no more fuss about it."

"I will consider," said Flora, with much emotion — "between this time and the same hour tomorrow I will consider, sir, and if you can find any words more expressive of heartfelt gratitude than others, pray imagine that I have used them with reference to my own feelings towards you for such an unexampled offer of friendship."

"Oh, bother — stuff."

The admiral now at once changed the subject, and began to talk of Charles — a most grateful theme to Flora, as may well be supposed. He related to her many little particulars connected with him which all tended to place his character in a most amiable light, and as her ear drank in the words of commendation of him she loved, what sweeter music could there be to her than the voice of that old weather-beaten rough-spoken man.

"The idea," he added, to a warm eulogium he had uttered concerning Charles — "the idea that he could write those letters my dear, is quite absurd."

"It is, indeed. Oh, that we could know what had become of him!"

"We shall know. I don't think but what he's alive. Something seems to assure me that we shall some of these days look upon his face again."

"I am rejoiced to hear you say so."

"We will stir heaven and earth to find him. If he were killed, do you see, there would have been some traces of him now at hand; besides, he would have been left lying where the rascals attacked him."

Flora shuddered.

"But don't you fret yourself. You may depend that the sweet little cherub that sits up aloft has looked after him."

"I will hope so."

"And now, my dear, Master Henry will soon be home, I am thinking, and as he has quite enough disagreeables on his own mind to be able to spare a few of them, you will take the earliest opportunity, I am sure, of acquainting him with the little matter we have been talking about, and let me know what he says."

"I will — I will."

"That's right. Now, go in doors, for there's a cold air blowing here, and you are a delicate plant rather just now — go in and make yourself comfortable and easy. The worst storm must blow over at last."

Chapter XXXI.

SIR FRANCIS VARNEY AND HIS MYSTERIOUS VISITOR. – THE STRANGE CONFERENCE.

Sir Francis Varney is in what he calls his own apartment. It is night, and a dim and uncertain light from a candle which had been long neglected, only serves to render obscurity more perplexing. The room is a costly one. One replete with all the appliances of refinement and luxury which the spirit and genius of the age could possibly supply him with, but there is upon his brow the marks of corroding care, and little does that most mysterious being seem to care for all the rich furnishings of that apartment in which he sits.

His cadaverous-looking face is even paler and more death-like-looking than usual; and, if it can be conceived possible that such a one can feel largely interested in human affairs, to look at him, we could well suppose that some interest of no common magnitude was at stake.

Occasionally, too, he muttered some unconnected words, no doubt mentally filling up the gaps which rendered the sentences incomplete, and being unconscious, perhaps, that he was giving audible utterance to any of his dark and secret meditations.

At length he rose, and with an anxious expression of countenance, he went to the window, and looked out into the darkness of the night. All was still, and not an object was visible. It was that pitchy darkness without, which, for some hours, when the moon is late in lending her reflected beams, comes over the earth's surface.

"It is near the hour," he muttered "it is now very near the hour; surely he will come, and yet I know not why I should fear him, although I seem to tremble at the thought of his approach. He will surely come. Once a year – only once does he visit me, and then 'tis but to take the price which he has compelled me to pay for that existence, which but for him had been long since terminated. Sometimes I devoutly wish it were."

With a shudder he returned to the seat he had so recently left, and there for some time he appeared to meditate in silence.

Suddenly now, a clock, which was in the hall of that mansion he had purchased, sounded the hour loudly.

"The time has come," said Sir Francis. "The time has come, he will surely soon be here. Hark! hark!"

Slowly and distinctly he counted the strokes of the clock, and, when they had ceased, he exclaimed, with sudden surprise —

"Eleven! But eleven! How have I been deceived. I thought the hour of midnight was at hand."

He hastily consulted the watch he wore, and then he indeed found, that whatever he had been looking forward to with dread for some time past, as certain to ensue, at or about twelve o'clock, had yet another hour in which to prey upon his imagination.

"How could I have made so grievous an error?" he exclaimed. "Another hour of suspense and wonder as to whether that man be among the living or the dead. I have thought of raising my hand against his life, but some strange mysterious feeling has always staid me; and I have let him come and go freely, while an opportunity might well have served me to put such a design into execution. He is old, too — very old, and yet he keeps death at a distance. He looked pale, but far from unwell or failing, when last I saw him. Alas! a whole hour yet to wait. I would that this interview were over."

That extremely well known and popular disease called the fidgets, now began, indeed, to torment Sir Francis Varney. He could not sit — he could not walk, and, somehow or another, he never once seemed to imagine that from the wine cup he should experience any relief, although, upon a side table, there stood refreshments of that character. And thus some more time passed away, and he strove to cheat it of its weariness by thinking of a variety of subjects; but as the fates would have it, there seemed not one agreeable reminiscence in the mind of that most inexplicable man, and the more he plunged into the recesses of memory the more uneasy, not to say almost terrified, he looked and became. A shuddering nervousness came across him, and, for a few moments, he sat as if he were upon the point of fainting. By a vigorous effort, however, be shook this off, and then placing before him the watch, which now indicated about the quarter past eleven, he strove with a calmer aspect to wait the coming of him whose presence, when he did come, would really be a great terror, since the very thought beforehand produced so much hesitation and dismay.

In order too, if possible, then to further withdraw himself from a too painful consideration of those terrors, which in due time the reader will be acquainted with the cause of, he took up a book, and plunging into its contents, he amused his mind for a time with the following brief narrative: —

The wind howled round the gable ends of Bridport House in sudden and furious gusts, while the inmates sat by the fire-side, gazing in silence upon the blazing embers of the huge fire that shed a red and bright light all over the immense apartment in which they all sat.

It was an ancient looking place, very large, and capable of containing a number of guests. Several were present.

An aged couple were seated in tall high straight-backed chairs. They were the owners of that lordly mansion, and near them sat two young maidens of surpassing beauty; they were dissimilar and yet there was a slight likeness, but of totally different complexions.

The one had tresses of raven black; eyebrows, eyelashes, and eyes were all of the same hue; she was a beautiful and proud-looking girl, her complexion clear, with the hue of health upon her cheeks, while a smile played around her lips. The glance of the eye was sufficient to thrill through the whole soul.

The other maiden was altogether different; her complexion altogether fairer — her hair of sunny chestnut, and her beautiful hazel eyes were shaded by long brown eyelashes, while a playful smile also lit up her countenance. She was the younger of the two.

The attention of the two young maidens had been directed to the words of the aged owner of the house, for he had been speaking a few moments before. There were several other persons present, and at some little distance were many of the domestics who were not denied the privilege of warmth and rest in the presence of their master.

These were not the times, when if servants sat down, they were deemed idle; but the daily task done, then the evening hour was spent by the fireside.

"The wind howls and moans," said an aged domestic, "in an awful manner. I have never heard the like."

"It seems as though some imprisoned spirit was waiting for the repose that had been denied on earth," said the old lady, as she shifted her seat and gazed steadily on the fire.

"Ay," said her aged companion, "it is a windy night, and there will be a storm before long, or I'm mistaken."

"It was just such a night as that my son Henry left his home," said Mrs. Bradley, "just such another — only it had the addition of sleet and rain."

The old man sighed at the mention of his son's name, a tear stood in the eyes of the maidens, while one looked silently at the other, and seemed to exchange glances.

"I would that I might again see him before my body seeks its final home in the cold remorseless grave."

"Mother," said the fairest of the two maidens, "do not talk thus, let us hope that we yet may have many years of happiness together."

"Many, Emma?"

"Yes, mamma, many."

"Do you know that I am very old, Emma, very old indeed, considering what I have suffered, such a life of sorrow and ill health is at least equal to thirty years added to my life."

"You may have deceived yourself, aunt," said the other maiden; "at all events, you cannot count upon life as certain, for the strongest often go first, while those who seem much more likely to fall, by care, as often live in peace and happiness."

"But I lead no life of peace and happiness, while Henry Bradley is not here; besides, my life might be passed without me seeing him again."

"It is now two years since he was here last," said the old man,

"This night two years was the night on which he left."

"This night two years?"

"Yes."

"It was this night two years," said one of the servant men, "because old Dame Poutlet had twins on that night."

"A memorable circumstance."

"And one died a twelvemonth old," said the man; "and she had a dream which foretold the event."

"Ay, ay."

"Yes, and moreover she's had the same dream again last Wednesday was a week," said the man.

"And lost the other twin?"

"Yes sir, this morning."

"Omens multiply," said the aged man; "I would that it would seem to indicate the return of Henry to his home."

"I wonder where he can have gone to, or what he could have done all this time; probably he may not be in the land of the living."

"Poor Henry," said Emma.

"Alas, poor boy! We may never see him again — it was a mistaken act of his, and yet he knew not otherwise how to act or escape his father's displeasure."

"Say no more — say no more upon that subject; I dare not listen to it. God knows I know quite enough," said Mr. Bradley; "I knew not he would have taken my words so to heart as he did."

"Why," said the old woman, "he thought you meant what you said."

There was a long pause, during which all gazed at the blazing fire, seemingly rapt in their own meditation.

Henry Bradley, the son of the aged couple, had apparently left that day two years, and wherefore had he left the home of his childhood? wherefore had he, the heir to large estates, done this?

He had dared to love without his father's leave, and had refused the offer his father made him of marrying a young lady whom he had chosen for him, but whom he could not love. It was as much a matter of surprise to the father that the son should refuse, as it was to the son that his father should contemplate such a match.

"Henry," said the father, "you have been thought of by me. I have made proposals for marrying you to the daughter of our neighbor, Sir Arthur Onslow."

"Indeed, father!"

"Yes; I wish you to go there with me to see the young lady."

"In the character of a suitor?"

"Yes," replied the father, "certainly; it's high time you were settled."

"Indeed, I would rather not go, father; I have no intention of marrying just yet. I do not desire to do so."

This was an opposition that Mr. Bradley had not expected from his son, and which his imperious temper could ill brook, and with a darkened brow he said, —

"It is not much, Henry, that I trespass upon your obedience; but when I do so, I expect that you will obey me."

"But, father, this matter affects me for my whole life."

"That is why I have deliberated so long and carefully over it."

"But it is not unreasonable that I should have a voice in the affair, father, since it may render me miserable."

"You shall have a voice."

"Then I say no to the whole regulation," said Henry, decisively.

"If you do so you forfeit my protection, much more favor; but you had better consider over what you have said. Forget it, and come with me."

"I cannot."

"You will not?"

"No, father; I cannot do as you wish me; my mind is fully made up upon that matter."

"And so is mine. You either do as I would have you, or you leave the house, and seek your own living and you are a beggar."

"I should prefer being such," said Henry, "than to marry any young lady, and be unable to love her."

"That is not required."

"No! I am astonished! Not necessary to love the woman you marry!"

"Not at all; if you act justly towards her she ought to be grateful; and it is all that is requisite in the marriage state. Gratitude will beget love, and love in one begets love in the other."

"I will not argue with you, father, upon the matter. You are a better judge than I; you have had more experience."

"I have."

"And it would be useless to speak upon the subject; but of this I can speak — my own resolve — that I will not marry the lady in question."

The son had all the stern resolve of the father, but he had also very good reasons for what he did. He loved, and was beloved in return; and hence he would not break his faith with her whom he loved.

To have explained this to his father would have been to gain nothing except an accession of anger, and he would have made a new demand upon his (the son's) obedience, by ordering him to discard from his bosom the image that was there indelibly engraven.

"You will not marry her whom I have I chosen for your bride?"

"I cannot."

"Do not talk to me of can and can't, when I speak of will and wont. It is useless to disguise the fact. You have your free will in the matter. I shall take no answer but yes or no."

"Then, no, father."

"Good, sir; and now we are strangers."

With that Mr. Bradley turned abruptly from his son, and left him to himself.

It was the first time they had any words or difference together, and it was suddenly and soon terminated.

Henry Bradley was indignant at what I had happened; he did not think his father would have acted as he had done in this instance; but he was too much interested in the fate of another to hesitate for a moment. Then came the consideration as to what he should do, now that he had arrived at such a climax.

His first thoughts turned to his mother and sister. He could not leave the house without bidding them good-bye. He determined to see his mother, for his father had left the Hall upon a visit.

Mrs. Bradley and Emma were alone when he entered their apartment, and to them he related all that had passed between himself and father.

They besought him to stay, to remain there, or at least in that neighborhood; but he was resolved to quit the place altogether for a time, as he could do nothing there, and he might chance to do something elsewhere.

Upon this, they got together all the money and such jewels as they could spare which in all amounted to a considerable sum; then taking an affectionate leave of his mother and sister, Henry left the Hall — not before he had taken a long and affectionate farewell of one other who lived within those walls.

This was no other than the raven-eyed maiden who sat by the fireside, and listened attentively to the conversation that was going on. She was his love — she, a poor cousin. For her sake he had braved all his father's anger, and attempted to seek his fortune abroad.

This done, he quietly left the Hall, without giving anyone any intimation of where he was going.

Old Mr. Bradley, when he had said so much to his son, was highly incensed at what he deemed his obstinacy; and he thought the threat hanging over him would have had a good effect; but he was amazed when he discovered that Henry had instead left the Hall, and he knew not whither.

For some time he comforted himself with the assurance that he would, he must return; but, alas! he came not, and this was the second anniversary of that melancholy day which no one more repented of and grieved for, than did poor Mr. Bradley.

"Surely, surely he will return, or let us know where he is," he said; "he cannot be in need, else he would have written to us for aid."

"No, no," said Mrs. Bradley; "it is, I fear, because he has not written, that he is in want; he would never write if he was in poverty, lest he should cause us unhappiness at his fate. Were he doing well, we should hear of it, for he would be proud of the result of his own unaided exertions."

"Well, well," said Mr. Bradley. "I can say no more; if I was hasty, so was he; it is passed. I would forgive all the past if I could but see him once again — once again!"

"How the wind howls," added the aged man; "and it's getting worse and worse."

"Yes, and the snow is coming down now in style," said one of the servants, who brought in some fresh logs which were piled up on the fire, and he shook the white flakes off his clothes.

"It will be a heavy fall before morning," said one of the men.

"Yes, it has been gathering for some days; it will be much warmer than it has been when it is all down."

"So it will — so it will."

At that moment there was a knocking at the gate, and the dogs burst into a dreadful uproar from their kennels.

"Go, Robert," said Mr. Bradley "and see who it is that knocks such a night as this; it is not fit or safe that a dog should be out in it."

The man went out, and shortly returned, saying, —

"So please you, sir, there is a traveler that has missed his way, and desires to know if he can obtain shelter here, or if any one can be found to guide him to the nearest inn."

"Bid him come in; we shall lose no warmth because there is one more before the fire."

The stranger entered, and said, —

"I have missed my way, and the snow comes down so thick and fast, and whirled in such eddies, that I fear, by myself, I should fall into some drift and perish before morning."

"Do not speak of it, sir," said Mr. Bradley; "such a night as this is a sufficient apology for the request you make and an inducement to me to grant it most willingly."

"Thanks," replied the stranger; "the welcome is most seasonable."

"Be seated, sir; take your seat by the ingle; it is warm."

The stranger seated himself, and seemed lost in reflection, as he gazed intently on the blazing logs. He was a robust man, with great whiskers and beard, and, to judge from his outward habiliments, he was a stout man.

"Have you traveled far?"

"I have, sir."

"You appear to belong to the army, if I mistake not?"

"I do, sir."

There was a pause; the stranger seemed not inclined to speak of himself much; but Mr. Bradley continued, —

"Have you come from foreign service, sir? I presume you have."

"Yes; I have not been in this country more than six days."

"Indeed; shall we have peace think you?"

"I do so and I hope it may be so, for the sake of many who desire to return to their native land, and to those they love best."

Mr. Bradley heaved a deep sigh, which was echoed softly by all present, and the stranger looked from one to another, with a hasty glance, and then turned his gaze upon the fire.

"May I ask, sir, if you have any person whom you regard in the army — any relative?"

"Alas! I have — perhaps, I ought to say I had a son. I know not, however, where he is gone."

"Oh! a runaway; I see."

"Oh, no; he left because there were some family differences, and now, I would, that he were once more here."

"Oh!" said the stranger, softly, "differences and mistakes will happen now and then, when least desired."

At this moment, an old hound who had lain beside Ellen Mowbray, she who wore the coal-black tresses, lifted his head at the difference in sound that was noticed in the stranger's voice. He got up and walked up to him, and began to smell around him, and, in another moment, he rushed at him with a cry of joy and began to lick and caress him in the most extravagant manner. This was followed by a cry of joy in all present.

"It is Henry!" exclaimed Ellen Mowbray, rising and rushing into his arms. It was Henry, and he threw off the several coats he had on, as well as the large beard he wore to disguise himself.

"The meeting was a happy one. There was not a more joyful house than that within many miles around. Henry was restored to the arms of those who loved him, and, in a month, a wedding was celebrated between him and his cousin Ellen.

Sir Francis Varney glanced at his watch. It indicated but five minutes to twelve o'clock, and he sprang to his feet. Even as he did so, a loud knocking at the principal entrance to his house awakened every echo within its walls.

Chapter XXXII.

THE THOUSAND POUNDS. – THE STRANGER'S PRECAUTIONS.

Varney moved not now nor did he speak, but, like a statue, he stood with his unearthly looking eyes riveted upon the door of the apartment. In a few moments one of his servants came, and said –

"Sir, a person is here, who says he wants to see you. He desired me to say, that he had ridden far, and that moments were precious when the tide of life was ebbing fast."

"Yes! yes!" gasped Varney; "admit him I know him! Bring him here? It is – an – old friend – of mine."

He sank into a chair, and still he kept his eyes fixed upon that door through which his visitor must come. Surely some secret of dreadful moment must be connected with him whom Sir Francis expected – dreaded – and yet dared not refuse to see. And now a footstep approaches – a slow and a solemn footstep – it pauses a moment at the door of the apartment, and then the servant flings it open, and a tall man enters. He is enveloped in the folds of a horseman's cloak, and there is the clank of spurs upon his heels as he walks into the room.

Varney rose again, but he said not a word; and for a few moments they stood opposite each other in silence. The domestic has left the room, and the door is closed, so that there was nothing to prevent them from conversing; and, yet, silent they continued for some minutes. It seemed as if each was most anxious that the other should commence the conversation first.

And yet there was nothing so very remarkable in the appearance of that stranger, which should entirely justify Sir Francis Varney, in feeling so much alarm at his presence. He certainly was a man past the prime of life; and he looked like one who had battled much with misfortune, and as if time had not passed so lightly over his brow, but that it had left deep traces of its progress.

The only thing positively bad about his countenance, was to be found in his eyes. There there was a most ungracious and sinister expression, a kind of lurking and suspicions look, as if he were always resolving in his mind some deep-laid scheme, which might be sufficient to circumvent the whole of mankind.

Finding, probably, that Varney would not speak first, he let his cloak fall more loosely about him, and in a low, deep tone, he said,

"I presume I was expected?"

"You were," said Varney. "It is the day, and it is the hour."

"You are right, I like to see you so mindful. You don't improve in looks since —"

"Hush — hush! no more of that; can we not meet without a dreadful allusion to the past? There needs nothing to remind me of it; and your presence here now shows that you are not forgetful. Speak not of that fearful episode. Let no words combine to place it in a tangible shape to human understanding. I cannot, dare not, hear you speak of that."

"It is well," said the stranger; "as you please. Let our interview be brief. You know my errand?"

"I do. So fearful a drag upon limited means, is not likely to be readily forgotten."

"Oh, you are too ingenious — too full of well laid schemes, and to apt and ready in their execution, to feel, as any fearful drag, the conditions of our bargain. Why do you look at me so earnestly?"

"Because," said Varney — and he trembled as he spoke — "because each lineament of your countenance brings me back to the recollection of the only scene in life that made me shudder, and which I cannot think of, even with the indifference of contempt. I see it all before my mind's eye, coming in frightful panoramic array, those incidents, which even to dream of, are sufficient to drive the soul to madness; the dread of this annual visit, hangs upon me like a dark cloud upon my very heart; it sits like some foul incubus, destroying its vitality and dragging me, from day to day, nearer to that tomb, from whence not as before,

I can emerge."

"You have been among the dead?" said the stranger.

"I have."

"And yet are mortal?"

"Yes," repeated Varney, "yes, and yet am mortal."

"It was I that plucked you back to that world, which, to judge from your appearance, has had since that eventful period but few charms for you. By my faith you look like —"

"Like what I am," interrupted Varney. "This is a subject that once a year gets frightfully renewed between us. For weeks before your visit I am haunted by frightful recollections, and it takes me many weeks after you are gone, before I can restore myself to serenity. Look at me; am I not an altered man?"

"In faith you are," said the stranger. "I have no wish to press upon you painful recollections. And yet 'tis strange to me that upon such a man as you, the event to which you allude should produce so terrible an impression."

"I have passed through the agony of death," said Varney, "and have again endured the torture — for it is such — of the re-union of the body and the soul; not having endured so much, not the faintest echo of such feelings can enter into your imagination."

"There may be truth in that, and yet, like a fluttering moth round a flame, it seems to me, that when I do see you, you take a terrific kind of satisfaction in talking of the past."

"That is strictly true," said Varney; "the images with which my mind is filled are frightful. Pent up do they remain for twelve long months. I can speak to you, and you only, without disguise, and thus does it seem to me that I get rid of the uneasy load of horrible imaginings. When you are gone, and have been gone a sufficient lapse of time, my slumbers are not haunted with frightful images — I regain a comparative peace, until the time slowly comes round again, when we are doomed to meet."

"I understand you. You seem well lodged here?"

"I have ever kept my word, and sent to you, telling you where I am."

"You have, truly. I have no shadow of complaint to make against you. No one could have more faithfully performed his bond than you have. I give you ample credit for all that, and long may you live still to perform your conditions."

"I dare not deceive you, although to keep such faith I may be compelled to deceive a hundred others."

"Of that I cannot judge. Fortune seems to smile upon you; you have not as yet disappointed me."

"And will not now," said Varney. "The gigantic and frightful penalty of disappointing you, stares me in the face. I dare not do so."

He took from his pocket, as he spoke, a clasped book, from which he produced several bank notes, which he placed before the stranger.

"A thousand pounds," he said; "that is the agreement."

"It is to the very letter. I do not return to you a thousand thanks — we understand each other better than to waste time with idle compliment. Indeed I will go quite as far as to say, truthfully, that did not my necessities require this amount from you, you should have the boon, for which you pay that price at a much cheaper rate."

"Enough! enough!" said Varney. "It is strange, that your face should have been the last I saw, when the world closed upon me, and the first that met my eyes when I was again snatched back to life! Do you pursue still your dreadful trade?"

"Yes" said the stranger, "for another year, and then, with such a moderate competence as fortune has assigned me, I retire, to make way for younger and abler spirits."

"And then," said Varney, "shall you still require of me such an amount as this?"

"No; this is my last visit but one. I shall be just and liberal towards you. You are not old; and I have no wish to become the clog of your existence. As I have before told you, it is my necessity, and not my inclination, that sets the value upon the service I rendered you."

"I understand you, and ought to thank you. And in reply to so much courtesy, be assured, that when I shudder at your presence, it is not that I regard you with horror, as an individual, but it is because the sight of you awakens mournfully the remembrance of the past."

"It is clear to me," said the stranger; "and now I think we part with each other in a better spirit than we ever did before; and when we meet again, the remembrance that it is the last time, will clear away the gloom that I now find hanging over you."

"It may! it may! With what an earnest gaze you still regard me!"

"I do. It does appear to me most strange, that time should not have obliterated the effects which I thought would have ceased with their cause. You are no more the man that in my recollection you once were, than I am like a sporting child."

"And I never shall be," said Varney; "never — never again! This self-same look which the hand of death had placed upon me, I shall ever wear. I shudder at myself, and as I oft perceive the eye of idle curiosity fixed steadfastly upon me, I wonder in my inmost heart, if even the wildest guesser hits upon the cause why I am not like unto other men?"

"No. Of that you may depend there is no suspicion; but I will leave you now; we part such friends, as men situated as we are can be. Once again shall we meet, and then farewell for ever."

"Do you leave England, then?"

"I do. You know my situation in life. It is not one which offers me inducements to remain. In some other land, I shall win the respect and attention I may not hope for here. There my wealth will win many golden opinions; and casting, as best I may, the veil of forgetfulness over my former life, my declining years may yet be happy. This money, that I have had of you from time to time, has been more pleasantly earned than all beside, wrung, as it has been, from your fears, still have I taken it with less reproach. And now, farewell!"

Varney rang for a servant to show the stranger from the house. And without another word they parted. Then, when he was alone, that mysterious owner of that costly home drew a long breath of apparently exquisite relief.

"That is over! — that is over!" he said. "He shall have the other thousand pounds, perchance, sooner than he thinks. With all expedition I will send it to him. And then on that subject I shall be at peace. I shall have paid a large sum; but that which I purchased was to me priceless. It was my life! — it was my life itself! That possession which the world's wealth cannot restore! and shall I grudge these thousands, which have found their way into this man's hands? No! 'Tis true, that existence, for me, has lost some of its most resplendent charms. 'Tis true, that I have no earthly affections, and that shunning companionship with all, I am alike shunned by all; and yet, while the life-blood still will circulate within my shrunken veins, I cling to vitality."

He passed into an inner room, and taking from a hook, on which it hung, a long, dark-colored cloak, he enveloped his tall unearthly figure within its folds. Then, with his hat in his hand, he passed out of his house, and appeared to be taking his way towards Bannerworth Hall.

Surely it must be guilt of no common die that could oppress a man so destitute of human sympathies as Sir Francis Varney. The dreadful suspicions that hovered round him with respect to what he was, appeared to gather confirmation from every act of his existence.

Whether or not this man, to whom he felt bound to pay annually so large a sum, was in the secret, and knew him to be something more than earthly, we cannot at present declare; but it would seem from the tenor of their conversation as if such were the fact.

Perchance he had saved him from the corruption of the tomb, by placing out, on some sylvan spot, where the cold moonbeams fell, the apparently lifeless form, and now claimed so large a reward for such a service, and the necessary secrecy contingent upon it.

We say this may be so, and yet again some more natural and rational explanation may unexpectedly present itself; and there may be yet a dark page in Sir Francis Varney's life's volume, which will place him in a light of superadded terrors to our readers.

Time, and the now rapidly accumulating incidents of our tale, will soon tear aside the veil of mystery that now envelops some of our *dramatis personae.*

And let us hope that in the development of those incidents we shall be enabled to rescue the beautiful Flora Bannerworth from the despairing gloom that is around her. Let us hope and even anticipate that we shall see her smile again; that the roseate hue of health will again revisit her cheeks, the light buoyancy of her step return, and that as before she may be the joy of all around her, dispensing and receiving happiness.

And, he too, that gallant fearless lover, he whom no chance of time or tide could sever from the object of his fond affections, he who listened to nothing but the dictates of his heart's best feelings, let us indulge a hope that he will have a bright reward, and that the sunshine of a permanent felicity will only seem the brighter for the shadows that for a time have obscured its glory.

Chapter XXXIII.

THE STRANGE INTERVIEW. – THE CHASE THROUGH THE HALL.

*I*t was with the most melancholy aspect that anything human could well bear, that Sir Francis Varney took his lonely walk, although perhaps in saying so much, probably we are instituting a comparison which circumstances scarcely empower us to do; for who shall say that singular man, around whom a very atmosphere of mystery seemed to be perpetually increasing, was human?

Averse as we are to believe in the supernatural, or even to invest humanity with any preternatural powers, the more singular facts and circumstances surrounding the existence and the acts of that man bring to the mind a kind of shuddering conviction, that if he be indeed really mortal he still must possess some powers beyond ordinary mortality, and be walking the earth for some unhallowed purposes, such as ordinary men with ordinary attributes of human nature can scarcely guess at.

Silently and alone he took his way through that beautiful tract of country, comprehending such picturesque charms of hill and dale which lay between his home and Bannerworth Hall. He was evidently intent upon reaching the latter place by the shortest possible route, and in the darkness of that night, for the moon had not yet risen, he showed no slight acquaintance with the intricacies of that locality, that he was at all enabled to pursue so undeviatingly a track as that which he took.

He muttered frequently to himself low, indistinct words as he went, and chiefly did they seem to have reference to that strange interview he had so recently had with one who, from some combination of circumstances scarcely to be guessed at, evidently exercised a powerful control over him, and was enabled to make a demand upon his pecuniary resources of rather startling magnitude.

And yet, from a stray word or two, which were pronounced more distinctly, he did not seem to be thinking in anger over that interview; but it would appear that it rather had recalled to his remembrance circumstances of a painful and a degrading nature, which time had not been able entirely to obliterate from his recollection.

"Yes, yes," he said, as he paused upon the margin of the wood, to the confines of which he, or what seemed to be he, had once been chased by Marchdale and the Bannerworths — "yes, the very sight of that man recalls all the frightful pageantry of a horrible tragedy, which I can never — never forget. Never can it escape my memory, as a horrible, a terrific fact; but it is the sight of this man alone that can recall all its fearful minutia to my mind, and paint to my imagination, in the most vivid colors, every, the least particular connected with that time of agony. These periodical visits much affect me. For months I dread them, and for months I am but slowly recovering from the shocks they give me. 'But once more,' he says — 'but once more,' and then we shall not meet again. Well, well; perchance before that time arrives, I may be able to possess myself of those resources which will enable me to forestall his visit, and so at least free myself from the pang of expecting him."

He paused at the margin of the wood, and glanced in the direction of Bannerworth Hall. By the dim light which yet showed from out the light sky, he could discern the ancient gable ends, and turret-like windows; he could see the well laid out gardens, and the grove of stately firs that shaded it from the northern blasts, and, as he gazed, a strong emotion seemed to come over him, such as no one could have supposed would for one moment have possessed the frame of one so apparently unconnected with all human sympathies.

"I know this spot well," he said, "and my appearance here on that eventful occasion, when the dread of my approach induced a crime only second to murder itself, was on such a night as this, when all was so still and calm around, and when he who, at the merest shadow of my presence, rather chose to rush on death than be assured it was myself. Curses on the circumstances that so foiled me! I should have been most wealthy. I should have possessed the means of commanding the adulation of those who now hold me but cheaply: but still the time may come. I have a hope yet, and that greatness which I have ever panted for, that magician-like power over my kind, which the possession of ample means alone can give, may yet be mine."

Wrapping his cloak more closely around him, he strode forward with that long, noiseless step which was peculiar to him. Mechanically he appeared to avoid those obstacles of hedge and ditch which impeded his pathway. Surely he had come that road often, or he would not so easily have pursued his way. And now he stood by the edge of a plantation which in some measure protected from trespassers the more private gardens of the Hall, and there he paused, as if a feeling of irresolution had come over him, or it might be, as indeed it seemed from his subsequent conduct, that he had come without any fixed intention, or if with a fixed intention, without any regular plan of carrying it into effect.

Did he again dream of intruding into any of the chambers of that mansion, with the ghastly aspect of that terrible creation with which, in the minds of its inhabitants, he seemed to be but too closely identified? He was pale, attenuated, and trembled. Could it be that so soon it had become necessary to renew the life-blood in his veins in the awful manner which it is supposed the vampyre brood are compelled to protract their miserable existence?

It might be so, and that he was even now reflecting upon how once more he could kindle the fire of madness in the brain of that beautiful girl, who he had already made so irretrievably wretched.

He leant against an aged tree, and his strange, lustrous-looking eyes seemed to collect every wandering scintillation of light that was around, and to shine with preternatural intensity.

"I must, I will," he said, "be master of Bannerworth Hall. It must come to that. I have set an existence upon its possession, and I will have it; and then, if with my own hands I displace it brick by brick and stone by stone, I will discover that hidden secret which no one but myself now dreams of. It shall be done by force or fraud, by love or by despair, I care not which; the end shall sanctify all means. Ay, even if I wade through blood to my desire, I say it shall be done."

There was a holy and a still calmness about the night much at variance with the storm of angry passion that appeared to be momentarily gathering power in the breast of that fearful man. Not the least sound came from Bannerworth Hall, and it was, only occasionally that from afar off on the night air there came the bark of some watchdog, or the low of distant cattle. All else was mute save when the deep sepulchral tones of that man, if man he was, gave an impulse to the soft air around him. With a strolling movement as if he were careless if he proceeded in that direction or not, he still went onward toward the house, and now he stood by that little summer-house once so sweet and so dear a retreat, in which the heart-stricken Flora had held her interview with him whom she loved with a devotion unknown to meaner minds.

This spot scarcely commanded any view of the house, for so enclosed was it among evergreens and blooming flowers, that it seemed like a very wilderness of nature, upon which, with liberal hand, she had showered down in wild luxuriance her wildest floral beauties.

In and around that spot the night air was loaded with sweets. The mingled perfume of many flowers made that place seem a very paradise. But oh, how sadly at variance with that beauty and contentedness of nature was he who stood amidst such beauty! All incapable as he was of appreciating its tenderness, or of gathering the faintest moral from its glory.

"Why am I here?" he said. "Here, without fixed design or stability of purpose, like some miser who has hidden his own hoards so deeply within the bowels of the earth he cannot hope that he shall ever again be able to bring them to the light of day. I hover around this spot which I feel — which I know — contains my treasure, though I cannot lay my hands upon it, or exult in its glistening beauty."

Even as he spoke he cowered down like some guilty thing, for he heard a fair footstep upon the garden path. So light, so fragile was the step, that, in the light of day, the very hum of summer insects would have drowned the noise: but he heard it, that man of crime — of unholy and awful impulses. He heard it, and he shrunk down among the shrubs and flowers till he was hidden completely from observation amid a world of fragrant essences.

Was it some one stealthily in that place even as he was, unwelcome or unknown? or was it one who had observed him intrude upon the privacy of those now unhappy precincts, and who was coming to deal upon him that death which, vampyre though he might be, he was yet susceptible of from mortal hands?

The footstep advanced, and lower down he shrunk until his coward-heart beat against the very earth itself. He knew that he was unarmed, a circumstance rare with him, and only to be accounted for by the disturbance of his mind consequent upon the visit of that strange man to his house, those presence had awakened so many conflicting emotions.

Nearer and nearer still came that light footstep, and his deep-seated fears would not let him perceive that it was not the step of caution or of treachery, but owed its lightness to the natural grace and freedom of movement of its owner.

The moon must have arisen, although obscured by clouds, through which it cast but a dim radiance, for the night had certainly grown lighter; so that although there were no strong shadows cast, a more diffused brightness was about all things, and their outlines looked not so dancing, and confused the one with the other.

He strained his eyes in the direction whence the sounds proceeded, and then his fears for his personal safety vanished, for he saw it was a female form that was slowly advancing towards him.

His first impulse was to rise, for with the transient glimpse he got of it, he knew that it must be Flora Bannerworth; but a second thought, probably one of intense curiosity to know what could possibly have brought her to such a spot at such a time restrained him, and he was quiet. But if the surprise of Sir Francis Varney was great to see Flora Bannerworth at such a time in such a place, we have no doubt, that with the knowledge which our readers have of her, their astonishment would more than fully equal his; and when we come to consider, that since that eventful period when the sanctity of her chamber had been so violated by that fearful midnight visitant, it must appear somewhat strange that she could gather courage sufficient to wander forth alone at such an hour.

Had she no dread of meeting that unearthly being? Did the possibility that she might fall into his ruthless grasp, not come across her mind with a shuddering consciousness of its probability? Had she no reflection that each step she took, was taking her further and further from those who would aid her in all extremities? It would seem not, for she walked onward, unheeding and apparently unthinking of the presence possible or probable, of that bane of her existence.

But let us look at her again. How strange and spectral-like she moves along; there seems no speculation in her countenance but with a strange and gliding step, she walks like some dim shadow of the past in that ancient garden. She is very pale, and on her brow there is the stamp of suffering; her dress is a morning robe, she holds it lightly round her, and thus she moves forward towards that summer-house which probably to her was sanctified by having witnessed those vows of pure affection which came from the lips of Charles Holland, about whose fate there now hung so great a mystery.

Has madness really seized upon the brain of that beautiful girl? Has the strong intellect really sunk beneath the oppression to which it has been subjected? Does she now walk forth with a disordered intellect, the queen of some fantastic realm, viewing the material world with eyes that are not of earth; shunning perhaps that which she should have sought, and, perchance, in her frenzy, seeking that which in a happier frame of mind she would have shunned.

Such might have been the impression of any one who had looked upon her for a moment, and who knew the disastrous scenes through which she had so recently passed; but we can spare our readers the pangs of such a supposition. We have bespoken their love for Flora Bannerworth, and we are certain that she has it; therefore would we spare them, even for a few brief moments, from imagining that cruel destiny had done its worst, and that the fine and beautiful spirit we have so much commended had lost its power of rational reflection. No; thank Heaven, such is not the case. Flora Bannerworth is not mad, but under the strong influence of some eccentric dream, which has pictured to her mind images which have no home but in the airy realms of imagination. She has wandered forth from her chamber to that sacred spot where she had met him she loved, and heard the noblest declaration of truth and constancy that ever flowed from human lips.

Yes, she is sleeping; but, with a precision such as the somnambulist so strangely exerts, she trod the well-known paths slowly, but surely, towards that summer's bower, where her dreams had not told her lay crouching that most hideous specter of her imagination, Sir Francis Varney. He who stood between her and her heart's best joy; he who had destroyed all hope of happiness, and who had converted her dearest affections into only so many causes of greater disquietude than the blessings they should have been to her. Oh! could she have imagined but for one moment that he was there, with what an eagerness of terror would she have flown back again to the shelter of those walls, where at least was to be found some protection from the fearful vampyre's embrace, and where she would be within hail of friendly hearts, who would stand boldly between her and every thought of harm.

But she knew it not, and onwards she went until the very hem of her garment touched the face of Sir Francis Varney.

And he was terrified — he dared not move — he dared not speak! The idea that she had died, and that this was her spirit, come to wreak some terrible vengeance upon him, for a time possessed him, and so paralyzed with fear was he, that he could neither move nor speak.

It had been well if, during that trance of indecision in which his coward heart placed him, Flora had left the place, and again sought her home; but unhappily such an impulse came not over her; she sat upon that rustic seat, where she had reposed when Charles had clasped her to his heart, and through her very dream the remembrance of that pure affection came across her, and in the tenderest and most melodious accents, she said, —

"Charles! Charles! and do you love me still? No — no; you have not forsaken me. Save me, save me from the vampyre!"

She shuddered, and Sir Francis Varney heard her weeping.

"Fool that I am," he muttered, "to be so terrified. She sleeps. This is one of the phases which a disordered imagination oft puts on. She sleeps, and perchance this may be an opportunity of further increasing the dread of my visitation, which shall make Bannerworth Hall far too terrible a dwelling-place for her; and well I know, if she goes, they will all go. It will become a deserted house, and that is what I want. A house, too, with such an evil reputation that none but myself, who have created that reputation, will venture within its walls: — a house, which superstition will point out as the abode of spirits — a house, as it were, by general opinion, ceded to the vampyre. Yes, it shall be my own; fit dwelling-place for a while for me. I have sworn it shall be mine, and I will keep my oath, little such as I have to do with vows."

He rose, and moved slowly to the row entrance of the summer-house; a movement he could make, without at all disturbing Flora, for the rustic seat, on which she sat, was at its further extremity. And there he stood, the upper part of his gaunt and hideous form clearly defined upon the now much lighter sky, so that if Flora Bannerworth had not been in that trance of sleep in which she really was one glance upward would let her see the hideous companion she had, in that once much-loved spot — a spot hitherto sacred to the best and noblest feelings, but now doomed for ever to be associated with that terrific specter of despair.

But she was in no state to see so terrible a sight. Her hands were over her face, and she was weeping still.

"Surely, he loves me," she whispered; "he has said he loved me, and he does not speak in vain. He loves me still, and I shall again look upon his face, a Heaven to me! Charles! Charles! you will come again? Surely, they sin against the divinity of love, who would tell me that you love me not!"

"Ha!" muttered Varney, "this passion is her first, and takes a strong hold on her young heart — she loves him — but what are human affections to me? I have no right to count myself in the great muster roll of humanity. I look not like an inhabitant of the earth, and yet am on it. I love no one, expect no love from any one, but I will make humanity a slave to me; and the lip-service of them who hate me in their hearts, shall be as pleasant jingling music to my ear, as if it were quite sincere! I will speak to this girl; she is not mad — perchance she may be."

There was a diabolical look of concentrated hatred upon Varney's face, as he now advanced two paces towards the beautiful Flora.

Chapter *XXXIV.*

THE THREAT. – ITS CONSEQUENCES. – THE RESCUE, AND
SIR FRANCIS VARNEY'S DANGER.

*S*ir Francis Varney now paused again, and he seemed for a few moments to gloat over the helpless condition of her whom he had so determined to make his victim; there was no look of pity in his face, no one touch of human kindness could be found in the whole expression of those diabolical features; and if he delayed making the attempt to strike terror into the heart of that unhappy, but beautiful being, it could not be from any relenting feeling, but simply, that he wished for a few moments to indulge his imagination with the idea of perfecting his villainy more effectually.

And they who would have flown to her rescue, – they, who for her would have chanced all accidents, ay, even life itself, were sleeping, and knew not of the loved one's danger. She was alone, and far enough from the house, to be driven to that tottering verge where sanity ends, and the dream of madness, with all its terrors, commences.

But still she slept – if that half-waking sleep could indeed be considered as any thing akin to ordinary slumber – still she slept, and called mournfully upon her lover's name; and in tender, beseeching accents, that should have melted even the stubbornest hearts did she express her soul's conviction that he loved her still.

The very repetition of the name of Charles Holland seemed to be galling to Sir Francis Varney. He made a gesture of impatience, as she again uttered it, and then stepping forward, he stood within a pace of where she sat, and in a fearfully distinct voice he said, –

"Flora Bannerworth, awake! awake! and look upon me, although the sight blast you, and drive you to despair. Awake! awake!"

It was not the sound of the voice which aroused her from that strange slumber. It is said that those who sleep in that eccentric manner, are insensible to sounds, but that the lightest touch will arouse them in an instant; and so it was in this case, for Sir Francis Varney, as he spoke, laid upon the hand of Flora two of his cold, corpse-like looking fingers. A shriek burst from her lips, and although the confusion of her memory and conceptions was immense, yet she was awake, and the somnambulistic trance had left her.

"Help, help!" she cried. "Gracious Heavens! Where am I?"

Varney spoke not, but he spread out his long, thin arms in such a manner that he seemed almost to encircle her, while he touched her not, so that escape became a matter of impossibility, and to attempt to do so, must have been to have thrown herself into his hideous embrace.

She could obtain but a single view of the face and figure of him who opposed her progress, but, slight as that view was, it more than sufficed. The very extremity of fear came across her, and she sat like one paralyzed; the only evidence of existence she gave consisting in the words, —

"The vampyre — the vampyre!"

"Yes," said Varney, "the vampyre. You know me, Flora Bannerworth — Varney, the vampyre; your midnight guest at that feast of blood. I am the vampyre. Look upon me well; shrink not from my gaze. You will do well not to shun me, but to speak to me in such a shape that I may learn to love you."

Flora shook as in a convulsion, and she looked as white as any marble statue.

"This is horrible!" she said. "Why does not Heaven grant me the death I pray for?"

"Hold!" said Varney. "Dress not in the false colors of the imagination that which in itself is sufficiently terrific to need none of the allurements of romance. Flora Bannerworth, you are persecuted — persecuted by me, the vampyre. It is my fate to persecute you; for there are laws to the invisible as well as the visible creation that force even such a being as I am to play my part in the great drama of existence. I am a vampyre; the sustenance that supports this frame must be drawn from the life-blood of others."

"Oh, horror — horror!"

"But most I do affect the young and beautiful. It is from the veins of such as thou art, Flora Bannerworth, that I would seek the sustenance I'm compelled to obtain for my own exhausted energies. But never yet, in all my long career — a career extending over centuries of time — never yet have I felt the soft sensation of human pity till I looked on thee, exquisite piece of excellence. Even at the moment when the reviving fluid from the gushing fountain of your veins was warming my heart, I pitied and I loved you. Oh, Flora! even I can now feel the pang of being what I am!"

There was a something in the tone, a touch of sadness in the manner, and a deep sincerity in those words, that in some measure disabused Flora of her fears. She sobbed hysterically, and a gush of tears came to her relief, as, in almost inaudible accents, she said, —

"May the great God forgive even you!"

"I have need of such a prayer," exclaimed Varney — "Heaven knows I have need of such a prayer. May it ascend on the wings of the night air to the throne of Heaven. May it be softly whispered by ministering angels to the ear of Divinity. God knows I have need of such a prayer!"

"To hear you speak in such a strain," said Flora, "calms the excited fancy, and strips even your horrible presence of some of its maddening influence."

"Hush," said the vampyre, "you must hear more — you must know more ere you speak of the matters that have of late exercised an influence of terror over you."

"But how came I here?" said Flora, "tell me that. By what more than earthly power have you brought me to this spot? If I am to listen to you, why should it not be at some more likely time and place?"

"I have powers," said Varney, assuming from Flora's words, that she would believe such arrogance — "I have powers which suffice to bend many purposes to my will — powers incidental to my position, and therefore is it I have brought you here to listen to that which should make you happier than you are."

"I will attend," said Flora. "I do not shudder now; there's an icy coldness through my veins, but it is the night air — speak, I will attend you."

"I will. Flora Bannerworth, I am one who has witnessed time's mutations on man and on his works, and I have pitied neither; I have seen the fall of empires, and sighed not that high-reaching ambition was toppled in the dust. I have seen the grave close over the young and the beautiful — those whom I have doomed by my insatiable thirst for human blood to death, long ere the usual span of life was past, but I never loved till now."

"Can such a being as you," said Flora, "be susceptible of such an earthly passion?"

"And wherefore not?"

"Love is either too much of heaven, or too much of earth to find a home with thee."

"No, Flora, no! it may be that the feeling is born of pity. I will save you — I will save you from a continuance of the horrors that are assailing you."

"Oh! then may heaven have mercy in your hour of need."

"Amen!"

"And may you even yet know peace and joy above."

"It is a faint and straggling hope — but if achieved, it will be through the interposition of such a spirit as thine, Flora, which has already exercised so benign an influence upon my tortured soul, as to produce the wish within my heart, to do at least one unselfish action."

"That wish," said Flora, "shall be father to the deed. Heaven has boundless mercy yet."

"For thy sweet sake, I will believe so much, Flora Bannerworth; it is a condition with my hateful race, that if we can find one human heart to love us, we are free. If, in the face of Heaven, you will consent to be mine, you will snatch me from a continuance of my frightful doom; and for your pure sake, and on your merits, shall I yet know heavenly happiness. Will you be mine?"

A cloud swept from off the face of the moon, and a slant ray fell upon the hideous features of the vampyre. He looked as if just rescued from some charnel house, and endowed for a space with vitality to destroy all beauty and harmony in nature, and drive some benighted soul to madness.

"No, no, no!" shrieked Flora, "never!"

"Enough," said Varney, "I am answered. It was a bad proposal. I am a vampyre still."

"Spare me! spare me!"

"Blood!"

Flora sank upon her knees, and uplifted her hands to heaven. "Mercy, mercy!" she said.

"Blood!" said Varney, and she saw his hideous, fang-like teeth. "Blood! Flora Bannerworth, the vampyre's motto. I have asked you to love me, and you will not — the penalty be yours."

"No, no!" said Flora. "Can it be possible that even you, who have already spoken with judgment and precision, can be so unjust? you must feel that, in all respects, I have been a victim, most gratuitously — a sufferer, while there existed no just cause that I should suffer; one who has been tortured, not from personal fault, selfishness, lapse of integrity, or honorable feelings, but because you have found it necessary, for the prolongation of your terrific existence, to attack me as you have done. By what plea of honor, honesty, or justice, can I be blamed for not embracing an alternative which is beyond all human control? — I cannot love you."

"Then be content to suffer. Flora Bannerworth, will you not, even for a time, to save yourself and to save me, become mine?"

"Horrible proposition!"

"Then am I doomed yet, perhaps, for many a cycle of years, to spread misery and desolation around me; and yet I love you with a feeling which has in it more of gratefulness and unselfishness than ever yet found a home within my breast. I would fain serve you, although you cannot save me; there may yet be a chance, which shall enable you to escape from the persecution of my presence."

"Oh! glorious chance!" said Flora. "Which way can it come? tell me how I may embrace it and such grateful feelings as a heart-stricken mourner can offer to him, who has rescued her from her deep affliction, shall yet be yours."

"Hear me, then, Flora Bannerworth, while I state to you some particulars of mysterious existence, of such beings as myself, which never yet have been breathed to mortal ears."

Flora looked intently at him, and listened, while, with a serious earnestness Of manner, he detailed to her something of the physiology of the singular class of beings which the concurrence of all circumstances tended to make him appear.

"Flora," he said, "it is not that I am so enamored of an existence to be prolonged only by such frightful means, which induces me to become a terror to you or to others. Believe me, that if my victims, those whom my insatiable thirst for blood make wretched, suffer much, I, the vampyre, am not without my moments of unutterable agony. But it is a mysterious law of our nature, that as the period approaches when the exhausted energies of life require a new support from the warm, gushing fountain of another's veins, the strong desire to live grows upon us, until, in a paroxysm of wild insanity, which will recognize no obstacles, human or divine, we seek a victim."

"A fearful state!" said Flora.

"It is so; and, when the dreadful repast is over, then again the pulse beats healthfully, and the wasted energies of a strange kind of vitality are restored to us, we become calm again, but with that calmness comes all the horror, all the agony of reflection, and we suffer far more than tongue can tell."

"You have my pity," said Flora; "even you have my pity."

"I might well demand it, if such a feeling held a place within your breast. I might well demand your pity, Flora Bannerworth, for never crawled an abject wretch upon the earth's rotundity, so pitiable as I."

"Go on, go on."

"I will, and with such brief conclusions as I may. Having once attacked any human being, we feel a strange, but terribly impulsive desire again to seek that person for more blood. But I love you, Flora; the small amount of sensibility that still lingers about my preternatural existence, acknowledges in you a pure and better spirit. I would fain save you."

"Oh! tell me how I may escape the terrible infliction."

"That can only be done by flight. Leave this place, I implore you! leave it as quickly as the movement may be made. Linger not — cast not one regretful look behind you on your ancient home. I shall remain in this locality for years. Let me lose sight of you, I will not pursue you;

but, by force of circumstances, I am myself compelled to linger here. Flight is the only means by which you may avoid a doom as terrific as that which I endure."

"But tell me," said Flora, after a moment's pause, during which she appeared to be endeavoring to gather courage to ask some fearful question; "tell me if it be true that those who have once endured the terrific attack of a vampyre, become themselves, after death, one of that dread race?"

"It is by such means," said Varney, "that the frightful brood increases; but, time and circumstances must aid the development of the new and horrible existence. You, however, are safe."

"Safe! Oh! say that word again."

"Yes, safe; not once or twice will the vampyre's attack have sufficient influence on your mortal frame, as to induce a susceptibility on your part to become coexistent with such as he. The attack must be often repeated, and the termination of mortal existence must be a consequence essential, and direct from those attacks, before such a result may be anticipated."

"Yes, yes; I understand."

"If you were to continue my victim from year to year, the energies of life would slowly waste away, and, till like some faint taper's gleam, consuming more sustenance than it received, the veriest accident would extinguish your existence, and then, Flora Bannerworth, you might become a vampyre."

"Oh! horrible! most horrible!"

"If by chance, or by design, the least glimpse of the cold moonbeams rested on your apparently lifeless remains, you would rise again and be one of us — a terror to yourself and a desolation to all around."

"Oh! I will fly from here," said Flora. "The hope of escape from so terrific and dreadful a doom shall urge me onward; if flight can save me — flight from Bannerworth Hall, I will pause not until continents and oceans divide us."

"It is well. I'm able now thus calmly to reason with you. A few short months more and I shall feel the languor of death creeping over me, and then will come that mad excitement of the brain, which, were you hidden behind triple doors of steel, would tempt me again to seek your chamber — again to seize you in my full embrace — again to draw from your veins the means of prolonged life — again to convulse your very soul with terror."

"I need no incentives," said Flora, with a shudder, "in the shape of descriptions of the past, to urge me on."

"You will fly from Bannerworth Hall?"

"Yes, yes!" said Flora, "it shall be so; its very chambers now are hideous with the recollection of scenes enacted in them. I will urge my brothers, my mother, all to leave. And in some distant clime we will find security and shelter. There even we will learn to think of you with more of sorrow than of anger — more pity than reproach — more curiosity than loathing."

"Be it so," said the vampyre; and he clasped his hands, as if with a thankfulness that he had done so much towards restoring peace at least to one, who, in consequence of his acts, had felt such exquisite despair. "Be it so; and even I will hope that the feelings which have induced so desolated and so isolated a being as myself to endeavor to bring peace to one human heart, will plead for me, trumpet-tongued, to Heaven!"

"It will — it will," said Flora.

"Do you think so?"

"I do; and I will pray that the thought may turn to certainty in such a cause."

The vampyre appeared to be much affected; and then he added, —

"Flora, you know this spot has been the scene of a catastrophe fearful to look back upon, in the annals of your family?"

"It has," said Flora. "I know to what you allude; 'tis a matter of common knowledge to all — a sad theme to me, and one I would not court."

"Nor would I oppress you with it. Your father, here, on this very spot, committed that desperate act which brought him uncalled for to the judgment seat of God. I have a strange, wild curiosity upon such subjects. Will you, in return for the good that I have tried to do you, gratify it?"

"I know not what you mean," said Flora.

"To be more explicit, then, do you remember the day on which your father breathed his last?"

"Too well — too well."

"Did you see him or converse with him shortly before that desperate act was committed?"

"No; he shut himself up for some time in a solitary chamber."

"Ha! what chamber?"

"The one in which I slept myself on the night —"

"Yes, yes; the one with the portrait — that speaking portrait — the eyes of which seem to challenge an intruder as he enters the apartment."

"The same."

"For hours shut up there!" added Varney, musingly; "and from thence he wandered to the garden, where, in this summer house, he breathed his last?"

"It was so."

"Then, Flora, ere I bid you adieu —"

These words were scarcely uttered, when there was a quick, hasty footstep, and Henry Bannerworth appeared behind Varney, in the very entrance of the summerhouse.

"Now," he cried, "for revenge! Now, foul being, blot upon the earth's surface, horrible imitation of humanity, if mortal arm can do aught against you, you shall die!"

A shriek came from the lips of Flora, and flinging herself past Varney, who stepped aside, she clung to her brother, who made an unavailing pass with his sword at the vampyre. It was a critical moment; and had the presence of mind of Varney deserted him in the least, unarmed as he was, he must have fallen beneath the weapon of Henry. To spring, however, up the seat which Flora had vacated, and to dash out some of the flimsy and rotten wood-work at the back of the summer-house by the propulsive power of his whole frame, was the work of a moment; and before Henry could free himself from the clinging embrace of Flora, Varney, the vampyre was gone, and there was no greater chance of his capture than on the former occasion, when he was pursued in vain from the Hall to the wood, in the intricacies of which he was so entirely lost.

Chapter XXXV.

THE EXPLANATION. – MARCHDALE'S ADVICE. – THE PROJECTED REMOVAL, AND THE ADMIRAL'S ANGER.

*T*his extremely sudden movement on the part of Varney was certainly as unexpected as it was decisive. Henry had imagined, that by taking possession of the only entrance to the summer-house, he must come into personal conflict with the being who had worked so much evil for him and his; and that he should so suddenly have created for himself another mode of exit, certainly never occurred to him.

"For Heaven's sake, Flora," he said, "unhand me; this is a time for action."

"But, Henry, Henry, hear me."

"Presently, presently, dear Flora; I will yet make another effort to arrest the headlong flight of Varney."

He shook her off, perhaps with not more roughness than was necessary to induce her to forego her grasp of him, but in a manner that fully showed he intended to be free; and then he sprang through the same aperture whence Varney had disappeared, just as George and Mr. Marchdale arrived at the door of the summer-house.

It was nearly morning, so that the fields were brightening up with the faint radiance of the coming day; and when Henry reached a point which he knew commanded an extensive view, he paused, and ran his eye eagerly along the landscape, with a hope of discovering some trace of the fugitive. Such, however, was not the case; he saw nothing, heard nothing of Sir Francis Varney; and then he turned, and called loudly to George to join him, and was immediately replied to by his brother's presence, accompanied by Marchdale.

Before, however, they could exchange a word, a rattling discharge of fire-arms took place from one of the windows and they heard the admiral, in a loud voice, shouting, —

"Broadside to broadside! Give it them again, Jack! Hit them between wind and water!"

Then there was another rattling discharge, and Henry exclaimed, —

"What is the meaning of that firing?"

"It comes from the admiral's room," said Marchdale. "On my life, I think the old man must be mad. He has some six or eight pistols ranged in a row along the window-sill, and all loaded, so that by the aid of a match they can be pretty well discharged as a volley, which he considers the only proper means of firing upon the vampyre."

"It is so," replied George; "and, no doubt, hearing an alarm, he has commenced operations by firing into the enemy."

"Well, well," said Henry; "he must have his way. I have pursued Varney thus far, and that he has again retreated to the wood, I cannot doubt. Between this and the full light of day, let us at least make an effort to discover his place of retreat. We know the locality as well as he can possibly, and I propose now that we commence an active search."

"Come on, then," said Marchdale. "We are all armed; and I, for one, shall feel no hesitation in taking the life, if it be possible to do so, of that strange being."

"Of that possibility you doubt?" said George, as they hurried on across the meadows.

"Indeed I do, and with reason too. I'm certain that when I fired at him before I hit him; and besides, Flora must have shot him upon the occasion when we were absent, and she used your pistols Henry, to defend herself and her mother."

"It would seem so," said Henry; "and disregarding all present circumstances, if I do meet him, I will put to the proof whether he be mortal or not."

The distance was not great, and they soon reached the margin of the wood; they then separated agreeing to meet within it, at a well-spring, familiar to them all: previous to which each was to make his best endeavor to discover if any one was hidden among the bush-wood or in the hollows of the ancient trees they should encounter on their line of march.

The fact was, that Henry finding that he was likely to pass an exceedingly disturbed, restless night, through agitation of spirits, had, after tossing to and fro on his couch for many hours, wisely at length risen, and determined to walk abroad in the gardens belonging to the mansion, in preference to continuing in such a state of fever and anxiety, as he was in, in his own chamber.

Since the vampyre's dreadful visit, it had been the custom of both the brothers, occasionally, to tap at the chamber door of Flora, who, at her own request, now that she had changed her room, and dispensed with any one sitting up with her, wished occasionally to be communicated with by some member of the family.

Henry, then, after rapidly dressing, as he passed the door of her bedroom, was about to tap at it, when to his surprise he found it open, and upon hastily entering it he observed that the bed was empty, and a hasty glance round the apartment convinced him that Flora was not there.

Alarm took possession of him, and hastily arming himself, he roused Marchdale and George, but without waiting for them to be ready to accompany him, he sought the garden, to search it thoroughly in case she should be anywhere there concealed.

Thus it was he had come upon the conference so strangely and so unexpectedly held between Varney and Flora in the summerhouse. With what occurred upon that discovery the readers are acquainted.

Flora had promised George that she would return immediately to the house, but when, in compliance with the call of Henry, George and Marchdale had left her alone, she felt so agitated and faint that she began to cling to the trellis work of the little building for a few moments before she could gather strength to reach the mansion.

Two or three minutes might thus have elapsed, and Flora was in such a state of mental bewilderment with all that had occurred, that she could scarce believe it real, when suddenly a slight sound attracted her attention, and through the gap which had been made in the wall of the summer-house, with an appearance of perfect composure, again appeared Sir Francis Varney.

"Flora," he said, quietly returning the discourse which had been broken off, "I am quite convinced now that you will be much the happier for the interview."

"Gracious Heaven!" said Flora, "whence have you come from?"

"I have never left," said Varney.

"But I saw you fly from this spot."

"You did; but it was only to another immediately outside the summer house. I had no idea of breaking off our conference so abruptly."

"Have you anything to add to what you have already stated?"

"Absolutely nothing, unless you have a question to propose to me — I should have thought you had, Flora. Is there no other circumstance weighing heavily upon your mind, as well as the dreadful visitation I have subjected you to?"

"Yes," said Flora. "What has become of Charles Holland?"

"Listen. Do not discard all hope; when you are far from here you will meet with him again."

"But he has left me."

"And yet he will be able, when you again encounter him, so far to extenuate his seeming perfidy, that you shall hold him as untouched in honor as when first he whispered to you that he loved you."

"Oh, joy! joy!" said Flora; "by that assurance you have robbed misfortune of its sting, and richly compensated me for all that I have suffered."

"Adieu!" said the vampyre. "I shall now proceed to my own home by a different route to that taken by those who would kill me."

"But after this," said Flora, "there shall be no danger; you shall be held harmless, and our departure from Bannerworth Hall shall be so quick, that you will soon be released from all apprehension of vengeance from my brother, and I shall taste again of that happiness which I thought had fled from me for ever."

"Farewell," said the vampyre; and folding his cloak closely around him, he strode from the summerhouse, soon disappearing from her sight behind the shrubs and ample vegetation with which that garden abounded.

Flora sunk upon her knees, and uttered a brief, but heartfelt, thanksgiving to Heaven for this happy change in her destiny. The hue of health faintly again visited her cheeks and as she now, with a feeling of more energy and strength than she had been capable of exerting for many days, walked towards the house, she felt all that delightful sensation which the mind experiences when it is shaking off the trammels of some serious evil which it delights now to find that the imagination has attired in far worse colors than the facts deserved.

It is scarcely necessary, after this, to say that the search in the wood for Sir Francis Varney was an unproductive one, and that the morning dawned upon the labors of the brothers and of Mr. Marchdale, without their having discovered the least indication of the presence of Varney. Again puzzled and confounded, they stood on the margin of the wood, and looked sadly towards the brightening windows of Bannerworth Hall, which were now reflecting with a golden radiance the slant rays of the morning sun.

"Foiled again," remarked Henry, with a gesture of impatience; "foiled again, and as completely as before. I declare that I will fight this man, let our friend the admiral say what he will against such a measure I will meet him in mortal combat; he shall consummate his triumph over our whole family by my death, or I will rid the world and ourselves of so frightful a character."

"Let us hope," said Marchdale, "that some other course may be adopted, which shall put an end to these proceedings."

"That," exclaimed Henry, "is to hope against all probability; what other course can be pursued? Be this Varney man or devil, he has evidently marked us for his prey."

"Indeed, it would seem so," remarked George; "but yet he shall find that we will not fall so easily; he shall discover that if poor Flora's gentle spirit has been crushed by these frightful circumstances, we are of a sterner mould."

"He shall," said Henry; "I for one will dedicate my life to this matter. I will know no more rest than is necessary to recruit my frame, until I have succeeded in overcoming this monster; I will seek no pleasure here, and will banish from my mind all else that may interfere with that one fixed pursuit. He or I must fall."

"Well spoken," said Marchdale; "and yet I hope that circumstances may occur to prevent such a necessity of action, and that probably you will yet see that it will be wise and prudent to adopt a milder and a safer course."

"No, Marchdale, you cannot feel as we feel. You look on more as a spectator, sympathizing with the afflictions of either, than feeling the full sting of those afflictions yourself."

"Do I not feel acutely for you? I'm a lonely man in the world, and I have taught myself now to center my affections in your family; my recollections of early years assist me in so doing. Believe me, both of you, that I am no idle spectator of your griefs, but that I share them fully. If I advise you to be peaceful, and to endeavor by the gentlest means possible to accomplish your aims, it is not that I would counsel you cowardice; but having seen so much more of the world than either of you have had time or opportunity of seeing, I do not look so enthusiastically upon matters, but, with a cooler, calmer judgment, I do not say a better, I proffer to you my counsel."

"We thank you," said Henry; "but this is a matter in which action seems specially called for. It is not to be borne that a whole family is to be oppressed by such a fiend in human shape as that Varney."

"Let me," said Marchdale, "counsel you to submit to Flora's decision in this business; let her wishes constitute the rules of action. She is the greatest sufferer, and the one most deeply interested in the termination of this fearful business. Moreover, she has judgment and decision of character; she will advise you rightly, be assured."

"That she would advise us honorably," said Henry, "and that we should feel every disposition in the world to defer to her wishes our proposition, is not to be doubted; but little shall be done without her counsel and sanction. Let us now proceed homeward, for I am most anxious to ascertain how it came about that she and Sir Francis Varney were together in that summer-house at so strange an hour."

They all three walked together towards the house, conversing in a similar strain as they went.

Chapter XXXVI.

THE CONSULTATION. – THE DUEL AND ITS RESULTS.

*I*ndependent of this interview which Flora had had with the much dreaded Sir Francis Varney, the circumstances in which she and all who were dear to her, happened at that moment to be placed, certainly required an amount of consideration, which could not be too soon bestowed.

By a combination of disagreeables, everything that could possibly occur to disturb the peace of the family seemed to have taken place at once; like Macbeth's, their troubles had truly come in battalions, and now that the serenity of their domestic position was destroyed, minor evils and annoyances which that very serenity had enabled them to hold at arm's length became gigantic, and added much to their distress.

The small income, which, when all was happiness, health and peace, was made to constitute a comfortable household, was now totally inadequate to do so — the power to economize and to make the most of a little, had flown along with that contentedness of spirit which the harmony of circumstances alone could produce.

It was not to be supposed that poor Mrs. Bannerworth could now, as she had formerly done, when her mind was free from anxiety, attend to those domestic matters which make up the comforts of a family — distracted at the situation of her daughter, and bewildered by the rapid succession of troublesome events which so short a period of time had given birth to, she fell into an inert state of mind as different as anything could be, from her former active existence.

It has likewise been seen how the very domestics fled from Bannerworth Hall in dismay, rather than remain beneath the same roof with a family believed to be subject to the visitations of so awful a being as a vampyre.

Among the class who occupy positions of servitude, certainly there might have been found some, who, with feelings and understanding above such considerations, would have clung sympathetically to that family in distress, which they had known under a happier aspect; but it had not been the good fortune of the Bannerworths to have such as these about them; hence selfishness had its way, and they were deserted. It was not likely, then, that strangers would willingly accept service in a family so situated, without some powerful impulse in the shape of a higher pecuniary consideration, as was completely out of the power of the Bannerworths to offer.

Thus was it, then, that most cruelly, at the very time that they had most need of assistance and of sympathy, this unfortunate family almost became isolated from their kind; and, apart from every other consideration, it would have been almost impossible for them to continue inhabitants of the Hall, with anything like comfort, or advantage.

And then, although the disappearance of Charles Holland no longer awakened those feelings of inclination at his supposed perfidy which were first produced by that event; still, view it in which way they night, it was a severe blow of fate, and after it, they one and all found themselves still less able to contend against the sea of troubles that surrounded them. The reader, too, will not have failed to remark that there was about the whole of the family that pride of independence which induced them to shrink from living upon extraneous aid; and hence, although they felt and felt truly, that when Admiral Bell, in his frank manner, offered them pecuniary assistance, that it was no idle compliment, yet with a sensitiveness such as they might well be expected to feel, they held back, and asked each other what prospect there was of emerging from such a state of things, and if it were justifiable to commence a life of dependence, the end of which was not evident or tangible.

Not withstanding, too, the noble confidence of Flora in her lover, and not withstanding that confidence had been echoed by her brothers, there would at times obtrude into the minds of the latter, a feeling of the possibility, that after all they might be mistaken; and Charles Holland might, from some sudden impulse, fancying his future happiness was all at stake, have withdrawn himself from the Hall, and really written the letters attributed to him.

We say this only obtruded itself occasionally, for all their real feelings and aspirations were the other way, although Mr. Marchdale, they could perceive, had his doubts, and they could not but confess that he was more likely to view the matter calmly and dispassionately than they.

In fact, the very hesitation with which he spoke upon the subject, convinced them of his doubts, for they attributed that hesitation to fear of giving them pain, or of wounding the prejudices of Admiral Bell, with whom he had already had words so nearly approaching to a quarrel.

Henry's visit to Mr. Chillingworth was not likely to be productive of any results beyond those of a conjectural character. All that that gentleman could do was to express a willingness to be directed by them in any way, rather than suggest any course of conduct himself upon circumstances which he could not be expected to judge of as they who were on the spot, and had witnessed their actual occurrence.

And now we will suppose that the reader is enabled with us to look into one of the principal rooms of Bannerworth Hall. It is evening, and some candles are shedding a sickly light on the ample proportions of the once handsome apartment. At solemn consultation the whole of the family are assembled. As well as the admiral, Mr. Chillingworth, and Marchdale, Jack Pringle, too, walked in, by the sufferance of his master, as if he considered he had a perfect right to do so.

The occasion of the meeting had been a communication which Flora had made concerning her most singular and deeply interesting interview with the vampyre. The details of this interview had produced a deep effect upon the whole of the family.

Flora was there, and she looked better, calmer, and more collected than she had done for some days past.

No doubt the interview she had had with Varney in the summer-house in the garden had dispelled a host of imaginary terrors with which she had surrounded him, although it had confirmed her fully that he and he only was the dreadful being who had caused her so much misery. That interview had tended to show her that about him there was yet something human, and that there was not a danger of her being hunted down from place to place by so horrible an existence.

Such a feeling as this was, of course, a source of deep consolation; and with a firmer voice, and more of her old spirit of cheerfulness about her than she had lately exhibited, she again detailed the particulars of the interview to all who had assembled concluding by saying, —

"And this has given me hope of happier days. If it be a delusion, it is a happy one; and now that but a frightful veil of mystery still hangs over the fate of Charles Holland, how gladly would I bid adieu to this place, and all that has made it terrible. I could almost pity Sir Francis Varney, rather than condemn him."

"That may be true," said Henry, "to a certain extent, sister; but we never can forget the amount of misery he has brought upon us. It is no slight thing to be forced from our old and much-loved home, even if such proceeding does succeed in freeing us from his persecutions."

"But, my young friend," said Marchdale, "you must recollect, that through life it is continually the lot of humanity to be endeavoring to fly from great evils to those which do not present themselves to the mind in so bad an aspect. It is something, surely, to alleviate affliction, if we cannot entirely remove it."

"That is true," said Mr. Chillingworth, "to a considerable extent, but then it takes too much for granted to please me."

"How so, sir?"

"Why, certainly, to remove from Bannerworth Hall is a much less evil than to remain at Bannerworth Hail, and be haunted by a vampyre; but then that proposition takes for granted that vampyre business, which I will never grant, I repeat, again and again, it is contrary to all experience, to philosophy, and to all the laws of ordinary nature."

"Facts are stubborn things," said Marchdale.

"Apparently," remarked Mr. Chillingworth.

"Well, sir; and here we have the fact of the vampyre."

"The presumed fact. One swallow don't make a summer, Mr. Marchdale."

"This is waste of time," said Henry — "of course, the amount of evidence that will suffice to bring conviction to one man's mind will fail in doing so to another. The question is, what are we to do?"

All eyes were turned upon Flora, as if this question was more particularly addressed to her, and it behooved her, above all others, to answer it. She did so; and in a firm, clear voice, she said, —

"I will discover the fate of Charles Holland and then leave the Hall."

"The fate of Charles Holland!" said Marchdale. "Why, really, unless that gentleman chooses to be communicative himself upon so interesting a subject, we may be a long while discovering his fate. I know that it is not a romantic view to take of the question, to suppose simply that he wrote the three letters found upon his dressing table, and then decamped; but to my mind, it savors most wonderfully of matter-of-fact. I now speak more freely than I have otherwise done, for I am now upon the eve of my departure. I have no wish to remain here, and breed dissension in any family, or to run a tilt against anybody's prejudices." Here he looked at Admiral Bell. "I leave this house tonight."

"You're a d——d lubberly thief," said the admiral; "the sooner you leave it the better. Why, you bad-looking son of a gun, what do you mean? I thought we'd had enough of that."

"I fully expected this abuse," said Marchdale.

"Did you expect that?" said the admiral, as he snatched up an inkstand, and threw at Marchdale, hitting him a hard knock on the chin, and bespattering its contents on his breast. "Now I'll give you satisfaction, you lubber. D — me, if you ain't a second Jones, and enough to sink the ship. Shiver my timbers if I shan't say something strong presently."

"I really," said Henry, "must protest, Admiral Bell, against this conduct."

"Protest and be d—d."

"Mr. Marchdale may be right, sir, or he may be wrong, it's a matter of opinion."

"Oh, never mind," said Marchdale; "I look upon this old nautical ruffian as something between a fool and a madman. If he were a younger man I should chastise him upon the spot; but as it is I live in hopes yet of getting him into some comfortable lunatic asylum."

"Me into an asylum!" shouted the admiral. "Jack, did you hear that?"

"Ay, ay, sir."

"Farewell all of you," said Marchdale; "my best wishes be with this family. I cannot remain under this roof to be so insulted."

"A good riddance," cried the admiral. "I'd rather sail round the world with a shipload of vampyres than with such a humbugging son of a gun as you are. D — e, you're worse than a lawyer."

"Nay, nay," cried they, "Mr. Marchdale, stay."

"Stay, stay," cried George, and Mrs. Bannerworth, likewise, said stay; but at the moment Flora stepped forward, and in a clear voice she said, —

"No, let him go, he doubts Charles Holland; let all go who doubt Charles Holland. Mr. Marchdale, Heaven forgive you this injustice you are doing. We may never meet again. Farewell, sir!" These words were spoken in so decided a tone, that no one contradicted them. Marchdale cast a strange kind of look round upon the family circle, and in another instant he was gone.

"Huzza!" shouted Jack Pringle; "that's one good job."

Henry looked rather resentful, which the admiral could not but observe, and so, less with the devil-may-care manner in which he usually spoke, the old man addressed him.

"Hark ye, Mr. Henry Bannerworth, you ain't best pleased with me, and in that case I don't know that I shall stay to trouble you any longer; as for your friend who has just left you, sooner or later you'll find him out — I tell you there's no good in that fellow. Do you think I've been cruising about for a matter of sixty years, and don't know an honest man when I see him. But never mind, I'm going on a voyage of discovery for my nephew, and you can do as you like."

"Heaven only knows, Admiral Bell," said Henry, "who is right and who is wrong. I do much regret that you have quarreled with Mr. Marchdale; but what is done can't be undone."

"Do not leave us," said Flora; "let me beg of you, Admiral Bell, not to leave us; for my sake remain here, for to you I can speak freely and with confidence, of Charles, when probably I can do so to no one else. You know him well and have a confidence in him, which no one else can aspire to. I pray you, therefore, to stay with us."

"Only on one condition," said the admiral.

"Name it — name it!"

"You think of letting the Hall go."

"Yes, yes."

"Let me have it, then, and let me pay a few years in advance. If you don't, I'm d — d if I stay another night in the place. You must give me immediate possession, too, and stay here as my guests until you suit yourselves elsewhere. Those are my terms and conditions. Say yes, and all's right; say no, and I'm off like a round shot from a carronade. D — me, that's the thing Jack, isn't it?"

"Ay, ay, sir."

There was a silence of some few moments after this extraordinary offer had been made, and then they spoke, saying, —

"Admiral Bell, your generous offer, and the feelings which dictated it, are by far too transparent for us to affect not to understand them. Your actions, Admiral —"

"Oh, bother my actions! what are they to you? Come, now, I consider myself master of the house, d — n you! I invite you all to dinner, or supper, or to whatever meal comes next. Mrs. Bannerworth, will you oblige me, as I'm an old fool in family affairs, by buying what's wanted for me and my guests? There's the money, ma'am. Come along, Jack, we'll take a look over our new house. What do you think of it?"

"Wants some sheathing, sir, here and there."

"Very like; but, however, it will do well enough for us; we're in port, you know. Come along."

"Ay, ay, sir."

And off went the admiral and Jack, after leaving a twenty-pound note in Mrs. Bannerworth's lap.

Chapter *XXXVII.*

SIR FRANCIS VARNEY'S SEPARATE OPPONENTS. – THE INTERPOSITION OF FLORA.

*T*he old admiral so completely overcame the family of the Bannerworths by his generosity and evident single-mindedness of his behavior, that, although not one, except Flora, approved of his conduct towards Mr. Marchdale; yet they could not help liking him; and had they been placed in a position to choose which of the two they would have had remain with them, the admiral or Marchdale, there can be no question they would have made choice of the former.

Still, however, it was not pleasant to find a man like Marchdale virtually driven from the house, because he presumed to differ in opinion upon a very doubtful matter with another of its inmates. But as it was the nature of the Bannerworth family always to incline to the most generous view of subjects, the frank, hearty confidence of the old admiral in Charles Holland pleased them better than the calm and serious doubting of Marchdale.

His ruse of hiring the house of them, and paying the rent in advance, for the purpose of placing ample funds in their hands for any contingency, was not the less amiable because it was so easily seen through; and they could not make up their minds to hurt the feelings of the old man by the rejection of his generous offer.

When he had left, this subject was canvassed among them, and it was agreed that he should have his own way in the matter for the present, although they hoped to hear something from Marchdale, which would make his departure appear less abrupt and uncomfortable to the whole of the family.

During the course of this conversation, it was made known to Flora with more distinctness than under any other circumstances it would have been, that Charles Holland had been on the eve of a duel with Sir

Francis Varney, previous to his mysterious disappearance.

When she became fully aware of this fact, to her mind it seemed materially to add to the suspicions previously to then entertained, that foul means had been used in order to put Charles out of the way.

"Who knows," she said, "that this Varney may not shrink with the greatest terror from a conflict with any human being, and feeling one was inevitable with Charles Holland, unless interrupted by some vigorous act of his own, he or some myrmidons of his may have taken Charles's life!"

"I do not think, Flora," said Henry, "that he would have ventured upon so desperate an act; I cannot well believe such a thing possible. But fear not; he will find, if he have really committed any such atrocity, that it will not save him."

These words of Henry, though it made no impression at the time upon Flora, beyond what they carried upon their surface, they really, however, as concerned Henry himself, implied a settled resolution, which he immediately set about reducing to practice.

When the conference broke up, night, as it still was, he, without saying anything to any one, took his hat and cloak, and left the Hall, proceeding by the nearest practicable route to the residence of Sir Francis Varney, where he arrived without any interruption of any character.

Varney was at first denied to him, but before he could leave the house, a servant came down the great staircase to say it was a mistake; and that Sir Francis was at home, and would be happy to see him.

He was ushered into the same apartment where Sir Francis Varney had before received his visitors; and there sat the now declared vampyre, looking pale and ghastly by the dim light which burned in the apartment, and, indeed, more like some specter of the tomb than one of the great family of man.

"Be seated, sir," said Varney; "although my eyes have seldom the pleasure of beholding you within these walls, be assured you are a honored guest."

"Sir Francis Varney," said Henry, "I came not here to bandy compliments with you; I have none to pay to you, nor do I wish to hear any of them from your lips."

"An excellent sentiment, young man," said Varney, "and well delivered. May I presume, then, without infringing too far upon your extreme courtesy, to inquire, to what circumstances I am indebted for your visit?"

"To one, Sir Francis, that I believe you are better acquainted with than you have the candor to admit."

"Indeed, sir," said Varney, coldly "you measure my candor, probably, by a standard of your own; in which case, I fear I may be no gainer; and yet that may be of itself a circumstance that should afford little food for surprise, but proceed, sir — since we have so few compliments to stand between us and our purpose, we shall in all due time arrive at it."

"Yes, in due time, Sir Francis Varney, and that due time has arrived. Know you any thing of my friend, Charles Holland?" said Henry, in marked accents; and he gazed on Sir Francis Varney with earnestness, that seemed to say not even a look should escape his observation.

Varney, however, returned the gaze as steadily, but coldly, as he replied in his measured accents, —

"I have heard of the young gentleman."

"And seen him?"

"And seen him too, as you, Mr. Bannerworth, must be well aware. Surely you have not come all this way, merely to make such an inquiry; but, sir, you are welcome to the answer."

Henry had something of a struggle to keep down the rising anger, at these cool taunts of Varney; but he succeeded — and then he said, —

"I suspect Charles Holland, Sir Francis Varney, has met with unfair treatment, and that he has been unfairly dealt with, for an unworthy purpose."

"Undoubtedly," said Varney, "if the gentleman you allude to, has been unfairly dealt with, it was for a foul purpose; for no good or generous object, my young sir, could be so obtained — you acknowledge so much, I doubt not?"

"I do, Sir Francis Varney; and hence the purpose of my visit here — for this reason I apply to you —"

"A singular object, supported by a singular reason. I cannot see the connection, young sir; pray proceed to enlighten me upon this matter, and when you have done that, may I presume upon your consideration, to inquire in what way I can be of any service to you?"

"Sir Francis," said Henry, his anger raising his tones — "this will not serve you — I have come to exact an account of how you have disposed of my friend; and I will have it."

"Gently, my good sir; you are aware I know nothing of your friend; his motions are his own; and as to what I have done with him; my only answer is, that he would permit me to do nothing with him, had I been so inclined to have taken the liberty."

"You are suspected, Sir Francis Varney, of having made an attempt upon the life or liberty of Charles Holland; you, in fact, are suspected of being his murderer — and, so help me Heaven! if I have not justice, I will have vengeance!"

"Young sir, your words are of grave import and ought to be coolly considered before they are uttered. With regard to justice and vengeance, Mr. Bannerworth, you may have both; but I tell you, of Charles Holland, or what has become of him, I know nothing. But wherefore do you come to so unlikely a quarter to learn something of an individual of whom I know nothing?"

"Because Charles Holland was to have fought a duel with you: but before that had time to take place, he has suddenly become missing. I suspect that you are the author of his disappearance, because you fear an encounter with a mortal man."

"Mr. Bannerworth, permit me to say, in my own defense, that I do not fear any man, however foolish he may be; and wisdom is not an attribute I find, from experience in all men, of your friend. However, you must be dreaming, sir — a kind of vivid insanity has taken possession of your mind, which distorts —

"Sir Francis Varney!" exclaimed Henry, now perfectly uncontrollable.

"Sir," said Varney, as he filled up the pause, "proceed; I am all attention. You do me honor."

"If," resumed Henry, "such was your object in putting Mr. Holland aside, by becoming personally or by proxy an assassin, you are mistaken in supposing you have accomplished your object."

"Go on, sir," said Sir Francis Varney, in a bland and sweet tone; "I am all attention; pray proceed."

"You have failed; for I now here, on this spot, defy you to mortal combat. Coward, assassin as you are, I challenge you to fight."

"You don't mean on the carpet here?" said Varney, deliberately.

"No, sir; but beneath the canopy of heaven, in the light of the day. And then, Sir Francis, we shall see who will shrink from the conflict."

"It is remarkably good, Mr. Bannerworth, and, begging your pardon, for I do not wish to give any offence, my honored sir, it would rehearse before an audience; in short, sir, it is highly dramatic."

"You shrink from the combat, do you? Now, indeed, I know you."

"Young man, young man," said Sir Francis, calmly, and shaking his head very deliberately, and the shadows passed across his pale face, "you know me not, if you think Sir Francis Varney shrinks from any man, much less one like yourself."

"You are a coward, and worse, if you refuse my challenge."

"I do not refuse it; I accept it," said Varney, calmly, and in a dignified manner; and then, with a sneer, he added, — "You are well acquainted with the mode in which gentlemen generally manage these matters, Mr. Bannerworth, and perhaps I am somewhat confined in my knowledge in the ways of the world, because you are your own principal and second. In all my experience, I never met with a similar case."

"The circumstances under which it is given are as unexampled, and will excuse the mode of the challenge," said Henry, with much warmth.

"Singular coincidence — the challenge and mode of it is most singular! They are well matched in that respect. Singular, did I say? The more I think of it, Mr. Bannerworth, the more I am inclined to think this positively odd."

"Early tomorrow, Sir Francis, you shall hear from me."

"In that case, you will not arrange preliminaries now? Well, well; it is very unusual for the principals themselves to do so; and yet, excuse my freedom, I presumed, as you had so far deserted the beaten track, that I had no idea how far you might be disposed to lead the same route."

"I have said all I intended to say, Sir Francis Varney; we shall see each other again."

"I may not detain you, I presume, to taste aught in the way of refreshment?"

Henry made no reply, but turned towards the door, without even making an attempt to return the grave and formal bow that Sir Francis Varney made as he saw him about to quit the apartment; for Henry saw that his pale features were lighted up with a sarcastic smile, most disagreeable to look upon as well as irritating to Henry Bannerworth.

He now quitted Sir Francis Varney's abode, being let out by a servant who had been rung for for that purpose by his master.

Henry walked homeward, satisfied that he had now done all that he could under the circumstances.

"I will send Chillingworth to him in the morning, and then I shall see what all this will end in. He must meet me, and then Charles Holland, if not discovered, shall be, at least, revenged."

There was another person in Bannerworth Hall who had formed a similar resolution. That person was a very different sort of person to Henry Bannerworth, though quite as estimable in his way.

This was no other than the old admiral. It was singular that two such very different persons should deem the same steps necessary, and both keep the secret from each other; but so it was, and, after some internal swearing, he determined upon challenging Varney in person.

"I'd send Jack Pringle, but the swab would settle the matter as shortly as if a youngster was making an entry in a log, and heard the boatswain's whistle summoning the hands to a mess, and feared he would lose his grog.

"D — n my quarters! but Sir Francis Varney, as he styles himself, shan't make any way against old Admiral Bell. He's as tough as a hawser, and just the sort of blade for a vampyre to come athwart. I'll pitch him end-long, and make a plank of him afore long. Cus my windpipe! what a long, lanky swab he is, with teeth fit to unpick a splice; but let me alone, I'll see if I can't make a hull of his carcass, vampyre or no vampyre.

"My nevy, Charles Holland, can't be allowed to cut away without nobody's leave or license. No, no; I'll not stand that anyhow. 'Never desert a messmate in the time of need,' is the first maxim of a seaman, and I ain't the one as'll do so."

Thus self-communing, the old admiral marched along; until he came to Sir Francis Varney's house, at the gate of which he gave the bell what he called a long pull, a strong pull, and a pull altogether, that set it ringing with a fury, the like of which had never certainly been heard by the household.

A minute or two scarcely elapsed before the domestics hurried to answer so urgent a summons; and when the gate was opened, the servant who answered it inquired his business.

"What's that to you, snob? Is your master, Sir Francis Varney, in? because, if he be, let him know old Admiral Bell wants to speak to him. D'ye hear?"

"Yes, sir," replied the servant, who had paused a few moments to examine the individual who gave this odd kind of address. In another minute word was brought to him that Sir Francis Varney would he very happy to see Admiral Bell.

"Ay, ay," he muttered; "just as the devil likes to meet with holy water, or as I like any water save salt water."

He was speedily introduced to Sir Francis Varney, who was seated in the same posture as he had been left by Henry Bannerworth not many minutes before.

"Admiral Bell," said Sir Francis, rising, and bowing to that individual in the most polite, calm, and dignified manner imaginable, "permit me to express the honor I feel at this unexpected visit."

"None of your gammon."

"Will you be seated. Allow me to offer you such refreshments as this poor house affords."

"D — n all this! You know, Sir Francis, I don't want none o' this palaver. It's for all the world like a Frenchman, when you are going to give him a broadside; he makes grimaces, throws dust in your eyes, and tries to stab you in the back. Oh, no! none of that for me."

"I should say not, Admiral Bell. I should not like it myself, and I dare say you are a man of too much experience not to perceive when you are or are not imposed upon."

"Well, what is that to you? D — n me, I didn't come here to talk to you about myself."

"Then may I presume upon your courtesy so far as to beg that you will enlighten me upon the object of your visit?"

"Yes; in pretty quick time. Just tell me where you have stowed away my nephew, Charles Holland?"

"Really, I —"

"Hold your slack, will you, and hear me out; if he's living, let him out, and I'll say no more about it; that's liberal, you know; it ain't terms everybody would offer you."

"I must, in truth, admit they are not; and, moreover, they quite surprise even me, and I have learned not to be surprised at almost anything."

"Well, will you give him up alive? but, hark ye, you mustn't have made very queer fish of him, do ye see?"

"I hear you," said Sir Francis, with a bland smile, passing one hand gently over the other, and showing his front teeth in a peculiar manner; "but I really cannot comprehend all this; but I may say, generally, that Mr. Holland is no acquaintance of mine, and I have no sort of knowledge where he may be."

"That won't do for me," said the admiral, positively, shaking his head.

"I am particularly sorry, Admiral Bell, that it will not, seeing that I have nothing else to say."

"I see how it is; you've put him out of the way, and I'm d——d if you shan't' bring him to life, whole and sound, or I'll know the reason why."

"With that I have already furnished you, Admiral Bell," quietly rejoined Varney; "anything more on that head is out of my power, although my willingness to oblige a person of such consideration as yourself, is very great; but, permit me to add, this is a very strange and odd communication from one gentleman to another. You have lost a relative, who has, very probably, taken some offence, or some notion into his head, of which nobody but himself knows anything, and you come to one yet more unlikely to know anything of him, than even yourself."

"Gammon again, now, Sir Francis Varney, or Blarney."

"Varney, if you please, Admiral Bell; I was christened Varney."

"Christened, eh?"

"Yes, christened — were you not christened? If not, I dare say you understand the ceremony well enough."

"I should think I did; but, as for christening, a —"

"Go on, sir."

"A vampyre! why I should as soon think of reading the burial service of a pig."

"Very possible; but what has all this to do with your visit to me?"

"This much, you lubber. Now, d — n my carcass from head to stern, if I don't call you out."

"Well, Admiral Bell," said Varney, mildly, "in that case, I suppose I must come out; but why do you insist that I have any knowledge of your nephew, Mr. Charles Holland?"

"You were to have fought a duel with him, and now he's gone."

"I am here," said Varney.

"Ay," said the admiral, "that's as plain as a purser's shirt upon a handspike; but that's the very reason why my nevey ain't here, and that's all about it."

"And that's marvelous little, so far as the sense is concerned," said Varney, without the movement of a muscle.

"It is said that people of your class don't like fighting mortal men;

now you have disposed of him, lest he should dispose of you."

"That is explicit, but it is to no purpose, since the gentleman in question hasn't placed himself at my disposal."

"Then, d — e, I will; fish, flesh, or fowl, I don't care; all's one to Admiral Bell. Come fair or foul, I'm a tar for all men; a seaman ever ready to face a foe, so here goes, you lubberly moon manufactured calf."

"I hear, admiral, but it is scarcely civil, to say the least of it; however, as you are somewhat eccentric, and do not, I dare say, mean all your words imply, I am quite willing to make every allowance."

"I don't want any allowance; d — n you and your allowance, too; nothing but allowance of grog, and a pretty good allowance, too, will do for me, and I tell you, Sir Francis Varney," said the admiral, with much wrath, "that you are a d—d lubberly hound, and I'll fight you; yes, I'm ready to hammer away, or with anything from a pop-gun to a ship's gun; you don't come over me with your gammon, I tell you. You've murdered Charles Holland because you couldn't face him — that's the truth of it."

"With the other part of your speech, Admiral Bell, allow me to say, you have mixed up a serious accusation — one I cannot permit to pass lightly."

"Will you or not fight?"

"Oh, yes; I shall be happy to serve you any way that I can. I hope this will be an answer to your accusation, also."

"That's settled, then."

"Why, I am not captious, Admiral Bell, but it is not generally usual for the principals to settle the preliminaries themselves; doubtless you, in your career of fame and glory know something of the manner in which gentlemen demean themselves on these occasions."

"Oh, d — n you! Yes, I'll send some one to do all this. Yes, yes, Jack Pringle will be the man, though Jack ain't a holiday, shore-going, smooth-spoken swab, but as good a seaman as ever trod deck or handled a boarding-pike."

"Any friend of yours," said Varney, blandly, "will be received and treated as such upon an errand of such consequence; and now our conference has, I presume, concluded."

"Yes, yes, we've done — d — e, no — yes — no. I will keel-haul you but I'll know something of my neavy, Charles Holland."

"Good day, Admiral Bell." As Varney spoke, he placed his hand upon the bell which he had near him, to summon an attendant to conduct the admiral out. The latter, who had said a vast deal more than he ever intended, left the room in a great rage, protesting to himself that he would amply avenge his nephew, Charles Holland.

He proceeded homeward, considerably vexed and annoyed that he had been treated with so much calmness, and all knowledge of his nephew denied.

When he got back, he quarreled heartily with Jack Pringle — made it up — drank grog — quarreled — made it up, and finished with grog again — until he went to bed swearing he should like to fire a broadside at the whole of the French army, and annihilate it at once.

With this wish, he fell asleep.

Early next morning, Henry Bannerworth sought Mr. Chillingworth, and having found him, he said in a serious tone, —

"Mr. Chillingworth, I have rather a serious favor to ask you, and one which you may hesitate in granting."

"It must be very serious indeed," said Mr. Chillingworth, "that I should hesitate to grant it to you; but pray inform me what it is what you deem so serious?"

"Sir Francis Varney and I must have a meeting," said Henry.

"Have you really determined upon such a course?" said Mr. Chillingworth; "You know the character of your adversary?"

"That is all settled, — I have given a challenge, and he has accepted it; so all other considerations verge themselves into one — and that is the when, where, and how."

"I see," said Mr. Chillingworth. "Well, since it cannot be helped on your part, I will do what is requisite for you — do you wish anything to be done or insisted on in particular in this affair."

"Nothing with regard to Sir Francis Varney that I may not leave to your discretion. I feel convinced that he is the assassin of Charles Holland, whom he feared to fight in duel."

"Then there remains but little else to do, but to arrange preliminaries, I believe. Are you prepared on every other point?"

"I am — you will see that I am the challenger, and that he must now fight. What accident may turn up to save him, I fear not, but sure I am, that he will endeavor to take every advantage that may arise, and so escape the encounter."

"And what do you imagine he will do now he has accepted your challenge?" said Mr. Chillingworth; "one would imagine he could not very well escape."

"No — but he accepted the challenge which Charles Holland sent him — a duel was inevitable, and it seems to me to be a necessary consequence that he disappeared from amongst us, for Mr. Holland would never have shrunk from the encounter."

"There can be no sort of suspicion about that," remarked Chillingworth; "but allow me to advise you that you take care of yourself, and keep a watchful eye upon everyone — do not be seen out alone."

"I fear not."

"Nay, the gentleman who has disappeared was, I am sure, fearless enough; but yet that has not saved him. I would not advise you to be fearful, only watchful; you have now an event awaiting upon you which it is well you should go through with, unless circumstances should so turn out, that it is needless; wherefore I say, when you have the suspicions you do entertain of this man's conduct, beware, be cautious, and vigilant."

"I will do so — in the mean time, I trust myself confidently in your hands — you know all that is necessary."

"This affair is quite a secret from all of the family?"

"Most certainly so, and will remain so — I shall be at the Hall."

"And there I will see you — but be careful not to be drawn into any adventure of any kind — it is best to be on the safe side under all circumstances."

"I will be especially careful, be assured, but farewell; see Sir Francis Varney as early as you can, and let the meeting be as early as you can, and thus diminish the chance of accident."

"That I will attend to. Farewell for the present."

Mr. Chillingworth immediately set about the conducting of the affair thus confided to him; and that no time might be lost, he determined to set out at once for Sir Francis Varney's residence.

"Things with regard to this family seem to have gone on wild of late," thought Mr. Chillingworth; "this may bring affairs to a conclusion, though I had much rather they had come to some other. My life for it, there is a juggle or a mystery, somewhere; I will do this, and then we shall see what will come of it; if this Sir Francis Varney meets him — and at this moment I can see no reason why he should not do so — it will tend much to deprive him of the mystery about him; but if, on the other hand, he refuse — but then that's all improbable, because he has agreed to do so. I fear however, that such a man as Varney is a dreadful enemy to encounter — he is cool and unruffled — and that gives him all the advantage in such affairs; but Henry's nerves are not bad, though shaken by these untoward events; but time will show — I would it were all over."

With these thoughts and feelings strangely intermixed, Mr. Chillingworth set forward for Sir Francis Varney's house.

*A*dmiral Bell slept soundly enough, though, towards morning, he fell into a strange dream, and thought he was yard arm and yard arm with a strange fish — something of the mermaid species.

"Well," exclaimed the admiral, after a customary benediction of his eyes and limbs, "what's to come next? may I be spliced to a shark if I understand what this is all about. I had some grog last night, but then grog, d'y'see, is a seaman's native element, as the newspapers say, though

I never read 'em now, it's such a plague."

He lay quiet for a short time, considering in his own mind what was best to be done and what was the proper course to pursue and why he should dream.

"Hilloa, hilloa, hil — loa Jack a-hoy! a-hoy!" shouted the admiral, as a sudden recollection of his challenge came across his memory; "Jack Pringle a-hoy? d — n you, where are you? — you're never at hand when you are wanted. Oh, you lubber, — a-hoy !"

"A-hoy!" shouted a voice, as the door opened, and Jack thrust his head in; "what cheer, messmate? what ship is this?"

"Oh, you lubberly —"

The door was shut in a minute, and Jack Pringle disappeared.

"Hilloa, Jack Pringle, you don't mean to say you'll desert your colors, do you, you dumb dog?"

"Who, says I'll desert the ship as she's sea-worthy?"

"Then why do you go away?"

"Because I won't be called lubberly, I'm as good a man as ever swabbed a deck, and don't care who says to the contrary. I'll stick to the ship as long as she's sea-worthy," said Jack.

"Well, come here, and just listen to the log, and be d——d to you."

"What's the orders now, admiral?" said Jack, "though, as we are paid off —"

"There, take that, will you?" said Admiral Bell, as he flung a pillow at Jack, being the only thing in the shape of a missile within reach.

Jack ducked, and the pillow produced a clatter in the washhand-stand among the crockery, as Jack said, —

"There's a mutiny in the ship, and hark how the cargo clatters; will you have it back again?"

"Come, will you? I've been dreaming, Jack."

"Dreaming! what's that?"

"Thinking of something when you are asleep, you swab."

"Ha, ha, ha!" laughed Jack; "never did such a thing in my life — ha, ha, ha! what's the matter now?"

"I'll tell you what's the matter, Jack Pringle, you are becoming mutinous, and I won't have it; if you don't hold your jaw and draw in your slacks, I'll have another second."

"Another second! what's in the wind, now?" said Jack. "Is this the dream?"

"If ever I dream when I'm alongside a strange craft, then it is a dream; but old Admiral Bell ain't the man to sleep when there's any work to be done."

"That's uncommon true," said Jack, turning a quid.

"Well, then, I'm to fight."

"Fight!" exclaimed Jack. "Avast, there, I don't see where's the enemy

— none o' that gammon; Jack Pringle can fight, too, and will lay alongside his admiral, but he don't see the enemy anywhere."

"You don't understand these things, so I'll tell you. I have had a bit of talk with Sir Francis Varney, and I am going to fight him."

"What the *wamphigher?*" remarked Jack, parenthetically.

"Yes."

"Well, then," resumed Jack, "then we shall see another blaze, at least afore we die; but he's an odd fish — one of Davy Jones's sort."

"I don't care about that; he may be anything he likes; but Admiral Bell ain't a-going to have his nephew burned and eaten, and sucked like don't know what, by a vampyre, or by any other confounded land-shark."

"In course," said Jack, "we ain't a-going to put up with nothing of that sort, and if so be as how he has put him out of the way, why it's our duty to send him arter him, and square the board."

"That's the thing, Jack; now you know you must go to Sir Francis Varney and tell him you come from me."

"I don't care if I goes on my own account," said Jack.

"That won't do; I've challenged him, and I must fight him."

"In course you will," returned Jack; "and, if he blows you away, why I'll take your place, and have a blaze myself."

The admiral gave a look at Jack of great admiration, and then said, —

"You are a d——d good seaman, Jack, but he's a knight, and might say no to that; but do you go to him, and tell him that you come from me to settle the when and the where this duel is to be fought."

"Single fight?" said Jack.

"Yes; consent to any thing that is fair," said the admiral, "but let it be as soon as you can. Now do you understand what I have said?"

"Yes, to be sure; I ain't lived all these years without knowing your lingo."

"Then go at once; and don't let the honor of Admiral Bell and old England suffer, Jack. I'm his man, you know, at any price."

"Never fear," said Jack; "you shall fight him, at any rate. I'll go and see he don't back out, the warmint."

"Then go along, Jack; and mind don't you go blazing away like a fire ship, and letting everybody know what's going on, or it'll be stopped."

"I'll not spoil sport," said Jack, as he left the room, to go at once to Sir Francis Varney, charged with the conducting of the important cartel of the admiral. Jack made the best of his way with becoming gravity and expedition until he reached the gate of the admiral's enemy.

Jack rang loudly at the gate; there seemed, if one might judge by his countenance, a something on his mind, that Jack was, almost another man. The gate was opened by the servant, who inquired what he wanted there.

"The wamphigher."

"Who?"

"The wamphigher."

The servant frowned, and was about to say something uncivil to Jack, who looked at him very hard, and then said, —

"Oh, may be you don't know him, or won't know him by that name: I wants to see Sir Francis Varney."

"He's at home," said the servant; "who are you?"

"Show me up, then. I'm Jack Pringle, and I'm come from Admiral Bell; I'm the admiral's friend, you see, so none of your black looks."

The servant seemed amazed, as well as rather daunted, at Jack's address; he showed him, however, into the hall, where Mr. Chillingworth had just that moment arrived, and was waiting for an interview with Varney.

Chapter XXXVIII.

MARCHDALE'S OFFER. — THE CONSULTATION AT BANNERWORTH HALL. — THE MORNING OF THE DUEL.

*M*r. Chillingworth was much annoyed to see Jack Pringle in the hall and Jack was somewhat surprised at seeing Mr. Chillingworth there at that time in the morning; they had but little time to indulge in their mutual astonishment, for a servant came to announce that Sir Francis Varney would see them both.

Without saying anything to the servant or each other, they ascended the staircase, and were shown into the apartment where Sir Francis Varney received them.

"Gentlemen," said Sir Francis, in his usual bland tone, "you are welcome."

"Sir Francis," said Mr. Chillingworth, "I have come upon matters of some importance; may I crave a separate audience?"

"And I too," said Jack Pringle; "I come as the friend of Admiral Bell, I want a private audience; but, stay, I don't care a rope's end who knows who I am, or what I come about; say you are ready to name time and place, and I'm as dumb as a figurehead; that is saying something, at all events; and now I'm done."

"Why, gentlemen," said Sir Francis, with a quiet smile, "as you have both come upon the same errand, and as there may arise a controversy upon the point of precedence, you had better be both present, as I must arrange this matter myself upon due inquiry."

"I do not exactly understand this," said Mr. Chillingworth; "do you, Mr. Pringle? perhaps you can enlighten me?"

"If," said Jack, "as how you came here upon the same errand as I, and I as you, why we both come about fighting Sir Francis Varney."

"Yes," said Sir Francis; "what Mr. Pringle says, is, I believe correct to a letter. I have a challenge from both your principals, and am ready to give you both the satisfaction you desire, provided the first encounter will permit me the honor of joining in the second. You, Mr. Pringle, are aware of the chances of war?"

"I should say so," said Jack, with a wink and a nod of a familiar character. "I've seen a few of them."

"Will you proceed to make the necessary agreement between you both gentlemen? My affection for the one equals fully the good will I bear the other, and I cannot give a preference in so delicate a matter; proceed gentlemen."

Mr. Chillingworth looked at Jack, and Jack Pringle looked at Mr. Chillingworth, and then the former said, —

"Well, the admiral means fighting, and I am come to settle the necessaries; pray let me know what are your terms, Mr. What-d'ye-call-'em."

"I am agreeable to anything that is at all reasonable — pistols, I presume?"

"Sir Francis Varney," said Mr. Chillingworth, "I cannot consent to carry on this office, unless you can appoint a friend who will settle these matters with us — myself, at least."

"And I too," said Jack. Pringle; "we don't want to bear down an enemy. Admiral Bell ain't the man to do that, and if he were, I'm not the man to back him in doing what isn't fair or right; but he won't do it."

"But, gentlemen, this must not be; Mr. Henry Bannerworth must not be disappointed, and Admiral Bell must not be disappointed. Moreover, I have accepted the two cartels, and I am ready and willing to fight; — one at a time, I presume!"

"Sir Francis, after what you have said, I must take upon myself, on the part of Mr. Henry Bannerworth, to decline meeting you, if you cannot name a friend with whom I can arrange this affair."

"Ah!" said Jack Pringle, "that's right enough. I recollect very well when Jack Mizen fought Tom Foremast, they had their seconds. Admiral Bell can't do anything in the dark. No, no, d — e! all must be above board."

"Gentlemen," said Sir Francis Varney, "you see the dilemma I am in. Your principals have both challenged me. I am ready to fight any one, or both of them, as the case may be. Distinctly understand that; because it is a notion of theirs that I will not do so, or that I shrink from them; but I am a stranger in this neighborhood, and have no one whom I could call upon to relinquish so much, as they run the risk of doing by attending me to the field."

"Then your acquaintances are no friends, d — e!" said Jack Pringle, spitting through his teeth into the bars of a beautifully polished grate. "I'd stick to anybody — the devil himself, leave alone a vampyre — if so be as how I had been his friend and drunk from the same can. They are a set of lubbers."

"I have not been here long enough to form any such friendships, Mr. Chillingworth; but can confidently rely upon your honor and that of your principal, and will freely and fairly meet him."

"But, Sir Francis, you forget the fact, in thus acting, myself for Mr. Bannerworth, and this person for Admiral Bell, we do much, and have our own characters at stake; lives and fortunes. These may be small, but they are everything to us. Allow me to say, on my own behalf, that I will not permit my principal to meet you unless you can name a second as is usual with gentlemen on such occasions."

"I regret, while I declare to you my entire willingness to meet you, that I cannot comply through utter inability to do so, with your request. Let this to forth to the world as I have stated it, and let it be an answer to any aspersions that may be uttered as to my unwillingness to fight."

There was a pause of some moments. Mr. Chillingworth was resolved that, come what would, he would not permit Henry to fight, unless Sir Francis Varney himself should appoint a friend and then they I could meet upon equal terms.

Jack Pringle whistled, and spit, and chewed and turned his quid — hitched up his trousers, and looked wistfully from one to the other, as he said, —

"So then it's likely to be no fight at all, Sir Francis What's-o'-name?"

"It seems like it, Mr. Pringle," replied Varney, with a with meaning smile; "unless I you can be more complaisant towards myself, and kindly towards the admiral."

"Why, not exactly that," said Jack; "it's a pity to stop a good play in the beginning, just because some little thing is wrong in the tackling."

"Perhaps your skill and genius may enable us to find some medium course that we may pursue with pleasure and profit. What say you, Mr. Pringle?"

"All I know about genius, as you call it, is the Flying Dutchman, or some such odd, out o' the way fish. But, as I said, I am not one to spoil sport, nor more is the admiral. Oh, no, we is all true men and good."

"I believe it," said Varney, bowing politely.

"You needn't keep your figure-head on the move; I can see you just as well. Howsoever, as I was saying, I don't like to spoil sport, and sooner than both parties should be disappointed, my principal shall become your second, Sir Francis."

"What, Admiral Bell!" exclaimed Varney, lifting his eyebrows with surprise.

"What, Charles Holland's uncle!" exclaimed Mr. Chillingworth, in accents of amazement.

"And why not?" said Jack, with great gravity. "I will pledge my word — Jack Pringle's word — that Admiral Bell shall be second to Sir Francis Varney, during his scrimmage with Mr. Henry Bannerworth. That will let the matter go on; there can be no back-out then, eh?" continued Jack Pringle, with a knowing nod at Chillingworth as he spoke.

"That will, I hope, remove your scruples, Mr. Chillingworth," said Varney, with a courteous smile.

"But will Admiral Bell do this?"

"His second says so, and has, I daresay, influence enough with him to induce that person to act in conformity with his promise."

"In course he will. Do you think he would be the man to hang back? Oh, no; he would be the last to leave Jack Pringle in the lurch — no. Depend upon it, Sir Francis, he'll be as sure to do what I say, as I have said it."

"After that assurance, I cannot doubt it," said Sir Francis Varney; "this act of kindness will, indeed, lay me under a deep and lasting obligation to Admiral Bell, which I fear I shall never be able to pay."

"You need not trouble yourself about that," said Jack Pringle; "the admiral will credit all, and you can pay off old scores when his turn comes in the field."

"I will not forget," said Varney; "he deserves every consideration; but now, Mr. Chillingworth, I presume that we may come to some understanding respecting this meeting, which you were so kind as to do me the honor of seeking."

"I cannot object to its taking place. I shall be most happy to meet your second in the field, and arrange with him."

"I imagine that, under the circumstances, that it will be barely necessary to go to that length of ceremony. Future interviews can be arranged later; name the time and place, and after that we can settle all the rest on the ground."

"Yes," said Jack; "it will be time enough, surely, to see the admiral when we are upon the ground. I'll warrant the old buffer is a true brick as ever was; there's no flinching about him."

"I am satisfied," said Varney.

"And I also," said Chillingworth; "but, understand, Sir Francis, any fault for seconds makes the meeting a blank."

"I will not doubt Mr. Pringle's honor so much as to believe it possible."

"I'm d——d," said Jack, "if you ain't a trump-card, and no mistake; it's a great pity as you is a wamphigher."

"The time, Mr. Chillingworth?"

"Tomorrow, at seven o'clock?" replied that gentleman.

"The place, sir?"

"The best place that I can think of is a level meadow half-way between here and Bannerworth Hall; but that is your privilege, Sir Francis Varney."

"I waive it, and am much obliged to you for the choice of the spot; it seems of the best character imaginable. I will be punctual."

"I think we have nothing further to arrange now," said Mr. Chillingworth. "You will meet with Admiral Bell."

"Certainly. I believe there is nothing more to be done; this affair is very satisfactorily arranged, and much better than I anticipated."

"Good morning, Sir Francis," said Mr. Chillingworth. "Good morning."

"Adieu," said Sir Francis, with a courteous salutation. "Good day, Mr. Pringle, and commend me to the admiral, whose services will be of infinite value to me."

"Don't mention it," said Jack; "the admiral's the man as'd lend any body a helping hand in case of distress like the present; and I'll pledge my word — Jack Pringle's too, as that he'll do what's right, and give up his turn to Mr. Henry Bannerworth; cause you see he can have his I turn arterwards, you know — it's only waiting awhile."

"That's all," said Sir Francis.

Jack Pringle made a sea bow and took his leave, as he followed Mr. Chillingworth, and they both left the house together, to return to Bannerworth Hall.

"Well," said Mr. Chillingworth, "I am glad that Sir Francis Varney has got over the difficulty of having no seconds; for it would not be proper or safe to meet a man without a friend with him."

"It ain't the right thing," said Jack, hitching up his trousers; "but I was afeard as how he would back out, and that would be just the wrong thing for the admiral; he'd go raving mad."

They had got but very few paces from Sir Francis Varney's house, when they were joined by Marchdale.

"Ah," he said, as he came up, "I see you have been to Sir Francis Varney's, if I may judge from the direction whence you're coming, and your proximity."

"Yes, we have," said Mr. Chillingworth. "I thought you had left these parts?"

"I had intended to do so," replied Marchdale; "but second thoughts are some times best, you know."

"Certainly."

"I have so much friendship for the family at the hall, that not withstanding I am compelled to be absent from the mansion itself, yet I cannot quit the neighborhood while there are circumstances of such a character hanging about them. I will remain, and see if there be not something arising, in which I may be useful to them in some matter."

"It is very disinterested of you; you will remain here for some time, I suppose?"

"Yes, undoubtedly; unless, as I do not anticipate, I should see any occasion to quit my present quarters."

"I tell you what it is," said Jack Pringle; "if you had been here half-an-hour earlier, you could have seconded the wamphigher."

"Seconded!"

"Yes, we're here to challenge."

"A double challenge?"

"Yes; but in confiding this matter to you, Mr. Marchdale, you will make no use of it to the exploding of this affair. By so doing you will seriously damage the honor of Mr. Henry Bannerworth."

"I will not, you may rely upon it; but Mr. Chillingworth, do I not see you in the character of a second?"

"You do, sir."

"To Mr. Henry?"

"The same, sir."

"Have you reflected upon the probable consequences of such an act, should any serious mischief occur?"

"What I have undertaken, Mr. Marchdale, I will go through with; the consequences I have duly considered, and yet you see me in the character of Mr. Henry Bannerworth's friend."

"I am happy to see you as such, and I do not think Henry could find a worthier. But this is beside the question. What induced me to make the remark was this, — had I been at the hall, you will admit that Henry Bannerworth would have chosen myself, without any disparagement to you, Mr. Chillingworth."

"Well sir, what then?"

"Why I am a single man, I can live, reside and go any where; one country will suit me as well as another. I shall suffer no loss, but as for you, you will be ruined in every particular; for if you go in the character of a second, you will not be excused; for all the penalties incurred your profession of surgeon will not excuse you."

"I see all that, sir."

"What I propose is, that you should accompany the parties to the field, but in your own proper character of surgeon, and permit me to take that of second to Mr. Bannerworth."

"This cannot be done, unless by Mr. Henry Bannerworth's consent," said Mr. Chillingworth.

"Then I will accompany you to Bannerworth Hall, and see Mr. Henry, whom I will request to permit me to do what I have mentioned to you."

Mr. Chillingworth could not but admit the reasonableness of this proposal, and it was agreed they should return to Bannerworth Hall in company.

Here they arrived in a very short time after, and entered together.

"And now," said Mr. Chillingworth, "I will go and bring our two principals, who will be as much astonished to find themselves engaged in the same quarrel, as I was to find myself sent on a similar errand to Sir Francis with our friend Mr. John Pringle."

"Oh, not John – Jack Pringle, you mean," said that individual.

Chillingworth now went in search of Henry, and sent him to the apartment where Mr. Marchdale was with Jack Pringle, and then he found the admiral waiting the return of Jack with impatience.

"Admiral" he said, "I perceive you are unwell this morning."

"Unwell be d——d," said the admiral, starting up with surprise. "Who ever heard that old Admiral Bell looked ill just afore he was going into action? I say it's a scandalous lie."

"Admiral, admiral, I didn't say you were ill; only you looked ill – a – a little nervous, or so. Rather pale, eh? Is it not so?"

"Confound you, do you think I want to be physicked? I tell you, I have not a little but a great inclination to give you a good keelhauling. I don't want a doctor just yet."

"But it may not be so long, you know, admiral; but there is Jack Pringle a-waiting you below. Will you go to him? There is a particular reason; he has something to communicate from Sir Francis Varney, I believe."

The admiral gave a look of some amazement at Mr. Chillingworth, and then he said, muttering to himself, –

"If Jack Pringle should have betrayed me – but, no; he could not do that, he is too true. I'm sure of Jack; and how did that son of a galipot hint about the odd fish I sent Jack to?"

Filled with a dubious kind of belief which he had about something he had heard of Jack Pringle, he entered the room, where he met Marchdale, Jack Pringle, and Henry Bannerworth. Immediately afterwards, Mr. Chillingworth entered the apartment.

"I have," said he, "been to Sir Francis Varney, and there had an interview with him, and with Mr. Pringle; when I found we were both intent upon the same object, namely, an encounter with the knight by our principals."

"Eh?" said the admiral.

"What!" exclaimed Henry; "had he challenged you, admiral?"

"Challenged me!" exclaimed Admiral Bell, with a round oath. "I — however — since it comes to this, I must admit I challenged him."

"That's what I did," said Henry Bannerworth, after a moment's thought; "and I perceive we have both fallen into the same line of conduct."

"That is the fact," said Mr. Chillingworth. "Both Mr. Pringle and I went there to settle the preliminaries, and we found an insurmountable bar to any meeting taking place at all."

"He wouldn't fight, then?" exclaimed Henry. "I see it all now."

"Not fight!" said Admiral Bell with a sort of melancholy disappointment. "D — n the cowardly rascal! Tell me, Jack Pringle, what did the long horse-marine-looking slab say to it? He told me he would fight. Why he ought to be made to stand sentry over the wind."

"You challenged him in person, too, I suppose?" said Henry.

"Yes, confound him! I went there last night."

"And I too."

"It seems to me," said Marchdale, "that this affair has been not indiscreetly conducted; but somewhat unusually and strangely, to say the least of it."

"You see," said Chillingworth, "Sir Francis was willing to fight both Henry and the admiral, as he told us."

"Yes," said Jack; "he told us he would fight us both, if so be as his light was not doused in the first brush."

"That was all that was wanted," said the admiral. "We could expect no more."

"But then he desired to meet you without any second; but, of course, I would not accede to this proposal. The responsibility was too great and too unequally borne by the parties engaged in the reencounter."

"Decidedly," said Henry; "but it is unfortunate — very unfortunate."

"Very," said the admiral — "very. What a rascally thing it is there ain't another rogue in the country to keep him in countenance."

"I thought it was a pity to spoil sport" said Jack Pringle. "It was a pity a good intention should be spoiled, and I promised the wamphigher that if as how he would fight, you should second him and you'd meet him to do so."

"Eh! who? I?" exclaimed the admiral, in some perplexity.

"Yes; that is the truth," said Mr. Chillingworth. "Mr. Pringle said you would do so, and he then and there pledged his word that you should meet him on the ground and second him on it."

"Yes," said Jack. "You must do it. I knew you would not spoil sport, and that there had better be a fight than no fight. I believe you'd sooner see a scrimmage than none, and so it's all arranged."

"Very well," said the admiral; "I only I wish Mr. Henry Bannerworth had been his second; I think I was entitled to the first meeting."

"No," said Jack, "you warn't, for Mr. Chillingworth was there first; first come first served, you know."

"Well, well, I mustn't grumble at another other man's luck; mine'll come in turn; but it had better be so than a disappointment altogether; I'll be second to this Sir Francis Varney; he shall have fair play, as I'm an admiral; but, d — e he shall fight — yes, yes, he shall fight."

"And to this conclusion I would come," said Henry, "I wish him to fight; now I will take care that he shall not have any opportunity of putting me on one side quietly."

"There is one thing," observed Marchdale, "that I wished to propose. After what has passed, I should not have returned, had I not some presentiment that something was going forward in which I could be useful to my friend."

"Oh!" said the admiral, with a huge twist of his countenance.

"What I was about to say was this, — Mr. Chillingworth has much to lose as he is situated, and I nothing as I am placed; I am chained down to no spot of earth. I am above following a profession — my means, I mean, place me above the necessity. Now, Henry, allow me to be your second in this affair; allow Mr. Chillingworth to attend in his professional capacity; he may be of service — of great service to one of the principals; whereas, if he go in any other capacity, he will inevitably have his own safety to consult."

"That is most unquestionably true," said Henry, "and, to my mind, the best plan that can be proposed. What say you, Admiral Bell, will you act with Mr. Marchdale in this affair?"

"Oh, I! — Yes — certainly — I don't care. Mr. Marchdale is Mr. Marchdale, I believe, and that's all I care about. If we quarrel today, and have anything to do tomorrow, in course, tomorrow I can put off my quarrel for next day; it will keep, — that's all I have to say at present."

"Then this is a final arrangement?" said Mr. Chillingworth.

"It is."

"But, Mr. Bannerworth, in resigning my character of second to Mr. Marchdale, I only do so because it appears and seems to be the opinion of all present that I can be much better employed in another capacity."

"Certainly, Mr. Chillingworth; and I cannot but feel that I am under the same obligations to you for the readiness and zeal with which you have acted."

"I have done what I have done," said Chillingworth, — "because I believed it was my duty to do so."

"Mr. Chillingworth has undoubtedly acted most friendly and efficiently this affair," said Marchdale; "and he does not relinquish the part for the purpose of escaping a friendly deed, but to perform one in which he may act in a capacity that no one else can."

"That is true," said the admiral.

"And now," said Chillingworth, "you are to meet tomorrow morning in the meadow at the bottom of the valley, half way between here and Sir Francis Varney's house, at seven o'clock in the morning."

More conversation passed among them, and it was agreed that they should meet early the next morning, and that, of course, the affair should be kept a secret. Marchdale for that night should remain in the house, and the admiral should appear as if little or nothing was the matter; and he and Jack Pringle retired, to talk over in private all the arrangements.

Henry Bannerworth and Marchdale also retired, and Mr. Chillingworth, after a time, retired, promising to be with them in time for the meeting next morning.

Much of that day was spent by Henry Bannerworth in his own apartment, in writing documents and letters of one kind and another; but at night he had not finished, for he had been compelled to be about, and in Flora's presence, to prevent anything from being suspected.

Marchdale was much with him, and in secret examined the arms, ammunition, and bullets, and saw all was right for the next morning; and when he had done, he said, —

"Now, Henry, you must permit me to insist that you take some hours' repose, else you will scarcely be as you ought to be."

"Very good," said Henry. "I have just finished, and can take your advice."

After many thoughts and reflections, Henry Bannerworth fell into a deep sleep, and slept several hours in calmness and quietude, and at an early hour he awoke, and saw Marchdale sitting by him.

"Is it time, Marchdale? I have not overslept myself, have I?"

"No; time enough — time enough," said Marchdale. "I should have let you sleep longer, but I should have awakened you in good time."

It was now the grey light of morning, and Henry arose and began to prepare for the encounter. Marchdale stole to Admiral Bell's chamber, but he and Jack Pringle were ready.

Few words were spoken, and those few were in a whisper, and the whole party left the Hall in as noiseless a manner was possible. It was a mild morning, and yet it was cold at that time of the morning, just as day is beginning to dawn in the east. There was, however, ample time to reach the rendezvous.

It was a curious party that which was now proceeding towards the spot appointed for the duel, the result of which might have so important an effect on the interests of those who were to be engaged in it.

It would be difficult for us to analyze the different and conflicting emotions that filled the breasts of the various individuals composing that party — the hopes and fears — the doubts and surmises that were given utterance to; though we are compelled to acknowledge that though to Henry, the character of the man he was going to meet in mortal fight was of a most ambiguous and undefined nature, and though no one could imagine the means he might be endowed with for protection against the arms of man — Henry, as we said, strode firmly forward with unflinching resolution. His heart was set on recovering the happiness of his sister, and he would not falter.

So far, then, we may consider that at length proceedings of a hostile character were so far clearly and fairly arranged between Henry Bannerworth and that most mysterious being who certainly, from some cause or another, had betrayed no inclination to meet an opponent in that manner which is sanctioned, bad as it is, by the usages of society.

But whether his motive was one of cowardice or mercy, remained yet to be seen. It might be that he feared himself receiving some mortal injury, which would at once put a stop to that preternatural career of existence which he affected to shudder at, and yet evidently took considerable pains to prolong.

Upon the other hand, it is just possible that some consciousness of invulnerability on his own part, or of great power to injure his antagonist, might be the cause why he had held back so long from fighting the duel, and placed so many obstacles in the way of the usual necessary arrangements incidental to such occasions.

Now, however, there would seem to be no possible means of escape. Sir Francis Varney must fight or fly, for he was surrounded by too many opponents.

To be sure he might have appealed to the civil authorities to protect him, and to sanction him in his refusal to commit what undoubtedly is a legal offence; but then there cannot be a question that the whole of the circumstances would come out, and meet the public eye — the result of which would be, his acquisition of a reputation, as unenviable as it would be universal.

It had so happened, that the peculiar position of the Bannerworth family kept their acquaintance within extremely narrow limits, and greatly indisposed them to set themselves up as marks for peculiar observation. Once holding, as they had, a proud position in the county, and being looked upon as quite magnates of the land, they did not now court the prying eye of curiosity to look upon their poverty; but rather with a gloomy melancholy they lived apart, and repelled the advances of society by a cold reserve which few could break through.

Had this family suffered in any noble cause, or had the misfortunes which had come over them, and robbed their ancestral house of its luster, been an unavoidable dispensation of providence, they would have borne the hard position with a different aspect; but it must be remembered, that to the faults, the vices, and the criminality of some of their race, was to be attributed their present depressed state.

It has been seen during the progress of our tale, that its action has been tolerably confined to Bannerworth Hall, its adjacent meadows, and the seat of Sir Francis Varney; the only person at any distance, knowing anything of the circumstances, or feeling any interest in them, being Mr. Chillingworth, the surgeon, who, from personal feeling, as well as from professional habit, was not likely to make a family's affairs a subject of gossip.

A change, however, was at hand — a change of a most startling and alarming character to Varney — one which he might expect, yet not be well prepared for.

This period of serenity was to pass away, and he was to become most alarmingly popular. We will not, however, anticipate, but proceed at once to detail as briefly as may be the hostile meeting.

It would appear that Varney, now that he had once consented to the definitive arrangements of a duel, shrunk not in any way from carrying them out, nor in the slightest attempted to retard arrangements which might be fatal to himself.

The early morning was one of those cloudy ones so frequently occurring in our fickle climate, when the cleverest weather prophet would find it difficult to predict what the next hour might produce.

There was a kind of dim gloominess over all objects; and as there were no bright lights there were no deep shadows — the consequence of which was a sameness of effect over the landscape, that robbed it of many of its usual beauties.

Such was the state of things when Marchdale accompanied Henry and Admiral Bell from Bannerworth Hall across the garden in the direction of the hilly wood, close to which was the spot intended for the scene of encounter.

Jack Pringle came on at a lazy pace behind with his hands in his pockets, and looking as unconcerned as if he had just come out for a morning's stroll, and scarcely knew whether he saw what was going on or not.

The curious contortion into which he twisted his countenance, and the different odd-looking lumps that appeared in it from time to time, may be accounted for by a quid of unusual size, which he seemed to be masticating with a relish quite horrifying to one unused to so barbarous a luxury.

The admiral had strictly enjoined him not to interfere on pain of being considered a lubber and no seaman for the remainder of his existence — threatened penalties which, of course, had their own weight with Jack, and accordingly he came just to see the row in as quiet a way as possible, perhaps not without a hope, that something might turn up in the shape of a *causus belli,* that might justify him in adopting a threatening attitude towards somebody.

"Now, Master Henry," said the admiral, "none of your palaver to me as we go along; recollect I don't belong to your party, you know. I've stood friend to two or three fellows in my time; but if anybody had said to me, 'Admiral Bell, the next time you go out on a quiet little shooting party, it will be as second to a vampyre,' I'd have said 'you're a liar.' Howsomever, d — me, here you goes, and what I mean to say is this, Mr. Henry, that I'd second even a Frenchman rather than he shouldn't fight when he's asked."

"That's liberal of you," said Henry, "at all events."

"I believe you it is," said the admiral; "so mind if you don't hit him, I'm not a-going to tell you how — all you've got to do is, to fire low; but that's no business of mine. Shiver my timbers, I oughtn't to tell you, but d — n you, hit him if you can."

"Admiral," said Henry, "I can hardly think you are even preserving a neutrality in the matter, putting aside my own partisanship as regards your own man."

"Oh! hang him. I'm not going to let him creep out of the thing on such a shabby pretence, I can tell you. I think I ought to have gone to his house this morning; only, as I said I never would cross his threshold again, I won't."

"I wonder if he'll come," said Mr. Marchdale to Henry. "After all, you know he may take to flight, and shun an encounter which, it is evident, he has entered into but tardily."

"I hope not," said Henry; "and yet I must own that your supposition has several times crossed my mind. If, however, he do not meet me, he never can appear the country, and we should, at least, be rid of him, and all his troublesome importunities concerning the Hall. I would not allow that man, on any account, to cross the threshold of my house, as its tenant or its owner."

"Why, it ain't usual," said the admiral, "to let one's house to two people at once, unless you seem quite to forget that I've taken yours. I may as well remind you of it."

"Hurra!" said Jack Pringle, at that moment.

"What's the matter with you? Who told you to hurra?"

"Enemy in the offing," said Jack, "three or four points to the sou-west."

"So he is, by Jove! dodging about among the trees. Come, now, this vampyre's a decenter fellow than I thought him. He means, after all, to let us have a pop at him."

They had now reached so close to the spot, that Sir Francis Varney, who, to all appearance, had been waiting, emerged from among the trees, rolled up in his dismal looking cloak, and, if possible, looking longer and thinner than ever he had looked before.

His face wore a singular cadaverous-looking aspect. His very lips were white, and there was a curious, pinkish-looking circle round each of his eyes, that imparted to his whole countenance a most uninviting appearance. He turned his eyes from one to the other of those who were advancing towards him, until he saw the admiral, upon which he gave such a grim and horrible smile, that the old man exclaimed, —

"I say, Jack, you lubber, there's a face for a figure-head."

"Ay, ay, sir."

"Did you ever see such a d——d grin as that in your life, in any latitude?"

"Ay, ay, sir."

"You did, you swab."

"I should think so."

"It's a lie, and you know it."

"Very good," said Jack; "don't you recollect when that ere iron bullet walked over your head, leaving a nice little nick, all the way off Bergen-ap-Zoom, that was the time — blessed if you didn't give just such a grin as that."

"I didn't, you rascal."

"And I say you did."

"Mutiny, by God!"

"Go to blazes!"

How far this contention might have gone, having now reached its culminating point, had the admiral and Jack been alone, it is hard to say; but as it was, Henry and Marchdale interfered, and so the quarrel was patched up for the moment, in order to give place to more important affairs.

Varney seemed to think, that after the smiling welcome he had given to his second, he had done quite enough; for there he stood, tall, and gaunt, and motionless, if we may except an occasional singular movement of the mouth, and a clap together of his teeth, at times, which was enough to make anybody jump to hear.

"For Heaven's sake," said Marchdale, "do not let us trifle at such a moment as this. Mr. Pringle, you really had no business here."

"Mr. who?" said Jack.

"Pringle, I believe, is your name?" returned Marchdale.

"It were; but blowed if ever I was called mister before."

The admiral walked up to Sir Francis Varney, and gave him a nod that looked much more like one of defiance than of salutation, to which the vampyre replied by a low, courtly bow.

"Oh, bother!" muttered the old admiral. "If I was to double up my back bone like that, I should never get it down straight again. Well, all's right; you've come; that's all you could do, I suppose."

"I am here," said Varney, "and therefore it becomes a work of super-erogation to remark that I've come."

"Oh! does it? I never bolted a dictionary, and, therefore, I don't know exactly what you mean."

"Step aside with me a moment, Admiral Bell, and I will tell you what you are to do with me after I am shot, if such should be my fate."

"Do with you! D—d if I'll do anything with you."

"I don't expect you will regret me; you will eat."

"Eat!"

"Yes, and drink as usual, no doubt, not-withstanding being witness to the decease of a fellow-creature."

"Belay there; don't call yourself a fellow-creature of mine; I ain't a vampyre."

"But there's no knowing what you may be; and now listen to my instructions; for as you're my second, you cannot very well refuse to me a few friendly offices. Rain is falling. Step beneath this ancient tree, and I will talk to you."

Chapter XXXIX.

THE STORM AND THE FIGHT. – THE ADMIRAL'S
REPUDIATION OF HIS PRINCIPAL.

"Well," said the admiral, when they were fairly under the tree, upon the leaves of which the pattering rain might be heard falling: "well —

what is it?"

"If your young friend Mr. Bannerworth, should chance to send a pistol-bullet through any portion of my anatomy, prejudicial to the prolongation of my existence, you will be so good as not to interfere with anything I may have about me, or to make any disturbance whatever."

"You may depend I shan't."

"Just take the matter perfectly easy — as a thing of course."

"Oh! I mean d——d easy."

"Ha! what a delightful thing is friendship! There is a little knoll or mound of earth midway between here and the Hall. Do you happen to know it? There is one solitary tree growing near its summit — an oriental looking tree, of the fir tribe, which, fan-like, spreads its deep green leaves across the azure sky."

"Oh! bother it; it's a d——d old tree, growing upon a little bit of a hill, I suppose you mean?"

"Precisely; only much more poetically expressed. The moon rises at a quarter past four tonight, or rather tomorrow morning."

"Does it?"

"Yes; and if I should happen to be killed, you will have me removed gently to this mound of earth, and there laid beneath this tree, with my face upwards; and take care that it is done before the moon rises. You can watch that no one interferes."

"A likely job. What the deuce do you take me for? I tell you what it is, Mr. Vampyre, or Varney, or whatever's your name, if you should chance to be hit, wherever you chance to fall, there you'll lie."

"How very unkind."

"Uncommon, ain't it?"

"Well, well, since that is your determination, I must take care of myself in another way. I can do so, and I will."

"Take care of yourself how you like, for all I care; I've come here to second you, to see that, on the honor of a seaman, if you are put out of the world, it's done in proper manner, that's all I have to do with you — now you know."

Sir Francis Varney looked after him with a strange kind of smile, as he walked away to make the necessary preparations with Marchdale for the immediate commencement of the contest.

These were simple and brief. It was agreed that twelve paces should be measured out, six each way, from a fixed point; one six to be paced by the admiral, and the other by Marchdale; then they were to draw lots, to see at which end of this imaginary line Varney was to be placed; after this the signal for firing was to be one, two, three — fire!

A few minutes sufficed to complete these arrangements; the ground was measured in the manner we have stated, and the combatants placed in their respective positions, Sir Francis Varney occupying the same spot where he had at first stood, namely, that nearest to the little wood, and to his own residence.

It is impossible that under such circumstances the bravest and the calmest of mankind could fail to feel some slight degree of tremor, or uneasiness; and, although we can fairly claim for Henry Bannerworth that he was as truly courageous as any right feeling Christian man could wish to be, yet when it was possible that he stood within, as it were, a hair's breadth of eternity, a strange world of sensation and emotions found a home in his heart, and he could not look altogether undaunted all on that future which might, for all he knew to the contrary, be so close at hand, as far as he was concerned.

It was not that he feared death, but that he looked with a decent gravity upon so grave a change as that from this world to the next, and hence it was that his face was pale, and that he looked all the emotion which he really felt.

This was the aspect and the bearing of a brave but not a reckless man; while Sir Francis Varney, on the other hand, seemed, now that he had fairly engaged in the duel, to look upon it and all its attendant circumstances with a kind of smirking satisfaction, as if he were far more amused than personally interested.

This was certainly the more extraordinary after the manner in which he had tried to evade the fight, and, at all events, was quite a sufficient proof that cowardice had not been his actuating motive in so doing.

The admiral, who stood on a level with him, could not see the sort of expression he wore, or, probably, he would have been far from well pleased; but the others did, and they found something inexpressibly disagreeable in the smirking kind of satisfaction with which the vampyre seemed to regard now the proceedings.

"Confound him," whispered Marchdale to Henry, "one would think he was quite delighted, instead as we had imagined him, not well pleased, at these proceedings; look how he grins."

"It is no matter," said Henry; "let him wear what aspect he may, it is the same to me; and, as Heaven is my judge, I here declare, if I did not think myself justified in so doing, I would not raise my hand against this man."

"There can be no shadow of a doubt regarding your justification. Have at him, and Heaven protect you."

"Amen!"

The admiral was to give the word to fire, and now he and Marchdale having stepped sufficiently on one side to be out of all possible danger from any stray shot, he commenced repeating the signal, —

"Are you ready, gentlemen? — once."

They looked sternly at each other and each grasped his pistol.

"Twice!"

Sir Francis Varney smiled and looked around him, as if the affair were one of the most commonplace description.

"Thrice!"

Varney seemed to be studying the sky rather than attending to the duel.

"Fire!" cried the admiral, and one report only struck upon the ear. It was that from Henry's pistol.

All eyes were turned upon Sir Francis Varney, who had evidently reserved his fire, for what purpose could not be devised, except a murderous one, the taking of a more steady aim at Henry. Sir Francis, however, seemed in no hurry, but smiled, significantly, and gradually raised the point of his weapon.

"Did you hear the word, Sir Francis? I gave it loud enough, I am sure. I never spoke plainer in my life; did I ever, Jack?"

"Yes, often," said Jack Pringle; "what's the use of your asking such yarns as them? you know you have done so often enough when you wanted grog."

"You d—d rascal, I'll — I'll have your back scored, I will."

"So you will, when you are afloat again, which you never will be — you are paid off, that's certain."

"You lubberly lout, you ain't a seaman; a seaman would never mutiny against his admiral; howsomever, do you hear, Sir Francis, I'll give the matter up, if you don't pay some attention to me."

Henry looked steadily at Varney, expecting every moment to feel his bullet. Mr. Marchdale hastily exclaimed that this was not according to usage.

Sir Francis Varney took no notice, but went on elevating his weapon; when it was perpendicular to the earth he fired in the air.

"I had not anticipated this," said Marchdale, as he walked to Henry. "I thought he was taking a more deadly aim."

"And I," said Henry.

"Ay, you have escaped, Henry; let me congratulate you."

"Not so fast; we may fire again."

"I can afford to do that," he said, with a smile.

"You should have fired, sir, according to custom," said the admiral; "this is not the proper thing."

"What, fire at your friend?"

"Oh, that's all very well! You are my friend for a time, vampyre as you are and I intend you shall fire."

"If Mr. Henry Bannerworth demands another fire, I have no objection to it and will fire at him: but as it is I shall not do so, indeed, it would be quite useless for him to do so — to point mortal weapons at me is mere child's play, they will not hurt me."

"The devil they won't," said the admiral.

"Why, look you here," said Sir Francis Varney, stepping forward and placing his hand to his neckerchief; "look you here; if Mr. Henry Bannerworth should demand another fire, he may do so with the same bullet."

"The same bullet!" said Marchdale, stepping forward — "the same bullet! How is this?"

"My eyes," said Jack; "who'd a thought it; here's a go! wouldn't he do for a dummy — to lead a forlorn hope, or to put in among the boarders?"

"Here," said Sir Francis, handing a bullet to Henry Bannerworth — "here is the bullet you shot at me."

Henry looked at it — it was blackened by powder; and then Marchdale seized it and tried it in the pistol, but found the bullet fitted Henry's weapon.

"By heaven, it is so!" he exclaimed, stepping back and looking at Varney from top to toe in horror and amazement.

"D — e," said the admiral, "if I understand this. Why Jack Pringle, you dog, here's a strange fish."

"Oh, no! there's plenty on 'um in some countries."

"Will you insist upon another fire, or may I consider you satisfied?"

"I shall object," said Marchdale. "Henry, this affair must go no further; it would be madness — worse than madness, to fight upon such terms."

"So say I," said the admiral. "I will not have anything to do with you, Sir Francis. I'll not be your second any longer. I didn't bargain for such a game as this. You might as well fight with the man in brass armor, at the Lord Mayor's show, or the champion at a coronation."

"Oh!" said Jack Pringle; "a man may as well fire at the back of a halligator as a wamphigher."

"This must be considered as having been concluded," said Mr. Marchdale.

"No!" said Henry.

"And wherefore not?"

"Because I have not received his fire."

"Heaven forbid you should."

"I may not with honor quit the ground without another fire."

"Under ordinary circumstances there might be some shadow of an excuse for your demand; but as it is there is none. You have neither honor nor credit to gain by such an encounter, and certainly, you can gain no object."

"How are we to decide this affair? Am I considered absolved from the accusation under which I lay, of cowardice?" inquired Sir Francis Varney, with a cold smile.

"Why, as for that," said the admiral, "I should as soon expect credit for fighting behind a wall, as with a man that I couldn't hit any more than the moon."

"Henry; let me implore you to quit this scene; if can do no good."

At this moment, a noise, as of human voices, was heard at a distance; this caused a momentary pause, and the whole party stood still and listened.

The murmurs and shouts that now arose in the distance were indistinct and confused.

"What can all this mean?" said Marchdale; "there is something very strange about it. I cannot imagine a cause for so usual an occurrence."

"Nor I," said Sir Francis Varney, looking suspiciously at Henry Bannerworth.

"Upon my honor I know neither what is the cause nor the nature of the sounds themselves."

"Then we can easily see what is the matter from yonder hillock," said the admiral; "and there's Jack Pringle, he's up there already. What's he telegraphing about in that manner, I wonder?"

The fact was, Jack Pringle, hearing the riot, had thought that if he got to the neighboring eminence he might possibly ascertain what it was that was the cause of what he termed the "row," and had succeeded in some degree.

There were a number of people of all kinds coming out from the village, apparently armed, and shouting. Jack Pringle hitched up his trousers and swore, then took off his hat and began to shout to the admiral, as he said, —

"D — e, they are too late to spoil the in sport. Hilloa! hurrah!"

"What's all that about, Jack?" inquired the admiral, as he came puffing along. "What's the squall about?"

"Only a few horse-marines and bumboat-women, that have been startled like a company of penguins."

"Oh! my eyes! wouldn't a whole broadside set em flying, Jack?"

"Ay; just as them Frenchmen that you murdered on board the Big Thunderer, as you called it."

"I murder them, you rascal?"

"Yes; there was about five hundred of them killed."

"They were only shot."

"They were killed, only your conscience tells you it's uncomfortable."

"You rascal — you villain! You ought to be keel-hauled and well payed."

"Ay; you're payed, and paid off as an old hulk."

"D — e — you — you — oh! I wish I had you on board ship, I'd make your lubberly carcass like a union jack, full of red and blue stripes."

"Oh! it's all very well; but if you don't take to your heels, you'll have all the old women in the village a whacking on you, that's all I have to say about it. You'd better port your helm and about ship, or you'll be keel-hauled."

"D – n your –"

"What's the matter?" inquired Marchdale, as he arrived.

"What's the cause of all the noise we have heard?" said Sir Francis; "has some village festival spontaneously burst forth among the rustics of this place?"

"I cannot tell the cause of it," said Henry Bannerworth; "but they seem to me to be coming toward this place."

"Indeed!"

"I think so too," said Marchdale.

"With what object?" inquired Sir Francis Varney.

"No peaceable one," observed Henry; "for, as far I can observe, they struck across the country, as though they would enclose something, or intercept somebody."

"Indeed! but why come here?"

"If I knew that I would have at once told the cause."

"And they appear armed with a variety of odd weapons," observed Sir Francis; "they mean an attack upon some one. Who is that man with them? he seems to be deprecating their coming."

"That appears to be Mr. Chillingworth," said Henry; "I think that is he."

"Yes," observed the admiral; "I think I know the build of that craft; he's been in our society before. I always know a ship as soon as I see it."

"Does you, though?" said Jack.

"Yes; what do you mean, eh? let me hear what you've got to say against your captain and your admiral, you mutinous dog; you tell me, I say."

"So I will; you thought you were fighting a big ship in a fog, and fired a dozen broadsides or so, and it was only the Flying Dutchman, or the devil."

"You infernal dog –"

"Well, you know it was; it might a been our own shadow, for all I can tell. Indeed, I think it was."

"You think!"

"Yes."

"That's mutiny: I'll have no more to do with you, Jack Pringle; you're no seaman and have no respect for your officer. Now sheer off, or I'll cut your yards."

"Why, as for my yards, I'll square 'em presently if I like, you old swab; but as for leaving you, very well; you have said so, and you shall be accommodated, d— —e; however, it was not so when your nob was nearly rove through with a boarding pike it wasn't 'I'll have no more to do with Jack Pringle' then, it was more t'other."

"Well, then, why be so mutinous?"

"Because you aggrawates me."

The cries of the mob became more distinct as they drew nearer to the party, who began to evince some uneasiness as to their object.

"Surely," said Marchdale, "Mr. Chillingworth has not named anything respecting the duel that has taken place."

"No, no."

"But he was to have been here this morning," said the admiral. "I understood he was to be here in his own character of a surgeon, and yet I have not seen him; have any of you?"

"No," said Henry.

"Then here he comes in the character of a conservator of the public peace," said Varney, coldly; "however, I believe that his errand will be useless since the affair is, I presume, concluded."

"Down with the vampyre!"

"Eh!" said the admiral, "eh, what's that, eh? What did they say?"

"If you'll listen they'll tell you soon enough, I'll warrant."

"May be they will, and yet I'd like to know now."

Sir Francis Varney looked significantly at Marchdale, and then waited with downcast eyes for the repetition of the words.

"Down with the vampyre!" resounded on all sides from the people who came rapidly towards them, and converging towards a center. "Burn, destroy, and kill the vampyre! No vampyre; burn him out; down with him; kill him!"

Then came Mr. Chillingworth's voice, who, with much earnestness, endeavored to exhort them to moderation, and to refrain from violence.

Sir Francis Varney became very pale and agitated; he immediately turned, and without taking the least notice, he made for the wood, which lay between him and his own house, leaving the people in the greatest agitation.

Mr. Marchdale was not unmoved at this occurrence, but stood his ground with Henry Bannerworth, the admiral, and Jack Pringle, until the mob came very near to them, shouting, and uttering cries of vengeance, and death of all imaginable kinds that it was possible to conceive, against the unpopular vampyre.

Pending the arrival of these infuriated town persons, we will, in a few words, state how it was that so suddenly a set of circumstances arose productive of an amount of personal danger to Varney, such as, up to that time, had seemed not at all likely to occur.

We have before stated there was but one person out of the family of the Bannerworths who was able to say anything of a positive character concerning the singular and inexplicable proceedings at the Hall; and that that person was Mr. Chillingworth, an individual not at all likely to become garrulous upon the subject.

But, alas! the best of men have their weaknesses, and we much regret to say that to Mr. Chillingworth so far in this instance forgot that admirable discretion which commonly belonged to him, as to be the cause of the popular tumult which had now reached such a height.

In a moment of thoughtlessness and confidence he told his wife. Yes, this really clever man, from whom one would not have expected such a piece of horrible indiscretion, actually told his wife all about the vampyre. But such is human nature; combined at with an amount of firmness and reasoning power, that one would have thought to be invulnerable safeguards, we find some weakness which astonishes all calculation.

Such was this of Mr. Chillingworth's. It is true, he cautioned the lady so be secret, and pointed to her the danger of making Varney the vampyre a theme for gossip; but he might as well have whispered to a hurricane to be so good is not to go on blowing so, as request Mrs. Chillingworth to keep a secret.

Of course she burst into the usual declarations of "Who was she to tell? Was she a person who went about telling things? When did she see anybody? Not she, once in a blue moon;" and then, when Mr. Chilling-worth went out like the King of Otaheite, she invited the neighbors round about to come to take some tea.

Under solemn promises of secrecy, sixteen ladies that evening were made acquainted with the full and interesting particulars of the attack of the vampyre on Flora Bannerworth, and all the evidence inculpating Sir Francis Varney as the bloodthirsty individual.

When the mind comes to consider the sixteen ladies multiplied their information by about four-and-twenty each, we become quite lost in a sea of arithmetic, and feel compelled to sum up the whole by a candid assumption that in four-and-twenty hours not an individual in the whole town was ignorant of the circumstances.

On the morning before the projected duel, there was an unusual commotion in the streets. People were conversing together in little knots, and using rather violent gesticulations. Poor Mr. Chillingworth! he alone was ignorant of the causes of the popular commotion, and so he went to bed wondering that an unusual bustle pervaded the little market town, but not at all guessing its origin.

Somehow or another, however, the populace, who had determined to make a demonstration on the following morning against the vam-pyre, thought it highly necessary first to pay some sort of compliment to Mr. Chillingworth, and, accordingly, at an early hour, a great mob assembled outside his house, and gave three terrific applauding shouts, which roused him most unpleasantly from his sleep; and induced the greatest astonishment at the cause such a tumult.

Oh, that artful Mrs. Chillingworth! too well she knew what was the matter; yet she pretended to be so oblivious upon the subject.

"Good God!" cried Mr. Chillingworth as he started up in bed, "what's all that?"

"All what?" said his wife.

"All what! Do you mean to say heard nothing?"

"Well, I think I did hear a little sort of something."

"A little sort of something? It shook the house."

"Well, well; never mind; it's no business of ours."

"Yes; but it may be, though. It's all very well to say 'go to sleep.' That happens to be a thing I can't do. There's something amiss."

"Well, what's that to you?"

"Perhaps nothing; but, perhaps, everything."

Mr. Chillingworth sprang from his bed and began and began dressing, a process which he executed with considerable rapidity, which was much accelerated by two or three supplementary shouts from the people below.

Then, in a temporary lull, a loud voice shouted, —

"Down with the vampyre — down with the vampyre!"

The truth in an instant burst over the mind of Mr. Chillingworth, and, turning to his wife, he exclaimed, —

"I understand it now. You've been gossiping about Sir Francis Varney, and have caused all this tumult."

"I gossip! Well, I never! Lay it on me; it is sure to be my fault. I might have known that beforehand. I always am."

"But you must have spoken of it."

"Who have I got to speak to about it?"

"Did you, or did you not?"

"Who should I tell?"

Mr. Chillingworth was dressed, and he hastened down and entered the street with great desperation. He had a hope that he might be enabled to disperse the crowd and yet be in time keep his appointment at the duel.

His appearance was hailed with another shout, for it was considered, of course, that he had come to join in the attack on Sir Francis Varney. He found assembled a much more considerable mob than he had imagined, and to his alarm he found many armed with all sorts of weapons.

"Hurrah!" cried a great lumpy-looking fellow, who seemed half mad with the prospect of a disturbance. "Hurrah, here's the doctor, he'll tell us all about it while we go along."

"For heaven's sake," said Mr. Chillingworth, "stop! What are you about to do all of you?"

"Burn the vampyre — burn the vampyre!"

"Hold — hold! this is folly. Let me implore you all to return to your homes, or you will get into serious trouble on this subject."

This was a piece of advice not at all likely to be adopted; and when the mob found that Mr. Chillingworth was not disposed to encourage and countenance it in its violence, it gave another loud shout of defiance, and moved off through the long straggling streets of the town in a direction towards Sir Francis Varney's house.

It is true that what were called authorities of the town had become alarmed, and were stirring, but they found themselves in such a frightful minority, that it became out of the question for them to interfere with any effect to stop the lawless proceedings of the rioters, so that the infuriated populace had it all their own way, and in a straggling, disorderly looking kind of procession they moved off, vowing vengeance as they went against Varney the vampyre.

Hopeless as Mr. Chillingworth thought it was to interfere with any degree of effect to stop the lawless proceedings of the mob, he still could not reconcile it to himself to be absent from a scene which he now felt certain had been produced by his own imprudence, so he went with the crowd, endeavoring, as he did, by every argument that could be suggested to him to induce them to abstain from the acts of violence they contemplated. He had a hope, too, that when they reached Sir Francis Varney's, finding him not within, as probably would be the case, as by the time he would have started to meet Henry Bannerworth on the ground, to fight the duel, he might induce the mob to return and forgo their meditated violence.

And thus was it that, urged on by the multitude of persons, the unhappy surgeon was expiating, in both mind and person, the serious mistakes he had committed in trusting a secret to his wife.

Let it not be supposed that we for one moment wish to lay down a general principle as regards the confiding secrets to ladies, because from the beginning of the world it has become notorious how well they keep them, and with what admirable discretion, tact, and forethought this fairest portion of humanity conduct themselves.

We know how few Mrs. Chillingworths there are in the world, and have but to regret that our friend the doctor should, in his matrimonial adventure, have met with such a specimen.

Chapter *XL.*

THE POPULAR RIOT. – SIR FRANCIS VARNEY'S DANGER. –
THE SUGGESTION AND ITS RESULTS.

*S*uch, then, were the circumstances which at once altered the whole
aspect of the affairs, and, from private and domestic causes of very deep
annoyance, led to public results of a character which seemed likely to
involve the whole country-side in the greatest possible confusion.

But while we blame Mr. Chillingworth for being so indiscreet as to
communicate the secret of such a person as Varney the vampyre to his
wife, we trust in a short time to be enabled to show that he made as
much reparation as it was possible to make for the mischief he had
unintentionally committed. And now as he struggled onward – apparently onward – first and foremost among the rioters, he was really doing
all in his power to quell that tumult which superstition and dread had
raised.

Human nature truly delights in the marvelous, and in proportion as
knowledge of the natural phenomena of nature is restricted, and unbri-
dled imagination allowed to give the rein to fathomless conjecture, we
shall find an eagerness likewise to believe the marvelous to be the truth.
That dim and uncertain condition concerning vampyres, originating
probably as it had done in Germany, had spread itself slowly, but
insidiously, throughout the whole of the civilized world.

In no country and in no clime is there not something which bears a
kind of family relationship to the veritable vampyre of which Sir Francis
Varney appeared to be so choice a specimen.

The *ghoul* of eastern nations is but the same being, altered to suit
habits and localities; and the *sema* of the Scandinavians is but the
vampyre of a more primitive race, and a personification of that morbid
imagination which has once fancied the probability of the dead walking
again among the living, with all the frightful insignia of corruption and

the grave about them.

Although not popular in England, still there had been tales told of such midnight visitants, so that Mrs. Chillingworth, when she had imparted the information which she had obtained, had already some rough material to work upon in the minds of her auditors, and therefore there was no great difficulty in very soon establishing the fact.

Under such circumstances, ignorant people always do what they have heard was done by some one else before them and in an incredibly short space of time the propriety of catching Sir Francis Varney, depriving him of his vampyrelike existence, and driving a stake through his body, became not at all a questionable proposition.

Alas, poor Mr. Chillingworth! as well might he have attempted King Canute's task of stemming the waves of the ocean as that of attempting to stop the crowd from proceeding to Sir Francis Varney's house.

His very presence was a sort of confirmation of the whole affair. In vain he gesticulated, in vain he begged and prayed that they would go back, and in vain he declared that full and ample justice should be done upon the vampyre, provided popular clamor spared him, and he was left to more deliberate judgment.

Those who were foremost in the throng paid no attention to these remonstrances, while those who were more distant heard them not, and, for all they knew, he might be urging the crowd on to violence, instead of deprecating it.

Thus, then, this disorderly rabble now reached the house of Sir Francis Varney and loudly demanded of his terrified servants where he was to be found.

The knocking at the Hall door was prodigious, and, with a laudable desire, doubtless, of saving time, the moment one was done amusing himself with the ponderous knocker, another seized it; so that until the door was flung open by some of the bewildered and terrified men, there was no cessation whatever of the furious demand for admittance.

"Varney the vampyre — Varney the vampyre!" cried a hundred voices. "Death to the vampyre! Where is he? Bring him out. Varney the vampyre!"

The servants were too terrified to speak for some moments, as they saw such a tumultuous assemblage seeking their master, while so singular a name was applied to him.

At length, one more bold than the rest contrived to stammer out, —

"My good people, Sir Francis Varney is not at home. He took an early breakfast, and has been out nearly an hour."

The mob paused a moment in indecision, and then one of the foremost cried, —

"Who'd suppose they'd own he was at home! He's hiding somewhere of course; let's pull him out."

"Ah, pull him out! — pull him out!" cried many voices. A rush was made into the house, and in a very few minutes its chambers were ransacked, and all its hidden places carefully searched, with the hope of discovering the hidden form of Sir Francis Varney.

The servants felt that, with their inefficient strength, to oppose the proceedings of an assemblage which seemed to be unchecked by all sort of law or reason would be madness; they therefore only looked on, with wonder and dismay, satisfied certainly in their own minds that Sir Francis would not be found, and indulging in much conjecture as to what would be the result of such violent and unexpected proceedings.

Mr. Chillingworth hoped that time was gained, and that some sort of indication of what was going on would reach the unhappy object of popular detestation sufficiently early to enable him to provide for his own safety.

He knew he was breaking his own engagement to be present at the duel between Henry Bannerworth and Sir Francis Varney, and, as that thought recurred to him, he dreaded that his professional services might be required on one side or the other; for he knew, or fancied he knew, that mutual hatred dictated the contest; and he thought that if ever a duel had taken place which was likely to be attended with some disastrous result, that was surely the one.

But how could he leave, watched and surrounded as he was by an infuriated multitude — how could he hope but that his footsteps would be dogged, or that the slightest attempt of his to convey a warning to Sir Francis Varney, would not be the means of bringing down upon his head the very danger he sought to shield him from.

In this state of uncertainty, then, did our medical man remain, a prey to the bitterest reflections, and full of the direst apprehensions, without having the slightest power of himself to alter so disastrous a train of circumstances.

Dissatisfied with their non-success, the crowd twice searched the house of Sir Francis Varney, from the attics to the basement; and then, and not till then, did they begin reluctantly to believe that the servants must have spoken the truth.

"He's in the town somewhere," cried one. "Let's go back to the town."

It is strange how suddenly any mob will obey any impulse, and this perfectly groundless supposition was sufficient to turn their steps back again in the direction whence they came, and they had actually, in a straggling sort of column, reached half way towards the town, when they encountered a boy, whose professional pursuit consisted in tending sheep very early of a morning, and who at once informed them that he had seen Sir Francis Varney in the wood, half way between Bannerworth Hall and his own home.

This event at once turned the whole tide again, and with renewed clamors, carrying Mr. Chillingworth along with them, they now rapidly neared the real spot, where, probably, had they turned a little earlier, they would have viewed the object of their suspicion and hatred.

But, as we have already recorded, the advancing throng was seen by the parties on the ground where the duel could scarcely have been said to have been fought; and then had Sir Francis Varney dashed into the wood, which was so opportunely at hand to afford him a shelter from his enemies, and from the intricacies of which — well acquainted with them as he doubtless was, — he had every chance of eluding their pursuit.

The whole affair was a great surprise to Henry end his friends, when they saw such a string of people advancing, with such shouts and imprecations; they could not, for the life of them, imagine what could have excited such a turn out among the ordinarily industrious and quiet inhabitants of a town, remarkable rather for the quietude and steadiness of its population than for any violent outbreaks of popular feeling.

"What can Mr. Chillingworth be about," said Henry, "to bring such a mob here? has he taken leave of his senses?"

"Nay," said Marchdale; "look again; he seems to be trying to keep them back, although ineffectually, for they will not be stayed."

"D — e," said the admiral, "here's a gang of pirates; we shall be boarded and carried before we know where we are, Jack."

"Ay ay, sir," said Jack.

"And is that all you've got to say, you lubber, when you see your admiral in danger? You'd better go and make terms with the enemy at once."

"Really, this is serious," said Henry; "they shout for Varney. Can Mr. Chillingworth have been so mad as to adopt this means of stopping the duel?"

"Impossible," said Marchdale; "if that had been his intention, he could have done so quietly, through the medium of the civil authorities."

"Hang me!" exclaimed the admiral, "if there are any civil authorities; they talk of smashing somebody. What do they say, Jack? I don't hear quite so well as I used."

"You always was a little deaf," said Jack.

"What?"

"A little deaf, I say."

"Why, you lubberly lying swab, how dare you say so?"

"Because you was."

"You slave-going scoundrel!"

"For Heaven's sake, do not quarrel at such a time as this!" said Henry; "we shall be surrounded in a moment. Come, Mr. Marchdale, let you and I visit these people and ascertain what it is that has so much excited their indignation."

"Agreed," said Marchdale; and they both stepped forward at a rapid pace, to meet the advancing throng.

The crowd which had now approached to within a short distance of the expectant little party, was of a most motley description, and its appearance, under many circumstances, would cause considerable risibility. Men and women were mixed indiscriminately together, and in the shouting, the latter, if such a thing were possible, exceeded the former, both in discordance and energy.

Every individual composing that mob carried some weapon calculated for defense, such as flails, scythes, sickles, bludgeons, &c., and this mode of arming caused them to wear a most formidable appearance; while the passion that superstition had called up was strongly depicted in their inflamed features. Their fury, too, had been excited by their disappointment, and it was with concentrated rage that they now pressed onward.

The calm and steady advance of Henry and Mr. Marchdale to meet the advancing throng, seemed to have the effect of retarding their progress a little, and they came to a parley at a hedge, which separated them from the meadow in which the duel had been fought.

"You seem to be advancing towards us," said Henry. "Do you seek me or any of my friends; and if so, upon what errand? Mr. Chillingworth, for Heaven's sake, explain what is the cause of all this tumult. You seem to be at the head of it."

"Seem to be," said Mr. Chillingworth, "without being so. You are not sought, nor any of your friends?"

"Who, then?"

"Sir Francis Varney," was the immediate reply.

"Indeed! and what has he done to incite popular indignation? of private wrong I can accuse him; but I desire no crowd to take up my cause or to avenge my quarrels."

"Mr. Bannerworth, it has become known, through my indiscretion, that Sir Francis Varney is suspected of being a vampyre."

"Is this so?"

"Hurrah!" shouted the mob. "Down with the vampyre! hurrah! where is he? Down with him!"

"Drive a stake through him," said a woman; "it's the only way, and the humanestest. You've only to take a hedge stake, and sharpen it a bit at one end, and char it a little in the fire so as there mayt'n't be no splinters to hurt, and then poke it through his stomach."

The mob gave a great shout at this humane piece of advice, and it was some time before Henry could make himself heard at all, even to those who were nearest to him. When he did succeed in so doing, he cried, with a loud voice, —

"Hear me, all of you. It is quite needless for me to inquire how you became possessed of the information that a dreadful suspicion hangs over the person of Sir Francis Varney; but if, in consequence of hearing such news, you fancy this public demonstration will be agreeable to me, or likely to relieve those who are nearest or dearest to me from the state of misery and apprehension into which they have fallen you are much mistaken."

"Hear him, hear him!" cried Mr. Marchdale; "he speaks both wisdom and truth."

"If anything," pursued Henry, "could add to the annoyance of vexation and misery we have suffered, it would assuredly be the being made subjects of every-day clamor."

"You hear him?" said Mr. Marchdale.

"Yes, we does," said a man; "but we comes out to catch a vampyre, for all that."

"Oh, to be sure," said the humane woman; "nobody's feelings is nothing to us. Are we to be woke up in the night with vampyres sucking bloods while we've got a stake in the country?"

"Hurrah!" shouted everybody. "Down with the vampyre! Where is he?"

"You are wrong. I assure you you are all wrong," said Mr. Chillingworth, imploringly; "there is no vampyre here, you see. Sir Francis Varney has, not only escaped, but he will take the law of all of you."

This was an argument which appeared to stagger a few, but the bolder spirits pushed them on, and a suggestion to search the wood having been made by some one who was more cunning than his neighbors, that measure was at once proceeded with, and executed in a systematic manner, which made those who knew it to be the hiding place of Sir Francis Varney tremble for his safety.

It was with a strange mixture of feeling that Henry Bannerworth waited the result of the search for the man who, but a few minutes before had been opposed to him in a contest of life or death.

The destruction of Sir Francis Varney would certainly have been an effectual means of preventing him from continuing to be the incubus he then was upon the Bannerworth family; and yet the generous nature of Henry shrank with horror from seeing even such a creature as Varney sacrificed at the shrine of popular resentment, and murdered by an infuriated populace.

He felt as great an interest in the escape of the vampyre as if some great advantage to himself had been contingent upon such an event; and, although he spoke not a word, while the echoes of the little wood were all awakened by the clamorous manner in which the mob searched for their victim, his feelings could be well read upon his countenance.

The admiral, too, without possessing probably the fine feelings of Henry Bannerworth, took an unusually sympathetic interest in the fate of the vampyre; and, after placing himself in various attitudes of intense excitement, he exclaimed, —

"D — n it, Jack, I do hope, after all, the vampyre will get the better of them. It's like a whole flotilla attacking one vessel — a lubberly proceeding at the best, and I'll be hanged if I like it. I should like to pour in a broadside into those fellows, just to let them see it wasn't a proper English mode of fighting. Shouldn't you, Jack?"

"Ay, ay, sir, I should."

"Shiver me, if I see an opportunity, if I don't let some of those rascals know what's what."

Scarcely had these words escaped the lips of the old admiral than there arose a loud shout from the interior of the wood. It was a shout of success, and seemed at the very least to herald the capture of the unfortunate Varney.

"By heaven!" exclaimed Henry, "they have him."

"God forbid!" said Mr. Marchdale; "this grows too serious."

"Bear a hand, Jack," said the admiral; "we'll have a fight for it yet; they shan't murder even a vampyre in cold blood. Load the pistols; and send a flying shot or two among the rascals, the moment they appear."

"No, no," said Henry; "no more violence, there has been enough — there has been enough."

Even as he spoke there came rushing from among the trees, at the corner of the wood, the figure of a man. They needed but one glance to assure them who it was. Sir Francis Varney had been seen and was flying before those implacable foes who had sought his life.

He had divested himself of his huge cloak, as well as of his low slouched hat, and, with a speed which nothing but the most absolute desperation could have enabled him to exert, he rushed onward, beating down before him every obstacle, and bounding over the meadows at a rate that, if he could have continued it for any length of time, would have set pursuit at defiance.

"Bravo!" shouted the admiral, "a stern chase is a long chase, and I wish them joy of it — d — e, Jack, did you ever see anybody get along like that?"

"Ay, ay, sir."

"You never did, you scoundrel."

"Yes, I did."

"When and where?"

"When you ran away off the sound."

The admiral turned nearly blue with anger, but Jack looked perfectly imperturbable, as he added, —

"You know you ran away after the French frigates who wouldn't stay to fight you."

"Ah! that indeed. There he goes, putting on every stitch of canvas,

I'll be bound."

"And there they come," said Jack, as he pointed to the corner of the wood, and some of the more active of the vampyre's pursuers showed themselves. It would appear as if the vampyre had been started from some hiding-place in the interior of the wood, and had then thought it expedient altogether to leave that retreat and make his way to some more secure one across the open country, where there would be more obstacles to his discovery than perseverance could overcome. Probably, then, among the brushwood and trees, for a few moments he had been again lost sight of, until those who were closest upon his track had emerged from among the dense foliage, and saw him scouring across the country at such headlong speed. These were but few, and in their extreme anxiety themselves to capture Varney, whose precipitate and terrified flight brought a firm conviction to their minds of his being a vampyre, they did not stop to get much of a reinforcement, but plunged on like greyhounds in his track.

"Jack," said the admiral, "this won't do. Look at that great lubberly fellow with the queer smock-frock."

"Never saw such a figurehead in my life," said Jack.

"Stop him."

"Ay, ay, sir."

The man was coming on at a prodigious rate, and Jack, with all the deliberation in the world, advanced to meet him; and when they got sufficiently close together, that in a few moments they must encounter each other, Jack made himself into as small a bundle as possible, and presented his shoulder to the advancing countryman in such a way, that he flew off it at a tangent, as if he had ran against a brick wall, and after rolling head over heels for some distance, safely deposited himself in a ditch, where he disappeared completely for a few moments from all human observation.

"Don't say I hit you," said Jack. "Curse yer, what did yer run against me for? Sarves you right. Lubbers as don't know how to steer, in course runs agin things."

"Bravo," said the admiral; "there's another of them."

The pursuers of Varney the vampyre, however, now came too thick and fast to be so easily disposed of, and as soon as his figure could be seen coursing over the meadows, and springing over road and ditch with an agility almost frightful to look upon, the whole rabble rout was in pursuit of him.

By this time, the man who had fallen into the ditch had succeeded in making his appearance in the visible world again, and as he crawled up the bank, looking a thing of mire and mud, Jack walked up to him with all the carelessness in the world, and said to him, —

"Any luck, old chap?"

"Oh, murder!" said the man, "what do you mean? who are you? where am I? what's the matter? Old Muster Fowler, the fat crowner, will set upon me now."

"Have you caught anything?" said Jack.

"Caught anything?"

"Yes; you've been in for eels, haven't you?"

"D — n!"

"Well, it is odd to me, as some people can't go a fishing without getting out of temper. Have it your own way; I won't interfere with you;" and away Jack walked.

The man cleared the mud out of his eyes, as well as he could, and looked after him with a powerful suspicion that in Jack he saw the very cause of his mortal mishap; but, somehow or other, his immersion in the not over limpid stream had wonderfully cooled his courage, and casting one despairing look upon his begrimed apparel, and another at the last of the stragglers who were pursuing Sir Francis Varney across the fields, he thought it prudent to get home as fast he could, and get rid of the disagreeable results of an adventure which had turned out for him anything but auspicious, or pleasant.

Mr. Chillingworth, as though by a sort of impulse to be present in case Sir Francis Varney should really be run down, and with a hope of saving him from personal violence, had followed the foremost of the rioters in the wood, found it now quite impossible for him to carry on such a chase as that which was being undertaken across the fields after Sir Francis Varney.

His person was unfortunately but ill qualified for the continuance of such a pursuit, and, although with the greatest reluctance, he at last felt himself compelled to give it up.

In making his way through the intricacies of the wood, he had been seriously incommoded by the thick undergrowth, and he had acciden-tally encountered several miry pools, with which he had involuntarily made a closer acquaintance than was at all conducive either to his personal appearance or comfort. The doctor's temper, though, generally speaking, one of the most even, was at last affected by his mishaps, and he could not refrain from an execration upon his want of prudence in letting his wife have a knowledge of a secret that was not his own and the producing an unlooked-for circumstance, the termination of which might be of a most disastrous nature.

Tired, therefore, and nearly exhausted by the exertions he had already taken, he emerged now along from the wood, and near the spot where stood Henry Bannerworth and his friends in consultation.

The jaded look of the surgeon was quite sufficient indication of the trouble and turmoil he had gone through, and some expressions of sympathy for his condition were dropped by Henry, to whom he replied, —

"My young friend, I deserve it all. I have nothing but my own indiscretion to thank for all the turmoil and tumult that has arisen this morning."

"But to what possible cause can we attribute such an outrage?"

"Reproach me as much as you will. I deserve it. A man may prate of his own secrets if he like, but he should be careful of those of other people. I trusted yours to another, and am properly punished."

"Enough," said Henry; "we'll say no more of that, Mr. Chillingworth. What is done cannot be undone, and we had better spend our time in reflection of how to make the best of what is, than in useless lamentation over its causes. What is to be done?"

"Nay, I know not. Have you fought the duel?"

"Yes; and, as you perceive, harmlessly."

"Thank Heaven for that."

"Nay, I had my fire, which Sir Francis Varney refused to return; so the affair had just ended, when the sound of approaching tumult came upon our ears."

"What a strange mixture," exclaimed Marchdale, "of feelings and passions this Varney appears to be. At one moment acting with the apparent greatest malignity; and another, seeming to have awakened in his mind a romantic generosity which knows no bounds. I cannot understand him."

"Nor I, indeed," said Henry; "but somehow tremble for his fate, and I seem to feel that something ought to be done to save him from the fearful consequences of popular feeling. Let us hasten to the town, and procure what assistance we may: but a few persons, well organized and properly armed, will achieve wonders against a desultory and ill-appointed multitude. There may be a chance of saving him yet, from the imminent danger which surrounds him."

"That's proper," cried the admiral. "I don't like to see anybody run down. A fair fight's another thing. Yard arm and yard arm — stink pots and pipkins — broadside to broadside — and throw in your bodies, if you like, on the lee quarter; but don't do anything shabby. What do you think of it, Jack?"

"Why, I means to say as how if Varney only keeps on sail as he's been doing, that the devil himself wouldn't catch him in a gale."

"And yet," said Henry, "it is our duty to do the best we can. Let us at once to the town, and summons all the assistance in our power. Come on — come on!"

His friends needed no further urging, but, at a brisk pace, they all proceeded by the nearest footpaths towards the town.

It puzzled his pursuers to think in what possible direction Sir Francis Varney expected to find sustenance or succor, when they saw how curiously he took his flight across the meadows. Instead of endeavoring, by any circuitous path, to seek the shelter of his own house, or to throw himself upon the care of the authorities of the town, who must, to the extent of their power, have protected him, he struck across the welds, apparently without aim or purpose, seemingly intent upon nothing but to distance his pursuers in a long chase, which might possibly tire them, or it might not, according to their or his powers of endurance.

We say this seemed to be the case, but it was not so in reality. Sir Francis Varney had a deeper purpose, and it was scarcely to be supposed that a man of his subtle genius, and, apparently, far-seeing and reflecting intellect, could have so far overlooked the many dangers of his position not to be fully prepared for some such contingency as that which had just now occurred.

Holding, as he did, so strange a place in society — living among men, and yet possessing so few attributes in common with humanity — he must all along have felt the possibility of drawing upon himself popular violence.

He could not wholly rely upon the secrecy of the Bannerworth family, much as they might well be supposed to shrink from giving publicity to circumstance of so fearfully strange and perilous a nature as those which had occurred amongst them. The merest accident might, at any moment, make him the town's talk. The overhearing of a few chance words by some gossiping domestic — some ebullition of anger or annoyance by some member of the family — or a communication from some friend who had been treated with confidence — might, at any time, awaken around him such a storm as that which now raged at his heels.

Varney the vampyre must have calculated this. He must have felt the possibility of such a state of things; and, as a matter of course, politicly provided himself with some place of refuge.

After about twenty minutes of hard chasing across the fields, there could be no doubt of his intentions. He had such a place of refuge; and, strange a one as it might appear, he sped towards it in as direct a line as ever a well-sped arrow flew towards its mark.

That place of refuge, to the surprise of every one, appeared to be the ancient ruin, of which we have before spoken, and which was so well known to every inhabitant of the county.

Truly, it seemed like some act of mere desperation for Sir Francis Varney to hope there to hide himself. There remained within, of what had once been a stately pile, but a few grey crumbling walls, which the hunted hare would have passed unheeded, knowing that not for one instant could he have baffled his pursuers by seeking so inefficient a refuge.

And those who followed hard and fast upon the track of Sir Francis Varney felt so sure of their game when they saw whither he was speeding that they relaxed in their haste considerably, calling loudly to each other that the vampyre was caught at last, for he could be easily surrounded among the old ruins, and dragged from amongst its moss grown walls.

In another moment, with a wild dash and cry of exultation, he sprang out of sight, behind an angle, formed by what had been, at one time, one of the principal supports of the ancient structure.

Then, as if there was still something so dangerous about him, that only by a great number of hands could he be hoped to be secured, the infuriated peasantry gathered in a dense circle around what they considered his temporary place of refuge, and as the sun, which had now climbed above the tree tops, and dispersed, in a great measure, many of the heavy clouds of morning, shone down upon the excited group, they might have been supposed there assembled to perform some superstitious rite, which time had hallowed as an association of the crumbling ruin around which they stood.

By the time the whole of the stragglers, who had persisted in the chase, had come up, there might have been about fifty or sixty resolute men, each intent upon securing the person of one whom they felt, while in existence, would continue to be a terror to all the weaker and dearer portions of their domestic circles.

There was a pause of several minutes. Those who had come the fleetest were gathering breath, and those who had come up last were looking to their more forward companions for some information as to what had occurred before their arrival.

All was profoundly still within the ruin, and then suddenly, as if by common consent, there arose from every throat a loud shout of "Down with the vampyre! down with the vampyre!"

The echoes of that shout died away, and then all was still as before, while a superstitious feeling crept over even the boldest. It would almost seem as if they had expected some kind of response from Sir Francis Varney to the shout of defiance with which they had just greeted him; but the very calmness, repose, and absolute quiet of the ruin, and all about it, alarmed them, and they looked the one at the other as if the adventure after all were not one of the pleasantest description, and might not fall out so happily as they had expected.

Yet what danger could there be? there were they, more than half the hundred stout, strong men, to cope with one; they felt convinced that he was completely in their power; they knew the ruins could not hide him, and that five minutes time given to the task, would suffice to explore every nook and corner of them.

And yet they hesitated, while an unknown terror shook their nerves, and seemingly from the very fact that they had run down their game successfully, they dreaded to secure the trophy of the chase.

One bold spirit was wanting; and, if it was not a bold one that spoke at length, he might be complimented as being comparatively such. It was one who had not been foremost in the chase, perchance from want of physical power, who now stood forward, and exclaimed, —

"What are you waiting for, now? You can have him when you like. If you want your wives and children to sleep quietly in their beds, you will secure the vampyre. Come on — we all know he's here — why do you hesitate! Do you expect me to go alone and draw him out by the ears?"

Any voice would have sufficed to break the spell which bound them. This did so; and, with one accord, and yells of imprecations, they rushed forward and plunged among the old walls of the ruin.

Less time than we have before remarked would have enabled any one to explore the tottering fabric sufficient to bring a conviction to their minds that, after all, there might have been some mistake about the matter, and Sir Francis Varney was not quite caught yet.

It was astonishing how the fact of not finding him in a moment, again roused all their angry feelings against him, and dispelled every feeling of superstitious awe with which he had been surrounded; rage gave place to the sort of shuddering horror with which they had before contemplated his immediate destruction, when they had believed him to be virtually within their very grasp.

Over and over again the ruins were searched — hastily and impatiently by some, carefully and deliberately by others, until there could be no doubt upon the mind of every one individual, that somehow or somewhere within the shadow of those walls, Sir Francis Varney had disappeared most mysteriously.

Then it would have been a strange sight for any indifferent spectator to have seen how they shrunk, one by one, out of the shadow of those ruins; each seeming to be afraid that the vampyre, in some mysterious manner, would catch him if he happened to be the last within their somber influence; and, when they had all collected in the bright, open space, some little distance beyond, they looked at each other and at the ruin, with dubious expressions of countenance, each, no doubt, wishing that each would suggest something of a consolatory or practicable character.

"What's to be done, now?" said one.

"Ah! that's it," said another, sententiously. "I'll be hanged if I know."

"He's given as the slip," remarked a third.

"But he can't have given us the slip," said one man, who was particularly famous for a dogmatical spirit of argumentation; "how is it possible? he must be here, and I say he is here."

"Find him, then," cried several at once.

"Oh! that's nothing to do with the argument; he's here, whether we find him or not."

One very cunning fellow laid his finger on his nose, and beckoned to a comrade to retire some paces, where he delivered himself of the following very oracular sentiment: —

"My good friend, you must know Sir Francis Varney is here or he isn't."

"Agreed, agreed."

"Well, if he isn't here it's no use troubling our heads any more about him; but, otherwise, it's quite another thing, and, upon the whole, I must say, that I rather think he is."

All looked at him, for it was evident he was big with some suggestion. After a pause, he resumed, —

"Now, my good friends, I propose that we all appear to give it up, and to go away; but that some one of us shall remain and hide among the ruins for some time, to watch, in case the vampyre makes his appearance from some hole or corner that we haven't found out."

"Oh, capital!" said everybody.

"Then you all agree to that?"

"Yes, yes."

"Very good; that's the only way to nick him. Now, we'll pretend to give it up; let's all of us talk loud about going home."

They did all talk loud about going home; they swore that it was not worth the trouble of catching him, that they gave it up as a bad job; that he might go to the deuce in any way he liked, for all they cared; and then they all walked off in a body, when, the man who had made the suggestion, suddenly cried, —

"Hilloa! hilloa! — stop! stop! you know one of us is to wait?"

"Oh, ay; yes, yes, yes!" said everybody, and still they moved on.

"But really you know, what's the use of this? who's to wait?"

That was, indeed, a knotty question which induced a serious consultation, and ending in their all, with one accord, pitching upon the author of the suggestion, as by far the best person to hide in the ruins and catch the vampyre.

They then all set off at full speed; but the cunning fellow, who certainly had not the slightest idea of so practically carrying out his own suggestion, scampered off after them with a speed that soon brought him in the midst of the throng again, and so with fear in their looks, and all the evidences of fatigue about them, they reached the town to spread fresh and more exaggerated accounts of the mysterious conduct of Varney the vampyre.

Printed in the United States
85799LV00003BA/88-105/A

9 781587 153648